RETURN

OF THE

BARONESS

"Yesterday is history. Tomorrow is a mystery.
Today is a gift that's why it is 'e
present." ER "Live every m   B"
KBD

SK Bentley Davis

Copyright © 2023 SK Bentley Davis

All rights reserved. No part of this book may be reproduced or transmitted in any form or by any means, electronically or mechanically, including photocopying, recording, or by an information storage and retrieval system without permission in writing from the author of this book.

ISBN: 9798868459405
Imprint: Independently published

Published by SK Bentley Davis

Edited by Dr. Ruth L. Baskerville

www.wwexcellence.org

Cover Design by Laurence Walden
jazzartdecor@yahoo.com

Creative Digital Art, ejcreate@mail.com

Introduction

"Each generation imagines itself more intelligent than the one that went before it, and wiser than the one that comes after it." George Orwell

My book, *Complicity*, ended on a sad note, with the demise of Jade and Bybel Ohara, the mother and father of Claudette. Both were professional gamblers in their own right. Very little was written about their four children whom they dearly loved. They knew each one of them well, as most parents know their children's strong points, as well as their weaknesses.

Prior to their passing, Jade and Ohara were on their way to becoming one of the wealthiest families in New Mexico, with the aid of Bix Toilet (Tulay), one of the twin sons of Abe Toilet, and the grandsons of Gideon Toilet. Bix was the President of the *New Mexico State Bank*, where his grandfather, Gideon, was founder and owner. Bix and twin brother, Bax, were chief advisors to the Ohara family.

Thanks to Bix and Francisco Vargo, one of the wealthiest men in New Mexico, the Ohara's had gone from owning a very lucrative gambling house to owning controlling interest in several mines of industrial minerals, sulfuric acid, molybdenum, gold, uranium, silver, and several oil wells on their ten-thousand-acre High Spade Ranch. Vargo helped turn that into thirty thousand acres! The Ohara's total wealth at that time was in excess of ninety-nine million dollars, which would become a billion dollars, thanks to Vargo.

He left his mining interest to Sean Michael, and fifteen thousand acres that bordered the Ohara ranch to Jean Phillipe. So, to put it in Latin, *addendo paginae defuit/* or adding the missing pages. Or as the French would say, *le reste de l'histoire/*, here is the rest of the story.

This is the continuing saga of the Ohara's, especially Claudette, who wanted to be a professional poker player like her mother, Jade. This is a story with a cornucopia of twists and turns that will test your emotions. It's a modern-day odyssey with Claudette's best friend, Jeru, who was like a sister to her. The odyssey begins in Santa Fe, New Mexico, and will take you to New Orleans, Paris, Monaco, Monte Carlo, and back to New Mexico. A fortune-teller in New Orleans had previously told Claudette that she would travel great distances and see many things and people, but eventually return from whence she came.

Furthermore, Claudette was told that she would sit at the top of an empire, along with her friend, Jeru, the native girl whom she met as a child. Due to tragic circumstances, including the murder of her two brothers, Sean Michael, and Jean Philippe, and also the attempted murder of her sister, Cielito, Claudette's life had become intertwined with the whole Blake family. The Blake matriarch, Blossom, was an unusual, Christian woman and a staunch believer in the *Holy Bible*, particularly Matthew 6:33: *"Seek ye first the kingdom of God, and his righteousness; and all these things shall be added unto you."*

You will experience murder, intrigue, paranormal happenings, love, romance, unbridled passion, betrayal, motherhood, and you'll meet a host of interesting characters, including lawyers, judges, politician despots and a most unusual family.

One of the best things Claudette will experience is learning life's greatest lessons from Blossom Benbow Blake, whose influence made a profound change in how Claudette viewed the world and her relations with others.

SK Bentley Davis

Table of Contents

1. "The Acorn Doesn't Fall Far From The Tree"   7
2. Claudette and Jeru in New Orleans   16
3. Sad News for Claudette   21
4. Return of the Baroness and the Duchess   28
5. The Adventure Begins!   33
6. Locations and Lifestyles and a Surprise   41
7. Nimrod bloom Means Trouble   55
8. The Kidnapping Plot   65
9. Murderers!   75
10. The Return to Sante Fe   90
11. Begg is Arrested!   101
12. Brinson's Plan and Blossom's Counsel   119
13. The Gathering   134
14. Hell-Fire Coming to the High Spade Ranch   150
15. A New Addition to the Family   165
16. Reorganizing and Rejoicing   184
17. "Get Me To The Church!"   204
18. Big Plans Materialized   222
19. Mature Relationships   247
20. Business, Marriage, and Business   276
21. Nimrod's Day in Court and Projects are Hatched   293
22. Prosperity and First Murder Trial   304
23. "Mercy, Mercy Me!"   309
24. The Extended Family Meets Mercy   318
25. Blossom Hears Truth, and Sarafina Meets Her New Mother   328
26. Claudette's Response to Nimrod   339
27. "Power Couples"   353
28. Claudette's Paranormal Encounters Revealed   369

Epilogue   387
How to Reach the Author   391

Chapter 1
"The Acorn Doesn't Fall Far From The Tree"

Two years after their marriage, Jade and Bybel Ohara had their first biological child, a boy named Sean Michael, who was the perfect likeness to his father. A year and three months later, Jean Phillipe was born, and he looked more like his mother. And a year after that came Claudette, a pretty little red-headed, green-eyed girl. The oldest child was Cielito. Jade adopted her, prior to her marriage to Bybel Ohara. She was a lovely child everyone who saw her expressed that she had "the look of love" about her. Jade and Ohara were so proud of all four children. They taught them to always be humble, respect older people, and treat everyone with kindness. They never looked down on anyone, and they never, ever talked loudly or bragged about their wealth.

Claudette would grow up to be stunningly attractive and shapely, like her mother. And just like Jade, Claudette's passion was Poker. Although she was quite wealthy and didn't need the money that came from winning, it was the winning at poker that meant more to her than anything -- other than Jeru, who had been her childhood friend since they were six years old.

Recall that Jeru is the child of Sarah Twotrees, a Mescalero Apache (It was thought that Sarah's parents were Cherokee and Mandingo.) and a very tall mixed-race fur trapper. That explained why Sarah was six feet six inches tall. While working as a prostitute at the *Dixieland Plantation Saloon* and moonlighting on her own so she did not have to split her earnings, Sarah Twotrees was impregnated by a very tall Black soldier, Jerusalem Mercy of the 9th Calvary Regiment of Buffalo Soldiers. They never had a chance to marry because the Regiment was moved to Montana.

Jerusalem loved Sarah and didn't mind that she was a prostitute, which was a lifestyle he believed would end once they were married. Sarah didn't mind that he was a Negro because she loved him dearly.

When Jeru was born, she was an unusually large baby -- so large and long that her delivery traumatized Sarah's body to the point that a year later she had to give up prostitution. It's only logical that by the time Jeru was fifteen, she was six feet, seven inches tall, and extremely attractive and shapely. At first glance, one would mistakenly assume that she was slow-witted and awkward, but that was far from the truth. Jeru was quick to learn, and her recall was flawless since she had a photographic memory. She also had the grace of a cat. She could move about and not make a sound, having been taught the way of a Warrior by her grandmother, Chaliapin, who was a Mescalero Apache female Warrior adept at stealing horses from the Mexicans and American soldiers. She spoke English and was often sent to negotiate with US Army officers.

From the time Claudette was four years old until she was ten, every night before she went to bed her mother would tell her stories about her grandfather, Jean Phillipe, who was a professional poker player. Jade admitted that she had always wanted to be like him. She told Claudette all about how she was living with her Grandmother Marie Le Beau after her father was killed in a duel, and how she went from the girl who cleaned the *Southern Belle Saloon* to the main attraction as the "Baroness of New Orleans."

Claudette delighted when her Mom shared how she came to be in New Mexico and met Claudette's father, Ohara. To be sure, Claudette loved her father, but she was so inspired by the stories that her mother told her. she could not wait to follow in her footsteps and make a famous name for herself.

As the children got older, Jade realized that the apartment above the gambling casino was inadequate. The girls would soon need their privacy, so she and Ohara discussed plans to build a house on the property of the gambling casino. The boys would eventually go to school for business and mining engineering at NMSU (New Mexico State University). Cielito would attend a Catholic university near Santa Fe since she was of Mexican heritage and Catholic.

Jade wanted Claudette to go to a finishing school in New Orleans, and Ohara thought it was a good plan too. However, he reminded Jade that Claudette would not go unless Jeru could go also. Jade said, "You are right, so I will ask Sarah if Jeru can go with Claudette to school in New Orleans when the time comes." Both girls were twelve years old at the time, so the adults had time to look for a suitable school.

The school to which everyone agreed was *Saint Augustine School*. "Our school was founded in1727 by the Sisters of the Order of Saint Augustine located in New Orleans. We enjoy the distinction of being both the oldest continuously operating school for girls, and the oldest Catholic school in the United States. Convinced that the education of women is essential to the development of a civilized, spiritual, and just society, the Augustine Sisters .... provide an exceptional education for its women .... a nurturing environment for the learning and development of the whole person.... The school offers the first retreat center for ladies, as well as the first classes for former enslaved females, free women of color, Creole, and Native Americans in the region."

Six months before the girls finished their primary education, Jade called the casino kitchen and asked Sarah if she could come to the house before the girls came home from school. Sarah arrived prior to the girls returning from school. Ohara said, "Sarah we are planning to send Claudette to a finishing school in New Orleans, and we know she will not want to go unless Jeru goes with her. So, with your permission, we will pay for her tuition, books, and clothing." Sarah began to cry. "Mr. Ohara, you all have done so much for us, and I don't know what to say." Jade smiled as she responded. "Say yes because you and Jeru are like our family. By getting educated, Jeru can go in any direction she feels like. 'The world would be her oyster'."

When the girls came into the parlor as they usually did, Ohara announced that the three adults had decided that the two girls would be going to finishing school in New Orleans. There was screaming and dancing and dancing and screaming.

Ohara read from the catalog, and when he finished, Claudette asked, "What is a Creole, father?" Ohara explained that Claudette and Jade were Creole, being persons of mixed heritage-- African, European, and Indian. Ohara said that Jade is French and African, and that Claudette and her brothers are French, African, and Irish. Sarah said that Jeru is French Canadian and Mescalero Apache and African.

Claudette couldn't be more satisfied, thinking she was going to school in New Orléans, which was her mother's hometown and the place where she got her start as a professional poker player. She was also going there with her best and only friend, Jeru Twotrees, which was short for "Jerusalem." The two had met as little girls at a school in Santa Fe, New Mexico. The White children made fun of Jeru because her clothes appeared to be dirty and too small for her, and they also made fun of her because of her dark red complexion. They called her a "red nigger."

This angered Claudette, who brought Jeru home from school with her the same day. Jade and Ohara immediately took the two of them, along with Cielito, to the clothing store and bought each four different dresses and shoes. Even though Claudette didn't need new clothes, her parents wanted to be certain that Jeru would not feel embarrassed by the situation.

The next day, Saturday, Sarah Twotrees, Jeru's mother, came by the casino with Jeru and the new clothes and shoes, saying she could not accept them because she had no way to pay for them. Jade and Ohara explained that it was a gift and would hurt Claudette if Jeru could not have the gifts.

Jade invited her to sit and have a cup of tea or something stronger. Sarah was embarrassed and felt the need to explain how everyone within fifty miles knew that she had been a prostitute, and a person like her should not be in the company of rich White people of their class in life. Jade laughed, which confused Sarah momentarily.

Jade took a sip of tea before speaking again. "Let me tell you a couple of things I was told a long time ago. We cannot all live as we wish, for most we live as we must.
You say you have been a prostitute. Well, it is hard to tell just by looking at me, but I have been a Negro all my life, so I know what it is like to be looked down upon. I had no friends as a child, except for a cat. so, we are happy that Claudette has Jeru." Ohara chimed in. "Now that we are in our new house, you and Jeru will be welcome. I would like to offer you a job anywhere in the casino.

Sarah said, "Oh no, Sir, that would not be right. Too many of your customers know who I am." "Well, if you can cook, we will have the head cook teach you some fancy dishes and you can work in the kitchen where no one will see you. "Oh, God bless you, Sir, thank you," as she crawled on her hands and knees over to Ohara to kiss his hand. Ohara jerked his hand back and told her to never let him or Jeru or any of his children see her do that again. "What you were or became, something I learned from Jade is that you are a child of God, and He will forgive and love and praise you, no matter what." Jade and Ohara were ecstatic that Claudette would have her friend near her, and they would have done anything to make Claudette happy.

In spite of the family's wealth, Jade and Ohara were parents who encouraged their children to find and pursue their own niche in life. Cielito, being the oldest, graduated first with a degree in

Liberal Arts, became the Head Mistress at the Jean Phillipe and Claudette Christophe School for Indigenous Children. As was mentioned earlier, the boys attended New Mexico State University. Sean earned a degree in Mining Engineering, and Jean earned a degree in Business.

Because Jean excelled in his studies and never took a break, both he and his brother graduated at the same time, and they also married the same day! The graduation party and wedding took place at the Ohara Estate on a beautiful summer day. Jean married Aiyana, an attractive, humble Pueblo young lady he met at NMSU. Sean married Gabriele, a Mexican young lady and devout Christian whom he knew from church since he was twelve years old.

After the marriage, the brothers went to work for Francisco Vargas. Vargas was very much acquainted with Jade and Ohara and was proud to have her two sons in his employ. Because of their work ethics, Vargas continued to give them increasing responsibilities. Sean became Safety Manager for all the mines owned by Vargas. Jean assumed the management of Vargas's vast cattle ranch. Jade, Claudette, and Jeru spent the whole summer going back and forth to Albuquerque shopping for clothes and all the necessary things the girls would need while at school in New Orleans. The school had sent Jade a list that included all the books they recommended, along with *Emily Post Guidelines for Good Manners and Etiquette*. This and some other similar books were to be used as a guide for proper social behavior.

When they were not shopping, Jade spent the afternoons helping them with some basic French, which would come in handy with street signs and menus in restaurants. One week before the girls were scheduled to leave, Ohara brought them together with Jade to present last minute instructions.

He said, "Now girls, listen to me carefully, and Jade, my darling, listen so if I miss something or make a mistake you can correct me. Girls, this trip is going to take five days. Your train is scheduled to leave from Albuquerque at 7 pm on the 20th of August and arrive in Dallas on the evening of the 23rd of August. In Dallas you will change trains and take the train to New Orleans, which should take two- and-a-half days. You must never lose sight of each other -- where one goes the other should go also, even to the restroom. Do not talk to strangers -- men or women. I am giving each of you one hundred dollars for emergency use only."

Jade chimed in. "Darling, I think we should contact Abe to get them a private car all the way to New Orleans. That way they will be the only ones in that car and will have their own restroom. Their meals will be served in the car, so, there would be no need for them to come in contact with the other passengers." Ohara agreed and exclaimed that he should have thought of that earlier. "I will get a hold of him right now."

Ohara was relieved after speaking with Abe. He advised Ohara that he should always consult with him or his son, Bix, after which he arranged for Claudette and Jeru to have their own nonstop train from Santa Fe to New Orleans for two thousand, five hundred dollars. It is too dangerous for those girls to travel by themselves, and besides, they will arrive two days earlier.

Ohara inquired as to how that could be possible. Abe's son, Bix, explained how once a week a train leaves Santa Fe nonstop for New Orleans, pulling twenty-five cars of freight. The girls' private car would be hooked up behind the engine and the mail car, with the freight cars behind the private car. By doing it that way they would not be in contact with the traveling public. Bix added, "Mr. Ohara, I don't know if you know it, but most of the Southwest public knows who you are and how wealthy you are. That's why Papa advised you to always let us handle things like this.

Ohara thanked him and said he felt at ease now. He explained it all to Jade and they were both relieved and proceeded to explain to the girls the change in their travel plans. They will have their own private car, complete with everything they could want for their comfort and safety. There will be a security person traveling with them to make sure they arrived in New Orleans two days earlier than they would have by using public transport, and they would be safe and on time.

Chapter 2
Claudette and Jeru in New Orleans

All five of the Ohara's, along with Sarah, were at the train station to hug, kiss shed tears, say goodbye, and give last minute instructions. The trip was several days, but the young ladies and their parents were glad they had the private accommodations throughout their journey. It was quite an adventure!

Upon arrival in New Orleans, Claudette and Jeru were delivered by cab to *Saint Augustine School for Girls.* The admitting Sister made the mistake of telling Claudette that students are not allowed to have servants, referring to the darker complexioned Jeru. Neither Claudette nor Jeru were used to overt racism, but Claudette was quick to tell the Sister that Jeru was not anyone's servant. "She is my friend, companion, and a fellow student at this school. My family paid for the two of us to get a formal education here, and if your school cannot do that, then you can return our tuition now and we will go elsewhere.

The Sister instinctively wanted to punish these rude and abrasive young women because she had never been spoken to in that manner without her being able to exert some physical force to subdue the temperament of such girls. However, she had received the full tuition for these two new students and couldn't afford to let her pride dictate her reaction to Claudette's pointed boldness. The Sister was stunned, but apologetic. She could see that this young lady could be a problem. So, she chose to apologize for her misunderstanding, almost stuttering as she groped for the words that expressed humility and regret. She found her words!

Despite the Sister's initial assessment that she would have problems with these two girls, she realized quickly that both girls were academically strong, and they learned fast. Claudette was quick to question the teachers. After eighteen months, the girls had adapted well to the routines of the Sisters, and they were praised for their academic successes. They were also very popular among their fellow students. Claudette and Jeru enjoyed the education they were receiving. Jeru enjoyed her math classes the most, and Claudette's favorite class was French. Neither of the girls appreciated liked the strict rules.

They often found themselves sneaking off campus to see the city of New Orleans. The School was located near a large cemetery, and as Claudette and Jeru were sneaking of campus one evening, they encountered and old woman near the cemetery. The old woman said, "Come here, let me tell your fortune." New Orleans, and much of Louisiana, was known for the practice of voodoo, and fortune-telling was a part of a ritual or thinking that Claudette and Jeru knew nothing about.

Claudette instinctively said, "No we have to hurry." The old woman responded, "No one is going to catch you. I know you. You are Marie Le Beau's granddaughter." Claudette asked how she knew that, to which the old woman replied, "I knew your

17

mother when she was a little girl and when she begin to gamble at the Belle. You look just like her." Claudette was suspicious, but a little nervous too. Her grandmother was dead. The old woman said, "Your Grandmother taught me all about voodoo when I was a young girl. Give me your hand."

Claudette complied, and the old woman began to tell her how she would travel great distances and return to New Mexico and sit atop an empire. Jeru attempted to convinced Claudette to leave the old woman, whispering that it might be dangerous for the two of them to be walking around New Orleans unescorted. Claudette assured Jeru that she had learned enough from the stories her mother told her since she was four years old that she felt like she knew New Orleans well enough to avoid the wrong places.

One evening, as Claudette left the library where she was writing a paper for her history class, she passed the bulletin board and saw something that caused her to run toward her room. She entered her and Jeru's room all excited. "Did you see it? Did you see it?" Jeru closed the book she was reading and inquired as to what it was that she was supposed to have seen. "Why, the Sisters are taking us on a tour of the French Quarters." "So, what is so great about that?" asked Jeru. "Don't you see, we can see the Southern Belle. My mother told me all about the French quarters and the Southern Belle. My mother told me all about how my grandfather gambled there, and years later so did she."

The two girls lay awake almost all night, as Claudette talked about how her mother had worked there as a child, and at sixteen, she showed up as the "Baroness" and for three years fooled everyone from New Orleans to Natchez. She had shot and killed a man in a duel for accusing her of cheating. No one ever knew that before claiming royal status, she was the young girl who cleaned the place and emptied and washed the spittoons. She got real pleasure in fooling all the men about her true identity. "She taught me everything I know about poker, so by the time I was six years old when we played poker, I was breaking even with her."

To Claudette, it seemed like Saturday would never come. It did, and the two girls were so giddy with excitement that they were talking a hundred miles an hour. As luck would have it, the tour started on Rue Canal one block from the Southern Belle. When they reached the Southern Belle, the owner, Jacque Le Feet, who was the grandson of Henri Le Feet, was out front washing down the sidewalk. As Claudette and Jeru walked by, he shouted, "Sacre bleu! You are her; you are the one in the painting." "What painting?" said Claudette. Le feet explained there was a painting of her in his establishment. "Step inside and you will see."

Claudette walked over to the Sister who was at the rear of the group and whispered that she had to use the public facility and this kind man said he would allow her to use his. "I will go in and come right back." The Sister said, "OK, but take Jeru with you. I will wait by the door." When the two went in and saw the painting, it was like looking in the mirror. Claudette and Jeru stood there with their eyes bulged and mouths wide open. They couldn't speak. A female voice with authority called out, "Girls! Come, stop lollygagging, and come along; this is no place for young girls." Claudette whispered to Le feet that they would return later. The two joined the rest of the girls' tour group all excited, whispering and giggling.

19

The Sister in charge stopped the group and said to Claudette and Jeru, "Stop acting like silly children or this will be the last time you will be allowed to accompany the rest of the girls on a tour. You two are beginning your last semester and we expect our senior young ladies to set the example for the younger girls." Claudette did not care. She and Jeru had finished their next-to-last semester and would be graduating soon.

Chapter 3
Sad News for Claudette

Two months before her graduation, Claudette received a letter from Cielito that their mother, Jade, was seriously ill, and their father, Ohara, was not in good health. They would not be able to attend Claudette's graduation ceremony. The news of her parents' health had a profound effect on Claudette. She found it hard to concentrate. Since the news did not describe their illnesses, she could only wonder if they were suffering from pain. That thought dominated her mind, emotions, and peace. She was praying over and over that they would get better. It did not matter about them attending the graduation ceremony. She was instructed to report to the Head Sister's office for not paying attention. There, she explained to the Sister the news she had received from home about her parents' condition. The Sister apologized and promised that a prayer would be said each evening and that she should light a candle for them.

Prior to Jade and Ohara's health declining, they had a meeting with their financial advisors, the Toilet twins, and based upon their legal advice, Jade and Ohara restructured their holdings and their will in order to protect their children and Jeru.

A week later, Claudette received a telegram from Cielito informing her that Jade had died, and that Claudette was needed at home right away. Wow, it seemed that Claudette and Jeru would miss the graduation ceremony after all. They didn't hesitate to focus entirely upon the parents instead of a graduation ceremony that instantly became less important than family health. Once again, the bank made arrangements for the girls to have a nonstop train from New Orleans. Why is it that shocking "news travel in twos." Claudette and Jeru were excused from school to be with family at this sad time.

Upon arrival home, Claudette was given the sad news that a day after the passing of her Mom, her Dad had died. Claudette was so grief-stricken that she spent most of the time over the next day locked away in Jade and Ohara's bedroom. She just lay in their bed surrounded by Jade's clothes. It was a sad and emotional time for the family. Just like Claudette, the other three siblings were grief-stricken. The boys had finished college and were married and employed by the wealthiest man in New Mexico. Cielito being the oldest of Jade and Ohara's children, felt it her duty to handle everything. She, too, was grieving and terribly sad, but there were arrangements to be made and people to call. Friends and employees offered comfort and condolement, including the aged Father Francisco, longtime friend, and spiritual advisor of both Jade and Ohara. Father Francisco, who was ninety-five, he felt the need to pay his respects and see if the family needed anything that he could furnish.

Sarah Twotrees, of course, was there. She loved Jade and Ohara and felt a tremendous loss when she heard of their passing. She felt she was indebted to Jade and Ohara for the love, kindness, and generosity shown to her and her daughter,

Jeru. Another important thing that Jade and Ohara had done before they died was to promote Sarah to Head Chef after the French chef had left for New York to open his own restaurant.

Because of their well-known reputation for philanthropy, and their sense of devotion to Santa Fe, Jade and Ohara were loved and respected by the community. They were first to assist those in need, and after a fire or other disaster occurred, it was Jade and Ohara who provided the town or the individual with money and encouragement. They gave to churches for their building funds. Their kindnesses and giving went on and on.

The funeral was a very sad affair. The family, friends, employees, and community felt a tremendous loss. The children decided that as soon as they could get a mausoleum built on the Casino property, Jade and Ohara's remains would be exhumed and placed in the mausoleum for their final resting place.

Sarah was deeply concerned now that both Jade and Ohara were gone. What would happen to Jeru and her? Would Jeru have to leave the school, and would Sarah lose her job? Everything was cleared up two days later when Bax read Jade and Ohara's Will, especially the part concerning the disposition of the Casino. Bax, being the Executor of the Ohara's estate, made public that the casino was to remain as it is. All employees would keep their positions. Only if anyone wanted to leave would Bax find a suitable replacement.

Cielito was to take over management of the casino, or to hire a suitable person as she saw fit. The boys would remain in their present positions of mine operations and ranch operations, and Cielito would continue as Head Mistress of the two schools. She would remain in the house and ensure that Sarah and Jeru were always welcome and considered a part of the family. This was a heavy load for someone in their twenties, especially for a female in the early Twentieth Century in America.

When Claudette and Jeru returned to school, Claudette told Jeru that although graduation was just a few days away, she was too distraught for graduation ceremonies and intended to stay in New Orleans. She was going to move off campus right away. Jeru said she would do the same, but Claudette said, "No, you must receive your diploma for your mother, Sarah, and you could join me after the ceremony." Jeru agreed, and the two separated temporarily.

Of course, after finding an apartment, Claudette went to the Southern Belle and began her career as a professional Poker player, making Le Feet happy. Now the Belle would be full every night now that the Baroness had returned. Claudette looked so much like her mother that the people saw her as the original Poker player. Business was "booming," as they say, and for Claudette, doing this was the only thing that helped her deal with her grief.

After graduation ceremonies had concluded, Jeru joined Claudette at the apartment. The few days they were apart was pure agony for both of them, and the two learned something about themselves. They could not be happy away from each other. They had developed a love for each other that could not be matched by anything on earth -- they were in love. Their love was not a sexual attraction, but a love like twin sisters might have, only deeper. Claudette told Jeru, "These few nights I found that when I am away, I miss you and find it hard sometime to concentrate, which is not good for a professional Poker player I learned that lesson from my mother, and it must have been hard for you too. They embraced, and Jeru said, "How did you know that I am feeling exactly the same way? Claudette responded that she just had a feeling.

"I tell you what. I will teach you how to deal Faro and we can be together every night." Jeru had no idea what Faro was, and Claudette smiled broadly before explaining. "Faro is a card game. Remember how good you were in all our math classes in school? Well, that's how easy Faro will be for you. Here, I will show you."

For the next several days Claudette taught Jeru something new and being very quick at learning and good at math, Jeru didn't take long before she was ready to make her debut at the Southern Belle. Prior to that, Claudette introduced Jeru to Bridget, who was the granddaughter of Madam Lizette and was now the owner of Madam Lizette Boutique. She instructed Jeru and Claudette in dress colors from which to choose, the right amount of cologne and fragrance to wear, and the best place on the body to attract men. When they made it clear they were not looking for a man, Bridget said, "Surely you understand that bees are attracted to flowers by their colors and smell. As professional gamblers, you are the exception, since all of the other customers are likely to be men."

After leaving Madam Lizette, Claudette informed Jeru that they had a couple of more stops to make. The first stop was the print shop to have Jeru's business cards printed. They were giggling with delight, as Claudette announced, "As far as the New Orleans gambling world is concerned, your name is Duchess Jeru Deuxarbres of the House of Bourbon." That was the information she instructed the print shop to print, and she asked how soon the cards would be ready. The proprietor informed her that it would take approximately two days. Claudette was pleased and thanked him.

Jeru asked her why the cards and the fake name, to which Claudette responded that she would explain when they got back to the apartment. The next stop was the Gunsmith Shop. Jeru looked at Claudette and asked what they were getting there. "Your protection." She purchased a Derringer with ammunition for Jeru, and they went home.

When they arrived, they dropped everything on the sofa. Claudette asked Jeru to sit at the kitchen table while she made tea. While the kettle was heating, she sat with Jeru and began to explain how they were going to live their lives as professional gamblers in a man's world. "First off, remember what Bridget said about all of our customers being men." She went on to explain the different men she would come in contact with, emphasizing the fact that the men do not like losing, especially to women. Some do not like playing against women, but none the less, Claudette and Jeru knew to never forget that they are operating within a man's world.

"I am not saying they are right in their thinking, but we have to use everything we have within reason to be accepted into their world. That is why the fake name. When you are speaking, speak with a French accent. My mother told me that. Flatter them often and pretend to be the weak, helpless female, but never lose your concentration. When they are losing, they will accuse you of cheating. When that happens look toward the bar and get the bartender's attention. If they make a move to put their hands on you, that is what the Derringer is for."

Claudette heard the kettle and moved toward the kitchen while still talking. After pouring the tea, she continued to stress to Jeru that she must never be afraid to protect herself. "I carry my Derringer in my bosom because it is easy for me to get to. My mother carried hers between her legs on the inside of her left garter belt. You should decide what works best for you. We have the advantage over most women who want to gamble, since we learned how to be charming in school." Jeru listened intently to everything Claudette was saying. She nodded to indicate understanding and acceptance of all she had heard.

Chapter 4
Return of the Baroness and the Duchess

Two days later, Jeru was ready to begin her career as a professional gambler. Claudette, with Jeru in tow, met with Le Feet, at which time Claudette demanded that Jeru become one of the Faro dealers, or else Claudette would have to go elsewhere. Of course, Le Feet had to agree. He did not mind having two gorgeous females working there, presuming that they would be an even bigger attraction for the Belle. It did not take long before Jeru became very popular and would spend time working the Roulette table, as well as dealing Faro. It was not unusual for men to leave the Faro table for Roulette when Jeru moved. They could be heard saying that she was so pretty and smelled so good that one couldn't help but to follow her.

All this attention was not lost on Jeru. She and Claudette reveled in their celebrity status at the Belle. It was not long before Claudette, like her mother, Jade, had a far-reaching reputation that brought exponential business to Le Feet. She and Jeru were the talk of the New Orleans gambling world, and they were known also as far as Mobile and Natchez. Jeru told Claudette she never imagined she would enjoy gambling as much as she did. They had become as popular as actors, singers, and dancers. It was not unusual to see some of those high-profile people in the Belle.

Their time at the Southern Belle had lasted about three years, when Claudette one morning, after looking at a gown she had worn before and notice there were small brown spots on the bottom, told herself that another of her expensive gowns had been ruined by careless, classless men. She became frustrated and just sat staring out the window and thinking that, while she was pleased to have established a reputation for high stakes gambling like her mother, she always knew that those men had class and manners. That was no longer the case at the Belle.

Claudette thought that she and Jeru needed to get away from that situation where they had to put up with smelly, drunk, tobacco-chewing, ill-mannered men. She decided right then and there to wake Jeru and tell her of her plan. She sat on the bed where Jeru was sleeping and asked, "How would you like to live in France?" Jeru said, "I am like Ruth in the Bible. I will go wherever thou goeth." The next day, Claudette placed two calls to her sister, Cielito, in Santa Fe. After getting all the latest news and telling her how she and Jeru were doing, Claudette informed her that she and Jeru were leaving New Orleans and going to live in France for a while. She asked Cielito to please let Sean and Jean know.

Cielito was a bit surprised, but she knew that Claudette and Jeru needed to have their freedom and expand their horizon. She advised her to call the bank to let them know she was going to France. Claudette said she intended to do that, and ended the call by saying that she loved Cielito and to please tell Sean and Jean Phillipe and their families that she loved them too. She said that she and Jeru would call Jeru's mother, Sarah, at the Casino.

Claudette called the bank and reached Bix Toilet, now is President. He told her that his father was retired, and that he was the President and CEO of both banks, in Santa Fe and Albuquerque. "Well congratulations, I am calling to let the bank know I am moving to France, Paris to be exact." Bix responded, "I am sure you will like it there, since I understand that was your grandfather's birthplace. As far as your finances are concerned, your family's net worth at is well over one hundred and ninety million. Your brothers continue to drill for more oil every day and the mines are producing at high capacity, with each well producing over one thousand barrels a day. You are on the way to becoming a billionaire! Now I know you are an independent-minded person, but I wish you would let me manage everything as it relates to money. Give me a month and I will have your trip arranged, including transportation, and hotel until you say you've found permanent accommodations. I will find you several villas and chateaus with servants."

Claudette was pleased with everything Bix intended to do, but said, "Two things: don't forget Jeru, who is coming with me. And why is it going to take a month to get everything set up for us?" Bix explained, "You can't just pick up and go. There are many things that must be taken care of. You must have ID cards with all your information and the name of who you want to be notified in case of an emergency. I have to contact the Bank of France and open a bank account for you to transact business. And you must give me or my brother, Bax, your Power of Attorney."

Bix told Claudette to go to any photo shop to have ID cards made, and the rest he would take care of. He promised to get the papers ready for her signature. Bix assured Claudette that the bank would take care of Jeru's needs, since she had a seven per cent stake in the Ohara fortune and was on her way to becoming a millionaire. When Bix added that each of the women would receive money each month, Claudette said that she had averaged five thousand dollars every two weeks at the Southern Belle, and that Jeru had two thousand dealing Faro. They planned to do better than that in France.

Just as Bix promised, a month and two weeks later, he contacted Claudette with the news that they were booked on the train, a private car from New Orleans to New York where they would travel by ocean liner on the SS France to Paris. Depending on weather, everything should take approximately fifteen days. They were beyond excitement at the thought of being off to their next adventure.

When they informed Le Feet of their plans to leave permanently and live in Paris, he was devastated. He begged them to stay, and even offered them half ownership in the Southern Belle. They turned down his offer, but they felt badly for him. Claudette said they would be around for a month, which would give him time to find someone to take their places. Le Feet quickly responded that no one could ever take their places.

The next few weeks were a busy time for Jeru and Claudette. A week after Claudette's conversation with Bix, a lawyer showed up at the Southern Belle searching for Claudette and Jeru. He explained to them he was an attorney doing a favor for his friend and colleague, Baxley Toilet, and he asked if they could come by his office the next day. He gave them his card with his address and phone number. Then he asked why these two lovely ladies were leaving New Orleans. Claudette carefully chose the words in her response. "New Orleans and the Belle are OK, but we are progressive and prefer a different class and a place where the customers are not trying to relive their past. We respect the common man, but the world is changing, and we want to grow with that change and experience what is on "the other side of the mountain."

The lawyer wondered if they had seen all of this country. Jeru said, "Sir, we consider ourselves to be well read, and it's only been a few years since humans were bought and sold like cattle and the original people were forced off their land and slaughtered because of White men's laws. So, I ask as a lawyer, are you a part of the problem? We know that the two of us can't do much here, but we need to see how the rest of the world lives." The lawyer's face got a little red and he loosened his collar while thanking them for their time and looking forward to their meeting the next day.

The next afternoon they were greeted with the greatest respect and signed the papers, after which the lawyer wished them God's speed in their future. A week later they boarded the train for New York.

Chapter 5
The Adventure Begins!

When Claudette and Jeru arrived in New York a limousine was waiting for them. Their baggage was already being brought to the limo, and the driver was waiting for them, holding a large sign with their names on it. They walked over to him and said,
"We are Miss Ohara and Miss Twotrees. The driver, Isaiah, told them that he knew them from the description given by Mr. Toilet. He admired their beauty and asked them to check to see if all their baggage were there. Everything was fine.

The ride to the docks was exciting for them. They were amazed at all the tall buildings and so many people. They asked the driver where all these people came from, and the driver responded, "Everywhere." He was amused at their naivete, and said, "I can see you are excited, so I will take you on the scenic tour. We have plenty of time, and I'll show you Central Park, Ellis Island, and the Statue of Liberty."

As the limousine moved along toward the docks, they caught a glimpse of the Statue and began to scream and point. At the dock, they were amazed at the size of the ship that would take them across the Atlantic Ocean to Paris, France. After the driver had their baggage delivered to the loading area, he turned and said, "Ladies, I don't know when I have enjoyed myself being in the presence of two of the most stunning females I've ever seen. Have a safe and pleasant voyage." They thanked him and gave him a really generous tip.

As they walked up the gang plank, they noticed two well-dressed, handsome men. They didn't know it, but the two were waiting for them. The one with the mustache introduced himself as "Jean Beauchamp, who showed them his badge and announced that his companion was Wilford Bunford. They were the security detail, and Claudette immediately said they didn't want any security. Beauchamp replied, "You might not want security, but you damn well need it!" Bunford said there were pickpockets and jewel thieves, even onboard this ship.

Beauchamp then escorted them to their stateroom, asking Jeru to stand between the two beds. When she moved, Bunford said, "Excuse me" and walked past her. She realized that he had opened her purse, and Beauchamp said, "That's lesson number one -- always keep your hand on the clasp or zipper on your purse. Number two is to watch the sounds in front and behind you, and if someone is going to pass to close to you, switch your purse to the opposite side of your body. Next, always be suspicious of people who walk up to you and start a conversation. Never take a drink they offer you, especially if it is from their bottle or container."

He told them that they were invited to dine at the Captain's table each night and they would be the ladies' escorts for dinner. Jeru wondered if they had the right attire to be guests at the Captain's table nightly, and Claudette reviewed the ship's amenities to see if there was a boutique. They called for the Stewart, who said, "Normally you would wear whatever you packed; however, since there are going to be several people of means and at least six royals onboard dining with the Captain each night, I suggest you dress formal." Claudette said they had gowns only suitable for gambling establishments, and she asked if there were any place nearby where they could purchase formal wear.

The Stewart said they could take a taxi to Channel's before the ship left in two days, and they followed his advice to ask for "Gisella." She was a tall, attractive woman about thirty-five years old, and she looked as if she had just stepped off the cover of a fashion magazine. Actually, she had been a top model for Channel. Claudette explained their dilemma. They wanted something that would set them apart from the other females.

Gisella escorted them to her showroom. Jeru admired Gisella's silk attire with dressy pants, admitting that she and Claudette had never seen dressy pants with matching kimonos for women. Gisella responded, "This is Channel's latest design. Soon, women all over Europe and America will be wearing this." In the showroom, models appeared in the same type of pants and kimonos in different colors and without kimonos, like Gisella was wearing. Others wore long, sleek gowns or short, frilly, and lacy gowns. Claudette and Jeru said they would take five pair of the slacks with matching kimonos, five different color blouses, and two each of the long gowns, and two each of the short ones. "How soon can you have them ready? We sail two nights from now."

Gisella took their measurements and said they could have everything ready the next day and would deliver it to them on the ship. That evening,

Claudette and Jeru decided to skip dinner at the Captain's table the first night and have dinner in their state room. Beauchamp would give the Captain the message they were tired and would join him and guests the next evening.

The next day, the Channel entourage arrived, complete with all the outfits and a Modiste, hairstylist and makeup person. The Modiste was there to make sure everything fit correctly, which it did. The two hairstylists and manicurists went to work. Claudette wanted her hair long, flowing, and covering her right eye. Her dress would be a long white gown with the black spots and a diamond choker and headband. Jeru wore her hair in a pulled back French roll to show the beautiful angle of her face and eyes. She liked the pants suit, so her choice was black slacks and a cream-colored blouse, with the long, black lace kimono with oriental lotus flowers, and the short and long white pearls together.

Shortly after hearing eight bells signaling dinner, the two with their escorts walked into the dining room and created quite a stir. Some of the female royals rose and left the table, as Beauchamp introduced Claudette and Jeru to the Captain and his seated guests. It was not known whether the stares were due to their beauty, or to the long cigarette holders they sported, or to their outfits, but over half the shipboard females followed the two when they went to the powder room.

There was one English woman at the table, Dame May Margo Shropshire, who was an independent-minded spinster and prolific writer of mystery novels. She moved next to Claudette and Jeru and introduced herself, Beauchamp signaled to them she was okay. Most people in England, France, and Belgium knew her and love her stories about a lovable crime solver named Barnaby Dorchester. She flashed a big grin. "I am intrigued by your manner of dress, which I presume are Channel 's latest creations, which I've always admired. I was what one might call a 'tomboy,' always wanting to wear pants, but, as you can see, now I am a fat, old spinster, so I have to settle for her fragrance."

Claudette asked her if "spinster" meant she never married, and Dame May Margo offered an explanation. "You see, I was in love with another female named Antoinette." Jeru interrupted, stating emphatically, "Claudette and I are in love. We have been since we were six years old, and we cannot live without each other." Dame May Margo said in a sad voice, "I know how you feel. Well, I am sure you know most people do not approve of that. They think it a mortal sin, and when Antoinette and I were eighteen, one of her family members found us making love and they locked her away. Sometime later, she committed suicide, and I had a nervous breakdown and was in an institution for three years. I spent the next ten years in seclusion, which is when I began to write. I created "Barnaby Dorchester," who became my friend and alter ego.

Claudette and Jeru quickly wiped their tears with their linen napkins, not wanting anyone to notice they were crying. Claudette said that sex had never been a part of her relationship with Jeru, revealing that both were virgin. Jeru added that there had been similar talk at their school in New Orleans, but she chose to ignore it.

Dame May Margo changed the subject. "Where are you all staying in Paris?" Claudette said it was the George Hotel. Dame was staying there, too. "How long will you be there? Maybe we can get together sometime, as I would like to hear more of your story. Maybe I will even write a story about you two."

For the next several days and evenings, Claudette and Jeru wore a different Channel outfit with different hair styles. There were several potential suitors trying to get close to them, but Beauchamp and Wilford made sure no one succeeded. Even some of the royals who left the table the first evening showed up for dinner at the Captain's table after noticing their popularity and celebrity status. Everyone warmed up to them because they were the talk of ship all the way to Paris!

They had not had that kind of reception since the Southern Belle in New Orleans. At the time, Santa Fe was several thousand miles away in distance and from their minds. Twelve days later the ship sailed into the harbor and docked. Beauchamp went to Claudette and Jeru's State Room and told them to stay in their room for two hours until most of the crowd had gone. "Wait for us near the top of the gang plank. You will be able to see me down on the dock. It will take some time to get all of your luggage, and then I will signal for you to come down."

When the young women arrived near the gang plank and focused their attention below, they could see Beauchamp talking to an attractive female wearing a white ermine stole and holding a small white dog. He reached in his coat pocket and showed her his badge before he turned and looked up and signaled for Claudette and Jeru to come down. When they reached the lower steps, the female with whom Beauchamp was talking said, "Hello, Mademoiselle Ohara and Twotrees." Claudette and Jeru were surprised at the attention they received when they set foot on French soil.

They were also surprised when this stunningly attractive, young, aristocratic-looking lady knew their names. They asked if she knew where females were allowed to gamble. The young travelers didn't discover until later that the attractive mulatto female to whom they had asked a question was a famous singer and dancer. Everyone in France and most of Europe knew of her.

She answered them in a sultry voice. "I can tell you are new here, and American to boot! Why, ladies, you are in Paris where there are no restrictions on you. Anything a man can do you can do as well."

Jeru and Claudette stood there unable to speak, thinking this lady was an aristocrat, from the way she dressed, and her fragrance was so alluring. Finally, Jeru asked her where she lived in Paris, and how they could see her again, and if she could help them get acquainted with the city. She said she was in a hurry, but she gave them her card and invited them to come by some evening to talk in between shows. "And you might visit the Café Afrique. The owners are Americans who meet there to socialize. Ask for Duncan."

From the card the girls could see her name was Candance (Candy Cane) Kane. She was an exotic dancer with the Folies Bergère. Claudette thought to herself, "What luck meeting such a well-known person on our first day in Paris." While Jeru waited for their luggage with Wilford, Claudette walked over to where all the taxi cabs were parked, chose one and asked the driver to move over to the dock where Jeru was standing with their luggage. Beauchamp voiced his displeasure with Claudette walking off, even though he could still see her. "Don't do that again! Please allow me to pick a taxi once again. You have to be careful."

Beauchamp spoke to the driver in French, and the driver opened the door and signaled to Claudette and Jeru to enter. His cab. Wilford sat in the back. Beauchamp watched the driver load the luggage, and then he sat up front with the driver. They were going to the George Hotel. At the hotel they were greeted and treated like royalty. The desk person greeted them as if he knew them, but in truth, Bix had given the hotel a description of the two beautiful ladies when he made their reservation. "We have the penthouse suite reserved for you and Mademoiselle Twotrees, and the gentlemen's room is just down the hall. How long does Mademoiselle plan to stay?" Claudette was quick to respond. "It depends on if the Casinos have Poker and Faro." "I am sure Mademoiselle will find that Poker is played in all the casinos in France."

Chapter 6
Locations and Lifestyles and a Surprise

After two months in Paris, Claudette was not satisfied, and Jeru said they should visit the *Café Afrique*. They were surprised to find that Duncan was not a man, but a very attractive blonde female who had left the states ten years ago, along with her lover, to escape persecution because of their lifestyle. Her lover was a Negro Jazz musician, and they opened the club and named it *Club Afrique*. Duncan, thinking the two were Lesbians, said, *"Ladies here in Paris we are not biased, you can live any lifestyle you wish. I think you would love the South of France, especially the Riviera."* After spending the evening in the club, Claudette and Jeru agreed to visit the South of France, especially the Riviera. The next day as they departed the hotel, Jeru asked the desk person to please put a note in Mademoiselle Shropshire's box, indicating that they were gone to the Riviera and would be back in two days.

The two-day visit to the South of France, especially Monte Carlo, was all it took for them to decide to move. The next morning, they returned to Paris to get their belongings and check out of the hotel. Jeru left a note for Dame May Margo, telling her they were leaving Paris and could be contacted in Monte Carlo, where they planned to buy a villa and hoped to hear from her soon. Before leaving the hotel Claudette sent a telegram to Bix stating that they planned to relocate to the French Rivera, and he should find them a large Villa with staff. Bix read the telegram, smiled, and shook his head before doing as Claudette had asked.

After two nights of playing Poker in Monte Carlo, Claudette had won a large sum and so did Jeru. They fell in love with Monaco and especially Monte Carlo. The next morning, Claudette sent a telegram to Bix, asking that he find a Villa in Monaco. Bix called the hotel to leave a message for Claudette to call him as soon she arrived. When Claudette and Jeru returned to the hotel, they got the telegram and went to their room. Jeru asked to speak with Bix after Claudette spoke. The phone was ringing, and Claudette, thinking it was Bix, said, "Hello, Bix, are you in France?" The voice said in an indignant tone, "Mister Toilet is in Santa Fe, New Mexico having dinner. Who may I say is calling?" "I am so sorry, but I forgot the difference in time. Tell him it is Claudette Ohara."

Bix took the phone from the maid, saying, "Claudette, my own true love! I found you two a Chateau/mansion, complete with staff, swimming pool and a great seaside view, and it has several bedrooms, a library, a guest house, and servants' quarters. It is not far from Monte Carlo. Oh, and also a fulltime chauffer. The staff think it will require at least two to three weeks to get it stocked and ready. It is an older, magnificent-looking building, but I was assured it is in good shape. It is the Chateau les Alpes, and once you see it you will know why the name. There is no need to hurry, and when all is ready you will be contacted, and the chauffer will pick you up."

Claudette passed the phone to Jeru, who said, "Mr. Toilet, have you seen or heard anything from my mother?" "As a matter of fact, I have. She visits the bank once a week to deposit her check minus fifty dollars, and the rest goes into her savings along with the money you send her. She appears to be in good health." She thanked him and hung up the phone. Shortly afterwards, Beauchamp knocked at their penthouse door and asked if he could come in. He announced, "I am afraid we must bid you ladies goodbye. You two have learned fast, and you will be moving to your Chateau soon. We received a call from Mr. Toilet telling us that there will be security there.

Jeru asked why they couldn't keep the two security guards with whom they had grown to feel totally safe. Claudette added, "We will pay to have your protection." Beauchamp said he would ask Wilford what he thought about the proposal, and within minutes, they had agreed to stay with Claudette and Jeru. Wilford added, "I don't know about Jean, but I am in love with the two of you and would marry either one of you. However, I know you are inseparable." Beauchamp admitted feeling the same way about these two beautiful ladies. Claudette and Jeru hugged them and thanked them both for understanding their love for each other. "Most people do not understand our love for each other and whisper behind our backs. But we could never exist without each other, and that would not be fair to any man."

Three weeks later, they got the call that they could be ready to move by 2:00 p.m. the next day. Claudette preferred 11:00 a.m. "I thought that since tomorrow is a special day, we could spend the rest of today shopping. I have something special I want to give you. It's your birthday, or have you forgotten?" All of a sudden Jeru bolted from the bed and hurried for the bathroom with Claudette in pursuit, asking if something was wrong. "No, no, but I get emotional when I think about you what you and your family have done for me and my mother. We are so blessed. I just wonder if I deserve it."

Claudette said, "Don't be silly, of course you do." Jeru stopped sniffling and said, "Do you think we are wrong to feel the way we do? I heard the whispers behind our backs, even when we were at St Augustine. Claudette tenderly responded that they would order room service and talk about this. They had a few silent moments before the food arrived, and after eating a little, Claudette said, "Jeru, you know I never gave that a second thought. I do know this -- life with you is the best thing to happen to me, and it would be an awful existence without you. Before we shop, we will go to the cathedral and talk to the priest if that will make you feel better." Jeru felt immediately comforted.

After breakfast, they stepped out of the hotel looking stunning as ever! Jeru hailed a taxi, and they were off to St. Catherine's Cathedral. They met Le Veau, the Sexton, who asked how he could be of assistance. They asked to see the Priest. Father David bid them welcome and asked about their needs, spiritual or otherwise. Claudette spoke up and said, "We needed clarification on the subject of love." Jeru added, "Father, we have a deep and abiding love for each other, and we want to know if it is a sin." Before Father David could speak, Claudette interjected that they were virgins with a non- sexual relationship, but they have loved each other since they were six years old.

Father David asked the ladies to sit, and then asked how familiar they were with the holy scriptures. "We are both Catholic and are confirmed and receive the Eucharist." Father David said that the holy scriptures teach us that God is love, and all who live in love live in God and God lives in them. "God is love, and He who abides in love abides in God, and God in him." Jeru said, "But Father, people say that we are wrong and are committing a sin." Father David raised his hand gently, as if to calm Jeru and Claudette with his next words: "My child, listen, God knows more of what is in your heart than any mere human does, and there is no wrong in the two of you having a deep and abiding love for each other. So do not be concerned with what others say. Go on loving, and remember that God is love, and all who live in love live in God. What you have is what the Greeks call 'Agape' love, which is the highest form of deep affection one person can have for another. Someone once said, 'When you kiss others with pure intentions, Agape love is sure to be found.' So, embrace, kiss, and stay in prayer, and may God be with you both." They thanked Father David for validating their lifestyle and their feelings for each other.

Jeru announced, "Claudette, my love, I am so happy. I feel free. I just want to live and breathe loving you! I love you! A million times!" They embraced and kissed, and Claudette said, "Let's shop until we drop!" They hailed a taxi, and in a loud and happy voice, they shouted, Palace du Casino, and broke out in uncontrollable laughter. The taxi driver thought two drunk females, and they were, in fact, drunk with mutual love.

"Driver, driver! Stop here at Cartier." When they entered the boutique, Claudette directed Jeru to see something she wanted them both to have. Claudette asked to see a heart-shaped diamond neckless, and she asked if the jeweler could cut the neckless in half. The jeweler shouted, "No!

Mademoiselle I will not destroy such fine work." Claudette clarified her request with a quick sketch showing that she wanted to wear half of it and Jeru to wear the other half. How long will it take and how much in dollars will it cost?" The jeweler said that the necklace was ten thousand dollars, and if the ladies wanted the same size carats and number of diamonds each, then he could make it in two days for that price, with a little more for the second gold chain.

Altogether, Claudette and Jeru bought diamond chokers and two love bracelets, and they requested engraving on the insides. One said, "Love forever, Jeru" and the other said, "Love forever, Claudette." They agreed Claudette would pay for the neckless since that was her Birthday gift for Jeru. They would pay for the choker and bracelets separately as gifts to exchange. The jeweler had the engraving done in three hours. They departed Cartier and went down the street to Channel and spent another large sum on the latest designs by Coco Channel.

On the way to the hotel, they discussed the logistics of having enough time to pick up their purchases, and pack to leave by eleven the next morning. Both were anxious to see the Chateau and meet the staff. The excitement and anticipation had them tossing and turning all night, but they were up by seven-thirty packing. They needed extra luggage for their gowns, so the desk clerk sent for that from the luggage store nearby. Jeru thanked him and gave him a very generous tip. The bellhop was appreciative of Jeru's generous tip, saying, "Thank you! Thank you, Mademoiselle." Jeru murmured how nice and thoughtful and polite the French are.

At exactly eleven o'clock, Hercule, their chauffer arrived. Everyone checked out successfully. Hercule addressed Claudette. "I am Hercule, your chauffer. I took the liberty to order a truck for all your baggage because I want you to be as comfortable as possible." Claudette excused herself and pulled Jeru into the bathroom. "Is he the most handsome man you have ever seen?" They composed themselves and walked out of the bathroom trying to pretend nothing had happened. They said that two gentlemen would be coming with them.

Beauchamp sat up front with Hercule. Wilford sat in the rear with Claudette and Jeru. Thirty minutes after they left the hotel, Hercule could see in the mirror that both ladies had fallen asleep. Two hours later the car and truck arrived at the chateau. Claudette and Jeru couldn't believe their eyes. It was like a fairy tale to see this huge mansion with a portico, and behind in the distance were the snow-covered Alps, and to the right a large swimming pool and tennis court. The guest house was large enough for a family of six. From the balcony was the beautiful blue waters of the Mediterranean.

The Butler, Brinson Dubois, stepped out followed by the staff. Brinson heartily welcomed everyone, and then introduced the staff: Chef Maurice, Maids Fannie and Monique, and Gardener Trudeau. Jeru Introduced Messieurs Beauchamp and Dunford as their personal bodyguards. The ladies needed to use the power room, with the entrance a mirrored screen with gold, Oriental lotus flowers. There were several elegant- looking chairs with a mirror the length of the wall trimmed in finely gilded traditional gold leaves. There were four private stalls, each equipped with two types of bidets.

After relieving themselves and exiting the powder room, Claudette and Jeru were given the tour of the chateau. They told Brinson that their hours were unusual because they were professional gamblers who leave about nine o'clock p.m. with bodyguards, and they return around three o'clock a.m. They liked to have breakfast around one-thirty p.m., a light lunch at four o'clock, and dinner at eight o'clock p.m. Their bodyguards would be in guest rooms, leaving the guest house for guests.

Beauchamp spoke about the fake tourists, as opposed to Claudette and Jeru, who were the "real thing." "Most Americans who come to Monte Carlo assume everyone here is rich and wears what appears to be expensive jewelry. Actually, most of their jewelry is fake, and some have lost their money on high stakes gambling. They come to Monte Carlo to sponge off of people like you, who have genuine wealth. They will marry you, or even kidnap you for ransom. The whole group decided that they were more like friends than employer/employees. Nevertheless, security and protection would always be the top priorities of Beauchamp and Dunford and Brinson.

Life in Monaco for Claudette was like a story book. She was with the love of her life, and the staff was adapting to her and Jeru's unusual schedule and the constant coming and going of famous, infamous, royalty and once-royal people from the casino. There seemed to be at least two or three yachts moored at the dock near their mansion in the Mediterranean Sea. The world being in the middle of World War II (or WW I?) did not affect Monte Carlo, as business was as brisk as always, with a mixture of famous characters, two or three spies, some delusional individuals who thought they could cheat the house, some criminal types, and of course, the usual, loveable rouges.

Claudette and Jeru were always the center of attention, and each evening they were the recipients of several marriage proposals. While they enjoyed their celebrity status, it never interfered with the concentration on their craft. In the beginning, the Monte Carlo staff was suspicious of Claudette's prolific winning, which became the subject of servants' gossip nightly. However, that soon subsided when it became obvious that she was a professional Poker player and there was no cheating. Management realized she and Jeru were a big attraction because whenever the two entered the building, it seemed to come alive with patrons commending them. The men would stand and kiss their hands while audiences often applauded.

As for Claudette, the affairs of Santa Fe and the rest of the world were far from her thoughts, except when she received the occasional letters from her sister, Cielito and her brothers sharing the latest family news. She would tell them all about Monaco, Monte Carlo, and the mansion in which they lived comfortably. Claudette begged them to come and visit, but they never did. Truth was that they were busy with business and family, on top of which Cielito's life centered around her two schools and the welfare of the Native American children.

With Jeru, it was different. She was always worried about her mother, Sarah, and wanted her to come and live with her and Claudette. Sarah had no thoughts of leaving Santa Fe or her job as head chef at the casino. At that time, none of the relatives had that adventurous spirit which Claudette and Jeru possessed, so each would go on enjoying the life they had carved out for themselves.

It was not long before an event happened that caused Claudette's brothers to rethink their way of life. Their first business was working for one of the wealthiest men in New Mexico -- Francisco Vargas. Vargas had never married or had children, and there were no known relatives. He had spent most of his life building his wealth without taking time for anything else, which was something he regretted when in Claudette's company. When Vargas was on his death bed, he called for the Ohara brothers, telling them he was proud of how they were building their wealth beyond what they inherited from their parents. He went on to tell them that relationships are more valuable than money. "Since my ranch and your ranch are next to each other, I am willing to give you five hundred head of cattle and fifteen thousand acres of my land that borders your ranch. I ask you to hire as many of my vaqueros' who remain in the area. I have willed to them money, land, and cattle. But I beg of you on my dying bed to please live your life by seeing the world and not letting your wealth define you."

To the Brothers Ohara, Santa Fe suited them just fine. Both were hard working and forward-thinking. No one knew that better than Bix Toilet, Bank President and advisor to the Oharas. His brother, Bax Toilet, was Chief Legal Counsel. The Ohara's holdings consisted of several highly successful ventures, including several Mines (some left to them by Francisco Vargas), a large cattle ranch, twelve high-producing oil wells, and a profitable gambling casino, with a combined value of two and a half billion dollars. He introduced them to a well-respected accountant and predictor of business trends, Streeter Finley.

Finley had reviewed their portfolios, and he said, "It is my recommendation that you look at incorporating, and afterwards look into more diversifying and maybe making the corporation a private family-owned entity. I can help you with that after the Toilets have time to study my proposal." Bix suggested that the boys take a month off and take the family on a memorable trip to Monaco to visit Claudette and Jeru. Cielito was unable to join them, but she was happy they would consider Bix's suggestion. Bix said he could have all their travel arrangements ready in a week.

The next evening, Cielito called Monaco to tell Claudette the good news, and they both screamed with excitement. Claudette was happy beyond belief! She called the staff together to tell them her two brothers were coming in a few weeks with their families, consisting of four adults and two children. She asked for suggestions as to how to make them feel welcome and what they could do to entertain them. Brinson mentioned a festival for the children, and museums and other sights for the adults. In at Monte Carlo, they could take a sight-seeing trip to Riviera and Niece. Brinson said, "If it pleases you, Mademoiselle, may I suggest that Hercule and Fannie take care of all of that." Claudette thanked Brinson for the suggestions. Her head was spinning with the thought of seeing her brothers and their children. One thing for sure was that she wanted them to see Monte Carlo on more than just one evening.

Three weeks later, Claudette received a call from Cielito informing her that the loved ones should arrive in approximately twelve or fifteen days. They would be on the SS France from New York to Paris. Claudette planned to be there to meet them. After the call from Cielito, she summoned Brinson and apprised him of the situation. He agreed to check for the next ten days as to the arrival of the SS France from New York and make arrangement for transportation for the family to Monaco. Brinson assured her that all arrangements would be made, and no detail overlooked.

The day finally arrived! The SS France was scheduled to dock at six o'clock p.m., and it was right on time. Claudette was so excited that she could hardly contain herself when she saw her brothers and their families moving toward the gang plank. Hercule had to hold her back from running up the gang plank to get to them. There were a lot of hugs, kisses, tears, and catching up on things back in Santa Fe. Brinson suggested the party retire to the automobiles, as it would be an hour or so before the baggage arrived.

There were plenty of nonstop conversations and excitement all the way to the chateau. Upon arrival, the brothers and their families were mesmerized by the size and scope of the chateau. The staff met them at the door, except for Chef Maurice, who was busy setting up the formal dining room for a light repast of Quiche Lorraine and tea) Brinson introduced them one by one and asked Claudette to introduce her brothers and family. After the light meal the mothers proceeded to prepare the children for bed while Claudette, Jeru and the brothers retired to the library for more conversation. The brothers tried to stay awake for their baby sister, but after two hours they retired to their bedrooms.

The next morning Brinson had the staff up early to prepare breakfast for the visitors, and Hercule and Fannie were planning to take them on their first sightseeing tour. The next two weeks were filled with exciting things to see and do. For Claudette, the pièce de résistance was the first night in Monte Carlo. She could hardly wait for her brothers to see her in action at the Poker table. They were amazed at her prowess and skill, but it was the reception she and Jeru received when they entered the casino that impressed them the most. They asked Brinson if they could hire a photographer to follow them around each night in the casino because they wanted pictures for the newspaper in Santa Fe. Brinson said he would check with the casino to see if it was okay. He learned that taking pictures was prohibited and he shared that information with the brothers, who suggested they could take pictures outside the casino. Brinson arranged for a photographer to follow them all going into the casino and coming out.

The next eight days would provide the Ohara family with hundreds of photographs of their visit with their sister, Claudette. It was a sad occasion when it was time for them to leave France. There were many tears, hugs, and kisses. Claudette reminded her brothers that they should receive three copies of the book of pictures soon -- one for each of her three siblings. The brothers thanked all the staff for all they did to make the vacation one to remember. Claudette held onto them as long as she could. They were the last to board the ship. Claudette insisted on staying until the ship left the dock.

Inside the car ride home the deafening silence was obvious. Claudette seemed to be distracted and withdrawn as she stared out the window the whole trip. When they arrived at the chateau, she was the first to exit and rushed inside to her and Jeru's bedroom. Jeru was conflicted as what she should do. She wanted to go to Claudette, but she felt she should let her have the moment before she tried to console her. When she entered the bedroom, she could hear Claudette crying. She lay on the bed next to her and embraced her without saying anything for minutes.

Claudette apologized to Jeru and said she loved her for allowing her to have those moments to herself. She said that when she watched her brothers go up the gang plank and turn to throw her a kiss, the wind picked up and she felt a chill come over her that made her feel as if that would be the last time that she'd see them alive. Jeru responded, "Oh, no, my love, don't think that! Why don't we plan to go back to Santa Fe once a year so you can visit with them, and I can see my mother? I feel a bit strange. You know, it's an ill wind that blows no good." Was this a premonition?

Chapter 7
Nimrod Bloom Means Trouble

    Meanwhile in New Mexico, Evil in the person of Nimrod Bloom crawled from under a rock. Nimrod was born into poverty in the Texas panhandle to a father who was not partial to pulling a cork (drunkard). His mother was a typical frontier woman with no schooling. She could not read or write and was subject to abuse, both physical and verbal, by all the authority figures in her young life and many in her adult life. By the time she was thirty, she was fully aware of her shortcomings, never having received kindness or grace. She was "old before her time."

    When Nimrod was ten years old, he was sick of seeing his mother beaten and cursed at, so he took matters into his own hands. While his father was sleeping off a drunken stupor, he took an iron skillet and busted both of his father's hands and one ankle. He left the house and the hard scrabble farm, and then he bounced between Texas and New Mexico. He learned to lie, cheat, and steal. Well, he had to if he was going to survive. By the time he was fifteen, he was taking whatever he wanted – a bully without a conscience. To him the point of a gun was the only thing he understood, and he used it to keep control of every circumstance in which he found himself. To him the law was just there to get in his way, until he was sentenced to five years in prison for attempted robbery. One would assume that prison had made a new man of him, because all of his spare time was spent reading the law. In truth, his reading was done to learn how get around the law next time.

Nimrod had started early planning his moves to become rich. He had associated with Hunt Dalton, who was in prison for assault and burglary, and Hezekiah Katz, known as "Copy Katz." Nimrod promised to teach Hunt to read and write. Hunt had two more years to serve, and Nimrod had three. Nimrod told him when his time was up, he was to go to Silver City, New Mexico and get a job and wait for him. He promised that they would be rich within a year.

Before prison, Nimrod had worked for a traveling minstrel show and caught onto the way the man and woman who did the magic show fooled the people who came to see the show. They would have the audience eating from their hand and not believing their own eyes. Over the few years of watching them, Nimrod became very good at "sleight of hand" tricks.

There was a preacher named Pearly Gates, who came to the prison to save the lost souls. Nimrod saw their sincerity and potential influence as his way out of prison. He told them that he had been reading the *Bible* and he wanted them to pray for him so the Lord would forgive him for all the evil things he had done. He wanted Pearly Gates and his wife to save him and those other wretched souls within and outside the prison.

Since they could only come once a week, Nimrod asked if he could hold service and have a nightly *Bible* study if it was alright with them and the Warden. The Warden approved, and before long, Nimrod was preaching so much fire and brimstone that the warden was sweating.

When Preacher Gates and wife made their next weekly visit, they found that the little chapel where they held service was filled to capacity with inmates. There was standing room only, and it appeared that their protégé could aid them much on the outside. Therefore, they began to talk to the Warden about letting Nimrod out for good behavior so he could do the Lord's work. The Warden had noticed a change in the attitude of those inmates who attended church service, so he petitioned the Governor to commute Nimrod's sentence and pardon him. The Governor thought it would be a wise political move, so he went ahead and got the press to cover this story and put a picture of him in the newspaper. Three days later, Nimrod walked out of prison a free man. Preacher Gates and his wife were at the front gate waiting for him with the proposal that he join them in their ministry. Nimrod thanked them, but said his plan was to go to prisons all over the West and minster to the inmates. He bade them goodbye and within a week, he was back in Silver City, New Mexico. That afternoon, he walked into Gramick's Dry Goods store where Hunt was working. Hunt immediately quit his job and walked out with Nimrod.

Hunt could not believe how Nimrod managed to keep his promise, but he would follow Nimrod anywhere. Nimrod said, "Tomorrow, I want you get a false beard and mustache and show up in a little town just south of Taos at exactly 10 o'clock. Go in the little bank and rob it for twenty dollars and say these words: 'I'm Nimrod Bloom and Jesus saves but Nimrod withdraws. Now I don't want to hurt anyone, so just relax, and give me just $20.00. I'm hungry and only want to take what I need.' When you leave the bank go to the eatery next door, eat breakfast, and go back to the bank and start crying. Say, 'The Lord told me it was wrong what I done, so I'm back with nineteen dollars and a quarter. I just got out of prison and had no money and was hungry. So, here I am, poor, simple Nimrod Bloom. Arrest me."

Hunt said, "You want me to go to jail for twenty dollars?" Nimrod responded, "You won't be in jail but a day or two. Didn't I tell you I would be out of prison before my time? Do this and we are on our way to more money than you have ever seen." Hunt reluctantly agreed to do just as Nimrod told him. At 10:00 the same day as Hunt was at the bank near Taos, the Bank of Las Cruces was robbed for seventy thousand dollars. Neither the money nor the holdup man was ever found, but nobody could suspect Nimrod because he was sitting in a small-town jail for robbing the local bank of $20.00. Nimrod was thoroughly corrupt, but he was smart.

The next day, A preacher by the name of Reverend Josiah Boone showed up in that small-town jail with his wife and told the Sheriff he knew this small-time crook, Nimrod Bloom and had ministered to him in prison. He and Mrs. Boone wanted to pray with him the Sheriff agreed. The Reverend prayed so loudly that people came in off the street. He asked the Lord to touch this Christian Sheriff's heart and let him release this poor boy because he was hungry and tempted by Satan. "I pray that if you, Sheriff, let your servant go, the Lord will shower you with blessings untold." Truth was that Nimrod could have been an effective pastor or evangelist, if not for his dark heart and scheming existence. His act actually had influence over weak-minded people full of guilt and seeking God!

The Sheriff, weeping, opened the cell door and let Hunt out, and Reverend Boone and his wife hugged him and saying, "Bless you, brother." By now, everyone was weeping. Nimrod checked his appearance to be certain that he looked like the Right Reverend Boone and not the infamous Nimrod Bloom. He whispered to Hunt that they must get out of there as soon as possible. When they got in the buggy, Nimrod introduced Hunt to Big Rump Cassie, who ran the Paradise Saloon and recruited prostitutes. "She's one of our associates and the rest of the group is waiting on the outskirts of town. Right now, we are headed to Silver City. The rest of you will go to the Paradise Saloon, Cassie will show you where it is. I have to make a stop and will see you all two days from now. Cassie will lay out our plans when all the group get here. Eat and drink and enjoy yourself because we own the place."

Two days later, true to his word he arrived in style in a yellow *Simplex Model 5* automobile loaded with several Edwardian suits, shoes, and shirts in the back of the car. A passenger dressed the same as Nimrod sat on the passenger side. Nimrod walked into the saloon and asked Cassie to have one of the boys get all his stuff and take it upstairs. "Is everyone here?" he asked. Cassie replied that all but two were there. "The person you call 'Copycat' never showed up."

A voice was heard coming down the stairs. "Copy Katz is here. Why he's a Ni..." Nimrod interrupted, saying, "I wouldn't use that term. Mr. Katz is just as precise with a straight razor as he is with a pen." Nimrod introduced his old prison mate, Hezekiah Copy Katz as the best forger in the world. He also introduced J. Arthur Begg, Esquire, but he paused mid-sentence and asked Cassie where Breed was. Cassie replied, "He's gone back below the border to pick you some more cherries." Breed traded with the Comancheros, who stole young Mexican girls and sold them to White traders, who sold them to Cassie, who forced them into prostitution. The girls were as young as ten years old, and they were Cassie's "cherries."

Nimrod was a disgusting pedophile and Cassie saved the youngest girls for him. Nimrod addressed the group gathered at the saloon. "After you depart today, Begg is your only contact with me. You will report to him for all of my instructions for jobs I want done. You will never come back here or mention my name from this day forward. Begg will take care of your needs and also pay you once a month. And each of you will buy suits, shoes, and shirts before you leave here, since you must look like businessmen.

Nimrod then turned to Cassie. "Let me have a look at my cherries." Cassie said there were three of them. "Breed said you can have two of them, but he will keep the one called 'Consuela' for himself." Nimrod responded with an attitude, "I will take all three. When he returns, pay him a little more and tell him we're moving our operation from Silver City to Albuquerque. Begg and I will be leaving today with Consuela. Two days from now, have everyone make their way there, not as a group but one or two at a time." Nimrod had disrespected Breed by telling everyone that he was taking Consuela with him, after Cassie said Breed intended to keep her for himself. This was the beginning of bad blood between Nimrod and Breed, and a life of hell for young Consuela.

Prior to leaving Silver City, Nimrod had a meeting with his lawyer, J. Arthur Begg, to discuss his interest in what he called a project forty miles north of Silver City. "Several mines owned by a company called the Ohara Brothers Mines, reputed to be worth millions. I want you to look into that for me. I want Hunt and Duce to muscle in on them and take over by the time we begin operating in the Santa Fe area." Begg said that taking the mines by force was not going to be easy. "Two years ago, they hired a nigger by the name of Jer Mercy as the superintendent of their operation. The first thing he did was to get the government to have army troops guard all the mines. So, the strong-arm method is not going to work."

Nimrod repeated his desire to get those mines by the time they moved in on Santa Fe. Begg told him that in Bonello County, the same owners of the mines owned a gambling casino and a thirty-thousand-acre ranch with close to one thousand head of cattle. "Rumor has it they have discovered oil on the ranch." Nimrod said for the moment they should concentrate on taking over Albuquerque. He gave Begg a map showing the land and farmland owned by Mexicans from Silver City to the northern border.

Several months later, on his return from Albuquerque to Santa Fe, Attorney Baxley Toilet felt an urgency to visit his twin brother, Bixley, at the State Bank of New Mexico Santa Fe. As he walked through the building, there was a chorus of "Good afternoon, Mr. Toilet," and of course he answered each one as he passed on his way to his brother's office. He stopped at the receptionist's desk where sat a well-dressed, pleasant-looking, middle-aged female who looked up and smiled and said, "Go right in, Mr. Toilet." Bax preferred to be announced, but his brother thought differently.

Bix spoke first. "Okay, okay, brother, what's on your mind?" Bax stood gazing out the window and finally spoke, "Brother, we got a storm headed our way. I'm not talking about the weather, but about trouble with a capital T." Bix asked to hear the details. Bax said, "I mean a storm of killing, stealing, claim-jumping and outright corruption by the name of 'Nimrod Bloom.' I just witnessed something in the Albuquerque courtroom that made me ashamed of my profession. From what I was able to learn, he came out of Silver City with his gang and began to run the land-owning Mexicans off their land. Those who would not leave would be burned out or murdered. From there he went to claim-jumping using the same tactics. It appears that he is moving into Albuquerque, and if he gets a foothold there, Bonello County and Santa Fe would be next. I am glad I got Jade and Bybel to redo their will before their unexpected passing."

Prior to the revelation about Nimrod Bloom, Bax had been working on the proposal presented by Streeter Finely, which was an almost ironclad structure that no one could lawfully lay claim to any of their holdings. He told Bix about his plan to put all of the Ohara's holdings into one corporation and a trust. Instead of each child having eleven percent and Jerusalem having seven percent, all the mines would be in the corporation, with all of the stock owned by the five. The casino and ranch would go into a trust, but the oilwells would remain owned by a joint venture of Ohara Oil and Consolidated Oil Corporation, with all the stock owned by four children and Jeru.

Bix said, "Well, brother, it appears we have no time to lose. Prior to Jade and Ohara passing, I had them place the casino and ranch in a trust, and all that is needed now is to turn Ohara holdings into a private inc. Now that the brothers Ohara have returned from Monaco and things have settled down, we should set up a meeting with Sean, Jean, and Cielito tomorrow. Claudette and Jeru are living in France, but we can function as proxy for them. Bix had his secretary contact the three Oharas to set up a meeting.

In the meantime, the brothers had a chance to further study Finley's plan, thinking it a good idea for him to be at the meeting with the Ohara siblings. The next day they all met. Bax told them what he knew about Nimrod Bloom, and Finley went through the details of his financial plan with them. Finley said his plan would secure their businesses and the children's financial future, and he and the Toilet brothers believed that with his plan, no one could legally take any of the things their parents had worked so hard for. Bax explained that Jade and Ohara, prior to their passing, had given him permission to place the casino and ranch in trust for the children's protection. "We ask you to be at my office tomorrow morning and tell no one where you are going. It won't be a problem for Sean and Jean, as their office is just a few blocks down from the bank."

After concluding the meeting, they went to Bax's office, after which Bix walked down to the Ohara brothers' office to tell them the plan. Sean greeted him and joked, "Do I owe the bank money?" Jean followed Bix back to the office to meet with Bax. Bax began, "Jean, there is a man named Nimrod Bloom going throughout New Mexico claim-jumping and running people off their land. He is slick and ruthless, and if the people do not sell, he burns them out or kills them. He already has a foot in Albuquerque, and I am afraid he is making his way into Bonello County and Santa Fe. I am going to fix it so neither you nor your siblings can sell unless all of you agree to sell."

Jean said, "I had three persons pay me a visit today asking about our mining operation and wanting to buy us out. One's name was Arthur Begg." Bax advised Jean to stall him by saying that it will take some time before he could get back to him. "That would give me time to get the papers registered with the state." The next morning the Ohara's had gathered at the bank with Bax and Bix, and after a thorough discussion the papers were signed and Bax dispatched a runner to his friend, Secretary of State Wallace Baffert, who understood and would expedite the entire process.

Chapter 8
The Kidnapping Plot

A month before the meeting with the Toilet brothers, the Ohara brothers had a great vacation with their sister, Claudette, in Monaco. However, now they were glad to be back and taking care of business. The building at 35 Santa Cruz Street had a newly painted sign on the door that read, "Headquarters Ohara Corporation." It housed the office of Sean Machel and Jean Phillipe Ohara. Over the door of the building hung a large clock that chimed loudly when it struck "12." It was about this time on a Tuesday when three men in suits, looking like "criminal types," walked in the door and asked to speak to the Ohara brothers. Sean introduced himself and asked if he could help them.

"You sure can. I am J. Arthur Begg. These two are my associates, Hunt Dalton and Duce Dawson, and we want to buy stock in your corporation." Sean said, "I am sorry, gentlemen, but Ohara Inc. is not mine alone. I and six others own the stock, on top of which this corporation is privately. There's no stock for sale.

Hunt blurted out, "Well, sell us your shares!" Sean quickly announced that they would need to discuss that with Mr. Bix Toilet, Chairman of the Board and CEO. He offered to let Chairman Toilet know about the three men, who reluctantly turned to leave because they had not gotten what they came for. Hunt said in a threatening voice, "Don't worry, we will be back; you can bet your life on that."

Jean came downstairs to report the discovery of another lucrative oil well, and then asked who Sean was talking to. Sean replied, "Three unsavory chaps with shifty eyes, two of whom appeared to be wearing shoulder holsters." The brothers needed to talk to Bax. Sean and Jean went to lunch, and while sitting at an outdoor café, they gazed in the distance at the snow caps on the Sangre de Cristo Range. They felt blessed to be born in Santa Fe, and thanked God for their late parents, their siblings and their wives and children. They began to realize what good medicine it was for them to have spent a month on vacation relaxing and unwinding.

Sean Michael finally said, "Brother, you know we have more money than we could ever spend …." Jean cut him off. "Brother, you are not thinking of selling our shares to those despots, are you?" "No! Never!" said Sean in a definitive tone. "I have been thinking of something Mr. Vargas said about his regrets before he passed away. I was thinking about how much time we take away from our wives and children putting in so much time in the office and being on the road checking the mining interest and the ranch. And we hardly ever spent time with mother and father when they were alive. Since we visited Claudette, we haven't found time for our family." Jean Phillipe agreed. "Why don't we take the time to do something with our families? I mean why not from now on take a break each weekend and take all of them on a trip?"

Sean Michael thought it was a great idea, and they could also attend the Fiesta De Santa Fe on Saturday, drive down to El Rancho De Las Golondrinas for the night, and drive back Sunday evening. Jean said, "I know the wives and children will be beyond excited." Jean Phillipe said that within an hour and a half, he should be able to finish looking over the numbers Consolidated Oil had sent them.

Sometime later, Jean Phillipe entered his building and was sorting his mail when the bell rang and the clerk and bookkeeper came inside. An hour later, Arthur Begg and his henchmen entered the building looking for Sean Ohara, claiming he was going to buy Sean's shares of Ohara Inc. Jean told him that his brother was not there, but that the stock was not for sale. "I'm afraid you are wasting your time." Hunt stepped closer to Jean, reaching inside his coat in a threatening manner, but Begg told him and Duce to leave the building.

Begg apologized for his associate's behavior and then asked for Bix Toilet. Jean said he might find him at the bank up the street, so Begg left. Jean immediately called Bix to warn him that Begg was on the way. As Begg stepped outside of the Ohara office building, Hunt angrily said, "Listen to me, you pip squeak, don't ever talk to us like that again or I will fill you so full of holes you will think you're a flour sifter!" Begg reminded both men that Nimrod had put him in charge, but nevertheless, Duce protested being talked down to in front of strangers. Begg redirected them to meeting Mr. Bix Toilet to take care of Nimrod's business.

When the three entered the bank, it appeared that Bix and his security team were prepared for them. When they walked toward the teller window, two men turned to walk away and bumped into Hunt and Duce. The men immediately apologized and pretended to brush off Duce's and Hunt's coats as a gesture of being sorry. Before Begg could reach the window, the two men signaled to a female security person acting as a teller, indicating that two of the three were armed. She relayed the information by hand signals to the loan officers nearest to Bix's office.

Begg had already surveilled the set up and could see a hall behind the loan officer. He proceeded to walk in that direction, asking to speak with Mr. Toilet. He told the officer, "I am Attorney J. Arthur Begg, here on corporate business and I do not have an appointment. I don't mind waiting." The loan officer stepped away, returning shortly to allow Begg to see Mr. Toilet. Hunt and Duce had to wait in the outer area.

Bix, already aware of what Begg was there for, asked Begg what he could do for him. Begg was interested in buying stock in the Ohara's corporation. Bix replied, "I assume you have spoken to the Principals who explained that the corporation is privately owned and therefore, there is no stock for sale unless all parties agree to release their collective 51%. This bank has no intention of selling its 49%."

Begg asked to look at the Articles of Incorporation, to which Bix responded that the papers are on file at the State office. Bix excused himself, adding, "If you make any progress, please feel free to come back and I will see what I can do to help you. Good day, Sir." When Begg, Hunt and Duce got outside, they argued briefly about why Hunt and Duce were excluded from the meeting. Begg said, "Shut up and listen. There were at least five Pinkerton men in there just waiting for one of you to do something stupid. "Mr. Bank President" thinks he is smart, but I will show him something.

The three men drove to the Secretary of State's office, and Begg asked the receptionist where he might find the Record Room for certificates of incorporations. The receptionist offered to help him, Hunt and Duce decided to catch a cab and go to the casino. Begg cautioned them not to start any trouble, and after giving him a dirty look, they left. After five hours of looking, Begg didn't find the Ohara's corporate filing, and was told he must leave as the office was closing for the day. As he walked to his automobile, it hit him they had to have a business license that would be easier to find. He would need at least two of their signatures for Katz, which meant that he must find their incorporation certificate.

As soon as Begg had made his way to the casino, he witnessed the bartender pointing a shotgun at Hunt and Duce, threatening to call the police. Begg rushed up to the bar with his hands raised, assuring the bartender that there was no need for police. He announced that he was their lawyer and would get them out of there right away. Begg pushed them towards the door, but Duce yelled back, "This ani't the last you will see of us. We going to own this place soon!"

Begg was so angry and disgusted that he cursed at the men. "Get the fuck outta here before you get locked up or killed! You know Nimrod is not going to like this." Duce immediately shot back with a threat of his own. "We ain't scared of Nimrod, and we definitely ain't scared of you." Hunt added that they were used to killing, so it wouldn't mean a thing for them to kill Begg or Nimrod or anybody else whom they felt had offended them. Begg had no response, as he knew they were dead serious!

They returned to their hotel, and Begg said he was going to the bar. Of course, the other two insisted on joining him, but he protested and asked them to stay in the room. Well, that was never going to happen. Hunt and Duce pushed right past Begg, heading for the bar. Actually, what Begg wanted was for these two to get drunk and pass out. It was a good plan, except that Begg didn't realize how much the two could drink. They ended up bringing more liquor to the room, where Hunt and Duce finally passed out. Begg took that opportunity to sneak down to the lobby to call Nimrod.

Cassie answered the phone, and Begg insisted on speaking to Nimrod. Begg reported, "First, three times I had to stop Hunt and Duce from screwing up things here. They are passed out drunk, and I'm in the lobby. I need you to give me thirty minutes and call the room until one of them answers. Ask to speak to me, and I will give you a report on where we are with the Oharas. Don't let them know I told you how they have been acting because they threatened to kill me."

Nimrod understood Begg's fear and agreed to call in half an hour. The phone rang, and Begg pretended to be passed out drunk so that Duce might wake up and answer. He did, and Nimrod asked to speak to Begg. Duce had to shake Begg a couple of times before Begg "awoke" and took the phone. Begg cleared his throat and sat up straight. "Hello, Boss. I want you to know I will soon have everything Katz needs, so have him to come to the Stockmen's Hotel in the morning and ask for me. After he does his job, I can wrap this thing up in a week or so."

Nimrod then asked to talk to Hunt, so Duce staggered over to shake Hunt. He wasn't happy about being awakened, so he snatched the phone. "Hello, Boss, man I hope you feeling as good as I am right now." Nimrod told him to shut up and listen. "It appears I hired the wrong man for the job if you're drunk. This job is too important for you to screw it up. I am sending Breed and his men, along with Cassie to take over the casino, so maybe Breed's men can handle this job." Hunt nervously assured Nimrod that he'd be fine in the morning.

Nimrod gave him one last chance, and Hunt said he wouldn't let him down. Hunt gave Begg a nasty look as he passed the phone back to him. Nimrod said, "I am sending Katz tonight, and he will get with you in the morning. It shouldn't take him more than an hour to do his job, and he'll call me when it's time for Hunt and Duce to begin their part. Once Mexican Bob and his gang of five have taken over the ranch, they will be ready for Hunt and Duce and the Ohara brothers. You all know what to do." Nimrod hung up.

Before Hunt returned the receiver to its cradle, he grabbed Begg by his robe and said, "I told you what I would do if you told Nimrod anything about us getting into trouble in the bar." Duce interjected that they were present when Begg spoke to Nimrod, so he hadn't betrayed them. Hunt simply said, "Oh, yeah," as he released Begg from his grip." Hunt mumbled in an almost inaudible manner that he would take care of Begg after he took care of the Oharas.

Early the next morning, a slender Black man entered the Stockmen's Hotel. The night clerk made the mistake of informing him that the hotel did not cater to "niggers." With the speed of a lightning bolt, Katz had leaped over the counter and had his straight razor on the clerk's neck, with his other hand tightly gripping his genitals. The clerk was paralyzed with fear and pain. Katz stared directly into the clerk's eyes, never releasing his tight grip, and said loudly, "When you address me, you better never call me 'nigger.' My name is Copy Katz, and you will address me as Mister Copy Katz!"

The clerk almost fainted by this time, but found enough strength to say, "Mr. Katz, Sir, what can I do for you, Sir, I mean Mr. Katz?" Katz lightened his grip on the man's genitals but didn't release him yet. "Pick up that phone and call Mr. Begg's room and tell him that Mister Copy Katz is here." The clerk stood there trembling, as he quickly complied. Katz told Begg to come down, and that he had some "garbage" for Hunt and Duce to get rid of. He was referring to the clerk, but Hunt said they needed to stick to Nimrod's plan and leave this clerk alone. Katz reluctantly agreed but stared back at the clerk with every step of his leaving the establishment.

The four of them got into the auto, with Begg and Katz up front and Hunt and Duce in the rear. On the way, Begg told Katz, "It shouldn't take more than one hour, and you can do your thing. We will stop at the city office, and I will find you another copy bearing all three signatures." Begg found the corporate filing of the Ohara corporation, and they all headed for the city business license office. Begg located the Ohara brothers' business license and Cielito's registration for the Jean Phillipe and Claudette Debose Christoph Schools. Begg handed Katz three blank bills of sale, and it took Katz a few minutes to copy the names.

Begg went to the Western Union office and called Nimrod. "We are preparing to leave for my office in Albuquerque to get the paperwork typed up and notarized." Nimrod responded affirmatively, but then asked Begg to take Hunt and Duce to the casino and leave them there. Breed and his people were there and had taken it over already. Nimrod asked to speak to Hunt again. "Proceed with your part of the operation. Breed is at the casino and knows to give you the keys to his car. I want those

Ohara boys taken today! They should be leaving for their quarterly meeting in Albuquerque, so you can kidnap them ten miles outside of Santa Fe and take them to the ranch where Mexican Bob and his people are. You might have to get the sister tomorrow."

Two days earlier, Breed, whose nickname was short for "half breed," and his gang had arrived at the casino and asked for the manger, Sarah Twotrees. When Sarah entered the room Breed was in, he made a kind of connection with her, due to his background. He noticed from her name and appearance that she was part Indian. He said, "Sister, are you the manager? I am proud of you." Sarah said, "Sir, I am sure I don't know you." He told her they had something in common. "I am called Breed, and the casino is under the new ownership of Mr. Nimrod Bloom. Call all the staff to the main room so I can tell them the good news." Breed told them the news and that all who wanted to stay could do so, depending upon their loyalty.

As Sarah was about to leave, Breed told her to show him around and acquaint him with where everything is and how everything works. Sarah replied, "Sir, I am the head chef and manager of the kitchen staff, waiters/waitress and the dining room. I have no knowledge of the rest of the casino, and I must get back to the kitchen in order to have food prepared when we open."

The door to the casino opened and the voice of females could be heard. Breed was surprised to see big rump Cassie and her girls. As they moved further inside, the last one to enter was a young Mexican girl struggling with several bags. Breed recognized Consuela, and rushed up to Cassie to ask what was going on. Cassie began to tremble because she knew Breed was ruthless. "I told

Nimrod what you said but he said he didn't care, and he was taking her."

Breed grabbed Consuela by the hand and pulled her to the kitchen with Sarah. He said, "Sister, this girl is mine and no one is to touch her, not even Nimrod! I want you to keep her with you at all times, so find something for her to do and you guard her with your life! She is not to go out in the main room, and they are not going to make a prostitute out of her." He didn't know that it was too late because Nimrod had already taken her. She was like the other girls, except that she was only about twelve at the time. Sarah was almost speechless, but agreed to whatever Breed told her to do.

Chapter 9
Murderers!

Four days later, Bax had a visit from the Ohara brothers' wives advising him that their husbands were missing, and they were supposed to have gone to their quarterly mine meetings in Albuquerque. The wives had received a call from Jer Mercy (short for "Jerusalem"), Superintendent of all the Mines, asking if the brothers had left for the meeting. The wives said they left two days ago. As they finished expressing their concerns, the women's voices began to fight back tears because they feared that something terrible had happened.

Bax said not to worry because he would find them. He added, "I want you to go home, pack some clothes for the children, and go to your families for a little while. It's just a precaution, so don't be alarmed. But do not tell anyone where you are going. I will be in touch."

About the same time Begg showed up at the bank but was told he would have to wait to see Bix, who was in a meeting with the city commissioners about the new downtown project. Bix's phone rang and it was Bax. There was a distinct nervousness in his voice as he announced that the Ohara brothers and Cielito were missing. The brothers never got to their quarterly meeting, and Cielito was last seen leaving her school with two men two days ago.

Bix and Bax thought it wise for Bax to come right over. When Bax arrived, Bix dismissed the commissioners to attend to "urgent matters." Bix said, "Let's get Begg in here and see what's on his mind." As Begg was making his way to Bix's office, Bix's secretary came in and whispered that Blossom was on the phone, saying it was urgent that she speak to Bix. He walked to his secretary's desk to take the call, asking her to hang up his phone. "What is it, Blossom?" She said, "I know you just buried your father, but I need you to come here right away, and bring Dr. Joe and your brother, Mr. Bax."

Bix discreetly told Bax to get rid of Begg. "Something has happened out at Blossom's place I got to pick up Dr. Joe. Tell Begg I have an emergency at home and must leave. Then join me at Blossom's place." Earlier that day at Blossom's place the whole family was in the field, along with JB's friend and employee, Al, watching the harvesting of their corn. Al was intrigued by the combine machine, which was taller than theirs. He climbed up on it to watch the seed company machine operator in action, but as he turned to get down, he saw something strange in the distance. Al beckoned to JB and signed for him to come up there.

JB climbed up on the combine in order to have the same landscape visibility that Al had. Al said, "Do you see what I see?" "I wonder what they are up to?" What they saw was a bunch of cows being moved, and they could see on the other side of the cows what appeared to be three men on horseback, each leading another person behind them. The three people appeared to be two men and a woman with their hands tied behind their backs. JB signed to Al that he fully understood what was about to happen. Before he could finish uttering those words, they both watched in horror as the men on horseback shot the two brothers dead. They shot Cielito too, but she didn't die.

As soon as it appeared to be safe, JB and Al rushed to the trio and confirmed that the Ohara brothers were dead. They hurried to stop Cielito's bleeding. JB sent Al back to the field to alert Blossom about what had just happened. Al was completely out of breath as he approached Blossom. He asked to speak to her privately because JB didn't want him to alarm Shy if she thought something had happened to her husband. Blossom asked Shy to get in the truck because they had to get back to the house in a hurry. At first, Shy protested, saying she would wait for JB to return before she came home. But Blossom had a nervous determination in her voice, as she told Shy, "Don't worry about JB, Honey, do as I say now. I am going to need your help the moment we get back to the house."

When they arrived, Blossom called the bank and told Bix she had an emergency. He and Bax and Dr. Joe would be there shortly. When Blossom got off the phone Shy asked if there was anything wrong with her husband, but Blossom assured her that JB was fine. "If the babies are asleep, I need you to start two large pots of water boiling, get those folded flour sacks out, and take my shears and begin cutting them up for bandages. Also, run out to the barn and bring me that piece of canvas." They didn't know that Al had already taken the canvas back to JB and Cielito.

Blossom asked Shy to bring her three sheets in the dining room, and before she returned with the sheets, JB, Al, and Juan were back. JB signed to Al to tell Juan to take the wagon to the barn, unhitch the mule, and push the wagon in the barn and close the door. JB and Al picked up Cielito and brought her into the house. She was still drifting in and out of consciousness. Blossom said to bring her into the dining room and put her on the table. JB signed that she had lost a lot of blood. Blossom told him to go into the garden and bring back a pot of okra. "Shy, when he comes back put the okra in that boiling water and watch it until it starts to get thick and slimy." Shy complied with every order from her mother.

Blossom found a small flour sack and put the okra in it. She started to squeeze it into a large bowl, and when she thought she had enough she told JB to get another big bowl and squeeze it until all the juice was out. She added a little water to cool the okra juice down. She brought it to the dining room and asked Shy to hold Cielito's head up. "We need her to drink this. It will substitute for some of the blood she lost."

It wasn't long before Bix and the doctor arrived. Everybody was busy, so Al went to the door and said they were all in the dining room trying to save the lady. Dr. Joe began checking Cielito's vital signs, while asking who had done this. Al said, "We don't know but JB saw them." "No! I mean who bandaged her up and put the pieces of aloe plant over the bullet holes?" It was JB who had ripped his shirt and made the bandage. "Well, you two might have saved her life. Blossom what is that you are having her drink?" Blossom said, "That's okra juice. I read somewhere that it is a suitable substitute for replenishing blood." "That's right. You know you all did so well that you probably didn't need me since the bullet went through." Blossom said they didn't have anything for pain, which Cielito would need as soon as she was fully conscious.

Al asked the doctor and Bix to come with him and JB to the barn. Bix said his brother was on the way and would come to the barn as soon as he arrived. Blossom asked Shy to bring her the rest of the okra juice and get some more from the garden. Blossom would listen for the babies in case they woke and cried.

Bax showed up and was directed to the barn with the rest of the men. Just as Bix asked where so many flies had come from, Al pulled the canvas back to reveal the bodies of the Ohara brothers. Bix, Bax, and the doctor gasped at the grizzly sight. "Oh, no! Not Sean and Jean Ohara!" Al said that JB had gotten there too late to stop the murders, but he saw it happen. He didn't know the names of the men who killed the brothers in cold blood. He was able to save Cielito.

JB signed and Al interpreted that, although JB didn't know the three men's names, he saw all three faces and could draw the whole scene well enough that the men's faces would be clear and identifiable. The doctor said, "Gentlemen, we have to dig graves and get those bodies under as soon as possible, or we're going to have a health problem on our hands. We can't wait for the corner or the police. I suggest we take that lime and spread it on the bodies, and the rest of it we spread all over the barn."

Bax told JB, Al, and Juan to bury the brothers while the other men discussed the best way to handle the situation. "We certainly don't want the ones who did this to know that we know what happened, and we can't let anyone know Cielito is alive. As soon as you get them buried, hurry back to the house. We have got a lot of planning to do."

The doctor interrupted. "Gentlemen, we need to talk outside until the three others come back, and I want them to strip, burn those clothes and shoes, and thoroughly wash from head to toe. I suggest you two do the same before you enter your house." Two hours later JB, AL, and Juan returned and did what the doctor suggested. Bix said, "Cielito must remain here for some time until the three men are apprehended. I will call Claudette tomorrow and tell her she should come home because her three siblings have been missing for some time. First, I will brief Brinson, the Pinkerton man posing as the butler."

Bax reminded them that somebody needed to talk to the wives of Jean and Sean, but he decided to tell them a story until these dangerous men were apprehended. "In addition, I will bring Chief Bywater up to speed and swear him to secrecy until JB completes drawing pictures of the murderers and the three men are apprehended. JB would report to the bank in the morning but would stay in the conference room in order to create the scene that would cause the three dangerous men to be apprehended fairly quickly. Nobody would be allowed to go near the conference room and distract JB for any reason.

The next morning Bix was at the bank early waiting with everything JB said he would need to recreate the scene. Bix called Monaco to speak to Brinson, but a female voice said Brinson was at Monte Carlo with Mademoiselles Ohara and Twotrees. Bix said, "When he returns quietly tell him to call Bix Toilet, no matter what time it is." The female voice said she would relay the message.

Three hours later JB emerged from the conference room and tapped on the glass door of Bix's office. Bix followed him to the conference

80

room, where JB pointed to the table. The scene he had recreated was very clear and graphic. Bix gasped and rushed out of the room to his office to call Bax. "Get over here. JB is finished, and you are not going to be surprised. Bring Bywater with you. Come to the back door because I don't want the employees to see you two." Bax convinced Bix that it would be better for the meeting to occur in his office.

Bix, JB, and Bywater arrived about the same time. JB laid out his work on Bax's conference table. Bax said to his brother, "You were right, this doesn't surprise me. That's two of them alright, with one missing. I believe he can tell us where we can find the others." Bywater was puzzled, but Bax said to take a look at this. Bywater looked at the two brothers and said, "Yes these three guys were arrested in Albuquerque last year.

They set fire to this Mexican farm, killed the grandfather, claimed the farmer sold to some guy named Nimrod, and ran the farmer off the place. Would you believe that the judge let them off? No one showed up at the trial, but this is Hunt Dalton, Duce Dawson, and Roberto Gomez, better known as "Mexican Bob."

JB was listening to Bywater, and then he handed Bix a note that said the victims of this gang were Al and his family. They were all a little stunned at this sad news. Bax asked Al if he had ever seen the men pictured there in JB's drawing. Al clearly recognized the men. His face grew tight as he said, "Those are the three who killed my father and burned me out." Bax asked if Al's family had sold any property to Nimrod, who responded with, "No, Sir, I don't know that person, but the others said they would kill the rest of my family if they ever saw my face again, which is why I am in Santa Fe."

Bax spoke with confidence. "They are going to see your face again, but they will not harm or kill your family. I can promise you that when they see your face it will be on the witness stand." Bax told Bywater that now they had two eyewitnesses to the murder of the Ohara brothers. He emphasized that everything they were discussing must stay right there. Cielito Ohara was shot but she is alive and hidden safely with Blossom until those three murderers are apprehended and locked up. "I will make sure they won't get bail!"

JB was asked to draw the three faces without the scene where the Ohara brothers were murdered execution style. JB signed affirmatively, which Al interpreted for everyone. He left to begin drawing. Bix said, "I think I know how we can find the three S.O.B.s. I will call Begg and tell him that our two stockholders who are in Europe don't plan to return to the States, and if the price is right, they will consider selling their shares. I'll tell him that that might entice the other stockholders to sell. I'll make it clear to Begg that he can come to the bank tomorrow and I will let him talk to the stockholders who can be present."

Bax turned to Bywater. "As soon as Begg walks in, you can arrest him and charge him with accessory to murder after the fact, fraud, forgery and arson and we can come up with several other things that might force him to tell us where his henchmen are hiding."

JB walked into the office and handed Bix the drawing. Bix looked at, it placed it on the desk, and told JB that it was perfect! Bywater and Bax moved closer to look at the drawing, and Bywater said, "They look so real! That boy is mighty smart for an Injun." Everyone stared at Bywater after his racist comment. Bix said sarcastically, "He is smart for a human being!" Bywater maintained his ignorance by saying, "Sorry, didn't know you was an Injun lover."

Bix sighed, unable to contain his contempt for Bywater. "Listen here! Were you ever invited to Washington, D. C. to be commended by Congress? Well JB has! Do you have over twenty thousand dollars in the bank? JB has! I would say that HE is pretty smart for a human being, wouldn't you?" Bywater turned red and backed away from the desk. Bax suggested that JB should sign and date the drawing, and others would sign as witnesses. They headed to Blossom's place to show the drawing to Cielito, whom Blossom indicated was conscious, although weak.

The brothers and Bywater left in one car. JB and Al were prepared to return to their jobs cleaning the bank, but Juan had already finished. JB made a walk through to ensure the job was done to his satisfaction, and it was. They left for home. JB looked at Al as they drove. He was quiet, and JB could tell Al was upset because his fist was tight, with his jaws clenched. JB pulled off the road and faced Al and signed, "It's going to be all right. I know you want to hurt someone, but don't think about that. Our day is coming. Mama will tell you that." Al hesitated before replying, "You are right, JB, I will get justice for my father when I point them out from the witness stand."

As Bax drove down the road towards Blossom's house, Bywater asked Bix how JB got that much money. Bix replied, "Our grandfather left it to him in his will, for taking care of him and our grandmother, and Blossom, JB's mother, cured him of gout." Bywater said, "Okay, but everybody knows that she ain't White, even if she looks it." Bax cut him off, insisting that he shut his mouth.

When they reached Blossom's house, Bax told Bywater to listen and not speak. Shy answered the door, holding one of her babies. JB had just driven up, and they all went inside to see Cielito, if she was awake. Shy told them, "Mama is with her, but I will check and see if she's finished." (Jim, given the time frame since Cielito was shot and lost much blood, it's not likely that she had a bath or entered the parlor standing up.) Cielito was too weak to sit up, but Blossom escorted the men to her bed. Bax said, "We don't want to upset you, Ma'am, but we need to ask you some questions and show you some drawings. Do you think you will be okay with that?" She said she would do her best. Bax asked her if she knew the men who kidnapped her and her two brothers. She didn't know them, but she remembered that she was taken as she left her office. She was unsure of the length of time she was held at a ranch but believed that her brothers had met them before. Bax asked if she could identify them if she saw them again. She seemed to become uncomfortable, almost frightened as she cried, "I don't want to see them again ever, ever again!"

Bax said they should pay for what they did, but he needed her help. Cielito was clearly weaker and needed to rest, but Bax asked if she could just look at a drawing and tell him if those faces are of the three kidnappers who murdered her brothers. Bax showed her the drawing, and her reaction was swift, and she screamed in pain and fear. "Take it away, take it away!" She broke down, and Blossom asked everyone to step outside the room until she could calm her down.

Blossom assured Cielito that she was safe and that those men would never hurt her again. She called out to Shy to make a cup of Chamomile tea.

Blossom was gently rubbing Cielito's head and temples while the tea steeped. Cielito seemed to calm down and took a few sips of the tea. Blossom chose her next words very carefully, determined not to upset Cielito again but wanting to know if she could identify the men in JB's drawing. "Drink this tea and you will feel better. Ms. Ohara you have to help Mr. Bax if you can. He wants to see those three men hanged, and from your reaction to the drawing, you identified them as your kidnappers. Remember what you did to help Mr. Bax stop the mistreatment of those Native children at those horrible schools? It was my son, JB, who saved your life, even though he was too late to save your brothers."

A few minutes after Cielito drank the tea she seemed relaxed and asked Blossom to let the men come back in. "I think I can deal with it now." Blossom brought everyone back into the room, and Cielito asked to see the pictures again. Bax held the drawings, and Cielito immediately said those were the two men who had kidnapped her. "They took me to the ranch where they had my brothers tied and gagged. The other one is the one who shot me." Bax asked if she would be willing to testify in court, and she said yes. Bax made sure she understood that she would have to stay there recovering in hiding until the men were found and locked up. "I am certain that they assume you are dead, and we want the whole gang to believe that. I say gang because there are more than just those three." Blossom said she could stay as long as need be.

Bax thanked Blossom and Cielito, and as the men left, he turned to Bix and Bywater and said, "Gentlemen, I think we got what we need. Let's leave the Blakes and Ms. Ohara in peace but make certain that there are police in plain clothes to protect them if needed. Before Bix left the house, he asked Shy he could see his namesake, which was one of the babies. Naturally, Bax asked to see his namesake also, and Shy smiled, but said they were asleep. They quietly entered the nursery area, where they both mentioned how these little ones have grown. They tiptoed out and left.

The next day Bix received a call from Brinson, and Bix relayed the horrific news that had just happened in Santa Fe. "I need Claudette to be here as soon as possible. The truth is that her brothers have been murdered and her sister is missing, but don't tell her that. Just say that the three of them have been kidnaped and I need her home as soon as possible. I am going to book passage for you all on the *LZ 127 Graf Zeppelin* Tht ride will take about three days, after which you will have a special train from New York to Chicago to Santa Fe. The conductor will be instructed to leave you all just outside of Santa Fe, and I will meet you all there. It should be daylight when you all arrive, but make sure the shades are down and don't allow anyone to approach you. These people are ruthless and have a wide network with eyes everywhere."

Brinson said there would be five travelers, since the ladies would insist on their personal bodyguards coming along. Bix was curious about their need for bodyguards. Brinson said they had hired the two whom he hired while they were in Paris. He added that they were good at their jobs. "Claudette and Jeru pay them from their earnings from Monta Carlo casinos." Bix said he hoped to see all of them in five days.

Four days later, Claudette and her party were on a nonstop train from Chicago bound for Santa Fe. The sound of the continues clickety clack noise made by the Atchison, Topeka, and Santa Fe Railway trains made its one-thousand- seven-hundred-mile journey from Chicago to Santa Fe akin to hypnosis on Claudette and Jeru as they occasional looked out the window of their private car that was provided by Bix Toilet, who was friend and advisor to the Ohara family.

That was especial so for Claudette Ohara. He had loved her from a young boy, although she was much younger. He loved her to this day, although he was married. Soon Claudette and Jeru were asleep. The two of them looked like two little girls on a sleep over, all hugged up together with heads laying against each other.

All of a sudden Claudette awakened and whispered to Jeru, "Wake up, Love." Jeru gathered herself and asked if they had arrived. Claudette relayed a dream she had just had. Do you remember when we were in New Orleans at the Southern Belle? It seemed there was this couple always sitting at a poker table near us playing poker with this man who appeared to have only one hand like my father. Jeru didn't recall that, saying she was dealing Faro at the Belle. "Yes, but you must have notice them in Paris."

Jeru couldn't recall this adventure, but she did remember one night at Monte Carlo, where Claudette was asking Brinson to find out who the threesome were who seemed to have the table near us every night." He inquired and was told, "It was the Grand Duke of Corsica and his daughter Duchess Jaiden and her husband, Sir John Bielby." Claudette said it was strange that she noticed them in three different places. "I began to have a feeling of kinship with them. "Maybe it was just as I was drifting off to sleep a few minutes ago and saw them again. It could it be the stress of my sister and brothers missing." Jeru said that was probably it.

It was not long before the porter/cook entered the car and inquired if Claudette and Jeru would care for dinner. He announced the menu of baked prairie chicken (squab) with stuffed baked potatoes, asparagus with hollandaise cream sauce or wine sauce, and for desert crème Brule. They said, "Oh yes, that sounds delicious." The porter made his way to the other car to announce diner to the men.

Claudette and Jeru made their way to the restroom to freshen up before dinner. When they returned, the conductor was waiting for them. He passed on the pleasantries of the day and advised them that the train was crossing from Missouri into Kansas in an hour and because there were only two engines and three cars, meaning that the wind would rock the cars a little more than usual. "Not to worry, you're safe. Most passengers take that time to sleep, and we should arrive in New Mexico around midday and Santa Fe about 2:00 p.m. Enjoy your dinner, ladies.

After dinner, the rest of the party had joined Claudette and Jeru in their car and were enjoying coffee and conversation when they began to feel the effects of the wind. The conductor entered the car and announced that due to the severity of the wind, the train would have to pull off into a siding for their safety. He stated that during all the years he had made this run, he had never seen the wind blowing this hard. "We will make up the time after the wind dies down."

Two hours later the winds seemed to subside, and the conductor knocked at the car door. The whole party, although asleep, happened to be in the seats in the one car where the conductor had last talked with them. Brinson got up and unlocked the door, and the conductor said the wind had died down and he made the decision to get back on schedule. He said they should encounter some more strong winds all the way through Kansas to New Mexico. Brinson said he would tell the others. The conductor said it was not necessary to lock the door. Brinson replied that, as the head of security he felt it necessary, since the train had stopped, and he was responsible for his party's safety.

The conductor said he understood and would signal the engineer to proceed. When the engine powered up and moved, it caused the cars to jerk, and the sleeping party was awakened and inquiring about what happened. Brinson assured them everything was okay. It was just the engine pulling from the siding to the main track.

Chapter 10
The Return to Santa Fe

Bix was explaining to Blossom that when Claudette and Jeru arrive in two days, they cannot be seen because of the serious danger surrounding the whole family. "I thought that if it is okay with you, they could stay here with their security persons, and I'm sure they will want to be near Cielito as she recovers from her gunshot wound."
Blossom replied, "Well, Sir, I know it is my Christian duty to help as I can, and certainly I want my family close to me, but I don't think we have enough room for all of them and the security persons.

They could stay upstairs, but we never furnished the upstairs, since there were just three of us living here when we moved in. Bix offered to have furniture sent out right away, enough for all four unfurnished rooms. Blossom was grateful for such a kind and speedy offer, adding, "I thank you, Mr. Bix, for taking care of all the furniture, but having these guests in our home must be cleared by JB because he is the man of the house." Bix promised to convey all of this to JB when he got back in town. "I also know that there's going to be a lot more people to feed, so I will make sure you have enough food." Blossom smiled. "Don't worry about that. We have enough food around here to feed a small army."

Bix looked a little hesitant about leaving, and then said, "Before I go do you think Shy would mind if I took a peek at the babies? And yes, I want to see my namesake first? Blossom grinned, telling Bix to follow her to see what Shy and the triplets were doing. "Shy, Mr. Bix wants to see the babies." Shy smiled almost as big as Blossom had a few moments ago. "You sure can come on anytime. Now that they are older, we think it's safe." "My goodness, Shy, they are growing like weeds! My, my, will you look at my namesake smiling? Must know I'm here." Bix reached over and kissed the little one and said, "Got to go because I need to catch JB before he leaves the new bank building."

After Bix left, Shy said, "Mama, Ms. Ohara has something to ask you if you have a minute." Blossom was already poised to say something to Shy. "Why yes, Honey, but can it wait until I can tell you and Ms. Ohara something? Mr. Bix wanted to know if we can accommodate Claudette, Jeru, and their security people here at the house until they catch that gang. I told him it was okay with me, but he will have to ask JB. Mr. Bix said if JB says it is okay, then he will send some furniture out this evening or early in the morning." Shy agreed that, with extra furniture coming, it was a good idea.

The next day, just as Bix had promised Blossom, around 10 o'clock, four trucks arrived with furniture, sheets, pillows, pillowcases, towels, and a truckload of groceries. Blossom asked Shy to show the men where and how she wanted it all arranged. Blossom would see after the babies and put away the groceries. Shy nervously replied, "Mama, maybe you should do that because I wouldn't know what to do." Blossom quickly came back with a response that gently pushed Shy out of her comfort zone. "Now, Honey, you are the woman of the house, so that is your responsibility. Maybe you can get Ms. Ohara to help you."

Two days later the train arrived and was in the siding. Bix and Bax had boarded the railcars and briefed Claudette and party of the situation, explaining that for their personal safety they would stay with Blossom and Cielito until the gang of murderers was caught and locked up. Claudette, still in shock and crying, said, "Please, can we go now? I want to see my sister." Bax said they must wait until dark. "That gang has eyes everywhere, so we cannot make assumptions or take chances. We have plans to arrest their lawyer tomorrow, and maybe we can find the three who kidnapped and murdered your brothers."

As they sat and waited for darkness, Brinson told Bix that he needed to talk to him and Bax. The three stepped out of the car to the platform. Brinson reported, "When we arrived in Chicago, there was a company man waiting for me who had a dispatch from headquarters instructing me upon arrival in Santa Fe to make plans to apprehend the culprits tomorrow. In the local newspaper there will be a story and a picture of me as J.W. Poteet, cattle buyer for the *Denaferd Ranch* of Montana, Wyoming, and parts of Canada.

I need you two to introduce me to the *New Mexico Stockman Association* and I will do the rest. One more thing -- when you arrest the lawyer I would like to be there. By the way, here is the dispatch that the company sent." Bix and Bax said they could arrange the meeting with the Stockman Association after they apprehend the lawyer, and they didn't need to see the dispatch for any verification.

It was dark enough for them to move the party. When they arrived at Blossom's farm, Bix suggested they wait on the porch and Cielito would come out to meet them, the reason being JB, as the head of the household, would be asleep, along with the babies. JB right now would have no idea that all these people were coming inside his home before he had a chance to formally meet them. So, it was a matter of respect for the man of the house.

Bix told them, "JB leaves around midnight for work, and meanwhile you all can go inside. Just be very quiet so you don't wake anyone while my brother and I go back to the siding to get your baggage and bring everything back here.

Cielito was inside watching for the lights from the two automobiles, and when the lights shone on the house, she opened the door and ran out to greet her sister first. She was crying and calling for Claudette, whom she hadn't seen in many years. Claudette ran toward Cielito with the same level of emotion. They must have stood outside the house crying and laughing and touching each other's face and hair, almost in disbelief that they were united again, albeit around a family tragedy. It was a good thing they were outside, or they would surely have awakened JB and the babies and everyone else inside!

The rest of the party remained inside the cars and allowed the two sisters to calm down before they got out of the cars and walked toward the house. From the kitchen Blossom heard an automobile, and instinctively she looked for Cielito to be sure she was safely inside. When she couldn't find her, Blossom became concerned, but only for a moment. She saw Claudette and Cielito outside in a big embrace as they wiped each other's tears.

Blossom realized that Bix had returned with Claudette and party. She asked everyone to come inside. "You all are welcome. The table is all set.

You must be hungry." When they entered, Bix said, "Claudette and party meet Ms. Blossom Blake." Blossom took a long look at Claudette, finally saying, "Your hair is still as red as it was when I delivered you, and as a grown woman you look like your Mama except for the hair." Claudette looked surprised, as Blossom said it was a little over twenty years ago.

    Jeru was next. Blossom said, "Well here is another one of my babies, and you look just like your Mama, all tall and pretty. I used to see her often when I worked at the bank, and she looked well the last time I saw her. You were one of longest babies I ever delivered." Now it was Jeru's time to be surprised. Every member of the party introduced themselves and then sat down to eat. Bix said that he and a couple of the men had to go back to the train to retrieve their baggage. After serving seconds to the hungriest persons at the table, and receiving praises for such a scrumptious meal, Blossom announced, "While I would like to take all the credit, praises go to Cielito and Shyanne, my daughter, who did everything.

    There came a knock at the door, and Brinson answered it. It was Bix and Bax returning with their luggage. They also shared a meal, after which Brinson inquired about the sleeping arrangements. Blossom asked Cielito if she would take care of that. Cielito asked everyone to follow her. Brinson stayed behind to ask the Toilet brothers if they could leave one automobile behind so he could get to town in the morning. Then he joined the others upstairs. Cielito said the guests could choose their bedrooms. Claudette asked Cielito where her room was, and Cielito said it was downstairs. Claudette said that would be where she and Jeru would sleep.

Brinson chimed in that for security reasons, he needed to be on the first floor, so everyone made the proper adjustments to assure that they were happy. Brinson returned to the kitchen to explain all this to Blossom, who said her son, JB, should be up in hour and a half and his wife would be up to fix him breakfast. Blossom stressed once more that JB was the head of her household and that he would need to meet everyone as soon as it was possible. Brinson told Blossom that he planned to talk with JB before he left for work, if she thought he wouldn't mind doing that. He also understood that JB was mute and communicated in sign language, and he, too, was fluent in sign language. He asked Blossom to leave a note for Shy so she would not be frightened when she saw Brinson in the kitchen. Blossom asked if Brinson was confident that he could catch the murderers, and Brinson replied, "The Pinkertons always get their man." Blossom said with pride, "My son saw all three of them, and he was too late to save the brothers, but he did save Cielito."

When Shy awakened, she saw the note Blossom left telling her that Mr. Brinson was in the dining room working. Shy could see Brinson busily writing and looking at a notebook. She cleared her throat to avoid startling Brinson, and introduced herself and said she would be in the kitchen if he needed anything. "JB, my husband, will be up in about thirty minutes." Brinson stopped what he was doing and said he was making notes for a meeting in the morning with the Toilet Brothers. "Do you think your husband will mind if I talk to him while he's eating breakfast? Shy said that she didn't think he would mind. Brinson said that Blossom told him that JB used sign language to communicate, and Brinson signed to Shy that he was fluent in signing.

Shy smiled and signed back, asking him if would care for breakfast. He declined, saying that after he talked with JB, he was going to get some sleep.

Shy started breakfast and then went to tell JB about Brinson being in the dining room and that he could sign. JB kissed her and thanked her. Shy went back to the kitchen and put biscuits from last night in the oven to warm. She made her husband a breakfast of two slices of ham, two biscuits, and a cup of coffee. She added some homemade jam to the breakfast tray, which she carried to the dining room. JB and Brinson were signing. She kissed JB on his forehead and said she was going to check on the babies.

JB told Brinson everything about the killing of the Ohara brothers and how he saved Cielito. He spoke about giving the Toilet Brothers drawings of the scene and what the three men looked like. JB had to leave for work, and Brinson was going to get a couple of hours of sleep before he met with the Toilet brothers. Before going to his room, he wrote a note for Blossom, asking if she would wake him after she finished in the bathroom in the morning.

A little later that morning, Blossom woke and saw the note Brinson left. She used the bathroom and then woke Brinson so that he could wash and shave and dress for a meeting with the Toilet brothers at ten o'clock. Blossom insisted that he eat some breakfast first. "How do you like your eggs, and how many would you like? While your eggs are cooking, I will get you a cup of coffee." Brinson was grateful for such personal attention, and he replied, "Two sunny side up eggs and coffee black."

When Blossom returned with his breakfast, she sat across the table facing him and said, "Tell me all about yourself." He was a Pinkerton detective whose full name was Brinson F. Dubois, and he was from Chicago. "My parents are French, and I was four and my sister was two when we came to America as a poor working family. My father was a street cleaner, and my mother was a maid for rich people who sponsored me to go to high school and college. We lived in a two-room apartment over a garage, which was something I was ashamed of, but I came to realize that one can be happy with little."

Blossom listened attentively to Brinson's story about his life. She decided to share something about her life. "I was born into slavery and was raped by a White man at eleven. My mother took me to this woman to see if I was pregnant, and that old woman made it impossible for me to ever have children. I came to New Mexico with General McKenzie and his wife and met my husband at seventeen. We lived in a one-room adobe shack, and we were so happy. I never prayed or asked God for material things, although I am a praying Christian woman. Everything I have, including my two children, was given to me by the grace of God."

Brinson appeared to be moved by Blossom's childhood trauma. He spoke of wealthy people and happiness, adding, "After getting to know Claudette and Jeru, I have found that as long as they have each other, they are extremely happy. I never found time for marriage." Blossom assured him that in time, love would find him. Blossom said Cielito was always looking out for others, and Brinson said he wanted to get to know her better. "I look forward to talking with you more, but now I must get to my meeting with the Toilet brothers."

After Brinson left, Cielito entered the dining room to sit with Blossom, who said she had just finished talking with Mr. Brinson. "He is an interesting man, and I can tell he is married to his job, but I told him love will find him." Cielito asked her how she could tell that, and Blossom responded, "You know the eyes reveal the depths of the soul. I could see in his eyes that he was not totally satisfied with his lot in life. His job consumes a lot of him, but there is an emptiness and something in his life that is missing. I can see that, just as I can see it in your eyes."

She went on to ask, "When the Good Lord created Adam, do you know what He did next?" Cielito said she considered herself to be a learned person but was sure she didn't know what God was thinking or saying. Blossom referred to the Holy Bible, quoting, *"It is not good for the man to be alone. I will make a helper suitable for him."* She explained the scripture: God decided that Adam should not live alone. So, you see Eve came from Adam. She was a part of him, so all of that was handed down to us humans and nothing can take the place of another human in our lives." Cielito said, "I think I understand. I have never given much thought to that." Blossom responded, "Child, it is quite simple. God is in all of us. The *Bible* says God is love and if that is the case, then we need to give someone else that love we have in us." Cielito at last understood. "Mama Blossom, you are so wise. How did you get all that knowledge about the *Bible*? Blossom said, "Since I was a girl, I have read a little of the *Bible* every night.

By this time the rest of the party to include Shy and the babies were coming to the dining room, and Blossom got up to fix breakfast for everyone. Cielito offered to help, but Blossom suggested she might spend time with her sister instead. "You might be right, but I believe what you said about grief and keeping busy helping you cope with grief. I will tell

Claudette that it might help her deal with her grief to sit in on the Bible study.

After breakfast Cielito asked Claudette and Jeru to help her with dishes so they could talk. Cielito told Beauchamp and Wilford they could remain in the dining room and have another cup of coffee. She suggested that Shy go about her routine and leave the babies with her. Shy agreed. Blossom could take the time to check her herb garden. Cielito said, "Oh, Mama Blossom, can we help you in the garden when we finish in the kitchen?" Blossom replied that she would be happy for their company.

The three ladies went to the kitchen. Cielito spoke first. "Now that we are alone, I want to tell you how fortunate we are to be with this unusual family. I am lucky to be alive because Blossom's son, JB, saved my life, although he couldn't save the boys. JB saw the three men who kidnapped us." She went on to tell them that her brothers were missing several days before they got her as she was leaving her office one morning.

"They took me to the ranch where the boys were tied and gagged. I am guessing but it seemed like two days had passed, and on the third day they put us on horses, and we must have rode for two hours before they finally stopped. We were blindfolded, so I had no idea where we were, but earlier I heard cows. So, I guess we were on the range and when we stopped, I didn't hear the cows, but I heard a woman screaming. JB told me it was a place called *Banshee Canyon*. I heard two shots and thought it must have been my brothers they shot. I knew I was next, but all of a sudden, I heard the woman scream really loudly and I felt the bullet strike me in my shoulder before I passed out. I thought I heard a rattle snake, but the next thing I saw was JB trying to tell me something. Then, I was here, and Mama Blossom was doing everything to save me from bleeding to death." Claudette said, "What they did to our brothers was awful. JB can draw really good. He drew the faces of those men for the Toilet brothers, and when they are captured, I will identify them in court."

    Cielito finished speaking: "I am telling you this because you need to know the truth and I know you are not used to this manner of living. I want you and Jeru to feel at ease with this family. As I said, they are simple, God-fearing Christian people who act like people are supposed to act with each other. I think that if you two stay busy, according to Mama Blossom, it will help you deal with your grief. I also believe that she received a telegram two days ago telling her that her husband who was in the army was missing and presumed dead. I could tell by her demeanor that she was worried, but it seemed to me that Blossom wouldn't let her mind think the words. Anyway, let's get done in here so we can go outside with her."

Chapter 11
Begg is Arrested!

Brinson arrived at nine o'clock a.m. at the old bank building. He was directed by a sign to the new building, which was five blocks away. When he arrived, the bank was not open, but as JB and Al were there doing their inspection of the job that the new crew had done, they opened the curtain to inspect the windows and saw Brinson outside the bank. JB recognized him and unlocked the door. He signed to Brinson that he expected Mr. Bix shortly. Brinson said he would wait outside, but JB heard Bix at the back entrance and asked Brinson to follow him.

Bix opened the door and told JB, "Son, I see you and Al are on the job and from what I can see, your crew did a good job on this floor. JB and Al thanked Mr. Bix and said that Mr. Brinson was there. Bix said, "Yes, I see him. Good morning, Brinson. My brother and Bywater should be right behind me." He turned to JB and said he needed him to come back around ten thirty after JB checked the other buildings. JB agreed.

Bax and Bywater came in as JB and Al left. Bix said, "Come on in and let's go to my office, since we have a few minutes before Begg shows up. "Brinson, this is Police Chief Bywater. Before Begg arrives down the hall from my office, there is a closet. I want you two to wait in there, and when you hear a knock on the door, come out and let's arrest this bastard." Bix called for his receptionist, who was surprised to see Brinson and Bywater. She asked how they got in there. Bix replied, "Don't be alarmed, Abigale, you know my brother Bax and Chief Bywater. The other gentleman is Mr. Brinson Dubois, Pinkerton detective. They are here to arrest Begg, whom we are certain was instrumental in the murder of the Ohara brothers. When he comes in and asks for me, call me from your intercom and tell me a Mr. Begg is here to see me. I will say bring him down once he enters the office you immediately go to the closet and knock on the door and go back to your office he should arrive around ten if JB and Al show up before he does have them to wait in your office, you got that. "Yes, Sir."

At ten o'clock a.m., Begg arrived at the old bank building and noticed a sign stating that the building was closed. All existing businesses were being directed to go to the new bank building address at 1000 New Town Street five blocks away. Begg left and made his way to the new location. It was now ten fifteen a.m. and Bix started to worry when his intercom came alive, and Abigale said that Mr. Begg was there to see him. Bix said to bring him on down.

Abigale opened the door for Begg. Bix said, "Come on in. You did bring the papers showing the Ohara brothers and their sister selling their shares to you, right?" "Yes, I have them right here," Begg said while touching his briefcase. Before Bix or Begg could say another word, Bywater and Brinson came into the room and announced, "J Arthur Begg, you are under arrest for forgery, fraud, theft, murder, and attempted murder, plus a host of other things that will be added. Begg was stunned at seeing the two men and hearing the crimes for which he was being accused. "I protest! I am a lawyer, and I know my rights." Brinson spoke up and said, "You are right, and one of those rights is a right to a speedy trial and that is just what you are going to get. Now we are willing to make a deal if you are. I can get two of the charges dropped if you are willing to cooperate, but if not, then you know as a lawyer that those two charges mean the electric chair. Either way, it's up to you." Begg was silent, as he slumped into a chair without saying another word. He understood fully what was happening, although his expression was one of defiance. A few minutes passed with nobody saying anything. Each person in the room made eye contact with another person, as if many speculative conversations were taking place.

At the end of what seemed an interminable silence, Bax said to Brinson, winking his eye deliberately, but quickly, "No, I want him charged with those last two crimes." Brinson asked what the rest of the men thought. Bix and Bywater agreed that Begg should be charged. Brinson told Chief Bywater to take Begg into custody, and Bywater handcuffed Begg's wrists behind his back. It was humiliating.

Bax told Bywater to pull his car up to the back entrance and make sure no one was around and when he got Begg to the jail. "Cover his head just in case someone sees him and recognizes him, you understand?" The next thing he said, he wanted to make sure Begg heard. He turned to Bix and said, "Brother, since you have a lot of pull, call a special session of the Grand Jury. I want this bastard in the chair before the month's end." Begg's eyes widened, but he quickly composed himself in order not to show he was concerned about the electric chair. He was confident that he had more pull and would beat the whole thing. Well, he appeared confident anyway.

Brinson said, "But gentlemen, we know there were three bastards who murdered the Oharas because the eyewitnesses saw three men. What if Begg tells us where they are hiding. He should get something for that information. Bix thought for a moment, and then said, "What about the man at the top? He's going to get away "scott free," and you know that to be true. I at least want Begg to be charged with accessory after the fact. Bax, as a lawyer, can we do that? Bax said, "Yes, we can! Let's go after the whole gang right now. I think I can get the Grand Jury to indict Begg within a couple of days. Meanwhile, before Chief Bywater and Begg reached the back door of the building, Bywater said, "Boy, it's good to be the bank owner because people jump when you say something." Before Bywater opened the door to the parking area, Begg said in a controlled, but nervous voice, "Take me back! I will cooperate. Bywater turned and went back to the office, just as everyone was preparing to leave. He gently pushed Begg inside.

Bax repeated his request to have Begg locked up, but Begg interrupted. "If you drop the accessory charges, I will cooperate." Brinson said that was a wise decision and had Bywater uncuff him. Speaking to Bax, he said, "Mr. Toilet, do you have someone to take his statement down?" Bax answered in the affirmative. He picked up the phone and called his office and told his secretary to come to the new bank and bring her stenograph machine. He instructed her to come to the back entrance. Bix asked Begg if he would care for some coffee, and Begg accepted, speaking in a shaky voice. Bix asked his receptionist, Abigale, to come to his office and bring the coffee pot and cream and sugar. She replied, "Right away, Sir."

Bax's secretary arrived fifteen minutes later and needed someone to get the machine from her car. Bax went to get it. While Bax was out Bix whispered to Brinson to question Begg, since he was a skilled interrogator. Bix said he would open his intercom and ask his secretary, Rosetta, to listen in and type what she heard. Brinson asked both ladies if they were ready, and then Begg began by given his name, date, and occupation. He was asked to read what a paper that said, "I was not threatened or coerced into making this statement. I voluntarily give this information.

Just as he was instructed, Begg followed the statement and began to recount what he knew about the murders. "I can't say for a certainty who committed the murders, but I believe that it had to be Hunt Dalton and Duce Dawson." Brinson asked him if he knew Dawson's real first name, and Begg said it was "Percival" or something similar. Brinson asked why he thought it was those two, and Begg replied, "Because my last contact with them was the first of September, and my boss had instructed me to drop them off at the casino. They had been drinking and were discussing kidnapping the Ohara brothers that day." Brinson asked for the boss' name. Begg hesitated for a few seconds before saying it was "Nimrod Bloom."

Brinson asked Begg how long he had been employed by Nimrod Bloom, and Begg said three years. "The last I heard from him, he was in Albuquerque, but I believe he is in Santa Fe at the Casino." Brinson asked, "Do you know how many times he had people murdered?" That direct question about Nimrod Bloom's record of murders caused Begg to pause briefly. He considered his next response carefully, and then said, "I never witnessed any of that, but I know he ordered it done. The records are in my office in Albuquerque." Brinson went on to ask if Begg knew a man called "Mexican Bob." Begg said the last he heard was that he and his gang had taken over the High Spade Ranch. Brinson asked where he could find the other named men. "I would think at the ranch, which is where they were to take the Ohara brothers." All the men looked at each other, remembering JB's drawing and Cielito's story of terror as she and her brothers were taken to a ranch and tied and left there before they were escorted on horseback to the place where the brothers were killed, and Cielito was shot.

Brinson said, "Now, what about these forged documents in your briefcase? We know that they're forged because you never saw the family members who supposedly signed them. Begg said he didn't copy those signatures, but a colored man named Katz did it, and he left the area for Mexico and South America as soon as he was paid. Brinson asked Begg if that was Hezekiah Katz, known as "Copycat." Begg confirmed and asked if they would drop the forgery charges. Brinson said, "Yes, but you must know that you will be charged with "aiding and abetting," and "conspiracy to defraud."

Brinson turned to Bax and asked if he had any questions. Bax asked Begg if he was willing to testify against Bloom. Begg hesitated, remembering how ruthless Nimrod Bloom had been. So, he posed a question to Bax, asking if he wanted me dead. "If I testify against him, he will have me killed. He has connections everywhere, including judges, police chiefs, senators, and congressmen, not to mention prison inmates. "Couldn't you just use the records in my office?" Bax said, "I don't know about that; I will have to study the records."

Brinson finally stated, "Gentlemen, that is all I have. I will make this suggestion: Chief Bywater, do you have officers in your employ whom you trust? Bix interrupted to ask Brinson if he could have a private conversation with him, and they stepped out of the office. Bix whispered, "I don't trust Bywater. Brinson replied, "Mr. Begg needs to be isolated from all the other prisoners. I noticed you have several of our operatives in your employ, and I wonder if you have a place where you can hold him until I can get another jail to house him." "Brinson said he would call the home office; they should have knowledge of a jail where he can be held in isolation. If you will let us have the use of your conference room and two of our operatives to guard him, I should hear from the home office soon." Bix said they could use Bax's conference room.

Meanwhile Bax was looking over the forged bills of sale and discovered the date on them was two days after the Ohara brothers was murdered. He recognized that Begg was a sly crook who knew how to cover his ass. Bix returned and asked Bax about the use of his conference room. Brinson was on the phone with his Chicago office trying to find a place for him. Bax agreed and turned to Bywater and said, "We are moving Begg to my office and two Pinkerton men will guard him. We are going to move him to a secure jail because if word gets out that we have Begg in custody, we will know it had to come from you, and you know what will happen to you. Do you understand?" Bywater softly replied, "Yes, I do." He was upset that he could be thought of as an untrustworthy man of the law, but he knew had to accept that or lose his job.

An hour later Brinson returned with good news. Headquarters had found a place at the Penitentiary of New Mexico, right there an hour outside of the city where Begg would be held in solitary until his trial date.

Begg was moved to Bax's conference room, and after dark he would be taken to the penitentiary. Brinson went back to the bank and sat with Bix to lay out his plan to quietly capture and arrest the other three bandits, after which he would raid the casino to get Nimrod and the rest of his gang. "I trust what Begg said about Nimrod having other people on his payroll, but I know the two operatives we've chosen will get Begg to the penitentiary with no problems. Bix corroborated Brinson's belief in the integrity of the operatives.

Brinson said he would leave now to work on his plans for going to the *High Spade Ranch*, but just as he was about to exit, Bix's phone rang, and the call was for Brinson. The voice on the other end said, "Sierra Oscar Sierra (a Pinkerton code SOS, which means a flash message from headquarters)." Brinson said, "Identify," and the voice said "McDonald Matthew, with a message to beware of J. D. Grimes, a member of the *Stockman Association,* suspected to be on Nimrod Bloom's payroll." The message ended with "Echo mike."

Brinson ask Bix if he was familiar with J. D. Grimes, and Bix said he had been with the Association about a year and owns a small spread up in the western end of the county. He was supposedly in good standing with the Association. Brinson said that call had come from one of his operatives inside the bank. He had just received a dispatch that Grimes was on Nimrod's payroll, and therefore, he was not to be trusted. Bix said, "Well, Begg is right to say this Nimrod has people everywhere." Brinson promised to check him out tomorrow at the *Stockman Association* meeting.

Thirty-five minutes later when Brinson arrived back at Blossom's farm, everyone was outside except Cielito and Beauchamp, who was in the kitchen preparing a lunch of French dishes to include dessert. Cielito was babysitting while Shy was going about her daily duty of farm management. Outside, Claudette and Jeru were in the herb garden with Blossom, who was giving them a tutorial in identifying different herbs and their medical use. Claudette asked Blossom where she acquired such a vast knowledge of herbs, and Jeru asked about Blossom's knowledge and understand of the *Bible.*

Blossom began by telling them about her life, saying that from the time she learned to read, her books were the *Bible* and a medical book that belonged to her father, who was a doctor and the plantation owner who raped her mother, Hermina when she was twelve years old. "Since I was a slave back then, I had no friends and no leisure time to play. I read those books every night before I went to bed.

When I came to New Mexico with General McKinzie and his wife, I didn't know anyone, so reading was my only company, and when I married my husband, Brownie, who was a soldier because of his duty, I was alone most nights." Everyone was listening intently to Blossom's story of slavery and rape and marriage. They were intrigued. Claudette said, "My sister said you can look in a person's eyes and learn a lot about them." Blossom smiled slightly because she knew she had a gift for seeing what people never spoke about themselves. "I don't know if that's all true, but what I do know is that the eyes can reveal the depth of one's soul."

Jeru asked, "When you look into my eyes, what do you see?" Blossom paused, as if forming her response before speaking it. "When I met you the second time ..." Jeru interrupted Blossom and asked when they had met the first time. Blossom said it was about thirty years ago, when she delivered Jeru. "What I am seeing now is love and happiness, but there is something missing."

Jeru interrupted again. "What are your feelings about me and Claudette?" Blossom said she only knew what they had told her. Claudette replied, almost defensively, "It is no secret we love each other and have since we were six years old. We've always been together and neither of us have ever had a man. Some people might see our relationship as wrong." Blossom responded, "If you have not noticed, I am not like other people. The *Bible* teaches us to not judge, and I live by that, and I've taught my children to do the same."

Jeru asked if Blossom saw the same thing in Claudette's eyes as in Jeru's, and Blossom said yes. Jeru asked Blossom what she thought was missing in their lives. Blossom said, "I can't say for sure; the only thing I can think of is that by now, most women your age have married and had one or two babies by now." Claudette affirmed the inseparability of Jeru and herself, adding that she didn't think any man would put up with that. Of course, you have to have a man to produce a baby.

Blossom told them that when she was eleven, my father let his overseer have her as a bed winch. Jeru inquired as to what is a bed winch "That's something you don't want to be. It is a girl or a women given for a man to satisfy his lust anytime and anywhere he wishes. A bed winch has no rights to her own body. Anyway, when my mother found out this man had raped me, she took me to this old woman to see if I was pregnant, and the old woman did something to where I could never give birth."

Claudette was puzzled that Blossom had two children. Blossom said, "Yes, but I didn't give birth. They were a gift from God, and I love them as if I did. Now let us change the topic by going to the vegetable garden and picking some vegetables for dinner. As they walked, Claudette stopped and looked off in the distance and asked Blossom if she could see two people standing out there. Blossom raised up and shaded her eyes before asking Claudette where she was looking. "They were standing near what looked like a small wooden fence." Blossom said that might have been some of Al's children going to place flowers where you Claudette's brothers are buried. Claudette looked completely surprised. "What!? You mean my brothers are buried out in a field like some animals?"

"My son, JB, made a drawing of the whole scene. Ask your sister. When Al and his brother brought their bodies down from the canyon the doctor said their bodies needed to be buried right away. Blossom began to cry. She said, "Child, they had no faces. The backs of their heads were gone, and hundreds and hundreds of flies covered their bodies." Claudette broke down sobbing and asked why Blossom was so descriptive. Jeru said, as she and Blossom were hugging Claudette, "Darling, you made her tell you. She did not mean to hurt you." Claudette finally said, "Forgive me, Blossom, it just seemed as if they were thrown away."

Blossom said, "I pray that God will forgive us both. Jeru. please help her back to the house and I will pick up the vegetables and follow. I need to make lunch. When they arrived and were making their way up the back steps, the aroma coming from the kitchen was strange. When they opened the screen door. to their surprise were four strange looking pies on the kitchen table, a large bowl of roasted vegetables, and two large bowls of mixed fruit salad. Beauchamp was taking a pan of croissants from the oven, and he turned and was surprised to see Blossom, Jeru and Claudette. "Mademoiselle Blossom, forgive me. I should have asked if it was okay to use your kitchen, but I thought I should be of some help to you."

Blossom said it was okay. Everything looked and smelled good. "I never saw dishes made like this, and I am not sure how my family will react to foreign dishes. We are so used to plan food." Jeru met Cielito as she was taking Claudette to the parlor. Cielito was alarmed and asked if Claudette was okay. Jeru said she was ok, and Jeru would I explain in a minute. As Jeru made her way back to the kitchen, Shy was coming downstairs to fix JB lunch. She asked Jeru about the great smelling kitchen. Shy was surprised to see Beauchamp wearing an apron. She had never seen a man cooking.

Jeru said that in France most cooks are men, and then she asked everyone to gather around so she could tell them what this was. "The four pies are what we call in France 'quiche.' The crescent-looking bread is called a 'croissant' and the rest is a fruit salad, and he made cream for the topping." All mouths were drooling with anticipation of eating this meal. She heard JB's car and asked everyone to help her bring the food to the dining room. Brinson and JB arrived, delighting at the smell of the food.

After everyone gathered in the dining room, Brinson shared good news. "We arrested the lawyer today, and we got him to tell us where the murderers are hiding. I expect to have them in a couple of days. Everyone cheered, but he cautioned them that the news had to stay right there in that room. "And when I get these three men, it does not mean it is all over."

Jeru suggested that each person taste a small portion of the food to see if they like it. Shy could see if the babies like a little of just the egg and cheese part. Blossom, Shy, JB, and Cielito tasted and then took a larger portion of quiche and roasted vegetables. Beauchamp was pleased, and Blossom said he could cook again – and again! JB signed that he had to go to the field, and Wilford asked to join him. JB kissed Shy, Blossom, Cielito, and the babies, and the two men left. Brinson told Wilford he needed to talk to him later. Cielito asked if he preferred hot or cold tea. Brinson replied, "Hot, of course. I don't think cold tea would taste that good." Blossom said, "Well, Mr. Brinson, you are in for a treat because throughout the South, most farm people and enslaved people drank sweet, iced tea, while only the rich and those who 'pretend' drank hot tea. I am not saying anything bad about rich people." Cielito said she would just bring in coffee and tea, and everyone could get what they wanted.

Cielito and Blossom went back into the kitchen. "I hoped you were going to come in the kitchen with me because I want to ask you something I been thinking about all morning, after listening to you and Brinson this morning. There is something about Brinson that I like, and I pray that when and if Claudette goes back to Monaco that he doesn't go. Blossom suggested that she tell him how she feels, but don't try to buy him.
Cielito asked her to explain.

Blossom said, "Some men do not like the idea that they are bought and paid for by a woman. Some men don't mind, but I feel that Mr. Brinson is a man of principles who is one of those men like the first kind I mentioned." Cielito said, "I need your help, Mama, so when you have your *Bible* study tonight, could you talk about that emptiness you were describing to me this morning? Blossom said, "I tell you what -- ask him if he would like to take a stroll with you this afternoon after you all come back. He probably will work on his plan to trap the other three men but tell him you would like to see it and listen to his plan carefully. Say it is brilliant and make him feel like he is the smartest man in the world, you know?"

Cielito looked down at the floor and sighed before responding to Blossom. "That's just it. I'm ashamed to say I am going on thirty-five and don't know anything about men or have ever been with one." Blossom said, "Daughter, make him feel like to you he is the most important man around, and you won't have to worry about your age. He won't notice. Now let's get back in there, and make sure you sit next to him and pour his tea." When Blossom and Cielito returned to the dining room, Cielito planned to do just as Blossom had instructed. Blossom brought in the tray with coffee and a pitcher of tea, while Cielito brought the cups and glasses. Wilford had moved next to Brinson, so she politely asked him if she could sit next to Brinson.

She poured a glass of tea and handed it to Brinson, who was surprised that it tasted good. Cielito asked if he would care to take a stroll the view outback when he finished his tea. "It's really beautiful." Wilford concurred, saying he planned to paint tomorrow, but Brinson reminded him that they needed to do something together tomorrow. Cielito looked disappointed, but Brinson said he and Wilford would take care of something when they returned from their stroll. Cielito stepped away to borrow a shawl from Blossom, and when they were out of sight of the men, Blossom winked and gave her the thumbs up. She asked Shyanne for her black lace shawl and some of her perfume. "Shy, honey, we need to fix up your big sister so she will be irresistible." She was, in fact, irresistible.

Several minutes later Shy entered the dining room first and said, "Ladies and gentlemen, may I present the beautiful and charming Senorita Cielito Guadeloupe Ohara! Cielito nervously entered the room and everyone let out a gasp. Claudette had never seen her all dressed up and wearing makeup, and her long black hair was pulled back from her face with one large braid across the top and raised in the back with a jeweled pin. Brinson walked over to her, kissed her hand, and said, "May I say you are a vision of loveliness; may I have the pleasure of strolling with you?" Cielito said with a shaky voice, "Why certainly, Sir." They started to walk toward the fields where they could see JB, Al, and Juan planting seeds for their winter wheat.

Brinson asked her if she wanted to go any further, since they were heading in the direction of the canyon, and it might bring up some unpleasant thoughts. Cielito responded, "As long you are with me, I am not afraid. I want to get to know more about you and I want you to come to know me." Brinson shyly said he was just a Pinkerton Detective for the last nineteen years. "I love my job and plan to do it as long as I can. What about you? I know you are wealthy and have two school for Native children." Cielito said she inherited her wealth from her parents, and she loves educating children. "My wealth is not who I am. I should be embarrassed to tell you that I am going on thirty-five and have never been with a man. You are the first man who has ever appealed to me. I put my job ahead of everything, and I live over my parents' casino. I do not have servants.

Brinson explained his involvement in the case involving Cielito and her brothers, saying he needed to focus and make no mistakes. Cielito understood completely, saying, "When it is all taken care of, I want to know that you will give us some consideration. I will wait for you. Let's head back and maybe sit in the swing on the front porch and you can tell me how you got the lawyer to tell you where the three were hiding and how you plan to catch them.

They arrived at the house before sundown and sat in the swing. Brinson said, "The men think they killed all three of you and got away with it. He shared some of his plan to catch them, and Cielito replied, "You are not only a man of principles, but you are smart and clever to boot." Brinson said he had had a most enjoyable evening, and that when he decided to search for a suitable mate, she would be the only name on the list. It was time for dinner.

After all the food Beauchamp had prepared was brought into the dining room and Blossom did the blessing, Jeru cleared her throat and began to tell everyone what they were about to taste. "The dish stacked high that looks like bread is called *Chicken Cordon Bleu*, which is chicken breast with sweet ham and cheese inside. Next is green beans vinaigrette with garlic breadcrumbs, and the yellow stuff is mustard *Dejon* sauce. There's roasted carrots and cinnamon and nutmeg sweet potatoes with creamy butter. Shy, for the babies, we have quiche and sweet potatoes.

Beauchamp was quietly waiting for everyone's comments on the food. Blossom stopped chewing to say, "Mr. Beauchamp, speaking for the Blake family, it is delicious. Maybe you might help me in the kitchen sometimes. Cielito reminded everyone that tonight was *Bible* study for the Blake family, and Blossom said everyone was welcome to attend. The men retired to the parlor and the women cleaned up.

In the kitchen Claudette and Jeru were interested in how things went with Cielito and Brinson's stroll. She said, "I told him some personal things about me, and he thanked me for my honesty; and the next thing he said almost scared me and my heart sank. He said at the moment he needed a clear head so that he made no mistakes in his case. I told him I understood and when everything is over, I would still be here."

At that moment Wilford entered the kitchen and Cielito whispered that she would finish sharing later. Time for *Bible* study. Blossom said she was not a preacher or teacher, but she had spent most of her life reading the *Bible* and a medical book that belonged to her father. She talked about the creation of mankind according last. The earth had to be made to support life, and Adam needed Eve to help him do as God commanded him to be fruitful and fill the earth. Our lives are empty without each other because we need to pass on that love of God that is in us The fruit that Eve ate was not an apple, but the fruit from the Tree of Knowledge -- good and evil.

After *Bible* study Cielito walked with Blossom to her room and thanked her for making her feel special tonight. She went upstairs to the room she shared with Claudette and Jeru. Cielito entered the room and fell backwards on the bed, smiling and gazing at the ceiling. Claudette and Jeru jumped on the bed to hear the rest of Cielito's story. She revealed that she was a virgin, and Claudette and Jeru said they were too. Claudette said they were so close that no man would put up with their relationship. They've had plenty of offers of marriage but declined them all. Cielito recounted Brinson's comment that this was a most enjoyable evening and when he decided to seek a suitable mate, her name would be the only one on his list." Jeru said, "Wow! I can't Imagine Brinson being romantic; he seemed so stiff."

Cielito asked about Beauchamp and Wilford, who seemed to be like faithful puppies. Jeru said they were their bodyguards when they first arrived in Paris and then Monaco. "Bix had hired Brinson and Hercule for us in Monaco, but we had gotten so used to them that we took them with us everywhere we moved. Wilford was the first to confess that he was in love with both of us, and Beauchamp felt the same way." The three of them stayed awake almost all night talking.

Chapter 12
Brinson's Plan and Blossom's Counsel

Truly, this had been an exceptional evening for a budding romance, but once the women had retired for the evening, Brinson and Wilford discussed plans for tomorrow. They needed to go over every detail of Brinson's plan to set up JD Grimes, perhaps after meeting him at the *Stockmen Association building*. The plan had to be meticulous, with contingency plans built in for emergencies, since both men knew they would only have one chance at making a "surprise attack." Pinkerton headquarters had warned Brinson that Grimes was connected to Nimrod.

Their plan would begin with Bix Toilet introducing the two them to Grimes as Mr. JW Poteet, Cattle Buyer, and young Doctor/ Professor Wilford Shipping Seymore. Dr. Seymore, although quite young, had earned the reputation as a highly respected Cattle Reproductive Specialist in England.

After meeting Grimes and spending some time talking with him and others, Brinson was to suggest that they get a drink at the casino. Brinson paused from explaining his plan to letting Wilford know that going to the casino was just a ruse to get a look at Nimrod and try to determine who is part of his gang. There should be some eye contact and "body language" between Nimrod and Grimes, once they supposedly meet for the first time, and that would give a big clue to Brinson and Wilford that they have the right crook with them and the right plan to bring Nimrod's operation down!

"If he falls for that introduction, I want you to be careful who you talk with, Wilford. I know that, according to Begg, there is large woman who goes by the name of "Big Rump Cassie," and she is very close to Nimrod. Wilford seemed a bit nervous, and he asked Brinson, "What if I am asked a question about cattle breeding." Brinson responded, "Remember that we are not interested in herd bulls, only heifer bulls. Herd bulls are mated with mature cows, but we want heifer bulls because of the short calving season. Try to be comfortable saying that, but I will add that you successfully mated a Welsh Black with an Angus/Hereford bull, so don't worry about anything.

Your main job is to convince Grimes that I am a little on the shady side. After I've had a drink, I will take out a flask and say that I would rather drink my own gin. When I go to the men's room, you say something to Grimes like, "Sir, I don't know you, but I do know him. I would be careful in making a deal with him. I was sent with him to make sure he deals straight. One of our partners, Lord Denaferd, trusts him, but Lord Chesterfield is concerned about the ranch's reputation. Get the picture? Wilford said he understood and would run it through his mind until he fell asleep. Brinson said they would continue to rehearse on the way to town in the morning, and both men went to bed to get some sleep.

The next morning, Brinson was up early. He went upstairs to check out Wilford's dress for the day. Wilford was in the bathroom tying his tie, and Brinson said to come to his room. Brinson headed back to his room but heard Blossom and Cielito preparing breakfast in the kitchen. He said with a smile that wanted to be a big grin, "Good morning. Why are you two beautiful ladies up so early?" Cielito blushed a little, but answered before Blossom could say a word. "We knew you had a very important job to do this morning, and we were not going to let you leave on an empty stomach." He might have blushed a little too, saying, "Well, thank you." He proceeded to his room.

Brinson searched his large trunk looking for some items of clothing he thought Wilford should wear. As a successful detective, Brinson needed to have plenty of disguises available, and so by this time in his career, he had every imaginable disguise in that trunk. He found what he was looking for: a tweed coat, bowtie, and glasses, just as Wilford knocked on his door. Wilford saw the outfit spread out on the bed and said, "Is that what you are going to wear?" Brinson replied, "No, that is what *you* are going to wear." Wilford was a bit cautious, but Brinson reminded him that he was going to be introduced as a Professor, so he must look the part. Wilford understood but insisted that he didn't wear glasses. Brinson said, "They are just glass, and you need them to make you look studious. Now go into the bathroom and look at yourself in the mirror.

Just as Wilford stepped out of Brinson's room Blossom was leaving the kitchen for the dining room. She saw Wilford and screamed, "Help! A strange man is in the house, and you better get out of here or I will throw this hot coffee on you." Brinson ran out of the room and yelled, "No, Blossom, it's Wilford, it's Wilford." He was secretly glad that this small disguise had fooled Blossom. By this time, the whole house was awake and making their way to where they heard Blossom scream. Brinson explained everything, after which he went to Blossom and hugged her and apologized. She calmed down, but said, "Lord a mercy, I thought it was one of those men after Cielito."

Brinson said in an assuring voice, "You don't have to worry about them because I plan to have them in custody in a day or two." Wilford took off the glasses and also went to Blossom to apologize, who responded, "It's okay, son, I know you didn't mean to scare me. God bless you. Please, you and Mr. Brinson sit and eat your breakfast." Blossom and Cielito went to the dining room and sat with Brinson and Wilford. Brinson explained that in is line of work as a detective, sometimes he uses disguises. "Sometimes you may see me with a beard and mustache, other times I might be dressed like a bum or acting like a drunk. Today we are going to the *Stockmen Association building* to meet this fellow who is one of those on Nimrod's payroll. He doesn't know that I know it, but if Wilford can get him to think I am a shady Cattle Buyer, he might put me on to the three men hiding out after murdering Cielito's brothers and shooting her. I have information that they are at your family's *High Spade Ranch*.

Cielito interjected with a shaky voice, "That is where they took me. They had my brothers tied and gagged, and they did the same with me." Blossom was seated nearest to Cielito, and she reached her arm across Cielito's back to give her comfort. Just as Brinson and Wilford was about to leave, the phone rang. Blossom asked Cielito if she would answer, and it was a female voice who asked to speak to Mr. Dubois. Cielito paused for a second, taken aback to hear a woman asking for Brinson. She asked, "Who may I say is calling?" The voice said, "Ma'am, please, I need to speak to him if he is still there. Tell him it's an SOS." Cielito said in a voice laced with a hint of sarcasm, "Mr. Dubois, it's for you. She said it's an SOS." Brinson noticed a dejected look on Cielito's face as he took the phone and said, "ID (identify)." "The voice said, "Hq said delay going to the casino. They want me to infiltrate." Brinson asked for her location, and when she gave it, he said he had a meeting at the bank, and she should meet him there. Brinson hung the phone up and turned his attention to Cielito. "That was Pinkerton business. What I told you last evening still goes. I have to hurry now, but I promise I will explain when I return. Cielito showed relief in her voice, saying, "Please be careful. I will worry until you return."

Blossom waited a few minutes after Brinson left and she heard the car leave. Then she went to Cielito, who was in the kitchen fixing her breakfast plate. "Daughter, when you finish breakfast, I am going to comb and brush your hair." Cielito answered, "Yes, Mama." Blossom went to Shy and JB's bedroom. Shy was changing the babies and dressing them for the day. She told Shy she wanted to check on the babies and see if Shy needed any help. Shy said, "Thank you, Mama, since these three have learned to sit up, they require watching or they will crawl off the bed. Blossom said she would get her namesake dressed.

She said, "Come here, you little Angel, let Grandmama put this dress on you." Blossom played with her and tickled her and held her up by the waist. When she finally attempted to put the dress on, she could see baby Blossom was outgrowing her clothes. She mentioned it to Shy in a diplomatic way. "I think it is time for us to make these babies some more clothes, and they need some starter shoes. What do you think?" Shy agreed. "I have been so busy. I am glad I have you. I know now I must prioritize my day so that I have time for them, so, I think I will stop working on the weekends. You think we can go to Willoughby's new store when it opens for business and get them shoes and cloth to make them several items of clothing?"

Blossom said, "Of course, but maybe you and JB might like for the five of you to do that. It's not that I don't want to go. I just thought you all need some family time." Shy responded, "Mama it is not family unless you are with us, so please don't think like that."

Blossom replied she was thinking that since they have company, one of them should be here. Shy volunteered that Cielito knew where everything was and could keep an eye on everything.

Blossom said, "I just thought of something. You should ask JB to make them a large fold-up crib. You can put a quilt on the floor and give them something to play with, and as you work, they will be right there with you wherever you are in the house. Once our company is gone JB can convert the bedroom that Mr. Brinson is in, into an office, or better yet, he can enclose the back or front porch and that might be better for an office.

Shy told her mother that she was so smart. "I thank God every night for sending me to you. Of course, there were tears of happiness from mother and daughter.

Cielito approached Blossom with her comb and brush, and Blossom suggested they sit on the back steps. Blossom asked Cielito to face her. "Daughter, I said that about combing your hair so the others wouldn't know I wanted to talk to you. Honey, I noticed that act of jealousy you displayed this morning. I don't think the others noticed it, but I feel you almost got off on the wrong foot with Mr. Brinson. There is something you have to understand. Trust is a big thing in a relationship, and Mr. Brinson's line of work brings him in contact with all kinds of people. You had no right to get jealous." Cielito interrupted, "Mama, just last night he said I am the only one on his list of a suitable mate, and when I answered the phone and it was a woman, my heart sank."

Blossom continued. "Some men might have taken that as mistrust. Honey, let me tell you something that happened to me when I got married. My husband, Brownie, being in the army and jealous, meant that we could not live on the fort. He rented this one room adobe shack, and I was happy with that because I was so much in love and anywhere was fine as long as he was there. Shortly after we were married, I went to work at the bank and gave the bank owner some medicine to relive him of gout. I helped his wife, too, but he wanted me to stay with his wife, despite the fact that I made it clear that I was married and had to be home for my husband at night. Because he trusted me and wanted me to take care of her, he gave me this house. When I went to pick up my husband, I had JB and Ms. Ula with me, and I told Brownie that she and the boy would be staying with us. He had a fit and said there was not enough room for them. That is when I told him the man at the bank had given me the house and I was moving that day into the house, and if he didn't like it I would have his clothe packed and ready for him because God had said I needed to take care of Ms. Ula and JB, and I was going to obey God.

He left because I had given him an ultimatum. We moved into the house without my Brownie, and I was brokenhearted because he wouldn't be here with us. The next day he showed up at the bank with an arm full of flowers and said he was sorry. Eventually, the old man from the bank, who was the Toilet boys' Grandfather, was brought to me to take care of for the rest of his life. JB shaved and gave him a bath every day and dressed him. When he died, he left JB twenty-four thousand dollars.

Brownie was jealous because he saw me as the prize. He was jealous when he came home one evening and the house was full of new stuff that JB had bought with some of the money the old man had willed to him. He knew I loved him, and JB was a Godsend for me, so he soon got over his jealousy because he learned that his jealousy was mistrust. He had no reason to mistrust me because I loved him and him alone."

Cielito asked Blossom if she thought that because of the way Cielito acted that morning, she had lost Brinson. Blossom said, "No, Child, didn't he say he would explain when he returned? And you helped the matter when you said to be careful, and you would worry until he returned." Cielito jumped up, grabbed Blossom, and hugged her, and almost caused her to fall off the steps. She repeatedly said, "Mama Blossom, I love you." Blossom then combed and brushed her hair so she would be pretty when Brinson returned later.

Meanwhile, at the Santa Fe Chapter of the *Stockmen Association*, Brinson's plan was beginning to bear fruit. Earlier, Brinson had met Grimes and asked if the Association had a bar. Grimes said it was upstairs. Just as they had rehearsed, Brinson asked if the bartender had *Calbert* gin, which he didn't. "I believe that is English." Brinson responded, "You are absolutely correct! I just so happen to have a flask in my pocket (actually watered- down gin). Brinson said he would drink his gin. Then he had to use the men's room, during which time Wilford would plant the seed of distrust between one of the Denaferd Ranch investors and Brinson.

Wilford immediately moved close to Grimes in a friendly, confident manner, and spoke enough words to cause Grimes to see Brinson as a shady operator Poteet (really Brinson). "Let me share with you some things I've heard about the shady deals Poteet has made. You heard of Lord Denaferd, I'm sure, and he didn't know much about counting cattle, you see, so he trusted Poteet." Grimes was listening intently. Poteet returned and Grimes got the men a table so they could talk further. "I think I can put you on to some guys that is right down your alley. They have some of the best mixed Angus and Hereford bulls in the State. Poteet asked how soon he could meet these boys. He leaned forward and almost whispered, "There is a large commission for each of them and one for you for putting us together. How soon can you get a hold of them?" Grimes said he would call them now, and he left to make the call. Fifteen minutes later, he said, "You are in luck. We can see them tomorrow."

Brinson, playing the character of Poteet as a master actor, paused, and said, "Wait a minute, you're not leading me into some kind of trap to be robbed. I heard you was a good and trusted man in the Association. Grimes said he could ask any of the men in the bar about his trustworthiness. The two shook hands to seal the deal.

The Stockman Association Stewart paged Mr. JW Poteet, saying, "Mr. Toilet said to tell you he was called away and to ask someone to give you a ride to the bank or the *Santa Fe Arms*. Grimes volunteered to give him and Wilford a ride, and they accepted. Grimes was happy about that because now he knew where they were staying.

As they were being dropped off at the Santa Fe Arms, Grimes offered to wait for them to check in and then take them to the bank. Poteet said they would walk to the bank, and Grimes left. Brinson told Wilford that he was suspicious of Grimes, and they couldn't go back to Blossom's that night. "I will get Bix to pick up a change of clothes for us and we will get rid of Grimes." Wilford asked how they could do that, and Brinson said they would strategize with Bix and Bax when they got to the bank.

When they arrived at the bank, Brinson made Bix aware that Grimes may be planning to put a tail on him. "Here is my plan. You have one of our operatives working for you by the name of "Highway." Have him come to your office." When Highway arrived, Brinson introduced himself and showed his ID. "I am told you are good at running interference, and I have a mission for you. It is early in the day, but in two hours Wilford and I are going to leave the bank as if we are going to Albuquerque. You see that *Packard* out there? "Yes, Sir, that is Mr. Toilet's automobile." "Yes, but he has loaned it to us, so you know what to do when we leave." "Yes, Sir, I do."

Brinson said the next thing was for them to keep Grimes occupied for most of the day so he couldn't go with them to the ranch. Bix said, "I have just the thing. The bank handles the Stockmen Association account and Grimes is on the Finance Committee. I will tell him there are some discrepancies and I need him to bring the books so we can correct them. I believe we can keep him occupied most of the day." Brinson said, "Good. Now I need to use your phone to call Blossom to tell her we won't be home tonight, and someone is going to come by and get Wilford and me a change of clothes. Bix offered to do that.

Brinson said, "When we have lost our tail, we will come back to the bank to get the clothes, and we'll change. He completed the call to Blossom. It was lunchtime, and Jeru answered. Brinson asked for Blossom. When she said, "Hello, Mr. Brinson, Cielito's ears perked up and her eyes revealed happiness. After Brinson gave Blossom instructions, he asked to speak to Cielito. "I know I told you I would explain that phone call this morning, I need to start by saying I won't be there tonight. The woman who called this morning was a Pinkerton agent who will be working on this case with me. Wilford and I must stay in town tonight, but I plan to see you tomorrow. I have to go now."

Cielito responded in an assuring voice, "Darling, please be careful and I will probably worry until I see you tomorrow." Cielito hung up and sat down at the table, where Claudette and Jeru said in unison, "Darling?" Cielito broke out into a big smile and said, "Yes, Darling!" Shy said, "Wait a minute, am I missing something?" Blossom interrupted everyone, saying kindly, "Now ladies, don't tease her. Love is in the air, and everything is going to be just fine."

Meanwhile in Santa Fe, Brinson was getting everything together. He called Highway back into Bix's office and explained he was sure the tail had to contact someone, so he would need at least two days. Highway said, "I can do a couple of things. I can shoot him up with enough juice to keep him out for two days and do the old drunk routine, or I can take him to Corrales and leave him." Brinson approved of either plan. "Ok, but make sure he could not recognize you." Highway said, "All he will remember is that the police stopped him. Right now,

I will check outside to see what I can see. Once I spot the tail, I will let you know, and you can leave.

Ten minutes later Highway returned and told Brinson, "This guy is stupid. He is wanted in Arizona. Give me time to get in my car so I can block him in, and I will arrest him and bring him inside. But my gut tells me that something is wrong. I believe they made you and they're setting you up." Highway went back out and moved his car to block the tail in. He walked over and said to the driver, "Get out of the car. You are under arrest. The tail got out his car and they went into the bank and into Bix's office. Highway said, "Gentlemen, this is 'Mr. Head,' also known as "MT." His record is as long as a rope without a knot in it. MT, it looks like this is it for you. It makes you a felon, a three-time loser. What are you doing here? I know you were not planning to rob the bank. Now if you want us to help you, it would be wise for you to come clean."

MT had certainly not planned to be arrested! He cleared his throat to give him more time to think of his answers. "Listen, all I know is I was to follow some Pinkerton Detective." Highway asked who hired him, and he said he thought the name was Grimes. "I overheard him talking about ambushing him." "Do you know who he was talking to?" "I don't know but it was a long way from here, maybe thirty miles." Just as the tail began to relax, thinking he had just cut a deal for himself, Bix announced, "Well, MT, it looks as though we are going to have to lock you up for a few days to help your memory."

At this time Bax walked in and said, "Boy am I glad I caught you, Brinson. Bax asked if he knew a female named "Lucky Street." Brinson said he did. She wanted to get word to you that headquarters in Chicago had contacted her to get to you and tell you that your cover is compromised by someone in

Chicago, so beware." Bix said, "I was planning on getting him over here to keep him busy all day so that he couldn't go with Brinson to the *High Spade Ranch*. We believe that is where the murderers of the Ohara brothers are hiding. Bax said, "You don't have to make up anything because I am going to have him arrested for conspiracy to commit murder." Brinson said, "Good, he might still be at the Stockmen building.

MT spoke up and said that was the place where he was to call him. Bax said he would get Chief Bywater over there and arrest him. Highway said, "You see, MT, your memory is coming back." Bax called the police station to summon Bywater to the bank immediately. Brinson told Wilford they had to change plans. "I have to get those three, so I am going to need a lot of fire power." Brinson asked how many operatives were in Albuquerque, and Bix said there were six. Brinson said he needed two of them. "Have them to drive up here later this afternoon and everyone meet me at Blossom's place." He said to Highway, wait here for the two operatives from Albuquerque and bring them to Blossom's place. Bywater promised Brinson he would bring the needed rifles and ammo Brinson had ask for. Brinson ask if he could bring two officers to Blossom's place later that day. As Bywater was about to leave, Highway asked him if he could lock up MT and not let Grimes know where he was. Bywater said, "Sure." Brinson said "Gentlemen, we must leave you now, but we will see you at Blossom's place later.

Back at Blossom's place, Blossom and Cielito were in the kitchen finishing the dishes. She told Cielito to go to Brinson's room and get him a change of clothes for tomorrow. She would do the same for Wilford. "Mr. Bix is coming to pick up everything, so make sure you send him his razor and a comb and brush, underwear, socks, and toothbrush. Cielito entered Brinson's room and could smell his aftershave. She went to the closet and began to lay out the things for him, but she was so overcome by her surroundings that she lay on his bed and sniffed his pillow, and then buried her face in it. Cielito got off the bed and began to fold stuff to put in a bag, when she heard Blossom say, "I thought you were not coming home tonight. We were getting your things together." Cielito heard Brinson say, "Change of plans," and her heart jumped as she ran to Brinson and began kissing him all over his face. Brinson was embarrassed, although he enjoyed those kisses.

He said that he needed to get with Beauchamp to bring him up to speed on the fast-moving events of the last two days. He told Blossom that he hated to have to call a meeting at her home for later that day. "There will be about ten men here. I will explain later, or you are welcome to listen when I brief Beauchamp." Cielito was still holding Brinson's arm when he asked her to come to his room to put the clothes back where they belonged. When they entered the room, he pulled Cielito to him and gave her a long kiss and motioned for them to sit on the bed. "Tomorrow, I have to do something dangerous. The two men who murdered your brothers and the one who attempted to murder you are planning on ambushing me tomorrow, so we had to change our plans. Tomorrow I must go after them to bring them to justice. I imagine there will be some shooting, but I don't want you to worry. When it is all over, I will come to you."

She buried her face in his chest and broke down crying. He gently caressed her and said, "Remember what I told you. I have to have my wits about me at all times, so please don't give me anything to worry about as I undertake this. I love you and, God willing, I will come to you safe and sound. I must go now and brief Beauchamp, so dry your eyes and be strong for me." She hugged him and said, "Yes, my love."

They left the bedroom and went into the dining room where Beauchamp was waiting for Brinson to explain everything to him. He said, "It's up to you, Jean Claude, I need your help and your expertise as a policeman." Beauchamp said without hesitation, "I am with you one hundred percent." Brinson thanked him with an embrace. He asked Cielito and Claudette if they could tell him the lay of the land around the ranch house. He said to Blossom, "When everyone arrived have the three ladies to stay out of sight. Blossom added that she thought JB had been there before and might be able to draw a picture of it.

Chapter 13
The Gathering

By two-thirty in the afternoon word of what was about to take place had spread. At the casino, Nimrod had gotten the news of Brinson's plan to arrest him and others for a host of crimes, including two murders and one attempted murder. Nimrod and Big Rump Cassie were busy gathering everything that might incriminate them, after which they were hurrying to get away before the hammer fell on them. However, Lucky Lucy Street, who was really an undercover Pinkerton detective, was having none of that.

As Nimrod and Cassie were rushing to get into their car, Lucky was waiting for them. Cassie looked alarmed, but Nimrod kept his composure. He said, "Get out of my way, you Black bitch." She gave him a grin instead of showing fear or any type of alarm, and then said, "I beg your pardon," as she placed her gun in his crotch. "It's Ms. Bitch to you, so get out of the car slowly, and put the bags down now!" Nimrod stared at her, considering that he might step on the gas to get away, in which case he risked being shot in a very sensitive area of his body. The thought of surrender was too distasteful, after all he had done to get away with his crimes.

Lucky Lucy Street sensed his thinking and leaned into the car, saying, "Nimrod, it would be a shame if I have to blow your nuts up into your back pocket, but I will do it, shame or not. And Ms. Big Ass, it is best you do the same or I will do the same thing to you; you will have two holes where your nipples used to be." Nimrod and Cassie did as she had instructed, slowly stepping from the vehicle while leaving all their incriminating evidence inside. "Both of you, get on your knees and crawl around to the other side of the car, and Nimrod, I suggest you call out to your cronies inside not to interfere, or I will have to kill you, and there's no preacher around to pray for your soul."

Inside the casino Breed watched what was taking place and he called his gang together and said they were getting out of there. One of his gang members said, "But we got to help Nimrod." Breed snapped, "Do you think he would make a move to help us? You can stay but I'm getting out the back way. The gang followed him, including the one who spoke about helping Nimrod.

To ensure that neither Nimrod nor Cassie had any weapons hidden, Lucky told Cassie to strip and get into the back seat and lay flat with her hands behind her head. Cassie scowled and mumbled something indistinguishable, but she obeyed. "Now Nimrod, strip and get behind the wheel and drive us to the police station, and don't try anything like wrecking the car or you will find yourself minus a couple or three things. Now, move it!"

As providence would have it, a policeman on patrol was passing by and saw Lucky with the gun and Nimrod naked getting into the car. He stopped and yelled, "Police! Drop it!" Lucky said she was a Pinkerton detective, and without turning, she pulled her ID and told the officer to come closer and look at her credentials. He cautiously moved in a little with his weapon drawn. When he was satisfied, he asked what was going on there. Lucky said, "Officer, this is the infamous Nimrod Bloom, and in the back seat you will find a woman called "Big Rump Cassie. I want the two arrested for murder and accessory after the fact, and I need them held in isolation." He said, "Yes, Ma'am." Nimrod thought for a brief moment that he was safe because he had many policemen on his payroll. He began to curse at Lucky and reach for his pants, but this policeman was honest because he handcuffed both Nimrod and Cassie before putting both of them in the back of his vehicle. Nimrod and Cassie were definitely going to jail!

Lucky followed behind the officer to ensure that these high-profile criminals were arrested and placed in isolation. However, at the police station, Nimrod did, in fact, meet up with corrupt officers and jail personnel who quickly moved the paperwork along until Nimrod and Cassie were out on bail. They were immediately picked up by "friends" who could have been current or former gang members loyal to Nimrod. Now, they were out on bail and had transportation.

Lucky was furious, but she had the presence of mind to call the bank for one of the Pinkerton operatives to follow Nimrod and Cassie, and to contact Brinson at Blossom's place if they stopped anywhere. Lucky needed to get to Blossom's home to tell Brinson and the others all that had happened.

Meanwhile, word had spread about the murders of the Ohara brothers and their sister, who miraculously was alive and hiding at Blossom's home while recuperating from a gunshot wound to her shoulder. People who knew and were fond of the Ohara family were calling the bank to confirm that the three siblings had been murdered. Bax, realizing the speed at which the news was traveling, reached out to the Ohara brothers' wives to alert them to the conversations among the townspeople. Of course, he had contacted them as soon as their husbands' bodies were found, but now he wanted them to avoid being in public for a while to protect their privacy. Nobody except Blossom's inner circle knew that Cielito was not dead, too.

The news included some partially true information about the impending capture of the murderers, and some unusual activity at Blossom's place. Some townspeople were making their way to Blossom's home when Bix was driving there. The road was full of automobiles, and he feared that this thing could get out of hand. When he finally arrived, Blossom asked what all these people were doing at her home. Bax replied, "It's okay, word of the murders went through the town like wildfire. Don't worry, Brinson and I will handle this." JB and Al could see all the cars and left the field in a hurry. JB signed to Blossom, "Mama what is going on?" Blossom said that people intown had heard that Mr. Brinson was going to arrest the men who killed the Ohara brothers, and they came to help." JB let out a sigh.

Blossom said, "You have seen the High Spade Ranch, so, do you think you can draw the ranch house and the surrounding area? JB signed that he could do that. Blossom told Brinson the news, and he was relieved because this would improve his chances of succeeding. He then turned to Bix to say that maybe he should speak to the crowd and introduce Brinson to them. Bix went out to the porch and began to speak: "Friends and neighbors, I am moved to see so many friends and neighbors of the Oharas. Like you, I was shocked when I learned of what happened to them right here in our fair county, and like you, I demand justice! I don't know what your intentions are, but you must let the law handle this. They will bring the murderers to justice. I need you to understand that whoever started this is interfering with the law and has placed several people's lives in jeopardy, even the Ohara wives and children. I am going to introduce you to one of the officials who will tell you as much as he can about the case, but after that, please go home.

Bix stepped back and Brinson stepped forward to say that they had two eyewitnesses to the murders, promising to have the criminals in custody within a day. He urged them to go home. The crowd disbursed, and Brinson asked Chief Bywater to have an officer walk guard around the house to ensure that everyone was gone. Bix noticed Dr. Joe's car was still there, so he went over and asked Dr. Joe why he was not leaving and who were the young ladies with him. Dr. Joe responded, "First, I am here to offer my service because, if there is going to be some shooting, you might need me. And these young colored ladies are physicians, actually surgeons hired by the BOIA to provide medical care at the reservations. Cielito might be interested in meeting them.

Bix said, "Let me ask Brinson about this." Brinson wasn't sure this was the best time for the surgeons and Cielito to meet. Remember, she was presumed to be dead, too. "I understand your intentions, however my concern is your safety, although your services might be needed at the ranch house. The teams will be leaving here around midnight. Where had you planned to spend the night?" Dr. Joe said they would sleep in the car, but Brinson asked Blossom to put them up for the night, and she graciously offered her settee and a comfortable chair for them to rest in.

Brinson selected Highway to patrol the perimeter of the house while they all went inside. Blossom told Brinson that it was dinnertime, and feeding everybody wouldn't be a problem. Brinson said, "OK, but I don't want to burden you no more than we have to, and by the way, thanks for keeping Cielito and Claudette out of sight. Please tell Cielito to come to my room for a minute." Blossom said, "Yes, Sir" in a voice like she was anxious to do that. Brinson excused himself and said he would be right back. Cielito knocked on the door and walked in. He grabbed her and kissed her and said, "I love you and I wanted to kiss you and tell you that because I am going to be quite busy the next several hours and I didn't want you to feel neglected." She said, "Oh, Darling, you have made me so happy." They kissed once more before he returned to the dining room and she to the kitchen. When Blossom went out to tell Dr. Joe and the doctors to come inside, she wanted Shy to meet these young ladies. Dr. Joe introduced them to Blossom as an Herbalist and a Midwife. They both expressed a need to talk with her later.

When Brinson walked back to the dining room, the group was standing around the table looking at a large piece of paper. It was the drawing JB had completed. Brinson thanked JB and began to ask him questions in Sign Language about different sections on his drawing. When he finished, he said, "OK, gentlemen, let's get down to business. I am going to assume that they know I am coming, and if you look at JB's drawing, there will probably be an early warning system in the form of someone hiding about here." He pointed at a place on the drawing. "We are going to use what I call 'The Three Little Pigs' method of attack. Remember when the wolf asked them what time they were going to the fair, and they said two o'clock, but actually went at eleven? We are going to be there earlier than they would imagine. In fact, we are going to have our team in place tonight and surround the place."

Brinson continued: "JB, do you know if there are any dogs there? JB signed that he didn't see or hear any, and Al agreed. Brinson asked JB, "If our teams left here and went cross country to the High Spade Range, about how far is it from your spread to the ranch house?" JB signed about fifteen miles by tractor, and it would be slow going in the dark. Brinson had a couple more questions. "How far would you guess the bunk house is from the main house?" JB looked at AL and signed that his guess would be about seventy yards.

At this time Blossom entered the room and said dinner was ready, but they had to eat in shifts and some of them could fix a plate and eat on the porch. AL interrupted Blossom and said he and Juan could go home for dinner, but she said, "You certainly will not! We are going to bring the food and dishes in, and you all do whatever pleases you."
Brinson moved JB's drawing to the parlor, as Cielito was bringing glasses and cups in. When she set the tray down, she was surprised to see the two young colored ladies, who had yet to be introduced to her as doctors assigned to serve the health needs of those on the reservation. Dr. Joe had asked that they meet Cielito, but Brinson thought that the introduction could wait.

Cielito wanted to fix Brinson a plate at the table, but since his men were eating on the porch, he felt the need to join them as their leader. She wanted them to eat together, but said she wouldn't do anything to worry him, so they would eat in separate areas. "Wilford and I don't have to be at the ranch until right before sunup, so you and I will have the rest of the evening for each other. So, what do you think?" She said, "I think I love you. No, I know I love you." She kissed him and went back to the kitchen humming. Shy looked at Claudette and Jeru and said, "Well someone is happy," and they all broke out laughing. She thought at first that they were laughing at her, but they quickly corrected any misunderstanding by saying they were very happy for her.

Cielito said, "Did you know there are two colored ladies in the dining room?" They were about to go to the dining room when Blossom walked into the kitchen and said, "What is going on ladies? We have hungry men to feed." They all said at the same time, "Yes, Mama," and began whispering among themselves as they carried the food into the dining room. Everyone enjoyed the dinner and thanked Blossom when they carried their empty plates to the kitchen, and some went back outside to enjoy a smoke.

As Cielito, Claudette, and Shy began to remove the dishes from the dining room, Dr. Joe said, "Ladies, it is my pleasure to introduce Doctors Cynthia K Smith and Joann Barker. Cielito, you might want to talk to them when you are finished. They are from the BOIA." Cielito said, "Of course," as they rushed to the kitchen to ask Blossom if, after the kitchen was cleaned, they could go to the parlor to talk with the two ladies." Blossom said yes, but she urged them to take their time because the ladies were not going anywhere.

Meanwhile outside, JB signed to Al that he wanted to talk to him away from the others. They excused themselves under the guise of having to feed the livestock, and they went to the barn for privacy. When they arrived, they surprised a person who was hiding in the barn and tried to run, but Al and JB caught him and took him to Brinson. Brinson was upset and asked Highway how this happened. Highway said he was with the police officers guarding the area, so Highway didn't inquire further. Bix came over to see what was going on, and when he saw the man, he said, "Ramon, what are you doing here?" Brinson said, "You know this person?" Bix replied that he was his secretary's husband." Brinson told Highway to take him to the back and find out what he knew and how much he had overheard. Highway said, "Glad to."

Brinson called the rest of the Pinkerton men and said, "I want a thorough search of this property, I mean every inch. Start at the house, then the chicken coup, hog pen, smoke house and barn, fan out and walk out two hundred yards in all directions." He turned to Bix and said, "Let's see how much this Ramon knows and who he is working for." Highway was giving Ramon a good physical interrogation when Brinson said to stop. Brinson told Ramon he was in a lot of trouble unless he would tell Brinson what he wanted to know, and that he could go to jail for a long time. "Now what were you doing here?" Ramon didn't say anything. Brinson asked Ramon the question in Spanish, and still Ramon didn't say anything. Brinson ask in Spanish if he was married, and Bix answered that he was married to Bix's secretary.

Brinson said, "Good. Highway, where he is going for the next twenty years, he won't need his penis because he is going to be someone's girlfriend! So, we are going to leave, Dr. Highway, so you can perform surgery." Highway reached into his pocket and pulled out his knife and said, "It ain't a scalpel, but it will do the job." As Brinson and Bix were turning to leave, Ramon yelled out, "I will talk, I will talk."

Brinson asked for his full name, how he knew about the meeting, and who hired him. Ramon said, "Ramon Estrada. I was hired by JD Grimes and heard about the meeting from my wife, but she didn't know she was telling me something she shouldn't. We were having lunch, and she was so happy to have this job. I always ask her about her day, and she tells me. She had no idea I was working for Grimes, who asked me to keep my ears to ground and report to him anything I heard. I am not a criminal. I just wanted the little the money he was paying me. I didn't hear anything you said except what Mr. Toilet said and what you said." Ramon stopped talking, but still breathed heavily because he was frightened and fearful of what Highway would do to him. Brinson said, "Take him to the barn, find some way to secure him, and we will decide what to do with him later. I will ask Blossom to fix him some food and I will have someone bring it to the barn and relieve you.

After JB and Al brought Ramon to Brinson, they went back to the barn. JB signed to Al that he wanted to show him something, JB opened the door to the tack room and showed Al the bow he had just finished. Al was amazed at the workmanship, saying, "Is there anything you can't do?" JB signed that there was more. He pulled out a quiver with several arrows in it. Al asked JB if it worked, and JB signed, "Of course, watch this." The other end of the barn was two hundred feet away. He put an arrow in and let go the arrow, which hit the barn wall with a thud so loud that it was heard in the yard where Brinson and Highway had interrogated Ramon. They heard the noise and started toward the barn. When JB and Al went to pull the arrow and saw Brinson through a crack walking toward the barn, Al ran out and said, "It's okay, JB was showing me his bow and arrow."

JB came out and signed to Brinson that he had forgotten something on the drawing. He signed that the hay barn was full of bales of hay. Brinson and JB went to the parlor where Brinson had left the drawing. JB began to sign: "When we get to the ranch house, we can set up bales of hay stacked three high at the back of the house and at the windows. I will be on the top of the hay barn, and when you arrive, I can shoot burning arrows into the bottom bale which will start a fire in case they try to escape through the back. When they see all that fire, they will think the house is on fire and might be inclined to surrender.

Brinson said, "I can't let you do that it is too dangerous and Blossom and Shy would never forgive me if you get injured." JB signed, "I will be on the top of the hay barn, and they won't see me. Besides, Al and Juan will be up there with me with rifles and ammunition. And I would guess that the gang will be at the house. The bunk house is where the vaqueros are, and they are not part of the gang. Brinson said, "JB, in the short time I have been here I've come to love you and your family, and if something happened to you, I would never forgive myself. Let me think about this and I will let you know."

JB signed, "Mr. Brinson, I was there and saw how those brothers were killed, and there is not a day gone by that I wished I could have been there soon enough to save them. I need to be a part of bringing them to justice." Brinson said, "JB, I guess you need that closure. I want you to stay out of sight and do not tell Blossom or Shy what you are going to do, just that you are going to take the team across the range and drop them off."

JB signed, "Sir, I have never lied to my Mama or wife and not about to start now. Rather than lie I will not say anything."

Brinson said, "OK, let's get the team together and I will break them down into teams of three." As they were making their way to the front of the house and calling the team together, everyone turned to see a set of lights coming down the road. Brinson thought, "Now who in the hell is this?" Bix said it looked like Bax's car. Brinson yelled, "Stand down, team." Bix said that was him "I don't know who is with him." When the car stopped and Bax exited, a female did the same. He asked Brinson if he knew Ms. Lucky Lucy Street because she had a message for him. Brinson said, "Not by sight, but we have talked. She is a pink (term used to denote female agents)."

Lucky said to Brinson, "Let's walk." They walked away. She said, "You are not going to like this. I had Nimrod arrested and the stupid police let him out on bail." Brinson said, "What! Well, I'll be darn." Lucky said, "Bax went to the station and raised hell and advised Chief Bywater that heads would roll as soon as we finished our business. I pulled an agent from the bank to tail Nimrod and Cassie, and he should call Blossom's house if they stop and make a call. If you haven't gotten a call here, then they must still be on the run. I figured I best get out here to tell you. I would not risk calling in case the agent was trying to call. And, by the way, can you use another gun?"

Brinson said, "Are you sure you're up to a shootout?" Lucky responded with confidence. "You are talking to a woman who shot expert with all weapons and qualified as a demolition expert." Brinson said she might as well join them, since he was getting ready to break the team into groups of three.

"Ok, team, here is how we are going to carry out this operation. You will be broken into three teams, and Pinkerton Detective Buford Highway will lead Team One, Jean Claud Beauchamp, veteran of the Paris, France Police, will lead Team Two, and I will lead Team Three. You will be happy to know we have a medical team led by Dr. Joseph Brubaker and assisted by Doctors Cynthia K. Smith and Joann Barker. They will setup an aid station well out of range and render any aid necessary. Team One and Two leaders, there are six Pinkerton agents from which you will pick two each. If you don't know it, the lone female is Lucky Lucy Street, who's highly qualified with tactical weapons to include a demolition expert, so do not think she is a weak link. Highway said he would take her.

Brinson explained the plan. "Gather around this drawing. As you can see there is a line of trees on each side of the driveway leading up to the ranch house, and according to JB, that driveway is about one hundred yards. Dr. Joe, you and your team will leave with me and setup right where the driveway curves. That should put you and your team out of range. I have yet to hear of a bullet going around a curve. Teams One and Two, you will leave here at midnight with JB. If you haven't noticed, he's mute but can hear real good. Al Gonzales will translate. Per JB's instructions, afterwards you will take up positions on either side of the house."

Highway asked who would cover the front and back. Brinson said Wilford and he would pull up in the front and exit from the car on the other side for protection. "When you leave tonight, JB will give instructions to secure the back. I will leave around three you should be able to see the car lights. I will shut them off and on so you will know it's me. Just as the sun rises, I will take my position, and by then you should hear gun fire coming from the house. That is when you open fire. If everything I've said is clear, I suggest you find a place to sack out. God willing, things will go well for us. Good night."

Bix asked Brinson, "What about me and Bax?" Brinson replied, "You two are too important. I need you to keep an eye on what is happing in town. Bix if your brother hasn't told you, Lucky had Nimrod arrested, but instead of holding him they allowed him to make bail and he got away. I need you all to deal with that while we deal with this situation."

Brinson, Dr. Joe, and his team went into the house where Blossom, Shy, Cielito, Claudette, and Jeru were sitting in the parlor anxiously waiting to talk to the female doctors. Blossom showed the ladies where they could freshen up first. Brinson went to the dining room to go over the details in his head, trying to see if he had forgotten anything. Cielito was anxious to get to Brinson, so she excused herself and went to the dining room and sat next to him. She kissed him on the jaw and asked if he was alright, after which they moved toward his bedroom.

At the same time, Blossom and the others were deep in conversation with the doctors. Dr. Joe finally said, "If you all don't mind, we have an early start in the morning, and I think the doctors and I need to check our medicine bags to see if we have everything we might need." Blossom went to get them sheets and Shy left to check on her husband and babies. Shy saw JB playing with the babies, and she smiled and thought, "God, what did I do to deserve such a man?" JB would have to get up in three hours to take the teams over to the High

Spade Ranch. He signed for her to come and lie down so he could kiss her. "With so much going on, I missed you and the babies."

In Brinson's room, he and Cielito were locked in each other's arms. She said Blossom suggested they say a prayer for everyone about to embark on a dangerous mission for justice. Brinson said that was just like Blossom, a most unusual woman with a most unusual family. Cielito responded, "She is so happy about us. She is constantly giving me advice, knowing I don't know that much about men and love. Did I tell you I am a virgin at almost thirty-five, and you are the only man I ever kissed?" Brinson pulled her even closer to him, saying, "I am not a handsome man and have never had time for anything but my job, so I guess you can say I am a virgin too. But when I get back, that's going to change. We have to find a preacher first."

Cielito raised up and looked at him and screamed, but he hurriedly and gently placed his hand over her mouth. There was a knock at the door, and Blossom was asking if everything was all right. Cielito invited her in, and when she whispered the news of a marriage to Mama Blossom, it was Blossom's turn to let out a muffled scream. Blossom opened the door and voiced to anyone who could hear her that everything was okay, and the noise was just an old woman being surprised. Then she turned to the couple and said, "Come here, you two, I couldn't be happier if you were my natural born."

Blossom returned to her room and prayed in silence, thanking God for Cielito finding love and happiness. She prayed once more: "Lord, I pray that if it is your will in Jesus' name, please let all the men come back safe." She lay down and fell asleep, and as always when she was troubled in her soul, Mama G would come to her. Mama G said, "Daughter, do not trouble yourself. The sprit will be with the men. But you have trouble coming that will be harmful to all mankind and many will perish. You must prepare and watch for this thing, which will come on the air. Because you have been warned, you and your children will be spared, but you must be ready to help others. Be not afraid -- the spirit of the Father will be with you. Sleep well, my daughter."

Chapter 14
Hell-Fire Coming to the High Spade Ranch

"After all the ideas and planning have passed, the time for action is nye. The strong hand of action finishes the plans and ideas put forward" (Author unknown).

In the Blake household there was a flurry of activity at the stroke of midnight. The teams that Brinson had assembled were preparing to act as they met Brinson, JB, Al, and Juan near the barn. Lucky Street had borrowed a pair of JB's pants and a shirt, and Brinson praised her for thinking ahead. He said to the team, "Now I will make this short. JB and I decided that you all will ride in the trailer pulled by the tractor, and once you get within a mile and a half from the house, you will switch to the mule and wagon because the tractor would make too much noise and will require light. The mules will get you close without noise. There should be no talking once you switch to the mule and wagon. JB will give you instructions, after which you will move to your designated positions, and you know the rest. Check your weapons and ammo now, and as the Spanish say it, *"Via con Dios"* (Go with God). See you in a couple of hours.

In the meantime, Claudette was awakened by the commotion downstairs, and she realized Cielito was not in bed with her and Jeru. She went downstairs to see where Cielito was, but instead saw Brinson coming from outside. She asked Brinson if he knew where Cielito was, and he replied, "Yes, please go back upstairs; she will be up in a minute." Brinson went to his room and found Cielito sleeping just as he had left her, He lay next to her, gently kissed her, and said, "Wake up, Love." She moved and stretched and asked if it was time for him to go. He told her to go upstairs because Claudette was looking for her. "I must get all my gear together since I will be leaving soon. I tell you what -- go upstairs get in the bed with Claudette and Jeru, and in an hour and a half come downstairs. I should be loading the car and waking Dr. Joe." She kissed him and said, "OK, Darling."

Two hours later Brinson woke up Dr. Joe and said maybe he and the ladies might want to wash up. "I am loading my gear and should be ready to leave in an hour." Dr. Joe said he would wake the ladies and let them use the bathroom first. When Brinson woke Wilford, Cielito heard him and was getting out of bed, when Claudette asked where she was going. "Brinson is leaving, and I want to kiss him and tell him I will be waiting for him; I'll be right back." Brinson was just leaving Wilford's room when she stepped out of the bedroom and reached for his arm. They went to his room so he could get his hat and coat and kiss Cielito. She asked if he had time for a cup of coffee, but he declined. Brinson, Dr. Joe, and Wilford went to the car.

By this time, JB and his team were a mile and a half from the ranch house and switched to the mule and wagon. JB signed his instructions and Al translated. Five minutes later they arrived at the hay barn. Juan moved to the corner to watch the bunk house, recognizing that it required twenty minutes to get the hay staked up against the house. Each team quietly went to their designated area and searched for concealment. JB, Al, and Juan reached their positions on the top of the hay barn, keeping their eyes fixed on the horizon while looking for the signal that Brinson was in position and waiting for the action to begin soon afterwards.

They didn't have to wait long. Off to the horizon, JB could see lights moving forward and then blinking twice. It was Brinson. All they needed now was to watch for the sun rising and they knew the action would start. JB had dipped his arrows in pitch, and all he needed was to light a match. He removed them and had Al and Juan to hold them and light them for him when he gave the signal.

The sun soon became visible over the mountains, and Brinson started to move. JB fired the first arrow and was holding his hand for the next one. By the time he had fired all five, Brinson was in front of the house calling for the gang to surrender. The hay on the back side of the house was turning into a blazing fire. He signaled for all the teams to open fire. Inside the house, the gang of eight began to return fire, but soon it became difficult, as they were receiving fire from three directions. Mexican Bob sent a man to check the back, and he returned and reported that the back of the house was on fire. The fire from the hay had set fire to the roof, and smoke was filling the back of the house. Mexican Bob announced, "I am going to surrender! Get me a white pillowcase, I will make a flag to wave.

Hunt Dalton said, "You do what you want to, but me and Duce is getting out of here! They dropped to their knees and crawled toward the back of the house to a bedroom. The fire had caused the glass to break in a window, so Hunt and Duce got a running start and crashed through the window into the hay that was still burning. They felt the heat, but jumped from the hay to the ground and began to run aimlessly. JB signaled to Al to shoot in front of them, but not to hit them. When Al shot in front of them, they stopped and ran in a different direction. JB fired an arrow and hit Duce in the right leg and quickly fired another and hit Hunt in his left leg. JB signed to Al to ask Juan to keep firing at the ground around them while they went down to get them. Al did as JB instructed. The two of them quickly climbed off the barn and ran over to Hunt and Duce, who were pleading for them to put out the fire. JB ask Al to hold his rifle on them while he pulled the arrows out of their legs. Al made them crawl toward the front.

    On the front side of the house Mexican Bob and four other gang members had surrendered. Beauchamp noticed two men crawling and urged Brinson to look. JB and Al had captured two and made them crawl to the front. Brinson started laughing. "Looks like they are wounded. Someone signal Dr. Joe and his team to come over because we have two wounded." Brinson said to JB and AL, "I heard firing behind the ranch house and thought maybe some of the gang was in the bunk house. Al replied, "No, these two crashed through the window and JB had me and Juan to fire around them to make them run in circles while he shot each one in the leg so they couldn't get away."

    Brinson asked where Juan was, and Al replied that he was bringing the vaqueros around and should be there shortly. At that moment, Juan showed up with twelve men of Mexican heritage, telling Brinson that these men were not part of the gang. "I will let Ernesto tell you the rest." Ernesto said, "Buenos Deas, Senior. I am Ernesto Mendez. I no speak English to good."

Brinson said he spoke Spanish, and Ernesto began to explain how the Ohara brothers hired all of them, and because of his knowledge of cattle he was made foreman until Bob and his gang came and took over. None of them were allowed near the ranch house, but they saw them take the two Ohara brothers and a lady away. "We don't know how the brothers got here, and after that day we never saw them again." Brinson said the lady was their sister, and that she was alive, although her brothers were murdered. JB, Al, and Juan saved the sister.

After hearing all that Ernesto had said, Brinson said, "Here's what I want you to do. Continue your position as foreman. The sisters will be out soon to talk to you, and I am sure they will insist you remain in your position. "Right now, I need you to loan us some ropes to tie this gang up. Ernesto said in Spanish that he would do that, and make sure the fire was out and start repairs to the house.

Brinson asked Al if he and Juan could bring the tractor and mule and wagon so they could move everyone over to Blossom's house. He asked Highway to check with Dr. Joe to see if he could have the two wounded gang members tied up. "Knowing them they will attempt to overrun Dr. Joe and the ladies and get away." Highway said they wouldn't get far because JB was watching them like a hawk. Highway walked over to where Dr. Joe and the lady doctors were attending to the wounded. Dr. Joe said he needed to get them to his office, since the arrow in one of them struck an artery and required medical attention as soon as possible.

Highway told Dr. Joe that he couldn't take them to his office just yet, and Brinson reinforced that statement. He called out for Lucky Street to come over. "Dr. Joe, I can't allow that, but you can ride with them in the mule and wagon, and if these ladies know how to get to your office, Lucky can drive your car and they can follow me to town. Dr. Joe agreed.

When Al and Juan arrived with the tractor and trailer, and the mule and wagon, the team had completed tying the gang members. Because of the wounds to Hunt and Duce, they tied their hands behind them and secured them to the wagon. JB and Dr Joe climbed into the wagon with Juan and waited for the team to load Mexican Bob and his gang of four on the trailer. Everyone was ready to leave.

Brinson walked over to Dr. Joe's car and said to Lucky, "Once we get in town I will turn to go to Blossom's place, and you should be able to find Dr. Joe's office. Dr. Cynthia said she knew the way to the office. When Brinson and Lucky arrived in downtown Santa Fe it was early the town was beginning to show signs of coming to life. Brinson turned north to the road that ran toward Blossom's place. Breakfast was over and Blossom, Claudette, and Jeru were washing dishes, while Shy was carrying out a diaper change. Cielito was in the dining room wiping off the table when she heard the sound of an automobile. She screamed that they were back. Everyone was rushing toward the door, with Cielito being the first out. She met Bax Toilet, who asked if everyone was back.

Cielito with eyes looking down answered in a disappointed tone. "No, we thought you were them." When she raised her eyes, she saw another car coming and her heart started to beat with great anticipation. As the car got closer, she could see it was Brinson. She started running and calling his name. As soon as he stepped out of the car, she jumped in his arms and started kissing all over his face and crying, "Darling, you are safe."

Blossom, Claudette, Jeru, and Shy were now outside, and Shy and Blossom asked where JB was. Brinson said he was with the wounded. Blossom and Shy started crying, thinking that JB must be hurt. Brinson clarified that two of the gang members were wounded by JB, who should be coming shortly. Brinson could hear the tractor and called out, "They're here now." At this time Al arrived with the tractor pulling the trailer with the team and Mexican Bob and his gang. When Cielito saw Mexican Bob, she fainted and Bob couldn't believe his eyes, since she was supposed to be dead. Brinson picked her up and went in the house. He lay her on the settee and began talking to her and trying to revive her. He yelled for some smelling salt, and Claudette rushed to Blossom's herb box and found the smelling salt. She rushed back and waved it under Cielito's nose.

She began to come around, reaching up and grabbing Brinson. "Darling, don't let him get me!" Brinson responded with compassion. "He can't hurt you, my Love, because I won't let him." She squeezed him with all her might. Brinson retrieved his hand, but he could see she was still shaking. He asked Claudette to sit with her and hold her until he got back. Cielito was still not comforted, so Brinson told her, "OK, you can come with me. I want you to sit in the swing with Claudette and I will be on the porch with you."

Meanwhile, JB and Juan arrived with Dr. Joe and the two wounded criminals Hunt and Duce. Blossom and Shy ran to him as Juan was driving the mule toward the front. JB jumped off the wagon and signed to Shy and Blossom to go to the front, and that he would explain later. He ran to the barn to get his van to carry Dr. Joe, Hunt, and Duce to Dr. Joe's office. Brinson told Highway to accompany them to be sure Duce and Hunt were locked up.

Bax interrupted, saying, "The police force has been disbanded, and the New Mexico National Guard is in charge, along with a small group of state policemen. They have sent a lawyer from the State Attorney's office." Brinson with great surprise said, "What?!" Bax responded, "After I heard they let Nimrod out on bail, I contacted the Governor, who activated a platoon of the National Guard and sent the local company in Santa Fe to take over and discharge the whole police force, including Chief Bywater."

Brinson said he knew about Nimrod getting bail, but right now he needed to get Hunt Dalton and Duce Dawson to Dr. Joe's office before they bled to death. Brinson signed to JB to leave. The whole household was coming at Brinson with questions, which was understandable. However, Brinson had much on his mind. "Please, everyone, I will be happy to answer your questions, but right now I need to get the team back to town so they can eat and get some sleep. And I must see about Cielito." Blossom said that everyone could have breakfast there, which made the team very happy.

Al asked for himself and Juan to be excused to go home, since they hadn't seen their families in a while. Brinson thanked them for their help and said, "Yes, you should go to your loved ones, and I must see about mine." He turned and looked at Cielito standing next to him, and he put his arm around her as he continued to speak to his team. Highway asked Brinson if the prisoners would be fed, and Brinson replied that they could eat after everyone finished.

Cielito asked Brinson if she could feed Mexican Bob. Brinson looked at her with great surprise and asked why. "A few minutes ago, you saw him and fainted." She said he should come in the house, and she would explain. She called her sister Claudette, Shy, Jeru and Blossom to the parlor. Cielito began by saying she wanted to feed Mexican Bob. Everyone was puzzled because this was the man who tried to kill her. She responded, "I know, I have learned according to Blossom that the Lord works in mysterious ways. After I fainted the thought came to me that his act of trying to take my life actually gave me life! I met you, Blossom, and your Bible studies taught me so much. Then I met my true love, so, you see, had that terrible thing not happened, I would never have come to love Blossom and her family, and you, my love." She squeezed Brinson's arm with affection.

"Can I tell them the good news?" Brinson blushed and said, "Please do." We are going to get married right away. Claudette giggled with glee, and said, "Sister, I am going to give the biggest and best wedding this town have ever seen!" Cielito thanked her, but said that on the advice of Blossom, they should do it the next day. "We are doing it now because we want to, without waiting until we have to." Shy said, "I know just how you feel, and we are so happy for you and Brinson." Claudette and Jeru hugged and kissed Cielito and Brinson.

Blossom interrupted the happy moment by reminding the ladies that they had men to feed. They all went to the kitchen and finished fixing breakfast. Just as they were beginning to serve breakfast JB returned with Agent Lucky Street. Brinson invited her to have some breakfast, adding that they were about to feed the prisoners. Cielito said, "Honey, I'm ready." Claudette and Jeru asked to help, and Brinson said it was all right, but they would have to feed the prisoners tied up and sitting in the trailer. The only utensil they could have would be a spoon -- no knife or fork.

When Cielito approached Mexican Bob, she had a smile on her face. Bob said sarcastically, "What the hell you smilin' about?" She looked him in the eyes and said, "Thank you." He replied, "For what?" Cielito never lost her composure. "For trying to kill me." Bob was visibly puzzled. She continued, "Had that not happened, I could have gone through the rest of my life never realizing the void of not knowing what it is to love another person and get married, yes married! You see, I have no fear of you because God is with me, and He has given me a protector for the rest of my life -- this man right here." She looked lovingly at Brinson standing next to her. "God put us together. He is my lover and protector, and after tomorrow, he will be my husband. That's why I thank you." Mexican Bob had nothing else to say, but he never apologized for attempted murder either.

After the prisoners were fed, the two Pinkerton agents resumed their position as guards. Cielito and the other ladies made their way to the kitchen with the dirty dishes. Brinson asked to speak to JB and Lucky. He apologized to JB, but needed to ask if his van could be used to transport the other prisoners to jail. JB signed that he could do that. Brinson said, "Give me a minute with Lucky." He wanted to know what the doctors had to say about Hunt's and Duce's condition. Lucky said, "Dr. Joann did surgery on their legs, but the arrows severed the leg muscles in both of them. She can reattach everything, and these criminals should begin to heal in a few days. They can't go anyplace, so trying to escape is impossible."

Brinson said that when Lucky takes these other guys to jail, she should see about getting eight sets of handcuffs to secure Hunt's and Duce's hands and legs to the bed. "If the doctors object, tell them it's that or they will be relocated to the jail immediately. When I wrap up things here, I will meet you in town, and by the way, I am recommending you all for a promotion and a citation for the job you've done here." Lucky said they just did what they get paid to do. Brinson replied, "I understand that; however, I could never have brought this to a successful conclusion alone, so you all made the difference. Thank you for a job well done. Now get out of here, before you see a grown man cry!"

Lucky and JB left with their prisoners. Cielito went out on the porch to tell Brinson he had a phone call. He hugged her and walked inside. The voice on the other end said, "Brinson, this is Angus Pinkerton, son of Allan Pinkerton who founded the agency." Brinson said, "Sorry, Sir, after all that has happened, I am still high, not drunk, but adrenalin." Angus said, "I just wanted to call and congratulate you on an outstanding operation." Brinson said, "Sir, I had a lot of help and I want to recommend Lucky and the other agents to receive public recognition for their outstanding work." Angus agreed, and then added, "When can we expect you back here? We have your office ready, Mr. Director!"

Brinson was clearly flattered, but said, "Not so fast, Sir, I need to ask my soon-to-be wife about that." Cielito looked up at him and kissed him. Angus' voice changed as he said, "New wife! When did that happen?" Brinson said, "Yes, Sir, it will take place in a day or so." Cielito gave him a puzzled look. He promised to send Angus his double AAR (After Action Report) sometime tomorrow.

Once he hung up the phone, Cielito said in a playfully serious tone, "Brinson Dubois, what did you mean in a day or so? Are we getting married tomorrow or not!" He kissed her and said, "Sweetheart, yes, we are getting married, but I think we need to talk about it. This is going to be a big and important step for us, and I want it to be something you and I will have fond memories of, something we can tell our children about. I can see there's a lot to do for you and all concerned, but listen, I want us to have our honeymoon right here with Blossom, after what you told me about Shy and JB's honeymoon. I want ours to be just as romantic, and I want us to plan on having children right away, and I was going to ask Blossom if we could stay here for a while, I would feel comfortable with you being here with Blossom when you get pregnant."

Cielito looked astonished at how quickly Brinson had moved the conversation from a wedding to a honeymoon and many children soon after. She questioned, "You are not going to leave, are you?" He replied, "No, I made up my mind that if they want me to be a Director it will have to be here in Santa Fe." Cielito hugged and squeezed him so tightly that he could hardly breathe. She said, "I love everything you said, so, let's talk to Blossom about this."

They went back inside searching for Blossom, with big grins on their faces. They found her sweeping the dining room floor. She looked up and asked, "What are you two grinning like Cheshire cats about?" Cielito said, "We have something to tell and ask you."
She related everything she and Brinson had discussed on the porch. Blossom said, "Let me sit

down." Brinson asked if something was wrong, but Blossom replied, "Oh, no, nothing is wrong. I can't get over you two wanting to spend your honeymoon here. You should go somewhere beautiful and romantic."

Cielito moved to sit close to Blossom, saying, "There is no place in our minds as beautiful and romantic as here. After Shy told me about how romantic their honeymoon was, I knew that was what I wanted, and when Brinson said what he said, I was thrilled. He thinks we should get married two days from now. There is so much to get done. I want you to make my dress, and I know Claudette wants to do much, and beside we have come to love you, Shy, JB and the triplets." Blossom said, "You know, now that I think about it, it makes sense. Let's tell everyone else."

Blossom called Claudette, Shy, Jeru, and Wilford. All showed up except Wilford, and Beauchamp who was sound asleep. Blossom said, "Cielito and Brinson have something to tell you all." Cielito and Brinson embraced each other, and then Cielito spoke. "We have decided to cancel the wedding for tomorrow..." Shy interrupted. "No! No! You can't do that." Blossom said to let her finish. Cielito continued. "We decided that you all probably want to do some well-meaning things and it is a happy occasion for you as well. We think the day after tomorrow will give you time to do what you were planning, and now you won't be rushed." The ladies started talking among themselves, when Blossom suggested they go into the kitchen and talk about what they wanted to do to surprise the couple.

While the others were discussing what they wanted to do, Claudette was on the phone talking with Bix Toilet. She asked him how long he was going to be at the bank. "I need you to do me a big favor. I will tell you when I see you this afternoon."

About then JB entered the kitchen, and Claudette said, "JB, you are just the man I need to see." JB knew Claudette did not know sign language, so he pulled out his note pad and wrote, "What can I do for you?" She said she needed him to build a sixteen-foot table and benches for the wedding reception that would take place the day after tomorrow. He drew something and handed her the paper, which she approved. JB wrote that it would have to be twenty-four feet long to avoid him having to do a lot of sawing. She asked how long it would take, and he replied that he could do it tomorrow afternoon. She said, "One last thing. Can you and Al pick up some things at Willoughby's tomorrow?" JB indicated he understood.

JB walked into his bedroom where Shy was busy working while the triplets were in the playpen that he had built for them. He picked up and kissed each one, but when he put baby Blossom down, she started to cry, which got Shy's attention. She jumped up and ran to JB and said she had a lot to tell him. He signed for her to go ahead. She said, "The grain supervisor said they can't get to us until the first of next week, and I just got off the phone with Al, who said it should not affect our yield. And Cielito and Brinson decided to not get married tomorrow, but the day after. And that's not all. They want to spend their honeymoon here, like we did." JB signed that the extra day would take the rush off everything.

"I am sure Mama would like that. I do, but right now, I am going to lie down for a few minutes I have been running since midnight. It's a good thing we have some good people working for us, Honey. They cleaned all the buildings without me, Al and

Juan being there. If only we had farm laborers like that, you wouldn't have to work so hard." JB signed that Willoughby's new store was opening tomorrow. "Today, they are having a sale at the old store to get rid of everything. Maybe when I wake up, we can go to town to see what they have left." Shy said, "I need to tell Mama because she was just saying we need to get cloth to make the babies some more clothes. They are growing so fast."

    Shy went to the kitchen where the ladies were and told Blossom about Willoughby's having a sale at the old store before the new one opened tomorrow. "Maybe we should go today to see what they have on sale." Claudette said, "That's a great idea. I was planning to go to see Bix, and Jeru, we can go by the Casino and see Sarah, and Cielito, you and Brinson can go to the church and talk to the Priest. It's just eleven o'clock."

Shy said that she had to change and dress the babies, and that she and JB would meet them at Willoughby's. Everyone left to comb hair, freshen up, and take care of things.

    Cielito went to Brinson's room and found him awake and writing his AAR. She asked him if that was something that had to be done right away, or could he do that later? He said it could be done later if she needed his attention now. She responded, "Honey, we are going to town, and you have to drive us, and while we are there we can see if the Priest can marry us." He said, "Give me a minute."

Chapter 15
A New Addition to the Family

No matter what we as humans plan, something always happens that causes us to alter our plans to deal with the "UFOs," not "unidentified flying objects," but "unforeseen occurrences." After Blossom and Claudette had assembled at the car, Brinson asked if that was everyone, and Blossom said JB and Shy would meet them there. Brinson said, "Well let's go," and they were off. A few minutes later, as JB and Shy were preparing to leave, Wilford came downstairs and asked where everyone had gone. Shy said they had gone to town and she and JB were leaving in a minute to meet them at Willoughby's store. Wilford asked to ride with them, and he sat in the back with the babies.

Blossom asked Brinson if he could stop at the church so they could talk to the priest. He responded, "You read my mind because that is just what Cielito and I had discussed. Claudette added, "Afterwards, Jeru and I will walk to the casino so Jeru can see her mother. We will meet you all at Willoughby's."

When they arrived at the church, Father Ignatius was out front with the gardener. When the group approached him, he turned and saw Cielito and cried out, "Holy Mother of God, Saints preserve us! Cielito, my child, forgive me, but the last I heard you were kidnapped and thought to be dead." She said, "No, Father, as you can see, I am very much alive, thanks to Blossom and her son, JB who saved my life." The priest asked what he could do for her, but Blossom spoke first. "Father, Cielito and the man standing with her want to get married." Father Ignatius said, "Yes, it will take a few minutes." Now it was Cielito who interrupted. "Not today, Father. We want you to marry us day after tomorrow at four o'clock at Blossom's house." He said, "I see. Come inside let me check my schedule with the parish secretary." After checking with the secretary, he asked her to block off his time at four o'clock for the wedding. He turned to Cielito and asked who was with her. She replied, "You have met my soon-to-be-husband, Blossom you know, and the two young ladies are my sister Claudette and her friend Jeru Twotrees."

    Father Ignatius said that the last time he saw the two of them was when they were going off to school in New Orleans. "Now that you're back, I expect to see you at Mass." Cielito said, "We will have someone to pick you up day after tomorrow at three." But he said he would have Ernesto drive him. He turned to the secretary to write that down. Father Ignatius asked Cielito what was so special about four o'clock, and she replied, "It is the time my life was spared, and it was around that same time that we fell in love." Father Ignatius smiled before saying, "I see, until then go in peace and love my child."

    Claudette and Jeru left right away for the casino, but when they arrived, they were appalled that the front facade needed a paint job, and the neon lights were dim. Jeru said, "My love, I can see you are thinking the same as I am." Claudette said,

"This won't do. I will talk to Cielito because we need to demolish the building and start anew." Jeru said, "Darling, why don't we plan on living here for six months, and six months in Monaco?" Claudette said, "Great idea, and when we rebuild, we can make it look like Monte Carlo." Jeru added that they should demolish the house and rebuild it to look like their chateau in Monaco.

When they opened the door to enter, there was an elderly woman on her knees scrubbing the floor. She looked up and saw Claudette and screamed, crossed herself, and said, "Mother of God save me! Ms. Jade is it you?" Claudette said, "Get up off your knees. I am Claudette, daughter of Jade and Bybel Ohara. I am one of the owners, and why are you scrubbing the floor?" The old woman spoke softly. "I was the greeter at this door, but the man who said he was the owner told me I was too old and ugly, so he made me do this." Jeru said, "Mother, you will be the greeter again."

When the woman first screamed, it was heard all the way to the kitchen, and most of the kitchen staff came running, including Sarah. Jeru saw her and cried, "Mama," and she ran toward her. Sarah had the same reaction when she recognized Jeru. They embraced and both were crying, Sarah was repeating over and over, "My baby, my baby." She asked Jeru why she didn't let her mother know she was coming. "When did you get here.?" Jeru said she had been there a month. Sarah was visibly disturbed. "You been here a month and just came to see me?" She started crying again. Jeru said, "Mama, let me finish. As I was about to say, we couldn't let anyone know until now for our safety and yours. The people who took over the casino are ruthless criminals who murdered the Ohara brothers and tried to kill Cielito, but Blossom's son, JB, saved her life, and they just caught the gang this morning and told us it was safe to leave Blossom's house." Sarah looked stunned at this news of danger and intrigue, but she was satisfied with her daughter's answer about not seeing her for a month.

Meanwhile, at Willoughby's the rest of the party had finished shopping and were waiting for Jeru and Claudette. Shy said, "Mama, why don't you all drive over to the casino and wait for them. It's been years since Jeru saw her mother. JB and I still have some shopping to do for the babies, so, we will see you when we get home." Blossom said, "You are right. If it is okay with Brinson, we will wait in the car and he can go in and let them know we are outside waiting, but they should take their time."

When they arrived, Brinson stepped inside and heard a scream, but he couldn't see where it came from. Sarah turned and it was Consuela, the young girl from the kitchen. Sarah asked what was wrong, and she replied, "It hurts." She was pointing to her genital area, and at that moment she fell to the floor. Sarah said that the baby was coming, and she instructed one of the staff to call Dr. Joe. Brinson ran back to the car and said they needed Blossom inside. Blossom immediately followed Brinson and saw right away what was about to happen.

She said, "Pick that child up and place her on this table and get me as many towels as you can find and some hot water." She asked if anyone had called for Dr Joe. "This child is burning up with fever. We got to get this baby out right now before she passes that fever to the baby." She told everyone to leave the room except Claudette and Jeru. She instructed them to stand on either side of the girl, with Sarah standing at her head to talk to her and try not to let her pass out. She raised the girl's legs to see how much she had dilated. She could see the baby's head, but the girl was not pushing. She instructed Claudette and Jeru to take her arms and wrap them around their waist, and Sarah to get on the table and straddle her and start at her chest and push toward her.

Blossom reached in and gentle pulled the baby's head, but since the child was not pushing, she needed to get the shoulders and pull it out. She could feel the shoulders, and she instructed Sarah to push harder. She was able to gently pull the baby out and quickly tie off the umbilical cord and cut it. She rushed to clean the baby and wrap it. By that time Dr. Joe had arrived. Claudette and Jeru said Consuela's arms were cold, and Blossom reported that Consuela was dead. Blossom asked, "Dr. Joe, check the baby first to make sure it isn't damaged. I had to reach inside her and pull the baby out by the shoulders." Joe said the baby seemed to be okay. He checked the mother and verified that she had been deceased for about an hour. "What I am concerned about right now is finding a wet nurse." Blossom immediately called Willoughby's and asked if Shy and JB had left. Ms. Willoughby said they were leaving now. Blossom asked to speak with Shy, who told JB that they needed to get to the casino in a hurry.

Blossom went back to the main room where Jeru was holding the baby, and Jeru asked Blossom if she could have the baby. Blossom said it was not up to her, but the mother's next of kin had to decide. Sarah said that Consuela had no kin here. "She was brought here by those people who claimed they were the new owners. I don't think she was related to them because they made that poor child a prostitute. She couldn't have been no more than twelve years old. The one called 'Breed' brought her to the kitchen and told me to keep her with me and watch over her and to not let her leave the kitchen and hide her from the one they called "Big Rump."

Blossom said, "Dr. Joe, I guess Sarah is the closest to being a kin so we should let her make the decision." Dr. Joe agreed with Blossom. Sarah said that if Jeru wanted her, then she should have her. With that settled, Blossom asked Jeru if she was sure she wanted the baby this is not going to be an easy job, all of your time is going to be raising this baby. Claudette said she would help with her. Dr. Joe asked Blossom if she had any fenugreek. She said, "Yes, I keep some as a midwife because occasionally some first-time mothers have a problem making milk."

When Shy and JB arrived. Blossom explained the situation to Shy and Shy agreed that since the triplets was seven months, she still had plenty of milk. She took the baby from Jeru and sought privacy to breast feed the baby. Jeru followed her and was watching her. Blossom said, "When we get home, I will give you medicine that will make you start to make milk."

Dr. Joe called the ladies together to discuss what they wanted do about the mother. "We have to decide where she will be buried." Cielito said she would pay for all of it. Claudette said, "I think we should place her body in the mausoleum with Mother and Father. We will be moving to the house, and that way her sprit will be close to the baby." Dr. Joe said he would wait there for the mortician and instruct him on their wishes. "When do you want the funeral to take place?" Brinson, who had been quiet through the whole thing, said, "How about three days from today, since we are getting married day after tomorrow and we don't want a funeral the same day as our wedding." They all looked at each other and agreed. Dr Joe said everything was settled and they should all go home. The baby would need to feed again soon.

Blossom said, "We can't leave until this baby knows her name." Jeru asked Blossom to give the baby a name, and Blossom asked everyone to gather around. "This baby girl shall be named 'Consuela Sarah Jade Twotrees Ohara.'" Jeru shouted to Claudette that it was a good name. They both hugged Blossom and thanked her. Blossom told everyone to line up, with Jeru following Blossom, then Claudette, and finally the rest of them. They all took part in the ritual, which was a tradition carried on since slavery. They would choose their baby's name before the master would arbitrarily claim a name for the slave child. As they began to leave, Jeru begged Sarah to come to the house that evening, and she promised that she would. Blossom asked Shy if she had brought bottles of milk with her, and Shy replied she had some bottles in her bag. Blossom took one in case the baby woke up before they got home.

Claudette suggested everyone could all go on ahead because she need to go to the bank to talk with Bix. Brinson agreed to drop her off. Blossom said to Jeru, "Move over closer to me; I want to show you something." She reached inside her blouse and pulled out a bottle of milk. "Take this bottle and place it under one of your breasts. Now understand that until your milk starts to flow you are going to have to feed the baby by bottle, and the secret is to never let the baby feel the bottle when you feed her. Let her lay on your left side so she can sense your heartbeat, and when she gets to be two or three days old, open your blouse and let her lay on you so she will get used to your feel and smell."

Thirty-five minutes later, they arrived at the house. Blossom told Jeru to make sure the baby's head was covered. She said, "For the next couple of months you and Consuela have to sleep with me because there is so much for you to learn before you move."

In the meantime, Beauchamp heard the voices and came to the front to tell everyone that lunch was ready. He noticed Jeru sitting and holding a bundle, and he asked her what it was. She replied with a small grin, "It is our baby, Consuela." Beauchamp recognized that the bundle was, in fact, an infant, and he was stunned. "What? We have a baby?" She said, "Yes, the four of us." He smiled and asked to see the child. Jeru consented, saying, "Blossom said I must keep her head covered; she's only a few hours old. Her mother died giving birth, which is how we got her, and we have to be careful with her until she gets older."

Blossom came to the parlor and told Jeru to follow her to the bathroom. She ran some warm water in the sink and instructed Jeru to lay the baby down and unwrap her. "Consuela needs a diaper change, and you and Claudette have to learn how to change diapers. You will be doing this several times a day." Jeru unwrapped the baby and held her nose and said, "Whew," since she had never been up close to a baby with a soiled diaper. Blossom told her to take the little wet towel and wash her bottom and dry her good. "I took some of the triplets' diapers. This one is ready so lift her by her feet and slide the diaper under her and pin it up. Now take her back to the bedroom and I have some blankets to wrap her in." Blossom spent an hour and a half telling her about babies, their needs, and how to care for a newborn. She told Jeru that after a diaper change, she should wash her hands really well.

"And don't let everyone touch Consuela because right now she doesn't have the things to fight off germs. When your milk starts, she will get those things from your milk." Blossom ended by saying to keep the baby in the bedroom until she is about six weeks old and keep her away from loud noises that will frighten her and make her nervous. Jeru asked when Blossom would give her the medicine to make her milk start, and Blossom promised to do everything when Claudette got back.

JB and Shy arrived later and brought several bags into the house, and Shy said that they had found several good items for the triplets, along with diapers, newborn gowns, and blankets for Consuela. Blossom stepped out of her room and invited Shy to join her and Jeru and Consuela. Shy came in the room and dropped two large bags on the bed. "We bought some things for Consuela. There are diapers -- you can never have enough of those -- and some little gowns, and here is something new, little rubber pants to go over the diaper so when the baby wets it won't get the bed or your lap wet. And Mama, JB will be in shortly. He had to bring the babies in, but we bought a rocking chair for the room.

Blossom acknowledged the extra efforts that JB and Shy had made on behalf of the newest family member. As Jeru began looking through the bags, tears of love and gratitude welled up in her eyes. She lay the baby down and hugged Shy and said,
"Thank you. The blankets and gowns are so pretty, and you all are such loving and compassionate people." Shy kind of stuck her chest out and announced, "We got that from our Mama." she reached and kissed Blossom on the forehead and turned back to Jeru. "By the way, we bought her

some nipples and bottles, and as soon as I get my brood settled, I will get the bottles and nipples washed and fix her three or four bottles that should hold her through the night.

Blossom was so proud of Shy. JB came inside and signed to Blossom and Shy that if someone would watch the babies, then he would bring in the rest of the bags and the rocking chair inside. Blossom agreed to do that. "Shy, why don't you stay with Jeru. I am sure she has questions to ask you since you are both mothers and Jeru can learn a lot from you." When Blossom left the room Shy said, "I don't know about that, but I will say that this is a twenty-four hour-a-day job and there will be times when you think you are at your wits end. According to Mama, a lot of women go through that, but I want you to know I am here when you feel like you can't take it anymore. You can always lean on me. You have taking on an awesome responsibility and that has revealed something about you and your compassion for others. I have the utmost respect for you."

Jeru asked if motherhood was really that hard, and Shy replied, "It is not hard if you keep in mind that out of all the women in the world, God has entrusted you with the life of this helpless being, and you have to give that life all of your love and attention. You'll still love others, but you will have a special love and responsibility for your child.

I will give you an example. A few months after I had the triplets, JB began to act as though he didn't care, at least it seemed that way to me. One night before he went to bed, he wanted to make love and I said I had to give the babies a bath and nurse them. Well, I went about doing that, and once I finished all of that and snuggled up to him, he just turned his back and began to snore. I thought he didn't want me anymore. It never dawned on me that he was feeling neglected. We both were hurt and not communicating. I talked to Mama about it and she explained to me that JB never had a man to teach him certain things about women. She talked to him and after that everything was right between us. I learned that a man has special needs and I had to find time for him."

Jeru said she didn't have a man, so therefore, she didn't have to worry about that. Shy stated that she had Claudette, after which Jeru became indignant, insisting that she and Claudette's feelings for each other weren't sexual, and neither of them had ever had a man or a woman. Shy apologized, but still made the point that up to now, they showered each other with love and attention. "However, taking care of the baby's needs will take a lot of your time, and Claudette might miss the love and attention you had previously shared so freely with each other." It was Jeru's turn to apologize. "It's just that we're sensitive about our relationship. Some people say it is a sin, but a priest in France told us that God knows our hearts better than a mere human, and we shouldn't put much stock in other people's opinions."

Jeru ask Shy how old she was, and Shy said she was nineteen. Jeru said she was thirty, independently wealthy, and well-traveled, but still lacked the wisdom Shy possessed. Shy responded, "One thing I noticed about you and Claudette is that your hearts are in the right place, and you are open to learning. The longer you are around Mama, the wiser you will become." Jeru asked how Shy could say that her heart is in the right place, and Shy touched her shoulder reassuringly. "First, if it wasn't, you would not have taken Consuela and Claudette would not have agreed."

Little Consuela began to move and was about to cry. Shy reminded Jeru to first check her diaper, while Shy prepared to nurse her and fix her some bottles. Jeru replied, "You are right, she is wet. Do you think I will ever learn?" They both laughed. Shy told Jeru that she had only been a mother for a few hours. There came a knock at the bedroom door, and Claudette entered saying a little loudly, "I come bearing gifts for all." Both Jeru and Shy said, "Shh! You will wake little Consuela." Claudette whispered an apology and left, saying she would be back. She went to the parlor where Bix was waiting with his arms full of bags. He asked where he could put them before going back to the car to bring in the rest. Claudette asked everyone to come into the dining room to see what she had brought them. She lined everyone up, with Cielito first and everyone else behind. "For the ladies, you have two bags full of personal female items. For the guys there are small envelopes for each of you, and inside are invoice slips for suits, shirts, sox, and ties. Tomorrow you can go into Willoughby's department store and pick out what you want. As you can see, the sales slips are marked "paid," so get what you want. Now for the triplets. Shy, I thought they had some cutie outfits for the babies, but you and JB can go in tomorrow and pick out what you like. I couldn't resist these." She laid out on the dining room table three little sailor suits for toddlers.

Everyone thought the outfits were cute. She urged everyone to accept her gifts because they came from her heart. "I am so happy that my heart is bursting. My sister has found love and is getting married, and then Jeru and I are mothers. Wilford and Jean Claude are fathers if they want to be. I thank Blossom, Shy, and JB specially. The lessons you have taught me about life, love, and compassion, and the way people should live and treat others, I will be eternally grateful, and I will love you all forever."

Claudette ended by saying that sometime in the next few months, she and the rest of her group would be moving. "I can't speak for the rest, but it will be a sad occasion for me. It is like leaving my family, so bringing these gifts to you all are very important to me. Mama Blossom, you have taught us that all of this is just material stuff, but all the things I do from my heart are my way of saying I love you and appreciate you." There were tears coming from every eye in the room. Blossom was about to speak, when Brinson asked if she could wait until he said something first. He reached out and pulled Cielito to him and said, "I guess I am going to have to get used to saying, 'we.' I guess I know Claudette and Jeru as adults better than the rest of you. Everything she said is coming straight from her heart, and what I am about to say is coming straight from my -- or our hearts. Cielito and I have talked it over after we are married, we plan to start having children right away. We plan on staying here, though not necessarily in this house. Blossom, we know you are a midwife, and we pray that you will be able to deliver all of our children. We want them raised near the Blake family."

There was some light chatter, all positive and loving all over the room. Brinson cleared his throat to indicate that he wasn't finished. "JB, I have not spoken to you about this, but if you allow us, we want to build you a new barn with living quarters above it for me and my family. Because of the kind of work I do, every once in a while, I will have business out of town and I feel my family being here with you all will put my mind at ease, and Blossom, I think it will be an honor if all of us can worship each Sunday and have dinner with you all."

Blossom was visibly moved by everything Brinson had just said. "Maybe I can say this without breaking down in tears. Some may say that what brought us together was a tragedy, and in a way it is true. But I rather see it as the handywork of God. I was told by my grandmother that by keeping God's commandments, I would be blessed beyond my wildest dreams, and there was a time when I thought that I was cursed by an old woman who had rendered me incapable of bearing children. But as it is said, God works in mysterious ways. Not only do I have JB, Shy and my grandbabies, but He added all of you as my children. I want you all to know as far as I am concerned, this is your home and you can come home any time you want; when you feel you can't go anyplace else, you can come here. Brinson, I know JB will be proud to have you living here." JB signed "Amen, Mama, and I know, Brinson, that with you living here, my mind will be at ease when I leave at midnight to go to work, knowing you are nearby. I know my family is safe.

Bix Toilet, who was quiet while others were speaking, said, "Just like the rest of you, I have tears in my eyes. But before I go, let me say that I need Claudette, Cielito, and Jeru to meet me at the bank tomorrow at ten, and Brinson should come, too." Claudette said Jeru was unavailable because they just had a baby. Bix expressed surprise and disbelief until Claudette explained everything. Bix said that Claudette could speak for Jeru, adding, "Also, the items you asked me to order for you will be ready tomorrow." She said some changes needed to be made, but she would explain tomorrow.

Beauchamp announced, "Since so much is going on and all of you have been busy, lunch is now going to be dinner!" He asked to speak with Blossom in the kitchen. Cielito told Brinson that they needed to go to his room to talk. In the kitchen, Beauchamp told Blossom that Claudette had asked him to prepare the reception meal, and Blossom was pleased. He said he planned to make a three-layer wedding cake and he estimated there would be twenty-five or thirty guests. He spoke about hors d'oeuvres, and Blossom asked what that was. He laughed, and said it was basically finger-sandwiches. Blossom was not familiar with that term, so she asked, "What is a finger sandwich and whose fingers?" He laughed once more and explained, "It is like cucumber sandwiches you eat with your hands." Blossom laughed, saying she must sound like a fool. But Beauchamp replied that sometimes he forgets that he was not in France. Blossom said, "Son, you go on ahead and fix what you want since you and Claudette know more about such goings on than I do." Blossom left the kitchen still laughing.

In Brinson's room, Cielito said, "I should have told you this when we first met, but you will find out tomorrow when we meet with Bix. Darling, I am wealthy." He said he figured that from Claudette. She said, "No, Honey, I mean really wealthy. Claudette and I are billionaires who inherited wealth from our parents. I own half of the new downtown Santa Fe and the bank own the rest. On our High Spade Ranch, we have a joint venture with Consolidated Oil Company, our oil wells continue to add to our wealth, and we own several mines that are producing." Brinson said, "Whew! I didn't know that!" She hoped that knowledge wouldn't make a difference in their relationship. "I'm not like

Claudette, whose profession causes her to dress and live a lavish lifestyle. But I don't wear fancy, expensive clothes. My whole life has been devoted to my schools. In addition, I built a school in Oklahoma for Native children. Bix will tell you that I have not touched my monthly dividend checks in the last seven years. I love you and I will be satisfied to live off what you make. You are going to be my husband and whatever you say, I will abide by it."

Brinson held her closer to him, and he looked into her eyes as he placed a finger over her lips in a gesture that indicated he had no issues with her wealth. He said, "Cielito, I love you and I loved you before I knew how rich you were. I don't want people to think I married you for your money, but it's important that. You know I'm marrying you because I love you with all my heart." Cielito said she wanted him to continue working as a detective, and that she wanted to have and raise his children right there with the Blake family. Brinson said, "My love, there is something I must tell you before the wedding. My full name is Brinson Francois Dubois. I never liked my middle name because I was teased as a child." Cielito said, "I think it is a beautiful middle name. Can I call you that instead of Brinson? Francois sounds loving and romantic." Brinson said no, but Cielito said, "OK, but if our first born is a boy, I want his name to be Francois."

Blossom and Claudette proceeded to her bedroom, where she found Jeru manipulating her breasts as Blossom had instructed her earlier. Blossom reached into her apron pocket and pulled out a bottle containing the herb medicine Fenugreek. "It will make a woman produce milk; however, in some women it has been found to heighten their desire for sex, and an almost uncontrollable desire to be with a man. Now, are you sure you want this?" Jeru said she would be the one to take the medicine, but Claudette thought they both should take it. "Consuela should see both of us as her mother." Jeru said she would come to know that as she gets older, but right now, Claudette has a better mind for business, and Jeru needs to sleep in Blossom's room for the next six weeks to properly care for the newborn.

Blossom agreed with Jeru that Claudette and Cielito should be the ones to take over the business, since their brothers were dead. Claudette finally agreed but asked to sleep in Blossom's room to be near Jeru and Consuela. Shy knocked gently to announce that dinner was ready, and everyone was in the dining room. When Blossom arrived, she told everyone, "We must make some adjustments for Jeru and Consuela. They need to sit away from us, so Jeru will sit at the head of the table close to the kitchen. So, now that is settled and let's eat." Beauchamp and Wilford brought in the food and a bottle of milk, asking Blossom to check the temperature. She squeezed a little on her arm and handed it to Jeru.

After asking for blessings, they began to eat until they heard a knock at the front door. It was Sarah and a young man, and when they entered, Jeru stood and said, "Mama." She moved toward her mother as the baby began to cry. Blossom cautioned her about making noise around Consuela. Sarah quietly said, "Hand me my granddaughter and you sit and eat." Blossom asked Sarah if she cared to eat. Sarah thanked Blossom but declined because she had already had dinner. However, her companion stated that he would partake. Sarah said, "Please excuse my manners, this is Rooster Roger Brownlee, the Casino manager. He was kind enough to drive me over here. I just wanted to get a peek at the little darling." Sarah wanted to feed Consuela, but Jeru said there was a special way she did that. "She is just a few hours old, and I am trying to get her to bond with me until my milk starts. If I let other people feed her, then it will confuse her. She needs to get used to me, and believe it or not, a baby does that by touch and smell and can tell it's me by my heartbeat."

Sarah said, "You learned all that in the last few hours?" Jeru said that after six weeks, her mother could spend as many hours as she wanted with the baby. Sarah said that her apartment over the Casino couldn't hold all of us, but Jeru said she and Claudette had decided to demolish the casino and the house, and to rebuild them both to look like the one they have in Monaco. Sarah asked what would happen to the people working in the casino. Jeru said Claudette would come by tomorrow and tell everyone of the plan.

Rooster asked if he and the others needed to get new jobs, but Claudette said that most of the staff would be paid three quarters of their earnings until they reopen. Dealers would receive a stipend, and if they wanted, they could deal some other place until the casino reopened. Sarah asked what happens to all the food, and Claudette said it would go to Cielito's two schools. All the gaming equipment would go to the old bank that's being converted into a warehouse for JB to store his cleaning supplies and equipment. Claudette apologized for just telling this part to JB, but he was happy with the plan. She explained that everything was happening so fast that there were the mining operations down near Silver City, and the ranch had to be reorganized. She lamented that she suspected the ranch hands had not been paid since her brothers' demise, not to mention how many heads of cattle had been sold without permission. And then there was the preparation for Cielito's wedding in two days, and the new baby. "I guess I should stop here."

After hearing Claudette, Blossom said, "Daughter, we will help you with whatever you want us to do. There is something to add to all of that, but I need to talk to you and Cielito about that alone." Meanwhile, Sarah was thinking she needed to leave in order to get an early start in the morning boxing up all that could be boxed and moving the food to the schools. She turned to Rooster and suggested he should organize the dealers to prepare all the equipment in the main gambling room to be loaded and moved to the warehouse when they received word that work was to begin.

Claudette, Cielito, and Blossom moved away from everyone. Blossom said, "We have to get with the wives of your brothers to plan a proper memorial for them. I hate to bring it up, but I feel it is fitting that we honor them. Their remains must be left where they were buried because they didn't have the benefit of a coffin. I suggest we do that after all of your business has been attended to." The two agreed. It had been a long, mostly happy day for everyone, Blossom said, "Cielito, before you get ready for bed, I need to measure you for your dress. I will cut the pattern tonight." Cielito indicated that she was ready now.

Chapter 16
Reorganizing and Rejoicing

"Tomorrow can never come too soon, but when it does arrive, it becomes a release from all the worries one had about it on yesterday."

As the morning sun rose over the mountains, the Blake household began to show signs of movement. Jeru and Consuela were awake for a diaper change and feeding time. Jeru went to the kitchen to get a bottle and warm it up, and then she returned to the bedroom and sat in the new rocking chair. Consuela was getting impatient and made it known by crying before Jeru could insert the nipple in her mouth. Her cries awakened Blossom, who reached over to shake Jeru, only to find that Jeru was not there. Blossom sat up quickly and saw Jeru sitting in the rocking chair feeding the baby. She smiled and lay back down, satisfied at what she saw.

Jeru said softly, "Good morning, Mama. Before you ask, I changed her diaper for the third time." Blossom said, "Okay, Little Mama, you are beginning to read my mind." She pulled the curtain back far enough to peak outside, and said, "Good morning, Daughter, looks like it is going to be a beautiful day." Jeru asked if it was okay for her to give the baby a bath. Blossom responded, "No, it is better to wait a day or so because she has a substance on her to protect her skin from drying out. As for you, I always recommend the mother to not use soap on her chest area, since the baby is still in the bonding stage and getting used to your smell. I don't want you to worry too much. You are catching on fast and asking the right questions. I'm going to wash up and get breakfast started, so, call me if you need help with anything."

Blossom stopped at Shy and JB's bedroom to peak in on Shy and the babies. She was surprised to see Shy up and at the dresser working, and the three babies were asleep. She whispered, "Shy, Honey, what are you doing up and working this early?" Shy said that she was working on government reports to mail in next week so she could get paid, and with so much to do and the babies still asleep, she thought it wise to complete the reports. Blossom responded, "I understand, but I don't want you to overwork yourself." Shy replied that in thirty days, Cielito would be sending three girls from the school to help.

Blossom made her way to the kitchen, only to find Beauchamp there. He greeted her in a polite fashion. "Good morning, Ma'am. I hope you don't mind, but I am making crepes, waffles, sausage, and bacon for breakfast. Blossom asked what crepes were, and Beauchamp said they were like pancakes, only lighter, and they could be stuffed with preserves or eaten like pancakes. "I thought that since I will be gone this morning, I would make enough so we can have some for lunch in case I am late getting back.   Blossom smiled. "Jean Claude, knock yourself out. I am going to use the dining room table for a few minutes to lay out the pattern and cut the cloth for Cielito's wedding dress."

After gathering all her stuff, Blossom began to lay out the front pattern on the cloth and pin it. Just as she began to cut there came an awful scream that scared her and caused her to make a deep cut into the cloth. She ran to her bedroom thinking something awful had happened to the baby. She burst into the room, with Claudette right behind her. Jeru was sitting on the bed holding Consuela with her breast in the baby's mouth, and she cried out, "Mama, I have milk! Look, I have milk!" By that time the whole house had descended on the bedroom. Blossom had to steady her breathing, and then she said, "Child, I know you are happy, but you scared the daylights out of me!" Jeru was not listening to Blossom. She was so happy that she couldn't stop talking about her milk. Blossom told everyone to go back to whatever they were doing.

When she went back to her work in the dining room and was about to finish cutting the cloth, she noticed she had cut too deep and there was no way to correct it. She just sat in a chair and started crying. Beauchamp heard her and went to see what she was crying about. She just pointed to the cloth and said, "I ruined it. I failed." He went to find Claudette, Cielito, and Shy. As he was doing that, a strange thing happened. Mama G's spirit came to Blossom. "Daughter, dry your eyes. You have not failed. You can't see me, as I usually come to you in your dreams when you are troubled. Let not your heart be troubled because sometimes when one thing goes wrong, it opens a door for something better to present itself. Stand up straight and tell Cielito what happend."

All three ladies showed up, along with Beauchamp, Shy ran to Blossom and asked her in a frightened and trembling voice if she was okay. Blossom explained how she came to cut too deeply into the cloth for Cielito's dress. Cielito comforted Blossom. "It is okay, Mama, Claudette and I were looking at one of her magazines she picked up while she was downtown. I think I want to have a Mexican wedding, so, let me get the magazine and show you." They all followed her upstairs. Claudette asked Blossom if she could make an outfit like the one that she pointed to in the magazine. "Not this color, but a color you like." Blossom said she and Shy could make it, except for the hat and boots. Cielito laughed and said she thought they might find the boots and hat at the Mexican Boutique.

"While we are in our meeting at the bank, maybe you can look around town and see what you can find. Which reminds me that it is eight thirty and we need to finish dressing and leave for our meeting. You should leave with us." Blossom said, "Let me change my dress and shoes and make sure Jeru and Consuela are okay. I will be ready when you all are ready." Claudette told Blossom that Wilford was there, and she would tell him. She went to Wilford's bedroom and knocked twice, but there was no answer. She opened the door and Wilford was not there. She called out, "Has anyone seen Wilford?" Now everyone was concerned and began to search in different rooms, but he was nowhere in the house.

Shy went to look out back, and she spotted him out back painting. She walked toward him, saying, "You had us worried. We were looking all over the house for you." He calmly responded, "I thought the sun rising over the mountain was so beautiful that I had to capture that scene." Shy looked at the half-finished painting and replied, "You're right, it is beautiful. Everyone is going to town, but I can see you probably want to continue painting. He said he did and would have breakfast and then return to his painting. When he went inside, she asked if he minded watching out for Jeru and the baby, and he said he would gladly do that. Shy went and announced that she had found Wilford outside painting.

After surveying the situation Shy asked if there would be enough room in the car for her and the triplets, and Brinson said absolutely. "Cielito and Claudette can sit up front with me and we will be ready to go." Blossom asked Brinson to take her and Shy to the old bank building. After he dropped Blossom and Shy and the babies at the old bank, he took Cielito and Claudette to their meeting with Bix. When they arrived, there was a conference room with several other men and the Ohara brothers' wives. Cielito warmly acknowledged her sisters-in-law before saying, "I know most of you, but let me introduce my soon-to-be husband, Brinson Dubos. Also, a couple of you have never met my sister, Claudette. After she introduced Claudette, the meeting started.

Bix began, "First I want Bax to give you the latest on status of Nimrod and his gang. Bax cleared his throat and began talking. "You will be happy to know that I have assembled some of the best trial lawyers around, since the murderers' trial will start next month. We are currently taking deposition of ten individuals, and within the next week we will have you, Cielito, JB, and Al to brief ahead of the trial. We need to get you ready for questions the defense lawyers will ask. Now as for Nimrod, his lawyer has petitioned the court for him to be tried separately from his gang. The bad news is that the Judge is Mason Stoddard, former Senator. The team and I have a problem with that because you know how politicians are -- wave a dollar at them and they will not only sell their soul, but they well sell the souls of their wives, kids, and Mamas."

Bix said, "Claudette, I want you to meet Architect Scott McKenzie whose firm is designing the new downtown Santa Fe. He has some suggestions for your casino. McKenzie stood and first congratulated Cielito and Brinson on their upcoming marriage, and then asked if they were satisfied with what his team was doing to the downtown area. Cielito responded that she was satisfied and trusted his judgment and vision for her. "Now, Ms. Claudette, I think demolishing the casino is not a good business move, but I recommend you redo the facade to look like Monte Carlo, and just clean and refurbish the inside to achieve the look you want. You have pure Italian marble, and the grout can be redone and sealed. The woodwork can be stained. I think my father did the original design work. My construction crew can redo the main floor in three days, so, there would be no need to close. And the outside work would take about three weeks, during which time your customers can enter the main floor and bar through the restaurant."

Claudette asked about the upstairs. He said they could gut the whole upstairs and it won't interfere with·her gambling customers. "Why don't we meet next week to look at it and you can tell me what you want upstairs?" Bix agreed with Scott. Claudette took Bix's hand in hers and said, "Bix, I have trusted your advice ever since I can remember so we will do it as you all have suggested."

Bix turned to the rest of the people assembled, and said, "Now that we have all that taken care of, I will turn the floor over to Streeter Finley. He was the business advisor to the late Ohara brothers. He also congratulated Cielito and her future husband. "I am looking forward to working with all six of you. Allow me to start with some positive news. All of your holdings are solid and continue to produce profitable returns, and you have some very good, faithful, and dependable employees."

Finley took a breath, as if getting the wind he needed to finish his report of good news. The mines continue to produce at a high capacity. All of them together for the year showed a net profit of twenty-five million dollars, compared to last year. The High Spade Ranch operation was doing well until the brothers disappeared, and I feel it will soon be in the black under the rightful owners. The joint venture with Consolidated Oil continues to show a healthy profit, and you now have fourteen oil wells. This year my prediction is that Ohara Inc will reach eight hundred million dollars!

Turning to next year, I had talked to your brothers prior to their demise about setting aside fifteen thousand acres for agriculture. The future is going to be soybeans, and I predict soybeans, like pecans, are going to sell at or above the price of wheat. That is according to a farm manager here in Santa Fe who has published articles in the Agriculture Department magazine about the many uses for soybeans. I suggest you get in touch with that person. Cielito asked the person's name, and Finley replied, "They just sign 'S Blake Farm Manager,' and I know nothing else." Cielito replied that "S Blake" was not a man, and she knows her as Shyanne.

Bix and Bax couldn't believe what they just heard. "You mean our Shy, JB's wife and Blossom's daughter? Bix said, "Gentlemen, you have got to meet this unusual family." As the meeting was adjourning and everyone was standing around talking, Cielito and Brinson asked Scott McKenzie if they could take a few minutes of his time. "We are planning on living with the Blakes, and we want you design a large barn with living quarters above. We want a very large area with a concrete floor and ceilings high enough for a combine machine to fit inside." He said, "I think I know what you are looking for. How many bedrooms and bathrooms upstairs?" She looked at Brinson as if to say that was his call. He said, "A large master suite with bath and three regular size bedrooms and one bath, two large office suites, and a lift." McKenzie asked when he could see the area, and Brinson looked at Cielito and asked what she thought. "Maybe two o'clock, and everyone agreed.

Meanwhile, Blossom and Shy were at the Mexican market with the babies. Blossom was carrying her namesake, while Shy was carrying the boys, one in the cradle board on her back and one in the front. As they moved along the different vendors, Blossom yelled, "Shy, that's it! Come on. She hurried to get there, as if someone would get there before she did. Blossom was already talking to the vendor when Shyanne arrive and saw what Blossom was so excited about. She said, "Uwe Mama, that is so pretty." What they were looking at was a Mexican female outfit of white with gold trim and gold designs on the Jacket and skirt.

This was a time Blossom wished she had her tape measure with her. She asked the vendor if she could use her chair for a few minutes. Blossom said, "Honey, you are about the same size as Cielito. Hand me the boys and try on the outfit." Shy said, "The jacket fits just right, but the skirt is little big." Blossom asked to see the back. "I can fix that." She asked the vendor the cost, which he said was fifty-five dollars. Blossom said, "My goodness, that is a lot." The vendor said it came with boots and a hat, which made the price acceptable. She said, "Shy, Honey, hurry to the new downtown and see if you see JB's or Al's van, and if they are still there, then have one of them to drive over here. I will stay here with the babies, but first open my bag and count out fifty-five dollars to pay for this." The vendor returned with the outfit, boots, and hat. Blossom paid her and said, "I am going to have to sit here until my daughter returns."

When Shy reached the area, she saw JB sitting in the van filling out a report. She spoke and signed, "Honey, I'm glad I caught you because Mama needs you to come to the Mexican vendor's market. JB signed with urgency, "Where are the babies and is Mama alright?" She told him that everything was fine. She had bought something for Cielito and didn't want her to see it. He told Shy to wait there for Claudette, and he would go to Blossom. At that moment Al drove up, and JB signed, "No, since Al is here, he can tell her. You get in the van." After conversing with Al, they left for the Mexican vendor's market.

After picking up Blossom and the babies, JB hurried back to the bank. The meeting was over, and Brinson, Cielito, and Claudette were coming outside with their sisters-in-law. They all shook hands and departed. Claudette asked Brinson if he could wait a minute, since she needed to give JB and Al some instructions. She walked over to JB's van and summoned Al. She said, "I will meet you all at Willoughby's Department Store. Drive around the back to the loading dock. JB and Al backed their vans up to the dock, waiting for Claudette. Five minutes later, the double doors to the loading dock opened. Claudette was there with several employees and a man in a suit. It appeared she was giving instructions. The workmen rolled out a small round table and two chairs, and loaded them, along with three large bundles into JB's van. She told JB to ask Al to assist in placing the table and chairs on the front porch.

"No, wait a minute, JB. She asked Al to move closer. "I don't know if you know this or not, but Cielito wants you two to give her away tomorrow. What I need to know is if both of you have suits." JB signed that he did, but Al didn't. She said, "You might as well come in the store and pick one."

Blossom said Claudette if you don't mind, I want to show you something before we go." She exited the van and opened the side door and opened the package with the outfit and said, "This is what I got Cielito for her wedding outfit." Claudette took a deep breath and hugged her and said, "Mama, you are a genius and a prophet. That is just what I was thinking when she said she wanted a Mexican wedding. I have already ordered a Mariachi band." Blossom replied, "When I was buying this, I saw some traditional Mexican suits for men, and I thought that while the men finish loading the rest of your stuff, Al can go with us to the Mexican vendor's market, and I will buy them suits. What do you think? She said that was great.

"Mama now we can't let Cielito see any of this. I want it to be a surprise and she is going be so pretty in that outfit! You have done so much that I can't let you pay for the suits, and I will pay whatever the white outfit costs. Blossom said, "I am the one who ruined her wedding dress. I think it's only right that I pay for her wedding outfit." Claudette said, "Okay, Mama, but I am paying for the men's suits. I want to go with you all so I can help them pick out the suits." Blossom said it was just down the street on the end of old town.

When they arrived, Claudette saw right away what she liked. It was a Black Mariachi jacket trimmed in white satin with black trouser and black boots. She asked Blossom and Shy what they thought, Shy liked it, except for the hat. Claudette said, "I agree, they don't need hats." She asked them to try on the boots and jackets. "If they fit, then that's all we need. As for the trousers, they might just need some alterations.

JB and Al tried on the jackets, which were a perfect fit, along with the boots. Claudette told the vendor that they would take five of them, same size boots, and all except the hats. The vendor said, "For you, Claudette Ohara, I will give you a special price of one hundred and twenty dollars." Claudette looked surprised. "How is it you know me?" He replied, "You don't remember me from school, but my name is Rolando Chavez. I was a poor, sickly kid back then, and I remember you taking up for the kids everyone was picking on. Whatever happened to the tall Indian girl. You fought several kids when they made fun of her."

Claudette realized immediately that Rolando was referring to Jeru. "We have been living together since we left finishing school, and she is a millionaire now and we recently adopted a baby. Tomorrow my sister, Cielito, is getting married and you are welcome to come; and you'll see Jeru. It was good seeing you after all this time, but we must go now. Hope to see you tomorrow." As she was leaving, he asked the location, and she responded, "At Blossom Blake's house. Ask anyone and they can tell you how to get there."

They made their way back to Willoughby's. Claudette found Brinson and Cielito at the jewelry counter picking out and trying on wedding rings. They had decided on the ones they liked and asked

Claudette for her opinion. Claudette almost "let the cat out of the bag" when she commented, "All I can say is this ring will go with the outfit ...." She stopped and rephrased her comment to say that it would go with any style or color Cielito chose.

She asked the clerk if there was a phone nearby, and she called the Blount Packard Dealership. BB Blount (Blue Bonnet Blount) answered the phone. "Mr. Blount, this is Claudette Ohara. Has my man Jean Claude Beauchamp been by?" Blount answered in the affirmative, saying he was finishing up the paperwork. "We had a slight problem. I was instructed by Bix Toilet to deliver the automobiles tomorrow; however, we have that straightened out now and he should be on his way shortly." She asked to speak to Beauchamp. "Listen, my dear, have you bought all of your groceries?" He hadn't, so she said she would meet him at Crowley's Food Market. When she went back to the jewelry counter, Brinson was paying for the rings. Claudette said, "I need you all to drop me off at the food market, but first drive to the back so I can see if Al is loaded.

When they made the short drive to the food store, Beauchamp was there. Brinson whistled, "Somebody has a brand-new Packard." Claudette said, "It is mine, and I will tell you all about it when I get home." She entered the market and began to search for Beauchamp, who said he had found almost everything he needed. "I might have to change my menu. It was my intention to stay with the wedding theme by making hors d'oeuvres using traditional recipes in the place of crackers and such. I wanted to use toasted tortillas, for example *foie gras* on toasted tortillas and so forth." Claudette asked how the car drove, and he responded that it was like a charm.

Next, they went to the Mexican market. When they arrived, Claudette rushed over to the cloth vendor and asked for Mr. Chavez, who had left for today. She said, "I see what I want," and she grabbed the items which cost thirty dollars. Claudette gave her two twenties and rushed away, yelling, "Keep the change!" They sped away for the casino.

When they arrived, she jumped out of the car and ran inside and called for all the on-duty employees to come to the main room. She didn't see Sarah, so she asked someone to get her because she had something important to say. When Sarah arrived, Claudette apologized, but said they had a change in plans. "We are not going to demolish the casino, but to refurbish the inside and upstairs and redo the whole front of the building. While the workmen are refurbishing the downstairs, gambling customers will enter through the restaurant entrance, so stop packing and go about your normal routine." There were cheers all around.

Beauchamp asked Sarah if he could talk to her in the kitchen. Sarah said, "This is it. You can get a better idea of what it is like once we put all this stuff back in place." He said, "It will do. I am going to ask for your help. As you know, Cielito and Brinson are getting married tomorrow, and I have been asked to prepare the reception dinner. An ordinary kitchen will be a challenge, but this kitchen is large enough for me and you. I promise not to get in your way; however, I will have to lean on your knowledge of traditional Mexican food as it relates to seasoning." Beauchamp said to Sarah, "I have a couple of more favors; I would like to leave all the food here until I return in the morning. Can you loan me two waiters and a cook who is good at carving? I plan to have a side of beef tomorrow." Sarah said, "Of course."

Claudette told Jean Claude they had much to do and needed to get to Blossom's place, where there were a flurry of activity going on. The table and chairs were on the porch with several parcels. JB and Al were bringing the table and benches around to the front yard. When Beauchamp noticed them, he asked Claudette if she could ask JB to make him a table like that to place the food and dishes on. JB signed, "Yes," before realizing that Claudette could not read sign language. He reached into his pocket and wrote, "Yes. How long and how wide?" Beauchamp responded that they would be the same size as those without the benches.

Claudette asked Beauchamp to help her take all the parcels on the table inside. She piled the packages so high that he could hardly see how to get inside. Blossom yelled that the dining room floor is wet with wax. Claudette and Beauchamp went into the parlor, both saying "Yes, Ma'am" to Blossom. Claudette began to separate the packages, with the first bundles going to JB and Shy's bedroom. It appears she had several bundles for everyone in the house.

When they made their first trip out back, they encountered Cielito, Brinson and Scott McKenzie discussing the location of the new barn and living quarters for them. Brinson asked Scott how long before they could see the blueprint. He said, "I can have them ready tomorrow, but since that is your wedding day maybe I can get them to you after the honeymoon." Cielito said, "No, Honey, I think tomorrow is better so that we can study them and get them back so he can get the building started right away." Claudette said Scott's blueprints could be a wedding gift. "We have the something old, the something new, something borrowed and yours can be the something blue."

Scott asked if she was that smart all the time, and her response was, "I heard Blossom say that a blind hog will root up an acorn every once in a while." "I don't know what that means, but you are as smart as you are beautiful." Beauchamp became a little jealous. He said, "Come on and show me where to put this stuff." Claudette said, "Why Jean Claude, I am flattered you are jealous." His faced turned red and he commented in French. She laughed and said, "I love you, too. You know you and Wilford are my men."

They entered the kitchen where there were three young Mexican girls wiping down walls and cabinets. Shy was busy polishing silverware. Claudette asked if they were Al's daughters, and they replied, "Si, senorita." Claudette commented, "You are you the ones who place flowers on my brother's grave?" They replied, "Si, Senorita." She said she had something to give them. She told Shy that she had new China and silverware for the reception, but Shy replied that they had enough of everything. Claudette asked how long those dishes and silverware had been a part of this household, and Shy replied, Mama had these things since before I came here." Claudette asked how Shy thought Blossom would feel if some of the China was accidentally broken. "Knowing Mama Blossom, she would be quick to forgive the person, but it would still hurt because these things have sentimental value."

Claudette said, "Shy, you are like Cielito. You are my sister and JB is the only brother I have now. I want desperately to be a part of this family, so, when you say I didn't have to do something it make me feel like you all think I am trying to buy my way into this family or trying to buy your love. I have learned enough from Mama Blossom that you can't buy love. It is no secret that I am wealthy, but what good is money if you can't spend it to help those you love?" Shy stopped polishing the silverware and walked over to Claudette and hugged and kissed her and said, "Sister, you have stolen my heart I love you and I will tell Mama and JB what you just said.

Beauchamp entered the kitchen and jokingly said, "Santa Claudette, we have more goodies to deliver. I need to warm up the food for dinner." She responded, "OK, my loving elf and helper, let's get to it." As they made their last trip, which was the China and silverware, they met JB and Al coming from the barn with the boards and sawhorses for the table Beauchamp had asked him to make. Beauchamp commented, "JB, you are a genius." JB and Al didn't acknowledge Beauchamp, since it was getting late in the afternoon, and they needed to finish because they had to leave for work at twelve midnight.

The flurry of activity at the Blake household came to a halt, Claudette went to Blossom's bedroom to check on Jeru and Consuela, remembering the rule about noise. She whispered, "How are my love and my baby doing?" Jeru answered, "We are well. I made at least seven diaper changes and have a bucket full of diapers to wash." Claudette said, "Don't worry about that. From now on the baby laundry will be my job. After dinner you show me, and I will take that off your list of things to do. I will watch "Connie" while you wash up. Jeru said she needed a longer time to wash up.

When Claudette entered the dining room, everyone was surprised to see her with the baby, and they asked about Jeru. Claudette said she went to wash up. "Remember, she is my baby also." Blossom said, "Please forgive us, it's just that Jeru is so particular about letting her out of her sight." Shy added, "You know we have had a busy day, and it can be nerve-racking. Today I had a conversation with Claudette, and she said something that made me think." Everyone's attention was on Shy. "The things she said made me dig deep-down and come to understand her better. She has suffered a tremendous loss, and she sees us as her family. When she does things for us and buys us stuff, she is not trying to buy our love. When we tell her she didn't have to do a particular thing, it's her way of giving what she has plenty of -- money, love, and herself. It's like Brinson said, 'She is giving from the heart.' I feel we owe it to her to accept her as she is. After all, material things should not change the loving and compassionate people we are." Everyone at the table stood and applauded, and one by one each person went by her and hugged her and hugged each other.

    Jeru entered the dining room and asked what was going on. Blossom said, "We are just showing a family member how much we love and appreciate her." JB signed and Shy translated, "I would love to stay but I have to be up in five hours for work." Claudette asked if Shy could stay for a few minutes to discuss some business matters involving JB and Shy. JB signed that was fine with him. Claudette started out by saying, "In business sometimes we don't realize the importance that each one plays. My brothers ran the Ohara corporation by giving their all, and it was no small job. Now that they are no longer with us, it is up to us three women -- Cielito, Jeru, and me -- to continue to keep it going. I am sure there are those who think we cannot do it, but we can with the help of everyone seated around this table. In case you all don't know it, we have a famous person among us. I didn't know it until today. Shyanne, will you stand please. I want to introduce to someone the government recognizes, along with the Agriculture Department, and that is none other than our own Shy."

Shy was surprised. Claudette continued, "Yes, the articles you have been writing to the Department of Agriculture are published in their monthly magazine. I know you have to get the babies ready for bed and take care of JB." Shy blushed, as Claudette spoke. "So here is what I want you and JB to consider. It was recommended to us today that we plant fifteen thousand acres of soybeans at the ranch and hire you to manage it. Think it over with JB and let me know. We need you, Sister. Now get out of here and see about the babies and your husband. I love you, Sister and am so proud of you. Good night."

Shy left the room, feeling worthy and important while keeping a humble spirit. "Now that that is taken care of, we have the casino and the mines and the downtown development to talk about. Cielito, as was suggested this morning, since you have taken the lead on that, I suggest you continue with that and your schools. What do you and Brinson think? Cielito looked at Brinson and asked what he thought. He said, "It makes sense to me, but can you do that and raise the children? She said, "We will give it a try."

Claudette said, "That leaves the mines. I don't think we should consider selling. I think we should do as Finley suggested -- make Superintendent Mercy a stockholder and let him continue to run the mines. According to Finley, under his management, the mines have run smoothly and with substantial uninterrupted profits. All in favor, say "Aye," and not in favor, say "Nay." Claudette proclaimed the "aye's" had it, and she declared the meeting adjourned.

Blossom said she had one more thing to bring up. "Brinson, I need you to go to your room and stay until we tell you that you may come out. Ladies, stay because I am going to need your help and opinion. Cielito, I need you to strip down, and I will be right back." Blossom departed to her bedroom closet and returned with two parcels. She removed the wrapping from the largest one. The ladies gasped and said, "Mama, that is so pretty!" Blossom told Cielito to try it on. Cielito was still "owing and awing" as she tried on the outfit which fit perfectly. Blossom said, "Turn around so I can see what it looks like from the back. Good. Good. Now try on the boots." She did, and they fit perfectly.

She stepped up on this chair so Blossom could see how the skirt hung with the boots on. Blossom opened another package with silk cloth of different colors -- pearl white, plain white and black. "I can make the blouse with a fancy puffed cascading collar or a straight pointed one with a bowtie, or you all give me some idea." Claudette left the room and returned with one of her diamond chockers. Cielito stepped down and Claudette asked her to turn around. She reached for the plain white silk cloth and draped part of it around Cielito's neck and fastened the chocker around her neck. She said, "Come, let's go to the bathroom and let her look at herself in the mirror." Cielito was brought to tears. Then, Jeru said, "Hold on. Here, Claudette, hold Consuela." She walked up behind Cielito and gathered her hair and braided part of it and pushed and wrapped it near the front the other to the top of her head in a rolled bun, and asked Cielito if she liked it.

Cielito said, "Hurry and get me out of this before I wet myself, and I want to hug and kiss all of you. I never knew what it would be like to have several females making me so pretty. I wish Shy were here. Blossom said she would cut the pattern for the blouse tonight and sew it after breakfast. "It's getting close to midnight, so, we should get to bed."

As Claudette and Jeru made their way to the bedroom, Claudette said, "I wish Shy could have been here, but think of how much fun it is going to be with all of us, including Mama Blossom, dressing one another, and doing make up. I can hardly wait." Claudette planned to do the baby's laundry in the washing machine, and as she finished her task and stepped out, she heard Cielito and Brinson sitting on the steps embracing and talking. She cleared her throat so as not to startle them. "Shouldn't you two be in bed, you have a full day tomorrow." Brinson replied, "We are too excited, but we will go in shortly." Claudette playfully replied, "You shouldn't be out here without a chaperone. Just joking, love you I am going to bed. Good night."

Chapter 17
"Get Me To The Church!"

At the stroke of midnight, JB and Shy's bedroom came to life. Shy went to the bathroom and proceeded to the kitchen to fix JB breakfast. When he arrived, Shy had his breakfast on the table. She said and signed, "Honey, I need to talk to you about something important." JB was listening. "Cielito, Claudette, Jeru and the Ohara's wives are the only ones left to run the corporation, and after you had gone to bed, they said Mr. Bix advised them to use fifteen thousand acres of the ranch for agriculture, And Mr. Finely said they should make me the farm manager, based on an article I wrote to the Department of Agriculture about soybeans. It would mean more money for us, but I don't care about that. As a woman, I want to try to see if I can do it. What do you think?"

JB signed, "Shy, you know how much I love you. Ever since we've been married you have shown me how smart you are, I know that you can do it. Why don't we talk it over with Mama and the three of us pray over it.' She said when she prays every night, she thanked God for JB and Mama. "I don't know what I did to deserve you and Mama, but let's talk tonight after the wedding." JB agreed, kissed his family, and left for work.

When Claudette awakened, she realized Jeru and the baby were missing. She thought they must be in the bathroom, and Jeru opened the door and said she was just washing Connie up. "Mama said maybe tomorrow I can start giving her a bath. I know I need one ever since I took the medicine to start my milk, and I have frequent hot flashes too." Claudette rocked Connie to give Jeru a chance to take a full bath.

About forty minutes later, Connie awakened and began to cry, which awakened Blossom. She sat up, rubbed her eyes, and called out to Jeru. Claudette responded that she had the baby and Jeru was taking a bath. When Jeru stepped into the bedroom, Blossom asked her if anything was wrong. She said, "Mama, I am okay, it's just I have these hot flashes and felt the need to take a full bath." Blossom apologized, saying, "Honey, I am so sorry, but with all that going on I plum forgot I have an herb that will help you with that. It has an unpleasant taste, so I will fix it in a tea for you and you can put a little honey in it. Now baby I am going to make a gallon and leave it in the refrigerator with a note for Jeru when you get those hot flashes. Jeru and Claudette said Mama was wise enough to be a doctor.

Blossom was flattered, but responded, "Daughters, God has given you all to me and it is my duty to take care of you. I need to get in the kitchen and start breakfast." They both said, "Thank you, Mama, we love you." Claudette said she would wake Jean Claude, so Blossom could have the bathroom all to herself. When Blossom closed the door, she dropped to her knees and began to pray. "Thank you, dear God, for these children. Please give me the wisdom and discernment to do what is right by them and help me to remain humble. They have come to see me as something special, but soon they'll know that I'm your handywork. You and I both know all the things you have made possible for me that I could never imagine that I, your humble servant, could think these blessing would be for me. Amen." She hurried and washed up and went to the kitchen.

Claudette asked Blossom if she had seen Beauchamp. "I went to his room, and he wasn't there, Mama, and he knew I had things to do in town." Blossom said there must be a reasonable explanation. At that time, the phone ranged it was Beauchamp calling from the casino. Blossom handed the phone to Claudette. She asked where he was, and he responded, "Did you get the note I left on the dining room table? I am at the casino. I left this morning around three to get in the kitchen before they closed, and my note said for you to call me, and I would come back to the house to get you. Are you ready?" She said she would be ready when he returned. "I love you." He said to get Wilford up so he could come and drive her back home.

Blossom said, "See, I told you there was a reasonable explanation. If I may, daughter, let me say that you must get to know your man because there will be times when people will come to you with accusations, and you have to be wise enough to know that what they are saying is what you have not seen in him." Claudette thought about Blossom's sage advice, and then said, "Mama, he is not my man in that way; you know Jeru and I love each other and have since we were six years old." Blossom responded, "I know, but I have heard both you and Jeru say that no man will put up with your relationship over that belonging to a husband and wife. Do you and Jeru ever consider marriage for your futures?

Claudette didn't choose to respond to that question but insisted that Wilford and Beauchamp have known them for three and a half years and accepted the women's closeness. Blossom had to acknowledge that Wilford and Beauchamp follow Claudette and Jeru around like little puppies, and clearly, they love them. "Most women I know would die to have someone to love them the way those two love you two. I'm just saying that it's natural for women and men in love to marry and form a union, which could have room for the love you and Jeru share. God has seen fit to bring you all to me and I love you like JB and Shy. Now come here let me hug you, Baby. Whatever God blesses you with, you'll accept it and make the best of it." Claudette said, "Mama, I don't know what we did to deserve you, but you are the best thing we could hope for. I better get Wilford up so we will be ready when Jean Claude gets here."

She went upstairs and kissed Wilford and said, "Thanks for loving me and Jeru and understanding. Now get ready because Jean Claude will be here shortly." She went downstairs humming, as Blossom said breakfast was ready.

Blossom said, "I want you to see something and tell me what you think." She went to the closet in the parlor and pulled out a blouse she made for Cielito. Claudette said, "Mama, this is gorgeous. She is going to look like royalty." Wilford entered the dining room and asked who was going to look like royalty. Claudette replied, "This is part of Cielito's wedding outfit, my dear." Wilford jokingly said, "That's going to be embarrassing; it is awfully short." Claudette looked at Blossom and said, "Very funny."

A knock at the front door caused all three to look in that direction. Blossom opened the door to see Beauchamp, who said he hoped Claudette and

Wilford were ready. Claudette yelled out that Wilford was finishing breakfast, to which Beauchamp said, "He is finished. Let's go because we are burning daylight." As Claudette walked past him, she reached up and kissed him. He had a puzzled look on his face, like Wilford when she kissed him earlier. Beauchamp asked what that was for, and she said, "That is for loving me and being understanding." He said, "Whatever it was, I love it, now let's get going."

In the car Beauchamp told Wilford what he needed him to do. "Claudette has some errands to run, and she needs to be back home by noon, so, when you drop her at home, I need you to come back and get me. I am sending most of the food ahead, so, Claudette, when it arrives make room in the refrigerator and in the cool house. I am bringing the cake with me and should be there about one thirty."

Blossom began to take Wilford's dishes to the kitchen, where she saw Jeru, who expressed that she wasn't hungry. Blossom said, "Nonsense, you have to eat, if not for yourself, you need to do it for Connie. Child, the milk your body makes comes from the food you eat, and she needs all the vitamins from that milk to continue to grow healthy." Jeru said she needed to take the diapers inside because it's going to rain. Blossom said she would do it, and it wasn't going to rain. Jeru asked how Blossom knew all of this. Blossom said, "The Almanac said it is not going to rain." Jeru asked her what an Almanac was, and Blossom said it is a book that Shy has that tells all about the weather and the moon and when to plant and when to harvest. "Finish eating and we can fold the diapers together."

Shy entered the kitchen and asked Jeru how baby Connie was doing. Jeru responded with a laugh, "Keeping me busy, between breast feeding, diaper changing, and laundry. Shy, you are something taking care of three babies, doing laundry, and running a farm and breast feeding too!" Shy said, "We are just about through breast feeding, since they are getting used to solid food, thanks to Mama." She picked each baby up and placed them in highchairs and went to the stove and spooned up three bowls of *Cream of Wheat*. She tested each one to make sure it was not too hot. Blossom said she would help feed them, and Jeru asked if she could feed one. Shy said, "Yes, only give them small portions."

In the meantime, Claudette and Wilford had dropped off Beauchamp at the casino and were headed to Claudette's first stop at the *Santa Fe Gazette* newspaper office to speak to the photographer about his time of arrival. And from there it was *Willoughby's* where she purchased more tablecloths and napkins and outdoor mesh food covering. From there they went by *Blount Automotive* to ensure the two automobiles she had ordered would be delivered at the right time. The owner, Mr. Blount, assured her they would arrive as she had requested. Wilford said, "It's none of my business, but who are the two autos for?" She said one was for Brinson and Cielito's wedding present from them, and the second one was for Shy. "Since she is going to manage the ranch, she has to learn to drive to take care of everything." He said, "Claudette, you are a good and compassionate person, and beside my deep and abiding love for you, that is one more thing I love about you." She said, "Stop the car!" He asked what was wrong, and she was blushing and said, "I want to hug and kiss you."

After that, she needed to find Al at the bank before he left from downtown. When they arrived, there was one of JB's vans parked near the bank. She asked him where Al was, and JB signed and wrote that he should be at the new *Wells Fargo* building. He gave directions, and she thanked him. "How long before you will be finished here?" He had a few more things to do and would see everyone at home.

When Claudette caught up with Al, he was about to leave to give JB a progress report on how long before the building contractors would be finished, so that they could get the cleaning crew in. She needed to ask him a favor. "I need two of your daughters to help me today, and I will pay them." Al said, "No need for that. I will get my two oldest. What time do you need them?" She said, "I am headed home now, so can you call and see if they can meet me at Blossom's house?" He said yes, and Claudette said she would see him at the wedding.

Claudette arrived home at noon time and she and Wilford unloaded the car before he went back to the casino to pick up Jean Claude. When she entered the house, it was quiet. She yelled, "Hey, where is everybody?" Shy stuck her head out of the bathroom and yelled, "Down here in the bathroom. I am doing Jeru's hair." Claudette walked to the door and said she liked that style. "Shy, can you do mine just like hers?" Shy said yes and told her there are two young girls waiting for her in the kitchen. Claudette said she would take care of them and come back for a hairdo.

Claudette went to the kitchen and asked the girls their names, which were Juanita and Carmencita. She began to show them what she wanted and how to place the tablecloths. Before she could finish talking, a van drove up and the driver asked for Ms. Claudette. He said, "Mr. Beauchamp said we were to deliver this food to you." When they opened the van door, she said, "My goodness, hold on, I am going to need some help." She went inside looking for Blossom, who was sitting in the rocking chair holding Connie and reading the *Bible*. She said in a desperate voice, "Mama, I need you. The food for the reception has arrived and it is so much that I need you to tell the men where to put it." Blossom said to put it on the kitchen table. She'd be there in a minute. "Baby don't panic. I am coming."

Blossom went to the kitchen to supervise. "What happened to Al's daughters?" Claudette said she had them working out front. Blossom said to get them. When Claudette returned with the girls, Blossom said, "Juanita, I want you to sit here and hold the baby. Claudette, Honey, look in the linen closet and bring me some tablecloths. When we run out of room on the kitchen table, we will put the rest of it on the dining room table. Come with me so we can extend the table with the leaf that's in the parlor closet." They extended the table together. Claudette said she learned something new from Blossom. Blossom laughed and said, "A blind hog will root up and acorn every once in a while." Claudette asked Blossom to explain that saying, and Blossom said, "It means if you keep working at something you will figure it out. Let's get this food moved in here."

Back at the casino, Wilford entered the kitchen as Beauchamp was putting the finishing touches on the wedding cake. He said to Wilford, "You are right on time. We will load the cake in the car, and you drive and take It easy, please, no bumps or quick stops." He gave instructions to the two chefs who were to bring the side of beef and pork. "I am taking the spits with me, so when you get there, I will have it set up and a good fire going. Don't forget to make the gravy. I will see you all at two o'clock sharp. Let's go, Wille boy."

They made it to the house without incident and removed the cake and the large carving knives, serving spoons, and forks. He said, "I need you to set the spits on the other end of the tables outside, about twelve feet away from the table without the benches and bring a load of wood and get a fire started under each spit." Wilford said, "Got it." Beauchamp remarked, "Pal, you have been a great help, and I thank you." Beauchamp went inside where Blossom and Claudette were bringing the last of the food to the dining room. Blossom said, "Mr. Beauchamp, I put the tomato things in the refrigerator; the other stuff should be fine if that is okay with you." He said, "It is, but how long is it going to take for you to call me Jean Claude." Blossom said she was just showing respect. He replied that he wanted to feel like one of her sons, and she said OK.

Beauchamp said, "Step outside and tell me what you think of the cake." Claudette and Blossom stepped out on the porch and gasped. Blossom said, "I've never seen anything like this. Claudette said, "It's simply beautiful, but right now, I am going to give this man a big kiss." She left and came back with a lace tablecloth and candle holders and the tablecloth to cover the cake. Wilford helped Jean Claude lift the cake while Claudette placed the lace tablecloth and candle holders on the table. Blossom placed the cover over the cake, and they went inside, where Shy was ready to do Claudette's hair.

About that time, the chefs arrived with the side of beef and pork, and Beauchamp told them everything was all set up for their cooking the meat. Shy said, "Hey, it is two o'clock and we need get upstairs and start dressing Cielito. Claudette, come on and I will finish your hair upstairs." When they got upstairs, Cielito was sitting in front of the mirror crying. She said, "Claudette, I am happy, but afraid I might not please Brinson." Blossom said, "You all go on with what you were planning to do because I need to talk to Cielito for a moment. "Come on, Baby, let's go to the bathroom. In what way do you think you might not please Brinson?" She said, "Mama, I have never been with a man, and I don't know what to do." Blossom suspected that was the issue. "Baby, a lot of girls and women have that fear, but making love is something that come naturally. But since you are a virgin, the initial act is going to hurt some and there will be some bleeding, but not like when it is your time of the month. By the way, when is your time?" Cielito said it was in ten days. "That is good 'cause you will be fertile and can get pregnant right away, but don't you worry. I guarantee you will please him, and everything is going to be fine. Go back in there while I get your blouse. We are going to get you dressed."

    Blossom returned with the blouse, and they all were helping Cielito into the skirt. Jeru and Shy remarked that the blouse was beautiful, and it fit just right. Shy said, "Someone, please get me a towel. I need to do her hair and while I am doing that you can do her eyes and makeup. It's almost three o'clock. After I leave, don't let her look in the mirror because she might start crying again. Once me and Mama get dressed and dress the babies and JB, we will come back and finish." Jeru said she needed to get Connie ready. Blossom reminded Jeru to stay on the porch when guests arrived. "We don't want people coming to peak at her. Remember, she is just three days old. I know you want to be with everyone else, but we have to think of her. After I say my few words that Cielito wants me to say, I will take her, and you can mix and mingle."

The wedding time was fast approaching. Claudette was running around as one thing after another popped up needing her attention. Her saving grace was Beauchamp, who had everything involving the reception dinner under control. Claudette asked him when he was going to get dressed, and he assured her that he wouldn't let her down.

At that moment the Mariachi band and news reporter and photographer arrived at the same time. The news person approached her first and introduced herself. "Ms. Ohara, I am Greta D. Gossiper (real name Greta Deigo), Social Reporter for the *Gazette,* and I believe you have read my articles or heard of me. Claudette, trying not to be impatient, said, "I am sorry I have not had the pleasure, but you must excuse me because I need to meet with the band first. Feel free to walk around and take as many pictures as you like." She went to the band leader and explained what and how she wanted the music to occur throughout the wedding. "The bride will appear at the top of the steps, and you will play the first note of '*Here Comes the Bride,*' and as she walks down the steps you will play *Cielito Lindo* until she faces the Priest. Then you stop. After the ceremony, feel free to go through the crowd and play whatever you chose until it is dark, and the reception is over. You and your band can eat as much as you want. Now tell me what I just told you."

He attempted to repeat her instructions, but the band leader got it all mixed up. He called his band together, and Claudette told them where to stand. She told them to play the beginning of 'Here Comes the Bride' and of "Cielito Lindo," and they played it. Claudette told the band Leader that she would be standing so he could see her. She would signal when to start and stop. He said, "Si, Senorita."

Claudette called Greta over and apologized, but the guests were arriving "I have to get dressed, but I will be happy to talk to you after the ceremony." She ran inside where Brinson, JB and Al were in the dining room adjusting their ties. "You all go out on the porch until we bring Cielito downstairs, and Brinson, you should not see her until she walks out of the door." The men took their places, as instructed.

Wouldn't you know it? Father Ignatius just showed up. She said, "Father, have a seat and I will be right back." She ran upstairs where Cielito was dressed and ready, and she paused to say, "Darling, you look wonderful. I would kiss you, but I don't want to mess up the great job the ladies did." Shy said, "Let me do your hair, but Claudette responded, "Only if you can do it while I am dressing. If no, I'm fine with my hair the way it is. I Just ran Brinson out of the dining room, so you all can take Cielito down. The Priest is sitting in the parlor." Blossom said, "All of us are dressed. Shy, try to fix Claudette's hair while she is getting dressed. Jeru, you, and I will take Cielito down and guard the front door, and I will watch the back door." Just as they were about to leave, Beauchamp came out of his room. Jeru said, "Jean Claude, get out of here, we are about to bring Cielito down." He said, "I'm going, I'm going."

When they got downstairs with Cielito, Father Ignatius saw her and said, "Cielito, this may be sacrilegious, but you could pass for the Blessed Saint Mary, the mother of Jesus." He asked the time. Blossom said they had about fifteen minutes, and that Claudette would show Father Ignatius where to stand.

About sixty seconds after he left, Claudette came down and rushed outside to show the Priest where to stand. "JB, you, and Al go inside. I will signal for you to escort Cielito out, and you'll bring her out this door and pause and walk her down the steps, and the Priest will ask who give this woman …. Both of you will step back, and the Priest will begin. When he finishes, Cielito wants Mama Blossom to say some words, and that will end the ceremony, and the reception will follow."

Claudette called Greta, the news reporter and photographer, and positioned them and said, "When she comes out the door, get me a real good shot, and when she gets to the steps, she will pause, and you can get another good shot. Once the ceremony starts, move here so that when the Priest finishes, you'll take a shot of them kissing, and when Blossom steps up to speak, get me a shot of that. Afterwards, feel free to take the pictures you want, and I promise that once the reception begins, I will be free to talk with you." Claudette stepped aside and signaled to JB and Al to bring Cielito out, and the band to do the few notes of *Here Come the Bride*, and when they pause at the top of steps, the band will play *Cielito Lindo*."

When the wedding guests saw Cielito, you could hear gasping, sighs, uh's and awes and whispers. She looked like the Blessed Madonna. When Brinson turned to look, he got weak in the knees, and Wilford and Beauchamp had to support him momentarily. He kept repeating in whispered tones, "God, she is beautiful!" Beauchamp whispered to get it together and be strong. The Priest began the ceremony with the usual, "Who gives this woman…." Just as Claudette had instructed, JB and Al said, "We do." And the Priest repeated some verses from the *Bible* before saying, "Do you, Brinson Francois Dubois, take this woman ...." He said, "I do," and the Priest asked Cielito Guadalupe Ohara if she took this man .... As he pronounced them man and wife, Cielito and Brinson grabbed each other and began kissing, while the crowd burst into laughter.

The Priest was embarrassed, saying, "Please, it is not time for that yet. Let me finish." Cielito and Brinson, with red faces, resumed their positions and the Priest continued with the ring ceremony and "What God has put together, let no man put asunder." He said, "I guess there is no need for me to tell you two to kiss, you've done that already." The crowd broke out in laughter, and the Priest asked if everyone could remain in their seats by request of the couple. "Here are some words of wisdom from Ms. Blossom Blake." Blossom stepped forward and said, "I can't remember the last time I have seen two people wanting to get their honeymoon started." Everyone laughed. "What you just witnessed is love, and I believe and pray that bond will never be broken. Here are some things the Creator of marriage says." She began to quote passages from the *Bible* about the duties of the wife and husband, and she said, "Our Savior the Son of God said the new commandment is to love," and she ended her comments with 1 Corinthians 13:1–3.

There was plenty of merriment and laughter and dancing and eating. Brinson said finally, "Friends, there's plenty of food and drink, but Cielito and I are going to cut the cake because, as you witnessed, we want to get our honeymoon started, so eat, drink, and enjoy. God willing, we will see you in a week." Claudette interrupted. "Hold it for one minute. Friends and neighbors, as the sister and sister-in-law, I know that these two love birds will take time in the next few days to open your gifts, but on their behalf, I want to thank you all for your gifts, and here is one they don't have to open. She raised her hand with a set of car keys and declared, "This gift is parked out there, and it is from me, Jeru, Jean Claude Beauchamp, and Wilford Dunford. We love you. Now get to honeymooning!"

Now that the ceremony was over, Claudette had time for Greta. She found her talking to Beauchamp and taking notes, She said, "Ms. Gossiper, I am free if you want to talk with me." Greta said, "Yes. Oh, Mr. Beauchamp, don't go anywhere. I will get back to you later., "Being French, you interest me. She turned to Claudette and said You put on an outstanding affair; believe me this is going to be front page news, or we might run an extra edition. Do you mind if we sit at the table?" Claudette replied, "Not at all, I need that about now.

Greta asked Claudette if she minded if she ate while she started her interview. Claudette joined her, as she hadn't eaten either. Greta said, "I want your whole story." Four hours later they were still talking. Greta said, "I think I have what I need. I must get back to the office and write this story for tomorrow's edition. Thank you, Ms. Ohara." Caudate went to Blossom's bedroom and fell across the bed. Jeru asked her if she was all right, to which Claudette responded that she was fine, but exhausted.

Meanwhile, Blossom and Shy were in the kitchen reorganizing and boxing all the dishes and silverware. Shy said, "Mama, I need to talk to you alone with JB. Can we go to our bedroom?" When they arrived JB was placing the last baby in the playpen, which was serving as their bed. Blossom said maybe they should go to the dining room or parlor to keep from disturbing the babies.

Shy asked Blossom if she recalled last night when Claudette said Mr. Bix and Bax and Mr. Finely had suggested that they set aside fifteen thousand acres of their ranch for farming, and that she hire Shy to manage the farm and the ranch. Blossom remembered the conversation. "Well, I want to try it. I told JB that I want to try it because if I can do it, then it will show everyone that women can handle big business as well as men. I don't want to do it for pride or glory or money, but for my daughter to know that she is not limited to what other people think she should be. Think about it, Mama -- five women running a billion-dollar corporation! I need to know what you think. JB has suggested I see what you think and the three of us pray for the right decision." Blossom said, "That is my son; he's something, isn't he? Let's pray now for guidance." They prayed aloud, and afterwards Blossom said, "Bedtime for us; good night my precious God-sent children."

When she went to her bedroom, Blossom found Jeru sitting in the rocking chair feeding baby Connie, and Claudette fast asleep and still dressed. Jeru said, "Mama, she came in here and just collapsed on the bed and has been like that for the last hour and a half. Looks like I will have to sleep in the rocking chair." Blossom said, "You will do no such thing; I will get my night things and go upstairs and sleep in her bed. Poor child has worked herself so hard the last three days. Let her sleep." She added, "Jeru, I am so proud of you; you have learned so much about becoming what I think is a really good mother." As Blossom was getting her night clothes and robe, Jeru stood and walked over to her and put one arm around her and said,

"Mama, I love you and I don't ever want to be too far from you." Blossom gently touched her. "I love you too, Baby; now while Connie is asleep, let me have her and you can take your bath." Jeru was most appreciative. Thirty minutes later, Blossom left to go upstairs, but stopped at Brinson's door and knocked slightly and whispered, "Good night and God bless."

It wasn't long before she was deep in sleep, and as usual, when she went to sleep with something on her mind, Mama G would come to her. This night was no different. She said, "Daughter, we heard your prayer asking for guidance. Well, here it is. Your daughter, Shy, is a smart and industrious one who will do good. Her accomplishments and success in this endeavor will serve as an inspiration to millions. Your world is changing, and you must come to accept it. You will see many who claim to be God-fearing believers, but the very things they claim worthy of devotion are false. You and I know you can't fool God, and they will be exposed by their works. You, daughter, continue to keep God's commandments and your reward shall be in heaven.

In my world, some of us are allowed to watch over our living loved ones in different ways. I come to you in your dreams, while some are allowed to be visible but not allowed to reveal who they are or speak directly to them, I have met two spirits that do that, which are the lost relatives of Claudette and Cielito. They see what effect you have on them, and their spirits are pleased. They wish for you to continue to work with Claudette. To them, she seems to show signs of the effect you have on her. She seems to understand love but has yet to understand the difference in love and romance, so keep working with her with compassion and understanding. Now rest well, my daughter."

Blossom, too, was exhausted, and these words of wisdom and comfort from her ancestors helped her fall into a deep and restful sleep.

Chapter 18
Big Plans Materialized

It was a nice autumn morning in Santa Fe as the sun began to appear in the Northeastern sky above the *Sangre de Cristo Range* of the *Southern Rocky Mountains*. There was a golden look to it, which made the forty-eight-degree temperature feel warmer. JB, with clipboard in hand and his three supervisors in tow, was making his daily inspection of the finished job, the three supervisors had checked off on their sheets that everything was complete and satisfactory. However, when he met with Al and Juan, JB noticed that they had written a question as to the cleanliness of the upper floor windows. Al stated that his crews didn't have experience doing outside high window cleaning, and he suggested JB contract with a professional window cleaning company. JB signed that he would talk it over with Shy. "In the meantime, let's leave a note for the owners that we are aware of the problem with the upper floors outside window and would like to meet with them to discuss how and what we need to do to correct the problem." He said that the Friday payroll would be ready at the usual time that afternoon.

JB departed for the *Santa Fe Gazette* office, which was still in old downtown Santa Fe. When he was about to go inside, he noticed the front page of the Friday *Gazette* with pictures of the wedding all over the front page. He purchased a copy and saw there were wedding pictures on all the pages, from top to bottom. JB got copies to bring home to the family, but first he checked off everything on the inspection sheet, indicating that he was satisfied with the job the crew had done. He signed it and left it on the receptionist's desk and headed home.

Everyone was in the dining room excepting Brinson and Cielito. JB signed to Blossom, "Mama, you gotta see this," and he handed her the newspapers. Blossom declared, "Lord, have mercy, Claudette you must see this." Everyone raced to where Blossom was sitting, and she gave all of them copies of the newspaper. She said, "I got work to do, and Shy, I need to speak to you and JB in the kitchen. The babies will be ok in the highchairs." The three moved to the kitchen and Blossom said, "Last night we prayed for guidance, and here is what Mama G said to me last night in my dreams. She said that it is okay for Shy to assume that oversight role, but she must be mindful of her other responsibilities." Shy said, "Mama, thank you, and I know if I stray from my obligations that you will point it out to me. I will do my best to make you and JB proud of me." JB signed, "Honey, we have always been proud of you." Blossom said "Amen."

Blossom went about her duties and Shy turned to JB and asked him if he brought the payroll money from the bank. JB signed that he hadn't. Shy said, "It's Friday. How am I going to pay the employees?" JB signed, "Hold on, let me go to the van." When he returned. he signed, "Honey, Mr. Bix gave me this." He handed her the large checkbook and signed, "He was concerned about me carrying around that much cash and said that too many people were aware of our success. The safest thing was to write checks, so, tonight he is leaving the payroll money in his office in individual envelopes, and he wants to discuss with us the advantage of paying every two weeks. All large companies are doing that. Also, he spoke to me about becoming a corporation." Shy said and signed, "Honey, that's too many things coming at me all at once." "Baby, this is what you will have to do if you are going to run that ranch and our farm and our cleaning company. I know you can do it. On top of those things, you have done a great job dealing with our government contracts, I don't know where I would have been if I didn't have you backing me up and being my voice." Shy said, "Come here and let me hug you, you are some kind of a smart man. I thank God every night and day for you."

Claudette entered the kitchen and asked, "Am I interrupting something?" Shy answered, "No, I was about to come to you to say that I am pleased that you asked me to manage the ranch, and I am up to the challenge. When do you want me to start?" Claudette replied, "I have to go to town to meet with Scott McKenzie about the renovation of the casino and house. The new car out there is yours, and Wilford is going to teach you to drive if it is okay with JB. He is so busy that I would not dare ask him to teach you. When I finish in town, I will come home." Then she turned to Blossom. "Mama, I want to get your permission to build Shy a large office on the back of the house. With all of her responsibilities, she is going to need that, and with the office at the house she can have the triplets with her at all times."

Blossom thanked Claudette for seeing the potential in Shy. "I know she will make you proud of her, as she has with JB and me. I think it is a good thing for her to have an office here so she will be near her children. Last night my grandmother, who has long passed, came to me in a dream and advised me to trust in your judgment in business matters and to love and support you." Claudette said, "Mama, thank you for your love and support. I will do my best to make you as proud of me as you are of JB and Shy, and I will love you and pray for your wisdom. Now, I need to get to town."

Just as she and Beauchamp were about to leave, Brinson and Cielito entered the dining room. Claudette said, "Well, I was wondering when you two might come up for air." Brinson and Cielito both blushed. Blossom jokingly said, "Now, Claudette, leave the honeymooners alone. They did a good thing for you last night and this morning." Claudette said jokingly, "From the sound of things, I am sure they did," causing the couple more embarrassment. Then Claudette asked, "Mama, what did they do for me?" Blossom went to the couple and hugged them and said, "They made you an aunt." The dining room erupted in laughter. As they both showed their discomfort at being made fun of, Blossom said, "Listen you two, we are not making fun of you; we are happy for you and love you so much. Please take it in that spirit. God knows we are so happy for you."

Brinson, feeling better about the joking, said, "I just want you all to know that we thank you for all you did to make this a happy occasion, and thank you for all the gifts and your prayers, and to show you we understand, I pray to God that we made you all aunts and uncles, and I will say this and I hope my darling wife is not embarrassed by it: I did my darnnest to give you all that title." The room once again erupted in laughter and all the men went to Brinson and raised his hand and cheered. Shy said, "Gentlemen, shhh, please; we have babies sleeping." Jeru spoke up and said, "Everyone, don't forget we have a burial to attend tomorrow at noon."

Claudette said, "Jean Claude, come on let's go, we are late already." Everyone began to depart for their duties. JB signed, "I need to see how the grainery people are doing and how far they are from completing their harvesting of the two hundred acres, and how soon before they can get started on the fifteen hundred." Shy said and signed, "Honey, don't forget to get the paperwork I need to get that to the Agriculture Department. Jeru said she had loads of laundry to do.

Brinson and Cielito decided to stroll around the part of the farm they had not seen. Blossom told them, "You love birds better take a jacket or coat, as it is little chilly out there." Cielito asked Brinson to bring the big envelope containing the blueprints that Scott McKinzie had left for them. Brinson responded, "Sure, my love, and where are your coat?" Cielito said, "My Lord, we have been so busy that I forgot to get my clothes from the house and bring them here." Blossom told her she could wear one of hers, and Cielito thanked her, saying, "I think when we come back, I will get Francois to take me to the house and I can get my clothes. Thank you, Mama." When she went to the dining room to ask Brinson if he was ready, he said, "Darling, come and look at this. Scott left us a rendering, along with the blueprints."

When they exited the house, Cielito said she was glad Mama suggested the coats because it was a little chilly. Brinson said, "Here, let's snuggle up as we walk together." Brinson commented on how beautiful this place was. Off in the distance they could see the chicken yard with peacocks and guinea hens all about. Cielito asked, "Honey, can we have all big windows facing this way, especially the ones in our offices?" Brinson answered, "Darling, you can have anything you want. I love you so much that if you ask for the moon, I will figure a way to get it for you."

She said, "Let's go and visit my brothers' graves. JB and Al buried them here after they brought me to Mama." Brinson ask her why they chose this place, and Cielito paused for a moment of grief before explaining that the condition their bodies was such that they had to be buried right away. "JB and Al built the fence, and Al's children come to place flowers. Claudette said we will get headstones and hold a memorial with their wives when we think enough time has passed and it won't hurt so much." Cielito pointed out Al's house before asking if they could leave. Brinson squeezed her hand before saying, "I know it's painful for you to come here. Let me hold you." They embraced for some time and then departed, proving that not enough time had passed.

Brinson changed the conversation as they walked. "My, love, hold me and kiss me until you make me shout to the heavens because I am in love with you, and promise me you will never let me go." They stopped and embraced for several minutes, and when they reached the house Claudette was there with Scott McKenzie and Shy discussing where to build Shy's office. Cielito interrupted, reminding Shy that she was going to have three girls from the school to assist her next semester, so it's crucial that her office be built as soon as possible. Scott suggested a plan building from Shy's bedroom to where the kitchen begins, and he added that she would need three or four phone lines.

Shy didn't want anyone entering her office through her bedroom, but Scott said there would be a door for entry from the outside. "The office will have a powder room, and you will have access to your children if they are in the bedroom, or there will be enough room for them in the office." Shy said, "Now I can live with that." Claudette said, "Then that's it! Scott, get busy. Can you get your crew to start tomorrow?" He said maybe.Brinson asked Scott if he could have a couple of minutes with him in the barn. "The only thing Cielito and I want in our offices are large windows facing the west, and if you can get one of your crews to start tomorrow and finish in six weeks, since you already have this blueprint, we will pay you and your crew a large bonus. He said, "I will see what I can arrange."

Claudette Shy if she was ready to go to the ranch. Blossom would watch the babies. Shy said, "Two things we have to understand. I will not go anywhere without my children, so if Mama can go with us, that is fine. Also, I have asked Al to meet us there so he can get the lay of the land and we can get started as soon as possible." Claudette responded, "Forgive me, little sister, I may have acted in haste. I understand how you feel but I want you to know I love you and am happy you are going to help me. Anytime you feel I have overstepped my boundary I know you'll call me on that. One of things I learned from Mama is love is slow to anger and it does not keep account of hurt feelings." Shy commented, "Yes, Mama has that effect on most people. Allow me to explain myself, since right now I am nervous. I know I can do this, but I must continue to do all the things I was doing, for fear that I might get so involved in trying to succeed that I ignore my other responsibilities."

Claudette was moved by Shy's vulnerability. "Little sister, I have faith in your talent and ability, so don't worry about anything. Just continue to do as you've been doing, and through prayer and perseverance you will succeed." Shy said, "According to Dr. Carver, in the right soil the yield should be around seventy bushels per acre; however, in my opinion, I feel that we should start with wheat and corn first. While I trust Dr. Carver's knowledge is correct and I know how Finley looks at things that are trending, when I do the math, here is the formula I use: CPATP against the SSPPB -- that is what does it cost per acre to plant, and the steady selling price per bushel. Right now, overseas there is a war going on, and while we are not in it yet, we will get in it, and corn and wheat are going to rise, and the price of commodities is going to drop. People still have to eat and the staples here are wheat and corn for bread and cereal, so the demand for those two items is going to be high, whereas the full potential of Dr. Carver's soybeans is yet to be discovered.

Claudette was almost speechless trying to follow Shy, but she did understand all of what she heard. "Whew! You are right, but when Jeru and I were playing poker in Monte Carlo, we were averaging ten to fifteen thousand a night and we played just about every night. It never occurred to me how much we were making, but it was the idea that I was a woman beating the men at their own game, and that's what we are going to do -- three women at the top of a corporation and succeeding! Come on, little sister, let's set the business world on fire!" They loaded up everybody and headed for the High Spade Ranch.

In the house, Cielito told Brinson that she needed to make a phone call to the school. "Administrative office, Ms. Nighthawk. How may I help you?" Cielito said, "Julieta, can you meet with me Sunday around ten a.m.?" Julieta replied, "Oh, Ms. Ohara, ..." Cielito interjected, "It's Mrs. Dubois."

Yes, Ma'am, Mrs. Dubois, I can meet you." Cielito asked her to include Margaret in the invitation, and she hung up. Brinson and Cielito made their way to the house on the casino property. Cielito asked Brinson how he liked the personal gifts that Claudette had given her. Brinson loved the see-through night gown and fancy underwear. "Darling, was it not obvious by my passionate love making that you were so beautiful and alluring, like a sex goddess. I want every night to be like I never want to stop making love to you." She acknowledged that, being a virgin, it was uncomfortable at first, just as Mama had said. "But then it was like you said, I didn't want you to stop." Brinson pulled the car off the road and started kissing and squeezing until they climbed into the back seat and made love, calling out each other's names. Afterwards, they adjusted their clothes and climbed back into the front seat and continued toward the Casino.

Cielito said playfully, "Francois, don't go to the house because those clothes we wanted to pick up reflect the old me, but the new me want to dress like a young woman. I want to wear perfume and cologne and sensual underwear and night gowns for you." Brinson smiled and said, "Somehow, saying 'darling, I love you' doesn't seem enough. You are my life, so let's go straight to Willoughby's and buy you a brand-new wardrobe and all the other things that go with that." She leaned back in the seat and said, "Yes, yes, and while we're in the store, let's go to the furniture department and furnish our new house and office." They looked at each other as if to silently suggest that they go into the back seat again, but they had things to do first.

At the High Spade Ranch, Claudette and the group arrived to discover that Al was talking with Ernesto. He said, "Boss lady, the only thing I found since I been here is that, before we can determine the scope of everything, we need an aerial photograph map so we can see the lay of the land. After that, we will be better able to tell if all fifteen thousand acres are usable, and it's going to take a lot of tractors and other implements, not to mention farm hands. By the way, what are we going to grow?"

Shy said, "Soybeans. Don't worry about the implements, tools, and farm hands because we will have all the equipment you need, and I will tell Claudette we are going to need the aerial map and I am sure she will take care of that right away. In the meantime, you and I need to meet every day for the next few weeks; in fact, tomorrow being Saturday, we have a burial to attend, but later on if you can meet with me, I would like to tell you all about soybeans and what your salary is going to be for this project." Al said, "Well, I do plan to slaughter two hogs in the morning, and I plan on giving you all half. I have to get with Blossom to grind up meat to make sausage, so while she is mixing the sausage meat we can meet." Shy said, "Good, see you tomorrow."

After finishing with Al, she went to where Claudette was talking with Ernesto. Claudette introduced Ernesto to Shy. "Shy, this is Ernesto Mendez, former ranch manager, Ernesto this is Mrs. Shyanne Blake, but we call her 'Shy.' She will be in charge of the farm and ranch, and she will pay you and the others. You will discuss all hiring and firing with her, but she will trust your judgment as it relates to the cattle and livestock." She told Shy that Ernesto was running the ranch when her brothers were alive. "I have explained our plan to set aside a portion of the ranch for agricultural purposes, and he will continue to handle the cattle and livestock, but he will report to you." She said to Ernesto, "I know you and your men have not been paid since my brothers were kidnapped and murdered, but I will have Bix and Finley take care of that. Now that I think of it, Ernesto, you will turn in time for you and your men to Shy, and she will make sure Finley gets that. Shy, Finley and the bank will handle the payroll from now on. Claudette adjourned the meeting after everyone understood their assignments and procedures.

As they walked to the car, Shy told Claudette that they were going to need an aerial map of the ranch as soon as possible, and Claudette immediately told Jean Claude to go by the bank so Bix and Finley could handle this today. At the bank, she explained what Shy needed, and Bix said there was one in her brothers' office. He gave her the key, and she rushed out the bank and over to her brothers' office. Shy noted that it was stuffy in there. Claudette found a large map in Jean's office on the wall behind his desk. Shy said, "It's huge. Will it fit in the car, and how do we get it down?" Claudette answered, "We'll have JB get it tomorrow when we come for the burial." She hugged Shy and said, "Little sister, we are on our way! Let's lock up and get home."

As they passed the casino, she noticed several men out front measuring and marking, and she thought Scott McKenzie was a man of his word. When they walked back to the car, Blossom said the babies were OK but hungry. "It's all right because we should be home in a few minutes." Shy said to give her one at a time and she would breast feed them until they get home.

At the house, Blossom noticed several vehicles in the yard and wondered who in the world was there. Jeru was on the front porch in the swing with little Connie. Blossom asked if she was keeping that baby's head covered, and Jeru said she was. Blossom detected a slight irritation in Jeru's reply, but Jeru quickly said, "I am sorry, Mama, I've been cooped up in the bedroom and have not taken the medicine this morning." Blossom, with much empathy, said, "Baby, it is a little early for her to be out at just six days old and I know you are going to want to take her to the burial tomorrow, so why don't you go in and have the tea now. By the way, who belongs to those trucks?" She said, "Mama, they are here digging and measuring for the new barn and Shy's office."

Blossom needed to fix lunch. Beauchamp was holding little Paul and walking right behind her. He volunteered, "Mama, you sit and rest. I can fix lunch really quickly." Blossom said, "All right, but fix some mashed potatoes and open a jar of peas for the babies. Shy, honey, I can feed the babies while you and Claudette continue your discussion." Shy remarked, "Mama, I can do that *and* talk with Claudette, but Blossom responded in a tired voice, "Please let me; with all the stuff going on I have not spent any time with them these last few days." Shy relented and did as Blossom had asked.

As Jean Claude went about preparing lunch, he inquired as to how Blossom was feeling. She said, "I am not tired, just worried about Shy taking on this project; that is a huge ranch." He answered, "It is, but, Mama, I know that Shy can handle it, just as she has with the addition of the extra fifteen hundred acres and the business end of the cleaning company. Besides, she will have lots of people doing all the work while she tells them what she wants done. The mashed potatoes and the peas are ready. I will help you feed them while my French-fried potatoes are cooking. I am making ham sandwiches to go with the potatoes, and mixed fruit, if that meets your approval." Blossom's approval was quick.

He insisted upon giving her a quick head massage, which she greatly appreciated. "I thank God all the time for you all. The love you have showed for me and my family, and the way you have accepted JB and Shy is heartwarming for me." Jean Claude checked his fried potatoes and ascertained that they were done. He dumped them out on a large tray and sprinkled some salt on them. He turned to Blossom and said, "Mama, the sandwiches are ready and so are the potatoes. I am going to run in to town and pick up a few things special for dinner tonight, which shouldn't take no more than an hour." Blossom said, "Okay, Son."

Meanwhile, Wilford had gone in search of a suitable place for a studio where he could paint. He went to the barn where he was told that JB did his sketching. Since the wide doors opened from both sides, he could see the Sangre de Cristo to the Northeast, and a great view of Banshee Canyon Wilderness to the East. JB rode up on his tractor, coming home from the field for lunch. Wilford asked to talk to him as they walked to the house. Wilford said, "I understand the barn is where you do your sketching." JB wrote, "Yes, I find it is quiet and there are no distractions." Wilford said he had seen some of JB's work. "Did you study to acquire that skill?" JB wrote that he had no formal schooling to support his gift for art.

Wilford said that JB's work reveals so much attention to details. "I wish I could do that. JB wrote, "You have a talent for painting landscapes. I've seen your work." But he wanted to move into doing portraits and needed a place for a temporary studio, since the weather was about to get colder and cause problems with his paint and canvas. JB advised that Wilford was welcome to share the barn. The men shook hands, and they went inside for lunch.

JB went about his usual ritual kissing Blossom and the babies first. He signed to Blossom, "Mama, they are getting heavy." She said and signed that she wouldn't be surprised to see them walking outside of the playpen before the end of the week. JB signed, "That will be something; I love you, Mama." He brought his lunch into the dining room where Shy was working. He kissed her and gave her the papers from the seed company, saying they should be finished next week. Shy asked, "So far, have we lost any of the crop?" JB responded, "The foreman said we are one of the few farms where they get all the corn and wheat from end to end." Shy said, "That's because Al knows what he is doing." He agreed and added that Mama thinks the babies would be walking outside the playpen by the end of that week. Shy stopped what she was doing and looked up at him and said, "Honey, they are pulling up and walking by holding onto the pen. Now eat your lunch so you can get back to the fields." JB signed that the potatoes were really good, and he got himself some more tea.

Jeru came in from the front porch and declared that something sure smelled good. Shy said, "Let me hold Connie while you eat." Jeru replied, "I appreciate that, Shy, but I have got to get used to holding her and doing other things." Shy asked her how her milk was flowing. She said, "Real good, but sometimes my right breast leaks and I worry that I'm wasting milk." Shy asked if she was nursing on the left side, and Jeru said she was, in order for the baby to get used to her heartbeat. Shy said Jeru needed to feed from both breasts and not to worry about leaking.

At that point, Claudette entered the dining room and kissed Jeru on the forehead and said, "Hello, my love, and how is our little girl doing?" Jeru exclaimed, "She's doing better than I am. I'm cooped up in the room, I have those hot flashes, and (she whispered to Claudette) I'm in a constant state of arousal. I have never had this feeling before." Claudette whispered back, "Remember, Mama said that was going to happened. We have to ask Mama what we can do about it."

Claudette turned to Shy, asking if she could talk to her while she was working. Shy said that she was listening, although she was finishing reports from the company that is harvesting their wheat. "They give us their guess as to the per-bushel yield, and I send it to the Department of Agriculture, which publishes the information for other farmers to look at. I also give them our cost per acre to plant, which determines what our profit is." Claudette asked how Sky knows that the grain people are not cheating her, to which Shy said that JB counts the trucks that leave the field, which are weighed at the mill and the figures match.

At last, Claudette to around to asking her question. "You know, I am a little nervous about taking control, but I remember something my mother told me, repeating something her father taught her about playing poker and winning. She said basically everything in life has a limit. There are only fifty-two cards in the deck, and if five people are playing, it all comes down to simple mathematics, those truck can only hold a certain amount, so you just do the mathematic. Little sister, that's how we are going to run this corporation. They talked for about two and a half hours, and now Beauchamp was cooking dinner and Blossom was taking a nap because the babies were asleep.

However, they did notice when Brinson and Cielito returned. Claudette asked where they had been all day, and she commented that Cielito's hair looked wild. Cielito ignored Claudette and said, "Francois, darling, please bring the bags with the lingerie into our bedroom and take the other bags upstairs while I talk to my loving, but nosy sister." Claudette said, "Lingerie?" Claudette, Shy, and Cielito went out on the porch. "Sisters, what you smell is all-day passionate lovemaking. You are looking at a new woman who is alive and loved. On our way to the house, we started kissing, caressing, feeling, rubbing and I don't know what else, but we found ourselves in the back seat of the car making love. Shy and Claudette said, "What!" She said, "And that was not the only time. I wanted the world to know that the man I love and the one who loves me and worships the very ground I walk on made love to me." Shy begin to fan herself. Cielito said she had heard of intimacy and read about it, but never knew it could be like this. "Last night was thrilling, but today I could feel his love -- it was euphoric, like I became intoxicated, and I have never had alcohol in my mouth. You should see the new wardrobe I bought and the cologne, perfume, and makeup too. I love all three of you I would hug you, but you have already told me I smell. After I take a bath, come to the bedroom and I will show you the lingerie; and we can go upstairs, and I will show the outfits I bought."

They went to Cielito and Brinson's bedroom, where Cielito emptied four bags on the bed. The fifth contained cologne and perfume, makeup, and a makeup mirror. Claudette held up a pair of underwear and said, "My, my, you are going to wear this?" Shy blushed and said she would be embarrassed to wear that in front of JB. Cielito said when Brinson saw the panties, he had a devilish grin and started acting like a cave man. Claudette and Shy started laughing.

Shy turned serious and said, "I will tell you a secret. The morning after our honeymoon night, we got up and had breakfast and went for a stroll near the canyon. JB and I made love several times right there in the grass. I was nervous and felt guilty because I just knew Mama knew." Cielito said, "Mama is nobody's fool. She was married and she knows what it's like to be in love and have the love of a man. Now, Claudette, allow me to say something that was not directed at you, since none of us as humans can help who we fall in love with. You and Jeru are special to all of us, no matter what anyone else thinks. I feel that God loves you, no matter what." Claudette thanked her. "As Mama said, we are still young, and we don't know what is around the next corner. I know that I am happy for you and Brinson, and I am happy with the change I see in you. Come on and show us what your new wardrobe looks like."

Cielito said, "It's just the fall and winter stuff. What I really want is you all's opinions on my new furniture for our living quarters and offices over the barn." Claudette said, as they were making their way upstairs, "Yes, and Shy, sometime next week I want you and the babies and Mama to come with me to pick out your office furnishings." When they arrived, Brinson was hanging Cielito's new wardrobe in the closet. "I hope you like the way I arranged the closet, dear." She responded, "I couldn't have done a better job, darling."

Cielito said that after dinner she would show Mama and Jeru her new things, but Shy quickly said she shouldn't show her lingerie." Cielito agreed, as she went to Brinson, and they kissed. Claudette said, "Wait a minute, you are not going to start the day over, are you? Shy laughed and said everyone should leave the happy couple alone. Cielito intended to bathe and put on a new outfit before dinner, so, she asked Brinson to use the bathroom downstairs, but he playfully replied that he wanted to bathe with her. "You know if you start that we will never get downstairs for dinner." He said, "You are going to be dinner for me," at which point the other ladies had left the room.

Cielito said, "Will you still love me when I am old and gray?" He said, "You know I have heard that the older the violin, the sweeter the music. Besides, I fell in love with you, not your hair color." She splashed water in his face and asked, "How are you going to get downstairs with no clothes?" He said, "I thought I might slip on your dress." Cielito laughed and said she would go downstairs and bring his clothes up. She stepped out of the tub, dried off, and noticed him looking at her with a satisfied look in his eyes. When she returned with his clothes, she went to the closet to pick what she would wear. She chose a plaid skirt with a white silk blouse and naval collar, and he wore brown slacks, a yellow shirt, and a light brown sweater.

They entered the dining room and everyone stood and applauded. The table was decorated, and Jean Claude said they all were saluting the couple for one day of marriage. He said as a joke, "And to think they said it wouldn't last." Everyone broke out in laughter. Jean Claude walked over to them and put out his arm to escort them to their chairs. He seated them and said, "My dear friend and spouse, this is our way of saying we wish you love, happiness, and blessings. To express my love for you two I have fixed a meal fit for a king and queen, so, everyone, please stand and raise a glass to the married couple while I toast them. May you have everything you want in life and want everything you have forever. And now I will serve you and your queen."

The main course was half prairie chicken with a light, white wine sauce, au gratin potatoes, French green beans almondine, and toasted French baguette with butter. Desert was a French vanilla cream custard sprinkled with nutmeg. Brinson asked Jean Claude how he knew this was his favorite, and Jean Claude responded, "In the words of our beloved Mama Blossom, 'A blind hog will root up an acorn every once in a while.' Amen."

As they were finishing dinner and engaged in conversation, the phone rang. It was the church calling to say that Father Ignatius would not be available for the burial tomorrow because he became ill and is on the way to the hospital, Claudette thanked the person and returned to the table with a sad look. "Father Ignatius is ill and can't do the burial tomorrow." Jeru said they had the best person who is close to God right there in the room. "For the sake of Connie and me, I want Mama Blossom to do it." Blossom felt certain that she couldn't take the place of a minister. But they all said, "Mama, you have to do it. We can't just bury her without some words being said." Blossom pleaded, "Let me pray over this and ask for guidance."

Once again, the phone rang. Father Ignatius had died. The household was shocked. Claudette explained that the Santa Fe Hospital would not take Mexicans. Cielito was visibly upset, and she asked to speak to Brinson privately. They left the dining room and went to their room. Cielito, with tears in her eyes, said, "Darling, this is one of those times I need you to help me make a decision. I have had plans in the works to build a clinic on the reservation for the Indians, but after hearing this news, I want to build a hospital in Santa Fe that will accept anyone needing care." He said, "Now that I am a tax- paying citizen of Santa Fe, I am compelled to stand up and speak out about injustices and be prepared to back it up with action." Cielito began to kiss him all over his face, exclaiming, "Darling, you are the kind of man I wanted and expected you to be. I love you a million times over." He said they should set a date to talk to Dr. Joe and the two lady doctors about it as soon as possible. In the meantime, he left to say goodnight to everyone in the dining room and thank Jean Claude for dinner.

That night, in Blossom's bedroom, Jeru asked Blossom why people are so mean. Blossom said, "I can't explain it; all we can do, child, is pray that we do not become like them." Jeru said, "I pray that things will change for Connie's sake. I guess seeing you, JB, and Shy has caused us to see that people don't have to be like that." Blossom added, "Honey I don't know if that will ever happen because those same people claim that they are God-fearing Christians. It is my belief that if those who can't accept the fact that people who don't look like them are God's creations, then the *Bible* says they are liars! You can't hate your fellow human beings whom you see all the time, and claim you love God and his Son whom you have never seen."

The next morning, everyone was up early and seated at the dining room table where Blossom announced she would say words at the burial. All of a sudden, they heard noise from JB and Shy's bedroom. Wilford said, "Stay seated, everyone, I will check it out." He came back in about two minutes and announced it was the workmen building Shy's office. Claudette said that in three or four weeks, Shy's office should be ready. Since everyone was dressed and ready, she called the mortician to meet them at the mausoleum in an hour and a half. When they arrived, JB, Sarah, and the mortician were there, and he backed up to the door of the mausoleum. Sarah unlocked the door and the mortician announced that he and his assistant were ready. They all moved on either side of the hearse and Blossom began. "Almighty God, we are here to commit this body and soul to your care. This child was too young to have committed any unforgiveable sin. I believe that the body and soul will perish, but the spirit belongs to God, so in a sense, the spirit never dies, but returns to God." She had likened this untimely death to that of Lazarus in the Book of John, Chapter 11.

The mortician asked, "Ma'am, are you a preacher?" Blossom said, "Goodness, no." He told her, "I have officiated many burials and never heard a preacher explain death that way. Everyone came toward Blossom, but she put her hand up and said, "Stand back and let me pray." Blossom prayed for forgiveness if she had overstepped her bounds and caused the mortician to think she was a preacher. She called JB and Shy, announcing that she was ready to go. JB was covering for Al and his brother slaughtering hogs, and he had one last building to check before he could leave. Shy had asked him to go by the bookstore for the latest Farm Report, the Department of Agriculture Magazine, and the New Mexico State College Ag. Newsletter. Last stop was the Western Union building. Claudette and Wilford met up with them, and she reminded Shy to go to Willoughby's to pick out her office furnishings. Blossom asked Shy to go with them, and she would wait for JB. But Shy instead insisted that they all go, and she would leave a note and key for JB to retrieve the aerial photo from her brothers' office.

Meantime Brinson and Cielito went to Dr. Joe's office to discuss building the hospital, and she told all three doctors about Father Ignatius' passing, and how it was a shame that the hospital would not admit him because he was Mexican. Dr. Smith said they should report them to the American Hospital Association, and Dr. Barker agreed. But Dr. Joe said, "Wait a minute, doctors, that is an awful policy, but we can't get involved in that; we have to use that facility, and if we create a problem, they may bar us from using their facility." Dr. Smith said they can't just stand by; they took an oath. Dr. Smith suggested that they let someone else report them. Cielito said, "Like us?"

Brinson said, "Sure, we can get that on the national wire, but in the meantime, we want to build a hospital that will admit anyone, so, if you all will guide us through that process, we will build a state-of-the-art facility and you all can run it. How soon can you get started? We will have Scott McKenzie to design it, and you will tell him what you want. Cielito added, "I own fifty percent of the land set aside for the new downtown, so land is no problem, and if that is not suitable, we will buy the land wherever you choose."

There were big smiles all around. They shook hands, and Brinson and Cielito departed. He asked her on the way to the car if there was anything else to do before they left town, and she said, "Let's go by the bank to see if Bix is in his office. I want to tell him about our plans, since the bank own half the land." As they were driving to the bank, Brinson asked about the size of the new downtown. "I believe it's about thirty square miles, but if Bix is in, he has a rendering of the project."

Cielito inquired as to what he was thinking, and Brinson said, "I was thinking I could get the company to open an office here, which is the only way I would accept the Director's position." Cielito asked if that position would take him away from home. "No, darling, there may be times when I'm asked to come to the main office in Chicago, but I would take you with me. I thought if a well-known company like the Pinkerton Detective Agency opened an office here, it would entice other large companies to do the same."

She thought about what Blossom had said about knowing your man, and she responded, "Sweetheart, you are so smart and sweet; I love you." She started to rub, grope, and put her hand inside his shirt and kissed him. He looked at her with that devilish look and started laughing and said, "Don't start something we can't finish."

Bix had left for the day, so they went on home. Everyone had returned from downtown and was getting ready for lunch. Claudette and Shy were at the dining room table studying the aerial map that JB had picked up from the Ohara office building, Jean Claude was in the kitchen preparing lunch, and Blossom was on the back porch with Al, who had brought over half of the two hogs he had slaughtered and was assisting Blossom to mix the sausage meat for both of them. Al also brought two hams and ribs for JB to smoke. He showed Blossom the pork chops, and she commented that Al was the best butcher she had ever seen. She declared the sausage meat was well seasoned. She took the chops in the kitchen and said, "Jean Claude, we are having old-fashioned baked pork chops with gravy and biscuits and turnips with corn tonight." He said that sounded mighty fine and delicious.

There came a knock at the kitchen door, and the person said they were almost finished working but needed to know what kind of heating and flooring Blossom wanted. She said, "Let me get the lady who belongs to that office." The workman put the same question to her, but Claudette interrupted. "Kind Sir, will you give us our options? He told them to follow him walking through the unfinished space. Shy asked what this little room was for. "This is your coat closet, and the other is your water closet or powder room. Now, as to the floor, you have a choice of carpet, tile, or a wood floor; however, I would recommend in the washroom that you choose tile and maybe wood and a throw rug. For heating you can choose steam, but if you chose that we have to build an addition to the office for the boiler." Claudette suggested to Shy that steam would be safer.

Without anyone noticing, Al had walked up and was quietly listening, but then asked, "Can the boiler explode?" The workman assured him that someone would explain everything to his satisfaction. The workman went on to explain how Shy would have access to her office. The workman finished giving details, along with a projected "move in" date.

Al asked Shy if she was ready to meet with him about the aerial map. Al asked where the "legend" was, and Sky asked, "What is a legend? Al took the map out of the frame and discovered that the map was folded at the bottom to fit in the frame. There was the legend. He explained "miles" and "acres," asking for a ruler to make measurements. "Watch this. I estimate starting five hundred yards away from the bunk house and measuring." Within a short time, he had laid out the area for cultivation and explained why it had to run in the direction he suggested. He also explained why it would not be profitable to plant the whole area in soybeans. "For the first year, we have to plant what we know will make a profit, so a large portion should be wheat or corn and the smaller soybeans. Ms. Ohara, I know that with your wealth you can afford to have a profit lose, but as a businesswoman, you can't afford it. Once it is out that females are running the Ohara corporation, there will be those waiting for you to fail. I will not let that happen, especially on this project. My best friend's wife is going to sit atop this project, and I will not allow her to be seen as a failure. I owe him and her too much."

Claudette was moved by Al's affection for Shy and JB. She said, "Al, we are in your hands, so, what is our next move?" Al said this huge undertaking will require at least ten tractors and other equipment. "I will make a list and you should order starting Monday morning. Prior to receiving the large equipment, I will have tested the soil and prepped it, that is tilling and harrowing. Healthy soil is the first step to a successful crop. Next, we will cover crop and I prefer buckwheat or sorghum. Once they are plowed up, they make good cattle feed. Tomorrow I will collect soil samples and Monday drop them off at the School of Agriculture and begin to hire the workers and test them on the equipment."

Chapter 19
Mature Relationships

In Blossom's bedroom, Jeru was feeding Connie and not paying attention when Shy walked in and offered to include Connie's diapers in her load. Jeru didn't answer because she was gazing out the window with a dejected and hopeless look, feeling guilty about something she hadn't yet chosen to share with Shy. Shy walked closer and called her name and shook her. She looked up and started to cry. Shy asked what was wrong. Blossom had talked with her about "baby blues" before, so, Shy kneeled in front of her looked her in the eyes, and said, "Honey, talk to me and let me help you. Let's go out back and sit on the steps, just keep the baby's head covered. As they left, Shy picked up the diaper hamper and they went to kitchen. Blossom was in there and sensed something was wrong. Shy signed to Blossom that it appeared to be baby blues, and she asked Blossom to put the diapers in the washing machine.

Shy sat Jeru down and put her arms around her and began talking to her in a soft voice. "Let me help you, honey." Jeru broke down again, insisting that no one could help her. Shy said there was nothing God couldn't help her with, and they could pray for the answer. Jeru said, "Claudette is not going to love me anymore. I am ashamed." Shy asked, "Do you want God's help? He will only listen if you sincerely admit your sin, which shows that you are repenting and truly sorry." Jeru said, "Me and Wilford did it. We made love." Shy was astonished, but said, "You mean Wilford took you." Jeru shook her head from side to side. "While all of you were gone to town, I could not stand the feeling of being aroused any longer, so I asked him to come in and I was naked, and I had to convince him, and the thing is we did it twice. I was so desperate that I would have asked any man who was here. Since I took that medicine for my milk, I have had hot flashes and wanted a man to make love to me." Jeru passed Shy the baby and wept into her skirt while hiding her face.

Shy said they needed to talk with Mama about this. "I will say this -- you were not making love, that was intercourse, and you are not the only woman to get those feelings. I can't speak for Claudette, but since I have come to know you two, I know she loves you and you love her. I want you to stop feeling guilty for needing a man, which is natural. Mama said that God said to Eve that she would crave her husband, and he told them to be fruitful and multiply, which is to have intercourse." Jeru said with a trembling voice, "I lied to Mama. I told her the reason I changed the sheets was that the baby messed on the bed, but the reason was that I bled on the sheets and tried to wash them." Shy responded, "When we talk to Mama tonight, you must tell her all of this, and she will forgive you and I believe Claudette will too."

Shy told Jeru to get herself together and go inside to hang the laundry out to dry. "After we talk to Mama you are going to feel better. When we finish hanging out the laundry, we can go to the room, and you can change the baby and think about what and how you are going to speak with Mama." Jeru asked Shy to tell Blossom the whole thing because she was too ashamed. Shy told Jeru that once she admitted what she had done, she would feel like a heavy load was off her shoulders and the guilt would disappear.

Shy shared a personal story. "When we were on our way home from Washington on the train, JB and I thought Mama was asleep and we were signing how we felt about each other and wanted to get married. We fell asleep in each other's arms. Mama woke up and saw us like that, and she cleared her throat loud enough to wake us. We realized we were embracing in our sleep, and we were embarrassed and quickly released each other and felt guilty. Mama said, 'No use trying to hide because I already saw what you two were signing, and even though you haven't done anything wrong, I knew it would come to this.' We told Mama we just wanted to get married, and she said we could get married when we got home. Honey, the guilt left us, and we were so happy. I love you, and no matter what, I know you are going to do the right thing."

That evening at dinner, Jeru cleared her throat and was about to speak. Shy whispered that she should speak after dinner. Everyone at the table was wondering what Jeru was about to say. Shy said, "This is women talk and doesn't concern you gentlemen." After dinner, Blossom asked the females except Jeru to help her clear the table and wash dishes. In the kitchen, Cielito asked what was going on. Shy said, "What Jeru has to say is something we need to be sitting to discuss, so, let's finish the dishes and clean the kitchen." Shy suggested the parlor might be a better place.

"Cielito, we certainly want your input, but you are still on your honeymoon, so we will understand if you feel inclined to leave." Cielito thanked them for understanding but agreed to stay a few minutes. They all sat down, and Jeru asked Claudette if she could hold her hand. She asked Blossom to hold the baby and she began to speak. "I want to ask for your forgiveness, prayers, and counsel." She looked Claudette in the eyes and said, "I have committed some improprieties, and on the advice of Shy I am here to confess and ask God to forgive me and my loved ones. First, I have lied, and worse, I have committed fornication." She began to cry and squeeze Claudette's hand. "I will not divulge the other person's name since he was not a willing partner. I will ask for his forgiveness also."

Shy walked over and hugged Jeru and whispered, "You are doing good; tell them why you were brought to that act." Jeru continued. "No one is to blame, but the medicine I was using to produce milk to save Connie's life also caused me to become aroused. I was warned that would happen, but I would have done anything to save my baby's life. I was not taking the medicine like I should have, and as a result, the desire caused me to seek relief." She dropped to her knees and began kissing Claudette's hand and begging for her understanding and saying she loved her. Claudette, with tears in her eyes, stood and said, "I need forgiveness because I also have committed a sin." Everyone was stunned. She said, "I need your forgiveness, Jeru. I love you more than anything. I did not take any medicine, so my sin was what Mama would call weakness of the flesh."

Blossom stood up and said, "Hold on here, I will not stand by and let you two agonize over something that is a natural act. You are not the first women this has happened to, even though I am not condoning what you did. What I am saying is that, as women, we all have weak moments. God said to Eve after she had eaten from the forbidden tree, 'For her rebellious act she would crave her man for the rest of her life.' And just like men, we have carnal desires, and we have to find ways to overcome them. I was married and used to intimacy with my husband, and I can't count the nights I wanted him so badly that I ached, but I prayed to God for help. My grandmother's sprit would come to me in my dreams and talk to me night after night, and eventually, I was able to overcome those moments through herbal medication. I have come to love you all so much that I won't allow you to live with your perceived guilt because you have confessed before Him and He has forgiving you. Shy, get me my *Bible.* I want to read something to all of you."

Blossom opened the *Bible* and began to read: "A woman was brought to Jesus by the Pharisees after being caught in the act of the offense of adultery. No one questioned whether or not she committed the act, so she was guilty. When Jesus said, 'Go and sin no more,' He was not expecting that this woman would leave her sinful flesh and never be tempted again. He was telling her to say no to the sin that dwells in her and stop the temptation from becoming a sin. So, let's compare your situation with hers. Her offense was adultery. Neither of you are married so yours would be fornication, which is a sin against customs. If a man commits fornication, he must marry the woman. Now that is going to be up to you all."

Jeru said, "Mama, I lied to you about the sheet. I washed it and tried to hide it." Blossom said, "Honey, I know; it is said that if it don't come out in the wash it will come out in the rinse, but that is not true with blood. Let's pray." They did and everyone said good night. Claudette asked Blossom a question. "Mama, you know that my confession was a lie, but I did it for Jeru's sake. I love her so much and I don't want her to carry that guilt." Blossom said she knew, but asked Claudette to seek God's forgiveness because He knows our hearts better than we do. Blossom said she was proud of Claudette and Jeru. "I think by next week you two can go back upstairs. Jeru has the making of a fine mother." Claudette hugged and kissed Blossom and said, "Thank you, Mama, for being so wise and understanding. I love you as much as my dearly departed mother."

Meanwhile, in the married couple's bedrooms, there were conversation going on. The Dubois were discussing the hospital they were planning. In the Blake's bedroom. JB was looking at his three babies and marveling at how fast they were growing. Shy was propped up in the bed reading the newsletter from the *New Mexico State University College of Agriculture* article about an experimental study of soybean as a food source. All of a sudden, she yelled, "Eureka!" JB turned and signed, "What's wrong, sweetheart? She said, "Darling I have found the key." She jumped out of bed and ran to Blossom's bedroom, knocking with an excited voice. "Claudette, we have to talk now!" Claudette came to the door holding Connie since Jeru was taking a bath. Shy asked Blossom to watch the baby since she and Claudette had some urgent business to discuss. Shy led the way to the dining room.

Sister, I have in my hand the answer to our wondering about soybeans." She handed the newsletter to Claudette and sat quietly as Claudette read it. She asked Shy to explain. "Don't you see, they have come up with a use for soybeans as a food source for humans. Look at all the different things they found. For example, take flour and think of all the dishes a cook could use that flour for. I say tomorrow after Mass, we go over to the school and find the two people and see if they will show us all the edible things they have made from soybeans." Claudette asked "So, what do we do with the information that is their discovery?" Shy responded, "Sister, remember at the reception how Jean Claude made all that stuff to taste like traditional Mexican food? We should take Jean Claude with us and let his mind go to work, and we introduce his food to the country by bringing food producers and the people from the agriculture department to the ranch and let them sample Jean Claude's dishes. We will be ahead of the game."

Claudette said "Hey, I see it now. Shy, in the words of Mama, the acorn doesn't fall far from the tree. I can see I won't get any sleep tonight. Good night, Sister, sleep well. We got this." Shy proceeded to her bedroom where the babies was asleep. JB returned from taking a bath, and signed "How did it go?" She said it went well. "You remember Claudette asked me to manage the ranch? She was advised to set aside fifteen thousand acres for agriculture purposes based on an article I sent to the *Department of Agriculture* on soybeans." JB added that soybeans were good for cattle feed.

She said, "That's true, but at the university two men have experimented with them and was able to produce edible food for humans." JB signed, "What kind of food?" Shy said that tomorrow after mass, she and Claudette would go over and try to find the men to see what they had come up with. JB signed, "I can watch the babies since Sunday night is a short night." Shy said, "No, honey, when I agreed to take this on it was with the understanding that I would not neglect my children or my husband or any of my responsibilities as a mother and a wife." JB asked if Shyanne remembered the first time she put her arms around his neck. She remembered. "I had blisters on my feet and Mama had you pick me up and bring me to the dining room. It was the first time I was touched by a male who did not plan on abusing me. Honey let's pray and thank God." They did, and afterwards, they enjoyed a night of intimacy.

Meanwhile In Blossom's bedroom she had fallen into a deep sleep and Mama G had told her not to agonize over her words at the burial of little Connie's mother. Remember that this woman is with Jesus. You made me proud the way you handled the situation with Jeru. I wish you could have been there when your daughter counseled her because it was like you speaking to her." Soon the whole house was quite everyone was sleeping peacefully.

The next morning everyone except for Wilford awakened and took turns using the bathrooms, giving Blossom first chance as she was going to fix breakfast. To everyone's surprise, the smell of food cooking was already coming from the kitchen. It seems that Jean Claude was preparing breakfast.

Brinson was going upstairs to use the bathroom, and Cielito volunteered to go too. Claudette and Jeru laughed, Blossom said, "Here, here they are still on their honeymoon, and if they were at a hotel they would be bathing together." Blossom asked if Wilford was all right, and Jean Claude said that Wilford wanted some time for himself. Blossom went about setting the table, all the time wondering if Wilford was OK. As she pondered it in her mind, it became clear what was wrong with Wilford.

Now, Blossom had to have some excuse for not attending Mass. Everyone was at the dining room table except Wilford. Shy asked if they should wait for Wilford, but Blossom said Wilford was not feeling well, so she would stay home and nurse him. Afterwards, she told Jeru to get the baby ready and be sure to cover her head. Jeru whispered, "Mama, should I go to confession?" Blossom replied, "Go, if you think it is going to make you feel better. You have already confessed and sought forgiveness from God, and we don't even know if we will have a Priest today." Claudette said, "Mama, you are right. Father Ignatius just died late yesterday."

They all had breakfast and loaded into separate cars and left. When the Dubois' arrived at the cathedral, the doors were closed. Cielito asked Brinson where the people were, and he said, "I can't answer that, my dear, but there's a notice on the door." He read the notice and returned to the car. He reported, "There is not going to be early Mass, but Mass will be celebrated later today. Since we are first to arrive, I will tell everyone else as they arrive. Claudette looked at Jean Claude and said, "I guess we can go back home." Jeru pleaded to wait and find out what time Mass was going to be, and Claudette said they would wait an hour. JB and Shy also decided to wait an hour.

Meanwhile, back at the house, Blossom went upstairs to talk with Wilford. She knocked on the door, but Wilford said "Please go away. I want to be alone." Blossom gently replied, "Son, it's me. Please let me in, as I know you are feeling guilty. I can help you." Wilford unlocked and opened the door; he had tears in his eyes. Blossom reached out and hugged him and suggested they go downstairs to talk. She asked to fix him some breakfast, but Wilford didn't think he could eat. Blossom insisted, saying he would feel better.

Blossom put her arms around him and asked him why he was feeling guilty. He said, "Mama Blossom, you know." She said, "I do, but if you tell me it is going to put you on the road to getting over your guilt." He told her the whole story, and he lifted his fork and began to eat. She said, "Son, what happened is nothing new; it's been around since the creation of humans, and it's called 'temptation.' What happened with you no man could have resisted, and Jeru admitted she seduced you." He said, "Mama, when I saw her like that, I wanted her." Blossom said, "Here is what you must do: pray for forgiveness and I want you and Jeru to talk. Don't tell her you are sorry about having intercourse with her because no woman wants to feel that what she offered was something you didn't want, even in a moment of passion. Tell her you wanted to make love to her, which is more than just intercourse."

Wilford said, "Mama, I have loved her for three years. Jean Claude and I both told Jeru and Claudette our feelings. We would not come between them, but we love both of them and would marry them in a heartbeat." He added, "I don't know if I could face anyone, I am so ashamed." Blossom told Wilford that Jeru admitted she tempted him, and she didn't tell anyone his name. "I will tell you this: now that you and Jeru have had a piece of the pie, it is going to be hard to resist, which could lead to more guilt and shame. Each time you see her, your mind will remember the sensation and splendor, and you will want and desire each other. Son, I suggest you ask for her hand in marriage."

Wilford said, "Mama, I can't do that; she and Claudette love each other, and I love both of them so much that I can't bring myself to come between them." Blossom shook her head slightly. "That might have happened already. If my calculation is right, we will know in six weeks if you want to or have to …. Sit down with Jeru, Claudette, and Jean Claude and the four of you talk and pray. I know it will work out." He pondered for a few seconds and declared "Mama, you are right. I feel so good now that I will have a second breakfast."

At the cathedral, Brinson. Claudette, Jeru, JB and Shy had waited an hour and a half and decided to leave, just as the mortician drove up with the body of Father Ignatius. They realized that there was no early Mass because the deacons were preparing the chapel to receive the body. Claudette suggested they go to the university to meet with the professors. Shy needed to go home first to clean up the babies, but Claudette said she would wait for her. Brinson said he and Cielito would run by the hospital and be home later. As the Dubois' drove by the hospital, there were police and newspaper reporters and cameramen. Cielito asked what was going on. He said, "While you all were meeting last night, I called the Chicago office and had them to run the story on the national news wire." They did not stop but drove home.

When JB and Shy arrived, Wilford was on the porch, asking for Jeru and Claudette. Shy informed him that they had gone to the university, and she added that it was good to see Wilford feeling better. She and JB went inside where Blossom was in the kitchen preparing dinner. Shy announced that she needed to change diapers and wash the babies off, and Blossom helped. "Why don't you leave them here while you are gone?" Shy declined. Blossom said, "I worry about what carrying three babies is doing to your back. You're such a petite thing." She laughed and said she was strong and want people to know how important her family is to her. "I will let JB carry the boys in the cradleboard, and I will carry little Blossom Shyanne." They finished dressing the babies, and Shy and JB started for the car. Brinson and Cielito were sitting in the car kissing. JB smiled and signed, "We still do that." She signed, "I love you with all my heart, mind, and strength."

They made their way to the university where Jean Claude was waiting. He said, "Come on let's hurry, this is so exciting, and you are going to be amazed what they have done." Claudette was talking to the professor, but when she saw Shy, she hurried over and grabbed her by the hand and Introduced her to Professor I. B. Moore, whom the students refer to as "thinking Moore." "Professor, this is my Farm Manager Mrs. Shyanne Blake and her husband, JB Blake. He is mute but has exceptional hearing and is a most intelligent young man. Please show Mrs. Blake all the food products you all have made from soybeans." The professor said, "Why don't we let her walk through, and my lab assistants can show and tell her what they are working on next."

The tour was about an hour, at the end of which the professor said, "Ms. Blake, I want you to meet my head lab assistant, Paul Daily." Paul said he knew Ms. Blake. "That is, I know of Ms. Blake. I was encouraged by the article you published in the agriculture department magazine." The professor realized she was "S. Blake." "We were impressed by your articles, especially the one on soybeans. All along, we were thinking you were a farmer, I mean we thought you were a man." He called out to the lab assistants to meet S. Blake. They all came over and introduced themselves and made comments about how they were impressed by her article.

Claudette, ever the deal maker, said, "Professor, let's talk business. Ms. Blake has plans to plant ten thousand acres in soybeans, and what you are doing here has put us on the road to making those acres profitable. As the CEO of Ohara Inc., I will give you as much research money as you need to continue your research experiments. I also want to introduce to you Jean Claude Beauchamp, who is an outstanding chef and excels in creating exotic dishes. He can take what you have come up with and create dishes that the whole country will salivate for. I will let Ms. Blake tell you more about her plan."

Shy said, "Sir, when Jean Claude has created several dishes, I plan to invite food producers from all over to include investors and people from the Agriculture Department to a luncheon, where I will reveal that nearly all the food they just ate came from soybeans. Professor Moore said, "Ms. Blake, you are a genius. Mr. Beauchamp, when can you start?" Jean Claude quickly responded, "Today if you can give me a copy of all the things you have created. I will create recipes for different food items." Claudette asked the professor if they could speak in private. "Professor Moore, you have to assure us that no one will speak of this until we can get this done. I will have my lawyers to draw up a contract giving you the right to your experiment. and Ohara Inc. the right to create dishes and recipes. We want to work with you." The professor said, "Ms. Ohara, I trust you and am looking forward to a long and successful relationship with you and the Ohara Corporation." Claudette advised Jean Claude that she would wait for him at the car when he finished with Professor Moore.

When Claudette, Shy and JB arrived at the car, Shy told Claudette, "Before we begin to strategize, I need to change diapers and give the babies some water." Then the two began to talk. Claudette said to remind her to get that list from Al today, and tomorrow she would have Bix order those items and put a rush on them. JB signed to Shy that Al had left the list for Claudette when they went home to change the babies. Shy relayed that to Claudette, who promised to talk to Bix by phone when they got home.

Jean Claude made his way to the car with a large box, followed by two lab assistants with a box under each arm. He said, "Ladies, this is going to be a piece of cake and pie. JB, I am going to need your help. I have five more boxes. Ladies, let's go home because I can't wait to get started." When they arrived, Jean Claude called for Wilford to assist him and JB carrying his boxes to the kitchen. He asked Blossom if he could speak with her, explaining everything and asking if he could do his experiments in her kitchen. He promised that it would not interfere with her plans, as most of his work would be done after dinner and he would clean up the kitchen afterwards. Blossom advised that if it was going to help Shy, then she was all for it. He said, "Today before dinner, I am going to make a pie for desert and ask everyone to taste and give me their feedback, but most of all I want your opinion as to what you think I need to add to make it perfect, because I know you are honest and will not spare my feelings." Blossom responded, "Son, you know how I feel about you, and I will give my honest opinion."

Claudette was on the phone with Bix. she apologized for calling him at home on a Sunday but explained what she needed. Bix said he would have someone on it tomorrow morning. Claudette said she planned to work out of her brothers' old office building and asked Bix what he thought. He said, "That will do in the short term; however, my opinion is that, as a large, successful corporation, you need to have your own office building as your corporate headquarters, with room to expand. You are going to have large and medium size companies seeking to do business with you, so your corporate image should reflect success, as well as your personal image." She asked, "Are you suggesting my building be located in the new downtown?" He said "No, what I envision is a building with a campus. Listen, your sister owns fifty percent of the development of the new downtown, which is about fifty-five acres, and I can subdivide the area and have ten acres for you right in the middle. All you will pay for is the building. Since Cielito owns the land, she will be able to recoup her investment from the other forty-five acres. *Consolidated Oil* is looking to open a division here, and I can put them next to you."

      Claudette needed a moment to follow everything Bix was saying. Then his voice got a little lower. "Listen, I am not a fool. I know there are going to be men at the head of large corporations just waiting to see you fail. They will try everything in an attempt to prove that a woman can't run a large corporation, including spreading malicious gossip. You have to make sure your name is not mixed up in anything they can use against you. Now, some may not understand your relationship with Jeru. It's not enough that we understand, we love you and Jeru. But it is up to you to make sure there isn't a hint of scandal, which can come from places you would never think of. I promise we will not let that happen. Lastly don't ever let them see you cry." Claudette said "Bix, I am indebted to you for the rest of my life." Bix replied, "It is the least I can do for the girl I have loved from the beginning." She said "You have always been a special friend and will always be. Enjoy the rest of your Sunday and I will see you tomorrow."

Wilford was hanging around while Claudette was on the phone, and when she hung up, he asked if he could speak with her, Jeru, and Jean Claude after dinner. She said she was sure that she and Jeru would make time for him and would ask Jean Claude as well. Wilford said he would ask him. He went to kitchen where Jean Claude was with Blossom. He asked Jean Claude if, after dinner, he could speak with him, Jeru, and Claudette about a private matter. Blossom said Jean Claude "You need to get back to his custard. I think it is going to need a pinch more nutmeg, and you can sprinkle it on the top and add a leaf of mint. I will get you some from my herb garden." He tasted the custard and said, "Mama, you are right." After she returned from outside with the mint, she told him to place one or two leaves on the top and let it sit for a while.

Jean Claude said, "Mama, Wilford sounded serious. Do you have any idea what he wants to talk about?" She said, "Yes, but he will tell you when he is ready. I will say that if you have learned anything from me, don't judge." He promised and asked her to taste the custard and render an opinion. She declared that it tasted just like her egg custard. Jean Claude was elated. He wrote the recipe down and asked Blossom if he could open a jar of her canned peaches to make a peach pie and use his ingredients for the crust. "Taste that flour and you tell me how you would make a flaky crust from it." She said "First, I would not use oil. I prefer lard to make a flaky pie crust." Jean Claude asked what kind of flavor she would you use if she wanted it to be different from regular crust. Blossom said, "You don't want the crust to have a flavor. Whatever fruit you use should give the pie the flavor. I don't know what kind of flour that is, but it is coarse enough to make Graham crackers and you can use the oil you have to make them and crumble them up and add butter and press it into your pan. That is what I use for my coconut cream pie." By the time it was time for dinner, Jean Claude had used several old Southern recipes and traditional Mexican recipes.

Blossom announced it was time for dinner. After all were seated and the blessing said, Jean Claude announced that he had prepared two special desserts for them. He asked Blossom to help him bring in the first desert, insisting that no one try it until each person had a cup in front of them. "I want to see the expression on your faces." Shy commented, "My, aren't we fancy, with a mint leaf garnish. We have to use all proper etiquette." Everyone laughed. Jean Claude said "Okay, everyone, take the first spoonful and tell me what you think it is. All of a sudden there were mmm sounds all around. Everyone was busy scooping up seconds. Brinson said this was the best egg custard he had tasted in a long time.

Jean Claude said, "I won't keep you wondering any longer. Yes, it is a custard, but not egg. Dear loved ones, this is a custard made from soybeans." "What! "was resounding around the table. Shy said, "Hold on, you mean you made this custard from the stuff you got from the university today?" "Yes, and that is not all. Mama, if you will help me bring in the second dessert." Claudette and Shy looked at each other and ran toward each other screaming. Blossom said they were scaring the babies. Shy and Claudette apologized, but quickly added, "Do you know what this mean?" Blossom said she didn't, asking them to try to control themselves. Claudette and Shy went to Jean

Claude and started kissing him and telling him he was a genius. He directed them to taste the pie. They had the same reaction. JB looked a little jealous at Shy kissing Jean Claude, but she signed and said, "JB, honey, what he has done and will continue to do will put us out in front of other farmers. He has taken what the professor discovered and found that the soybean can be used as a food source for humans." JB got up shook his hand. He turned to Shy and asked for forgiveness. She signed and responded, "It is okay, baby, it makes me feel good to see you are jealous." She kissed him and said, "I love you and you gotta know you are the only man for me."

Blossom asked Shy if she would help her clear the table, but Jean Claude volunteered. Blossom said, "No, son, you sit right where you are I will be back in a minute." When she returned, she said, "Wilford, Son, the floor is yours." Wilford began by acknowledging that Jeru and Claudette knew what this was all about. "Jean Claude, a few days ago while everyone was gone to town, I entered Mama's bedroom and Jeru was in there and I caught her at a moment of passion. We had intercourse, but afterwards, we felt ashamed and guilty because I felt like I had betrayed your trust, as well as Claudette's. I was not ashamed of having intercourse with Jeru because, when I saw her like that I was aroused and wanted to make love to her. When I said we had intercourse I was wrong because, to me, I was making love to her. I wanted to talk to the three of you because Jeru, I want to marry you. I know how you and Claudette feel about each other and I want to ask that you will forgive me." Jeru, with tears running down her face, stood and said It didn't happen like he said. Wilford interjected, "Jeru, my love, please let it go."

But she refused to let him take the blame for something she initiated. "He was outside the window painting, and I asked him to come inside, and I stripped, and it was I who started the whole thing. I felt bad that I had betrayed you two. So, I sought advice from Mama, which is why I asked the women to listen while I confessed." She went on to say, "Wilford, I was ashamed of the initial act, but I want you to know the second time it was different. We kissed, touched, and caressed, and I felt loved and wanted and didn't want you to stop. Claudette, I know you lied when you said you had done the same thing with Jean Claude. You did it to try to make me feel unashamed and ease my guilt. I thank you for that and I will always love you." Claudette said, "And I will always love you."

Blossom said, "Jean Claude, let me say that what happened was not unusual. Women will always desire men and men will always desire women. It is natural. I am not condoning what happened, nor am I judging. If one is not married, the person will feel he or she has done something wrong. Both of you have confessed and I know God will forgive you. Jeru, I don't want to embarrass you so I will whisper this to you."

Everyone looked lovingly at the others, giving Blossom and Jeru a little privacy. "How many days after you had intercourse did your cycle start?" Jeru answered, "I believe it was a week and three days." Blossom said she may be pregnant and would know in six weeks. Blossom turned back to the other three and said, "Now all four of you are grown and you can make up your own minds, but my thoughts are you should get married. Jean Claude spoke. "Claudette, Jeru, you both know how much I love you and would marry either one of you, but I don't want to marry either one of you for any reason other than you want and need me. You've said no man would put up with you because of your love for each other. Well, here are two men who have for over three years loved you both. I feel that both of you feel something, and when you show me that you want and need me, I want to marry you."

He gave everyone a chance to process all that he said. Then he spoke again. "I had planned to tell you tomorrow after I talk with Professor Moore. I plan on being gone for three weeks collecting recipes from different ethnic groups, which will be the first time in over three years that we will be apart. Maybe by then you can get in touch with your feelings. I know I will miss you, and I believe you will miss me too." Claudette asked Jean Claude if she could talk with him later, and he said he would like that. Blossom asked all of them to pray on it. "I will get out of your business, but remember, I love all four of you and so does God, no matter what you decide."

When everyone had gone, Claudette asked Jean Claude to step outside. Claudette reached and held his hand and began to spill her soul to him. "I have never been with a man or a woman, and that may sound strange, given my age, but I guess I never got past the little girl stage. Yes, I have gambled all over and I guess I was putting up a front, but to be honest, I am afraid of rejection and probably thought that being with and loving Jeru was safe because she is Indian, French Canadian, and African. You probably don't know this, but I am part Negro. My mother was Creole, and her mother was mixed Negro and White. I do love you and I am scared. If you reject me, it will hurt, but by the grace of God I will get over it. Since I have been here with Blossom and her family, I am mature enough to deal with anything."

Jean Claude looked her in the eyes and said "The first day I saw you walk up the gang plank of that ship, I thought you were the most beautiful female I had ever laid eyes on, and before the night was over, I fell in love with you. Jeru, Wilford, and I never discussed which one of you we preferred. I guess fate has settled that. Right now, I want to kiss you and make love to you all night." With tears in her eyes, she said "Go ahead and do both." He said he wouldn't feel right making love in Blossom's house before they were married. Claudette said, "If we confess our love and take an oath and ask God to bless our union, that should suffice. We can tell everyone in the morning we have stood before God and pledged ourselves to each other and plan to have a ceremony when I return. Mama has already kicked us from her bedroom -- just kidding – and she told Jeru yesterday that she has made good progress and is going to be a fine mother and we can go back upstairs."

Jean Claude said, "Good, what are we waiting for?" They kissed and caressed each other for a long time and went inside arm and arm. He told her to take a bath first, but she said it takes women longer than men, so he should go ahead. Claudette went to Brinson and Cielito's room and knocked on the door and said "Sister, it's me. Can I talk to you for a second?" Cielito came to the door and Claudette whispered in her ear, while quickly placing her hand over Cielito's mouth because she expected her to scream. Cielito was jumping up and down and trying to remove Claudette's hand from her mouth. Claudette told her how she and Jean Claude had asked for God blessings on their union, and they made and oath that they would marry when he returned from his three-week trip.

She asked Cielito if she could borrow a set of her lingerie.

They went back into the room and Cielito asked Brinson if he could go to the parlor for a short time, since she needed to discuss something with Claudette. He complied. Cielito laid out all of her lingerie on the bed and said to take what she wanted. Claudette said, "Just for tonight. I plan to buy my own tomorrow while I am downtown, and Jean Claude is not leaving until Tuesday." She selected a see-through night gown. Cielito gave an approving smile, and said, "Don't buy too much. Remember I owe you and when you tell everyone in the morning, they are going to be so happy and begin making plans." She kissed Claudette and said, "I'm so happy for you." Claudette folded the garment up as small as she could, in case she encountered someone on her way back to the room.

When she arrived, Jean Claude was in the bathroom so, she laid the gown out on the bed so he would see it when he returned. She gathered her comb, brush, lipstick, and cologne and sat in her terry cloth robe waiting for him. He walked over and picked up the lingerie and said, "Wow!" He grabbed her and threw her on the bed and started kissing her, but she gently pushed back saying she had to get ready.

Claudette went to her and Jeru's room and tapped on the door. Jeru stuck her head out and announced that Connie was asleep. Claudette asked why she was sweating, and Jeru was quick to say it was hot in there. Claudette whispered what she had told Cielito, and Jeru softly responded, "Oh, darling I am so happy for you, but let's discuss it in the morning." She hurried to the bathroom so she could finish and get her a "taste of the pie." When she returned to the room, her cologne began dancing in Jean Claude's nose. He grabbed her and did not give her time to put on the gown. She told him to be gentle since she had never had sex before. "You should take it slow ad easy because it is going to hurt me. After that, you can take me like you want to."

The next morning Blossom was surprised that Jean Claude was not in the kitchen, so she began preparing breakfast. Upstairs, Jean Claude and Claudette were about to leave for breakfast when their door opened at the same time the door to Jeru's bedroom opened and quickly closed, as if someone was pepping out. She grabbed him by the hand and said, "Come on, let's go down and tell everyone the great news." They found Blossom in the kitchen dishing up food to take to the dining room. Claudette walked up to Blossom and kissed her and thanked her, and so did Jean Claude. She inquired as to what all this was about, but Claudette said she'd reveal everything in a few minutes.

Shortly after that Jeru came down carrying Connie and a diaper hamper. She wished everyone a good morning. Three minutes later, Wilford came down with a sheepish look on his face and took a seat next to where Jeru normally sat. Shy was already there feeding the triplets. When Blossom entered with the last of the food, she took her place at the table and began to ask for the blessings. Claudette was about to burst, as Blossom said "Amen." Claudette stood up and asked for everyone's attention. At the same time Jeru stood to make her announcement but offered Claudette to go ahead.

"Loved ones, you are looking at a new woman, thanks to Mama. I am no longer that naïve, selfish girl, but a grown woman in mind and body, and soon to be a married woman." She had Jean

Claude to stand with her. Everyone at the table except Jeru and Cielito were surprised. Blossom asked, "When did that happen?" Claudette and Jean Claude went on to explain how they had sworn an oath before God that they loved each other and wanted to be married and asked Him to bless their union. Jean Claude added, "And we prayed, we promised to make it legal the day I return in three weeks. I will be leaving tomorrow evening and I ask that you all pray for us and my safe return." Claudette said, "If you want to plan a ceremony, you have three weeks to prepare." Jeru spoke up and said, "Please, everyone, you might as well plan a ceremony for two because Wilford and I decided last night to get married. We were going to do it today but if it is okay with Claudette, we will do it three weeks from now". Claudette wouldn't have it any other way. Everyone was happy and going around the table kissing, hugging, shaking hands, and congratulating, and then they finished breakfast. Claudette said, "Too bad we don't have any wine. I want to toast Mama for opening my eyes and making me the changed woman you see before you." Jean Claude said they did have a bottle of wine he used for one of the dishes he made for Brinson and Cielito's wedding. Brinson said, "Well what are you waiting for? Get it, man!" Shy said she would get the glasses.

After the toast, Blossom stood and proclaimed, "Thank you all. I won't claim any credit as it was all the work of God. I am happy that all of you have come to recognize the power of prayer and seeking first the Kingdom of God because everything else is like watered down liquor. It smells ok, but once you taste it you realize it is not what you expected."

Claudette offered to help Blossom clear the table, but Blossom said she could handle everything. Claudette said, "I need to talk to you, Mama, and I don't need to leave until the bank opens." While they were washing dishes, Claudette asked Blossom if what she and Jean Claude did was enough to please God. Blossom replied, "If you and Jean Claude were honest and sincere, then I believe that was pleasing to Him. Honey, you can't fool God." Claudette said, "Based on what I learned from you, I know that last night when Wilford brought us together to openly confess his feelings and Jean Claude said what he said, I saw something in me that I didn't like and I wanted to change because I could lose my only chance to be with a man who understood my relationship with Jeru, and who truly loved me and put up with my immaturity and selfishness in expecting everyone to cater to me. I believe that is what you could see in me when you talked about the emptiness you saw in my eyes. I know in my heart I am no longer that person and thank you, Mama, I will love you forever."

Blossom took Claudette by the hands and looked in her eyes and said "I believe you are right. When I look in your eyes, I can see the depth of your soul and yes, you are no longer that person. What I see now is a happy, fulfilled, confident woman who knows she is loved." And she hugged her and said, "Daughter, I will love you forever." When they let go of each other Claudette was crying. Blossom handed her a napkin to dry her eyes, which Claudette said were tears of happiness and joy. "I plan, with your guidance, to run my marriage and this company with *Bible* principles in mind."

Jean Claude stuck his head in the kitchen and reminded Claudette they needed to go. He stepped all the way in the kitchen and hugged Blossom and thanked her again. He reached in the refrigerator and retrieved two covered dishes, and he and Claudette left for town. On the way they talked about their activity last night, and Claudette asked him if everything he expected happened because she didn't know what to do. He said, "Honey, you were magnificent. If we didn't have to go to town for meetings, I would have suggested we stay in bed all day." She started to fan herself at the thought of that.

When they arrived at the bank, he kissed her and said if his meeting ended before hers, he would wait in the car. Claudette insisted that he could come into the bank and find her. Claudette walked inside the bank and started toward Bix's office. The receptionist said Mr. Toilet and Finley were waiting in the conference room and there was coffee and tea available. Claudette thanked her and gave her instructions that if her husband came in looking for her, she should direct him to the conference room.

Bix and Streeter Finley were setting up easel boards around the room. Bix said, "Claudette, my love, come on in. We just have a few more displays to set up." Claudette wanted to look around. Bix noted, "I can't recall you looking so ravishing and happy and serious about business." Claudette replied, "Don't you think it is time for me to get serious about business if I am going to sit atop the corporation?" Bix said Streeter could get started. He placed a stack of folders on the table and took one off the top and said "I will do this by the charts, and you can follow along. The folders are for you to take to your office so that you can refer to them when you need to. First, I will talk about the state of the corporation. As you can see, the combined divisions are approaching three billion dollars, with the main contributor being Ohara Oil. Production is up 77% over last year. The next is Ohara Mining Division, the next highest contributor. All ten continue to increase production, thanks to Jer Mercy leadership. The casino earnings dropped due to the fraudulent takeover, but I predict that next quarter earnings will increase under your leadership. There was no way for me to determine the High Spade Ranch due to that same fraudulent ownership problem. However, with the agriculture initiative, I project a 200% increase in revenue in the third quarter."

Bix asked if Streeter could hold off until further reporting until after lunch. The receptionist whispered to Claudette that her husband had arrived, and Claudette said to show him in. Claudette took him by the arm and said, "Gentlemen, may I introduce my husband, Jean Claude Beauchamp." *(Jim, do you want Claudette to say Jean Claude is her husband before they are married? The press covered the last wedding because this is a powerful family.)* Bix with great surprise exclaimed, "What! When did that happen?" He rushed over to shake Jean Claude's hand and congratulate him. "I hope you are not too jealous, as I have loved this woman since she was a little girl." He reached out and hugged her and congratulated her.

The receptionist announced that lunch arrived. Bix thanked her and said, "I hope you all don't mind, but to save time I took the liberty to order lunch from the casino. Claudette looked at Jean Claude and said, "Gentlemen, we might as well tell you and swear you to secrecy. Professor I. B. Moore at the university has found that soybeans can be used for a food source for humans. My darling husband who is an extraordinary chef is working with him to perfect recipes/ In fact, he is embarking on a three-week trip to different regions to collect traditional recipes where he will create a book of recipes for dishes using soybeans." Streeter couldn't contain himself. He shouted, "If he can do that, then why you are putting soybeans on the same level as wheat and corn? This is revolutionary and I need to do a deep study of this."

Claudette reminded everyone not to speak a word of this outside that room. "It is going to be approximately six months before we harvest our first crop of five thousand acres." Finley thought she agreed to plant fifteen thousand acres. Claudette replied, "Because of the initial cost to plant, the head of our agriculture division advised me to plant ten thousand acres in wheat to recoup the cost of planting the soybeans, and that way we will be able to show a profit for our first year." Bix was clearly impressed with Claudette. "I never knew you had a head for business." She said, "Bix, you are looking at a new person. I am not that selfish, self-indulgent person I was two days ago." Finley finished his presentation.

Claudette asked, "What can you tell me about my farm equipment?" Bix said, "Before you leave today, I should have some word for you." Bix keyed his intercom and asked the receptionist to have someone come and remove the dishes. Finley began. "Ms. Ohara ..." Claudette interrupted him and said, "Mrs. Beauchamp please." He apologized. "Mrs. Beauchamp, the next thing is what is called an organization chart. In your stack of folders there is one where I have laid out how this should work. It is what all big corporations use, and it shows you all the divisions. Reading from left to right, It gives a suggested yearly budget. As I said you have a copy of the folder, so now I will move to your Corporate headquarters. Here is Scott McKenzie's rendering of what it should look like, pending your approval. This next page is the plat of ten acres."

Claudette said, "Hold on. I thought it was to be two stories." Streeter said the length of the building was ninety yards and the width seventy yards. McKenzie thought maybe the initial building should be one story, and as the corporation grows and the economic paradigm changes, there can be a second story as reflected on the last page rendering. "As an advisor, I thought his recommendations were sound and in keeping with other corporations of this size. It is state-of-the-art and projects a positive acceptable image." Claudette said they would study everything and get back to him in a day or so.

Bix offered to check on the equipment before they left. "Baxter, what can you tell me about that farm equipment I had you order?" Baxter responded that the factory representative in Cincinnati assured him it should arrive by the end of the week if there was no problem with the railroad. Bix thanked him and asked Claudette, "Is that fast enough for you?" She replied, "Yes, I believe Shy should have the farm workers in place by then." Finley said, "By the way, we will take care of the payroll until you have all of your pieces in place." Jean Claude said, "Thank you, gentlemen, we must be on our way."

Chapter 20
Business, Marriage, and Business

Out at the new barn, the contractors were on their last room to paint. When they noticed Cielito and Brinson, they asked if they approved of the job they were doing, offering to walk them through to see if they had any questions. Cielito asked if they could start with the offices. Brinson said "Darling, I like the placement of the large windows and the glass wall that separates our office." The contractor added, "There will be curtains on both sides in case you get tired of looking at each other." Cielito gave him a dirty look, but he cleared his throat and said he was just joking. In the offices, the phone installer was setting up the phones, and Brinson asked if these were the phones that had multiple lines. The workman said, "This type is the latest; it has five lines, and I just installed three of them yesterday in the new office next door." Cielito asked if they would have a separate line for the living area, and the response was that they would have a phone in the bedroom and kitchen.

The contractor stated that this job should be finished by the end of next week and they could inspect everything. "If everything meets your standards, this job will be completed with three weeks to spare." Brinson looked at Cielito and said, "I am satisfied so far, how about you?" She agreed. "I guess we need to go to town and buy furniture." The contractor said, "After we finish painting the last bedroom, all that is left is the power company and the boiler company to connect your system, and that should be finished by Thursday evening. Friday morning, we will do our inspection tour which will take about an hour, and you can have furniture delivered Friday."

Brinson and Cielito were getting ready to go to town but decided to ask Blossom to join them. On their way, they notice in the distance what appeared to be Wilford and Jeru sitting on a stool holding Connie. Brinson said he must be doing a portrait of his new family. He turned to Cielito and said, "Honey, why don't we talk with him about looking at some of his paintings for our house and offices." "Great idea, darling."

When they arrived, Blossom was in the kitchen preparing dinner. They walked in and hugged and kissed her. Brinson asked Blossom if she would like to go to town with them. She responded affirmatively, but said, "Don't you think it is a little late today? Besides, we have to see Jean Claude off." Cielito said Mama was right. By the time they did that, it would be too late.

Upstairs Claudette was packing for Jean Claude to leave on his trip. He returned to the bedroom and after taking a bath he walked up behind Claudette and put his arms around her and kissed her on the neck. She said, "Hey, none of that; you just had a bath, and you want to smell fresh on the train." He let her go and lay on the bed and reached out to her, and then he pulled her to the bed and looked her in the eyes. She asked him what was wrong. "I don't feel I should make this trip.

Leaving you just doesn't seem right, and I have this feeling of dread.

Jean Claude looked away momentarily. "Why don't I start right here with some of Mama's recipes and go to the library and see if I can find some cookbooks." He confessed to Claudette, "Darling, I don't know what I was thinking, but I made that decision before we decided to get married, even though I loved you and you said you cared for me but now it is different. In the bathroom I began to think of how miserable I would be away from you that long."

Claudette looked lovingly at Jean Claude before she turned away from him. He could hear her sniffles, and he asked her, "Did I say something wrong?" She said, "No, you said something right. I just heard something that made me know what it means when a man really loves a woman. What you are about to embark on meant a lot to what we are trying to do, but while it is important, it is not as important as taking you from me for three weeks. Jean Claude, I love you and thank you for loving me."

Jean Claude said, "Baby, we need to tell everyone that I will not be taking the train tonight and we can have the ceremony right away." They went to find Jeru and Wilford and find out when they want to have the ceremony. They went to Wilford's room and tapped on the door but there was no answer. He opened the door and realized the room was empty and thought they must be downstairs. They went downstairs and asked Blossom if she had seen them. She said she saw them earlier walking outside near the old barn. They spotted Wilford and Jeru walking toward the barn, with Jeru holding Connie in one arm and the other was around Wilford's waist. They looked like a couple in love. Wilford carried his easel and a canvas.

They were surprised to see Jean Claude and Claudette. Wilford said, "Shouldn't you be getting ready for your trip?" Jean replied, "I am not going. I don't want to be away from Claudette that long, which is why we were searching for you two to ask when you would like to have the marriage ceremony.

Jeru rushed over to Claudette, hugged her, and said, "Of course, my darling, we wouldn't think of having a ceremony without you two. Let's hurry to the house so we can tell everyone." Wilford needed to drop his stuff in the barn. Claudette asked to see his artwork, but Wilford said the paint was still wet.

Jeru couldn't contain herself. She proudly said, "It is a wedding picture of me and Connie." Wilford held the picture up for them to look at it. Jean Claude and Claudette stood in amazement with their mouth opened because the painting showed Jeru in a traditional and colorful Indigenous dress holding Connie in a cradle board. When they were able to speak, Jean Claude asked Wilford if he could paint them in their wedding attire and do another one showing the five of them. "That is, if it's all right with you both. I don't want to take anything from you two, but since we have been together for a long time, we know what Jeru and Claudette mean to each other, and Jeru, I don't want you to feel I have taken Claudette from you, although she is a changed person. All four of them hugged and walked to the house arm in arm.

Blossom said, "You all are just in time for dinner so we can get Jean Claude to the station." Claudette hugged Blossom and said "Don't worry about that Mama. We will tell you about it at dinner. Can I help you with something?" Jeru added,

"Mama, I would help you, but it is time for a diaper change. Blossom said, "It's okay, you all go and wash up and tell the honeymooners dinner is ready and tell Shy and JB. Claudette said she need to run upstairs."

When she came downstairs. she picked up the phone and asked Blossom to listen in. She called Shy's number in her office, and Shy answered "Ohara Agriculture, Ms. Blake, how may I help you?" Claudette said, "Yes, Ma'am, I wanted Mama to hear you. You sure did sound business-like; I love you, sister." Shy laughed. "Claudette, I will get you!" Blossom had tears of pride and joy in her eyes. Claudette said they would give her more tears of joy at dinner.

Blossom brought in the last of two bowls of chicken and dumplings and took her seat. After all the rituals were completed and the Amens said, Jean Claude said, "Mama, that sure smells good and you have given me another dish for the soybean. I can make the dumplings from soy flour. I got to have all your recipes. You are going to save my marriage if you do that." Blossom asked what he was talking about. He said, "Sorry, Mama, and everyone I am not leaving tonight because, while collecting recipes is important to the venture, it is not as important as my wife." He looked at Claudette and proclaimed, "Spending three weeks away from her is not right. I realized I love her too much for that. I think Wilford and Jeru might have something to say."

Wilford stood and looked at Jeru and spoke. "Darling, please stand. Since Jean Claude is not going on this trip, I feel that we should make our marriage legal as early as tomorrow. What do you all think and how soon do you think we should hold the joint reception ceremony?" Cielito, Brinson, JB, and Shy stood and applauded. Wilford asked Blossom if she thought it was the wise thing to do. She said "Son, whatever you all decide is the wise thing to do. I feel the rest of the family owes you all a wedding ceremony, so tell them your reasons for wanting to make it legal right away and you all come to an agreement." JB signed, "Shy can speak for me. I need to bathe and get some sleep." Wilford said, "I don't need to go into our reason, as it should be obvious. We feel that tomorrow we would go to the cathedral and ask the priest to marry us, and whatever you all want to do for us we will be happy with your timetable."

Cielito and Brinson said, "We think everyone should check your calendars because, remember, we still have the memorial, and the trials will be starting soon. We should be moving into our place this Friday. Claudette has a host of things she needs to get done for the corporation and Shy has a full load with the planting and harvesting, and Claudette, I don't know if you mentioned it to Jeru and Wilford about taking charge of all things dealing with the casino. "

Claudette responded, "No, I have not, but since you brought it up, now is a good time to ask them. Jeru, Wilford, what do you think of that?" Wilford said, "Allow us to think on it and we will get back to you." Brinson cautioned, "It's not that we don't want to take time from our schedules, but this came up all of sudden. Maybe the four of you can do as Wilford said and we can do a ceremony next Saturday or Sunday. Mama can say some words like she did for us, which will give us a week to get presents." All agreed. Jeru asked Jean Claude and Claudette if they preferred Saturday or Sunday afternoon.

Jean Claude asked Mama Blossom what she thought. Blossom responded, "Don't let what I am about say influence you. My thought is wherever we are in our lives, we should make it as simple as possible. All four of you are surrounded by friends and loved ones, and after you have legalized your marriage, as I have said before, the rest is just watered down liquor. I Can bake a cake and fix a special dinner like I did for Shy and JB. That was almost two years ago, and they were just as happy and still are. You asked me and that's my say. All of you are on the verge of doing something that is going to benefit all mankind and I hope you are doing it, not for fame, but when you stand before your Maker. He will have nothing to say but, "Well done, my faithful and loyal servant." They all stood and applauded.

Blossom said "Please don't do that. I was only saying what the sprit put in my mind and heart. When I first realized what that old woman back in Georgia did to me, I held hatred for her, but look what God has done! He brought all of you to me and I love you and am so proud to see what you all have done and are about to do. There is not a day or night that passes without me thanking God for all of you."

Wilford said they should take Mama's advice. "I say Saturday afternoon. I have not talked it over with my wife, but I am willing to take the job if my wife agrees. Jeru said, "I will do whatever my husband wants to do." Claudette said "Now that is settled. Guys, I need you to begin teaching us ladies how to drive, including Mama." Blossom said she was too old, but Jean Claude said "Nonsense, Mama, we want you to have the freedom to go when and where you want to." They all agreed. Jeru suggested they have family prayers now.

That night, Blossom had a visit from Mama G, who told her, "Granddaughter, we are so proud of you and the change in those children's lives. In the morning you are going to have visitors at your front door, and just because they are different do not refuse them. They are mainly for Cielito and Claudette, so, be prepared to accept them as part of the family. Also, prepare yourself for a run for your money. You are going to have a hard time keeping up with those triplets. They will be walking by tomorrow. Sleep well, Granddaughter."

The next morning Blossom was up early preparing breakfast. Jeru was up early to do laundry, but before she went to the kitchen, she stopped at Shy and JB's bedroom. She knocked on the door and didn't hear an answer, so, she pushed the door to find nobody there. She moved to the office to find Shy at her desk working. She stuck her head inside and said, "Little sister, you need to get JB to put a bell on your bedroom door." Shyanne said she was trying to get some work done before she woke the babies for breakfast."

Jeru told her that she would get some laundry washed before breakfast while Connie was asleep. "Honey, I wish I had a camera to catch Wilford sleeping with Connie in his arms. I never knew it would be like this, I am so happy. I'll take your laundry too." Shy said, "Thank you, I hope you know how much I appreciate and love you, little sister."

In the kitchen Blossom was finishing breakfast and Jeru was loading the washer. Blossom heard a noise that sounded like it came from the front door, and she thought about her dream last night. When she opened the door, she called out to Jeru to come quickly. Jeru hurried to the front. What they saw were two pups and a mama wolf out in the yard with three other pups there, too. Jeru stooped to pick up one, but Blossom said, "Wait, let's see what mama wolf will do." Jeru picked up one and the mama just stood watching. Blossom picked up the other one and the wolf turned and walked away with the other three.

Blossom said, "Well, I'll be! It was like she wanted us to pick them up." Blossom thought that was what Mama G was talking about. Claudette walked into the dining room and could see Jeru and Blossom at the door. She walked to the door as Blossom and Jeru turned with the two pups that were making noise like they were crying. Claudette reached for the one Jeru was holding, and it tried to lick Claudette. She asked for the other one, which stopped crying and licked Claudette. Blossom was surprised and told Claudette to take them in the kitchen and warm them some milk.

Claudette said she needed to wash her hands and left for the bathroom. The pups stopped with the milk and followed her. When Jean Claude came down for breakfast, he noticed Claudette with the two pups and asked where they came from. "Mama said a mother wolf left them on the porch." He said, "No, wild animals don't do that." Jeru confirmed that when they picked them up, the wolf turned with the other three and left like she wanted them to stay here. Claudette added that they seem to follow her everywhere she goes. She had to leave after breakfast for a meeting, so, Blossom said that on the back porch was a wooden crate. She would place two towels in there and that should hold them. Jean Claude brought the crate in, and Blossom placed two towels in and told Claudette to bring the pups over and put them in the crate.

As soon as Claudette did that and walked away, both pups began to howl, but stopped when she walked back to the crate. Blossom asked the time of Claudette's meeting. She said, "Ten or ten-thirty but Jean Claude has to go to the university after he drops me off." At that moment, the phone rang, and Jean Claude answered. "It's for you, darling. It was Streeter Finley asking to set their meeting back to 1:00 p.m. so he could finish her organization chart. Jean Claude would be finished at the University by 12:00 p.m., so she asked Streeter if they could make their meeting for 1:30 p.m. He said yes.

She turned to Blossom for help with the pups. Blossom said, "I think I know what is going on. When everyone leaves, I am going to try something." Blossom asked Cielito if they could take Jeru and Wilford with them to show them the furniture. Wilford thought the four of the would go to the Cathedral this morning so he could meet with the priest to ask if he could perform their marriage at four o'clock. Everyone agreed.

After everyone was gone, Blossom asked Claudette to get her coat and bring the pups to the kitchen. Blossom mixed an egg with a small amount of sausage meat and told Claudette to cut a hole in the nipple and pour the mixture into a baby bottle, after which she began to put the bottle to one pup's mouth. Blossom said the mother wolf would chew a piece of meat regurgitate it this was the way their mother would feed them, and this is the way Claudette would have to feed them. That is the way she would have to feed the pups for the next week. Blossom said to get the pups and follow her. After they passed the barn, the pups stopped and began to urinate and have a bowel movement. Blossom put arms around Claudette and said, "Honey, I want you to see something and do not be afraid."

They approached the area where the Ohara brothers were buried, and the pups became excited and went to the area and laid on the ground. Blossom said they were acting like when Claudette picked them up and they tried to lick. They were trying to express love the only way they knew how. Claudette said, "You mean they know who is buried there? How did you know they would act like that, Mama. I'm afraid." Blossom asked, "Are you afraid of your brothers?" Blossom said she didn't know it last night, but in her dream, her grandmother told her that a stranger would leave two visitors at her door, and she should not turn them away but take them in and treat them like family. "I just put two and two together. You can't mention this to anyone, so, erase this from your mind and take care of your business. And when you return, ask everyone to hold the pups and see how the pups react to them. Make sure Cielito is last and when you notice how they act toward her, do not act surprised.

Claudette composed herself after she was a little shaken. "Mama, I think I am beginning to understand that these pups are my brothers." Blossom said they might be the spirits of her brothers. "We as humans can only understand things that are three dimensional, but our brains are not equipped to understand the spirit realm. For example, we know there is the wind, but can we see it? We know it is the wind because we see the results. As I said, clear this from your mind because you have work to do, and the first trial starts in a few days." As they walked back to the house, Claudette noticed the pups stopped to urinate, which Blossom acknowledged was marking their territory.

When they arrived, Jean Claude was just returning from the University. Claudette went to him and kissed him and said he was back early. He said the professor was called to an emergency faculty meeting. He asked what she had been up to, and she said they went for a walk and Mama explained some things about the pups that she didn't know. She went upstairs to change, and he offered to follow. She said, "No, you rascal, you wait right here. When she left the room, the pups began to act up. Jean Claude picked up one who still howled until Claudette returned. He thought that was odd behavior.

Jean Claude said, "Darling, I have to show you something and I don't want you to get upset." Claudette said if it was about the trial, then she knew about that. He said, "Remember how I told you I was dreading going on the trip? Look at the headlines in the paper." She took the paper and screamed and began crying, hugging, and kissing him. Blossom and Shy came running. Blossom read the headlines and hugged both of them and repeated over and over, "Praise God." Shy read it too. "Train from Santa Fe bound for Chicago derailed … fifteen dead, thirty-five seriously injured." Shy did just like Blossom, repeating, "Praise God."

Cielito and Brinson had seen the headline and rushed home to tell everyone. Blossom said, "I'm glad you're back because it's time we as a family prayed and thanked God for sparring our loved one." JB arrived home for lunch and noticed that everyone had heard the news. They all stood and held hands and hugged and silently prayed. Claudette held onto Jean Claude and would not let go. The phone ranged again and this time Shy answered as she was on the way to the kitchen to fix JB a sandwich for lunch. It was for Claudette. It was Streeter Finley informing her that he had remembered that her husband was to take a trip the day before. Claudette cut him off and said that Jean

Claude had decided not to take the trip, so he was not on the train. Streeter said, "If you want to cancel our meeting and do it tomorrow, I understand." She said, "Thank you, Streeter, but I think I need to stay busy so let's go with our plan to meet at one-thirty. I will see you shortly."

Brinson told everyone that they had talked to Bax and Cielito does not have to testify at this trial. Nimrod is charged with conspiracy, fraud, and numerous other things. The murder trial starts next Friday. Bax said to tell JB, Cielito, Mama, Al, and Juan that he will take depositions from them this week. Wilford told Claudette that the priest could perform their marriage at four o'clock. Claudette asked Jean Claude to pick up the crate and they would go. He asked, "Darling, are you planning to take them with us?" She said, "Yes, I learned today that they are special to me." She winked at Blossom and said, "Love you, Mama."

The rest of the household went about their business. Wilford and Jeru went upstairs, and he took Connie and kissed her on the forehead. Jeru asked, "Honey do you love her?" Wilford replied, "Just as much as the ones we are going to have." She hugged and kissed him and said she had no idea it was going to be like this. Wilford said Connie was asleep, so, they lay across the bed. Jeru said, "Babe, I been thinking I want our children to be raised near Mama. I was thinking about the house on the casino property. Why don't we demolish it like Claudette said and build a luxury hotel and have all kinds of frills that will bring tourists to town? I have the money, and we can buy some property up the street from here and the four of us can live there. Let's talk it over with Claudette and Jean Claude after the marriage."

In town, Streeter showed Claudette the organization chart. "I filled in suggested names to head the different divisions we had all agreed to establish. Jer Mercy would be Senior Vice President of the Mine Division and Shyanne Blake the SVP of Agriculture. Now as you will notice, I add Jeru Twotrees to the Entertainment Division." Claudette asked when they established an entertainment division. Streeter said, "That's the casino and Bix and I have some things we need to talk over with you that will bring tourism to downtown Santa Fe."

Claudette said there would be a name change. "Jeru is going to be Mrs. Dunford by five o'clock today and I would think she will want her and husband to be joint heads of casino operations." He said that was fine. Streeter continued. "We discussed adding a luxury hotel on the property, it's a great idea to have Scott McKenzie change the façade to look like *Monte Carlo*, and on the inside, we'll add more roulette wheels and a section for slot machines." Claudette interrupted. "I have heard those things are run by gangsters." Streeter said that was true if you get them from Chicago. "We looked into the manufacturer out of San Francisco and found they have no connections with gangsters." Lastly, I suggest my son head your personal division unless you have someone else in mind. It is what I call a 'non-revenue' division."

Claudette said she needed to stop for now, as she had another important meeting to attend. Finley asked what was in the crate, and Claudette said, "Something very important to me." She and Jean Claude left to meet Jeru and Wilford. They were surprised to see the whole family there waiting.

After the ceremony, Wilford asked the priest how old the baby needed to be to get baptized. The priest asked the age of the child, and Wilford said one month. The priest said he would baptize the baby now. Wilford said they adopted Connie after her mother died in childbirth. Her last name would be "Dunford." After the wedding and baptism, Wilford suggested they ride home with Claudette and Jean Claude. Blossom said to either let Cielito take Connie with them or take the pups. "Connie doesn't need to be around the pups until we have them checked." Jeru and Wilford agreed that Connie should ride with Cielito and Brinson. As they drove home, Jeru and Wilford told Claudette and Jean Claude about their idea about the Casino and the house. Claudette said she had just had a meeting with Streeter, who suggested the same thing. Jeru and Wilford were just thinking of ways to increase revenue if they were going to be in charge.

 Jeru then spoke of buying land across the street from Blossom's and building a house that the four of them could live in and raise children near Mama Blossom, just like Cielito and Brinson did. Claudette and Jean Claude broke into simultaneous laughter, saying, "We are reading each other's mind. Jean Claude and I were discussing that on the way to the Cathedral. Jean Claude said, "I told Claudette that I agreed with everything Streeter said. My darling wife's response was that if we build the hotel, we would have to get rid of the house and have nowhere to live." Claudette said they would discuss it with the family after dinner.

 The whole family arrived at home the same time and there was a lot of hugging and kissing and congratulations. Everyone went inside while Claudette and Jean Claude let the pups out of the crate. They urinated and ran around toward the rear of the house. Claudette guessed where they were going and placed them back inside the crate.

In the house, the rest of the family commented on the smell and inquired what was cooking. Blossom had cooked a roast before she left for town. "All I have to do is open some of my canned vegetables and dinner is ready." After diaper changes the triplets surprised everyone by running away from Shy, laughing as she chased them to Blossom in the kitchen. She grabbed them and Shy walked them to the dining room and placed them in the highchairs.

Claudette asked Blossom if she should feed the pups. Blossom said to wait until after dinner. Claudette told her how they were running outside and looked like they were heading up to where they were this morning.

After dinner Wilford told Blossom about their plans. Blossom said she was pleased that they thought so much of her, JB and Shy. She thought most of that land belonged to the Toilets. Jean Claude said that he and Wilford would talk to Bix tomorrow. Claudette said Bix might be in court. "Remember the trial for Nimrod is tomorrow. I will call him and find out if he has time to talk after dinner, and if he can, we can do it from Shy's office if it is okay with her. Shy said ok. Wilford asked her why they would use Shy's office, and Claudette said she has four phones and all four of them could be on the same line.

Claudette dialed Bix's home number, and he responded, "Claudette, my true love, what can I do for you?" She said, "We want to talk to you about a stretch of land you own across from Blossom." He confirmed it was a hundred and thirty acres. She signaled for Jean Claude and Wilford to speak up. Wilford said, "Mr. Toilet, we want to buy it.: Jean Claude didn't say anything because he didn't like Bix referring to his wife as his "own true love."

Bix responded, "I'd be happy to sell it to you. How does two dollars and fifty cent an acre sound? Wilford said it sounded good and Jean Claude shook his head in silent agreement. Bix said it would be a couple of days to get the papers done, and he would be in court tomorrow.

Jeru and Wilford were happy. He held Connie in one arm and picked Jeru up with the other arm and was spinning her around and kissing her and Connie. Claudette was trying to talk to Jean Claude, who hung the phone up and went upstairs with Claudette following. In the room he turned to her and asked why Bix called her his "own true love." She said "Darling, you are jealous, but you continue to make me happy."

He snapped, "You are damn right! How would you feel if a woman said that to me?" She said, "I would be jealous but that would only prove how much I love you and realize you must be something if some another woman said you were her own true love. Honey, Bix has said that since I was a little girl you are the only man for me. I feel you owe Wilford and Jeru an apology for the way you acted. If you truly love me you would trust me. Mistrust will ruin a marriage and we just legalized our union. Remember how men reacted to me and Jeru in France and especially at *Monte Carlo*?" He admitted he was jealous then, but she was not his wife. She said it was okay to be jealous but not angry. He said, "You are right, darling. I will apologize to Wilford and Jeru, and I will apologize to Bix."

Chapter 21
Nimrod's Day in Court and Projects are Hatched

"Friday morning, ten a.m. November 21, 1920, The bailiff announced all rise, the Honorable Mason Stoddard Presiding Judge Superior Court of New Mexico. All persons having business with this court are hereby recognized." The Judge asked the bailiff to announce the first case on the docket. The bailiff stated, "The State versus Nimrod Bloom, charged with conspiracy to commit murder, conspiracy to commit fraud, forgery, and theft by trespassing."

The Judge ask Nimrod to stand, and he asked if he understood the charges. Nimrod replied, "No." Stoddard asked if he was represented by council, and he responded, "Yes." The Judge said, "Mr. Bloom, you will address me as 'Your Honor.' Who is your attorney?" "Your Honor, I am council for the defense, J. Douglas Cess of the firm of *Cess Poole and Drane* of Silver City, New Mexico. Stoddard asked the attorneys and the accused to approach the bench. He asked Cess if he made his client aware of the charges, and Cess said, "I did, Your Honor." Stoddard asked Nimrod to state what charges he did not understand. Nimrod put on his act. "Your Honor, I am just a poor, uneducated farmer."

Kirkland Flowers, the Lead Prosecutor, interjected, "Your Honor, If I may, I have records to show that Mr. Bloom is neither poor nor a farmer." The Judge was visibly annoyed, and giving Cess a stern look, he said, "Mr. Cess, get out of my court and don't come back until you have made your client understand the charges. And your client is remanded to the custody of the County Sheriff until I set bail. In addition, I am charging the two of you one hundred and fifty dollars for contempt." As the bailiff was removing Nimrod, he looked at the prosecution table and grinned. Mr. Flowers asked Bax and the rest of the team if they saw that. "He knew what he was doing; it's an old trick, the accused must understand the charges before we can proceed. I need to get back to my office. I received a letter from the defense team for the murderers, and I will let you know what they are asking. They claim they plan to call twenty witnesses. We can start tomorrow deposing them. I plan to charge all of them with perjury.

Bix hurried back to his office and called his real estate agent, instructing him to draw up a contract for the one-hundred-and-thirty-acre plot on the east side of Buckhorn Road. "I will tell you what name to put on the contract later." He asked his secretary to call Claudette at the Ohara Brothers building. Two minutes later, she said, "Ms. Beauchamp on the line, Sir." He picked up the phone and, as usual, said, "Claudette, my own true love." She said, "Bix, you caused a bit of a problem last night by saying that. Jean Claude was on the line and became angry." Bix said he would apologize. "Anyway, I called to ask how you want to show the name on the deed and contract." She said,

"Wilford Dunford and Jean Claude Beauchamp." "Ok my love, sorry, Ms. Beauchamp, I will have this ready tomorrow." Claudette said she thought he would be in court all day and tomorrow, but Bix informed her, "You know Nimrod pulled a trick and the Judge locked him up and threw his lawyer out of court, so we have to wait until the Judge sets another date.

Meanwhile, Jeru and Wilford were at the Casino with Scott McKenzie and Streeter Finley discussing their plans for the Casino and luxury hotel. Scott said he would have a rendering in a week. Wilford said, "I am a painter. I will sketch something, and you can go from there." Streeter said he and Bix would get the necessary permits for approval from the City County and the State. Wilford ask Streeter "to Find out who owned the land in a twelve-block radius. Streeter asked why and Wilford replied that he would know the reason when he did his sketch. On the way out, Jeru whispered, "Honey, you are so smart. We are going to have smart children." He said they would get it from their beautiful mother. Did I ever tell you how beautiful you are? The first time I saw you it was like looking at a beautiful delicate flower. She said stop it you going to make me cry. He said go ahead you are even beautiful when you are crying.

As they were walking to Claudette's office, they saw a car dealership, and Jeru suggested they go there to buy a car. They stopped at *Bob Smith Ford Cars.* Wilford made known that he wanted to buy a car and drive it home that day. The salesperson offered a new *Ford Model T* for nine hundred dollars, but Wilford offered eight hundred dollars with a full tank of gas. The salesman responded, "Eight hundred and fifty and I will fill it up with gas. Mr. Dunford, let's go to my desk and fill out the paperwork." It required about an hour for the paperwork and the new auto to be owner ready. As they drove away, Jeru said, "Darling, this is the first thing we bought as married people. I love you Wilford. He said they should go by the office and let Claudette know they have a car and are heading home. She was thrilled and hugged them both she told them that soon they would be part owners in one hundred acres of land. They were so happy they danced around in circles. She announced, I have to get back inside to Sean and Jean. I hear them." Jeru asked what in the world Claudette was talking about, and she said it was the pups that she named "Sean" and "Jean." Jeru said in a relived voice, "I was about to ask if you had lost your mind." Claudette said not yet.

They left Claudette and headed home. When they turned on Buckhorn, Wilford wondered where their land started and ended. When they pulled into the yard JB was right behind them. He wrote, "Is that your car?" Jeru smiled and said, "Yes." He congratulated them. The three of them went inside where Blossom was in the kitchen. They all kissed her, and JB went to Shy's office where her girls were working while the triplets were in their playpen. When they saw him, they said, "Dada." JB looked surprised and signed to Shy, "They spoke!" She signed back that that was not all they could do.

He ran to the kitchen all excited and signed to Blossom, "Mama, they talked." He hugged her and ran back to the office where now he heard noises like someone beating on the wall. Shy said, "Don't worry, honey, they are making another door to enter the office from the kitchen instead of our bedroom but come let me show you this." She asked Baby Blossom, "Who am I?" She said, "Mama." JB was beside himself. Shy suggested they have lunch so he could get to the field, and she could get back to work. "Juan will assist you today; Al is moving equipment from the siding to the ranch." She turned to the girls still working and said lunch was ready.

At the dinner table, JB, Blossom, and Shy were conversing in sign language, discussing all the news from town, plus Wilford and Jeru getting a new car. Shy's employees asked how they could learn sign language. Shy said they had a lot of work to do, but maybe Mama could teach them. JB signed, "Where are Brinson and Cielito?" Blossom said they were at the new barn moving in and might stop in for lunch. JB signed, "I am sure going to miss them at mealtimes." Brinson and Cielito had just walked in, and Brinson signed, "JB, Little brother, we are only a hundred yards away and we expect to see you all soon for dinner with us. By the way why don't you all come over later today and see how everything looks?" Cielito added they would be back this evening for dinner.

At Claudette's office, Jean Claude showed up and announced he was finished for the day and wanted to take her to lunch. She chose the Casino. "Get the crate, and my knight in shining armor, save me from the starvation dragon!" He bowed and said, "Me lady, your carriage awaits." Inside the restaurant Bix was having lunch with a group of men from the town council. He noticed Claudette and Jean Claude and beckoned for them to come over to meet the council members, and he divulged to her that the contract for the land should be ready around three o'clock and the surveyor was on his way to mark the boundaries. She thanked Bix, as Jean Claude whispered in his ear, "I apologize for my attitude last night."

After lunch they returned to the office, and Jean Claude asked what was upstairs. Claudette said, "That was my brother, Jean Phillipe's office." He asked if she minded if he used the office to work on his book of recipes, and she responded, "I am sure Jean Phillipe is far removed from caring." An hour later Scott McKenzie showed up with one of his draftsmen and blueprints of a revised rendering of the Ohara Corporate headquarters building and campus. Claudette liked the building and called out to Jean Claude to come and look at the revised rendering. He said, "Darling, I am pleased if you are." She told McKenzie, "I guess you are getting tired, but we have several more projects." He said, "That is what I am in business for. I welcome all the work you can give me." She thanked him and he left.

Claudette went upstairs and the pups were doing their best to follow her. Jean Claude was busy writing. She interrupted with a sultry voice and said, "Hey, you, how would you like to pick me up? I am available for the right price and can show you a good time." He asked the cost, and she replied, "One deep, long kiss and some hugging and squeezing. How about right now?" She said playfully, "Not in front of Sean and Jean. They're trying to come up the steps. Now close that book and take me home; it's after three." He said, "Here are the keys. It's time for you to learn to drive." They started downstairs and she picked up the pups to go out so they could pee. When they finished, she picked them up and put them in their crate.

Jean Claude opened the car door for her, and she slid into the driver's side and asked, "What next?"
He explained all about the clutch and the gear post position, and he let her go through the motion. He

explained the safety, hand, and arm signals. "Now let's go." Like most learners she had a problem getting used to the clutch. He assured her that she was doing okay. She was nervous, but as they left town and got on the highway she began to calm down and turned to him. He said she must keep her eyes on the road and get used to talking without taking her eyes off the road. She continued to ask him if she was doing good, and he assured her she was doing good for a first-time driver.

The closer they got to the house, the more excited she became, and when she pulled up in the yard, she almost had an accident. Jean Claude had to grab the wheel to keep the car from hitting the house. He calmly told her to stop the car and explained about stopping. She apologized and just wanted to hug and kiss him. She jumped out of the car and ran in the house. "Mama, I drove the car home! I need to tell Shy and Cielito." Blossom said, "Calm down, honey, you might hurt yourself. Where are the pups?" Claudette was so excited that she left them in the car. Just then Jean Claude came in with the pups.

At dinnertime the family began to gather. Normally, Shy was last to enter with the babies, but this evening Jeru and Wilford were last. Wilford entered carrying an easel and several large pieces of paper. He and Jeru were dressed up, and Claudette asked why they were all dressed up. Jeru said, "We just had a festive attitude, but we have something to show everyone." After dinner Wilford stood and set up his easel and placed the first piece of paper. "I must thank JB who taught me to sketch. Claudette, Jean Claude we need your feeling on this." Speaking to Blossom and family, he said, "As you know, we now own the land across Buckhorn -- one hundred and thirty acres. My beautiful wife,

Jeru, and I discussed it and we have come to love Blossom and her family, so, we want to be near you all and want our children to get to know and love all of you as we do. This sketch is my version of what the house may look like."

Jean Claude stood and asked Claudette to stand with him. He said, "Family, we feel the same as Wilford and Jeru." Wilford continued. "Claudette The next piece shows some things we came up with since you asked us to head the Casino operations." He revealed the next sheet of paper, and everyone was surprised and began asking questions. He said, "Jeru and I felt like if our name was going to be associated with the Casino, it had to be something that would produce growth for a long time to come. So, we came up with this name: *Ohara's Monte Carlo at Santa Fe*. And the luxury hotel would rival any one in France. We decided to name the hotel *Ohara's Luxury Hotel* and have things that people would flock to and bring their children. In addition, all the stores next to the hotel and Casino would be high end stores such as *Channel, Tiffany,* and *Cartier*. Right next to us is Oklahoma, where oil has produced several millionaires who need some place to spend all that money and flaunt their affluence. This project will attract people from as far away as New York and Europe as well."

Wilford looked around to find unanimous approval for all his ideas. "The next one is the inside of the Casino. We thought the main gambling room would be expanded to include more roulette tables and all kinds of card games and a whole wall of slot machines and more female dealers. Of course, it all depends on your approval, Claudette." She said, "Wilford, you have said it all, so go full speed ahead. And one more thing, everyone-- I drove home today!" Everyone stood and applauded.

After dinner they had a *Bible* study where Blossom talked about the three slaves in Matthew 24:14-30 and ended by saying, "Children, just like the three slaves, the Lord has blessed all of you with gifts and you should learn to do as the slave that doubled his master's money. Gifts and blessings can be wisdom and empathy and compassion. Be humble in all you do, which does not mean thinking less of yourself, but thinking of yourself less. And lastly, remember, 'For those who are given plenty, Plenty is expected from them.' I love all of you and am so proud of you. Good night and don't forget to pray."

Cielito and Brinson walked to their house over the new barn and discussed what Blossom talked about, and he promised to teach her how to drive starting tomorrow. She smiled and said, "Honey, I can drive. I have a car at the school." He responded, "I guess that takes care of that." Upstairs Wilford asked Jeru if she was ready to learn to drive, but she asked him to wait until Connie was a little older. He agreed.

The next morning after breakfast, Claudette was at the dining room table going through her folders and found the real estate contract. She called out to Wilford that she had something for him to sign. He looked at the paper and realized it was for the land. He got excited and called Jeru to hurry to the dining room. When she arrived, he grabbed her and kissed her and said, "We are landowners!" Now she was excited. There came a knock at the front door it was the surveyor he asked for Mr. Dunford and Beauchamp. Wilford identified himself. The surveyor handed Wilford the map and boundaries of the land, which is staked off for the owners to see. Wilford asked the surveyor if he could show him the boundaries. The surveyor agreed.

Two hours later he came back with the map. Jeru asked him how it looked he said he would tell her after he came back from the barn. Sometime later Wilford returned to the house and called Jeru to the dining room. He had laid out his sketches. "Honey, you are not going to believe this! You see where I sketched the house? It's directly across the street from here and there is a big pond near the end of our property."

Jeru went to get Blossom and Shy to share the sketches. Shy was on the phone with Al, who was telling her that the equipment was on site, and they would spend the rest of the day harrowing and disking. He went on to say, "I figure it is going to take a week to get that done, and by the way, the Consolidated people have delivered a five-hundred-gallon tank, and the trucks are here filling the tanks." Shy said to make sure they left the bill for her to pay. Al replied he would drop it off later. She instructed the office workers to watch the babies while she joined Jeru in the dining room. Jeru showed her everything about the land and the house that would be directly across the street. Shy hugged her and told her how happy she was for her and Wilford.

Things were going well, and it would not be long before they break ground. That evening when everyone arrived home, Wilford asked if they wanted to see the layout of the land and his sketches. Claudette begged off saying she needed to meet with Shy and Al but said that whatever Jean Claude thought would be ok with her. She went to Shy's office. "Hey, little sister, I see you are still hard at work." Shy replied, "Sister, when you love what you are doing it ain't work." Claudette went to the playpen and kissed the babies, as the pups tried to squeeze through the bars to get in with the babies. Claudette picked the pups up and said, "Not before you get your shots tomorrow."

Shy and Al gave her the latest news about the equipment and fuel tanks and how soon they would plant the cover crop. "It will be up by January, and we will plow it under and be ready to plant the spring wheat and soybeans." She said Jean Claude was making great progress on his recipe book. "I spoke with Scott McKenzie today and gave him permission to hire as many contractors as he could find to work on the headquarters building, and to do the same for the Casino project. I will talk to Wilford tonight about doing a painting of the project so we can create a magazine advertising the land on the strip and cover all the surrounding states and New York."

She added that she didn't know why she's been so tired lately. Shy laughed and asked Al to cover his ears, and she said, "I do, it's from making love all night." Claudette immediately blushed and said, "Why sister, be ashamed." Shy gave out an audible laugh and said, "I know how it is and there is the evidence in the playpen." Claudette stood up and embraced Shy. "Let me get out of here. I love you. "

Chapter 22
Prosperity and First Murder Trial

"Time is a brisk wind, for each hour it brings something new." Paracelsus

This is such a profound statement, especially when applied to the Blake household these days. Everything was moving so fast! The triplets are walking and talking, Cielito and Brinson live in their new barn house and their hospital is being built, Cielito and Jeru are pregnant, and little Connie is a toddler. And so are the wolf pups!

Scott McKinzie hired contractors and artisans from all over the Southwest to complete all of the projects assigned by Claudette and Wilford, which included their home. Scott became quite wealthy, to say the least. The Ohara Corporate headquarters building was completed and quickly became the talk of the town. Claudette moved into the space and began hiring to fill the jobs openings. The Mayor and Town Council were ecstatic over the number of jobs created by Ohara Inc. Of course, JB got the contract to clean and maintain the building.

Shy's project was moving smoothly. Thanks to Al, all fifteen thousand acres were planted, and crops were growing. A big luncheon would soon take place, at which Jean Claude's soybean recipes and recipe book would be featured. To speed things up Shy and Claudette decided to purchase soybeans from the university for the luncheon. That luncheon was so successful that the leaders of several food-producing companies who were impressed by Shy's presentation sought contracts with *Ohara Agriculture Divisions* to buy the first soybean crop.

At the same time, Brinson launched his security company and received a lucrative contract from Ohara Inc. to provide security for the headquarters and the Monte Carlo Casino and the Luxury Hotel. Several large companies who specialized in securing and selling luxury items purchased land to build boutiques on the Monte Carlo strip. Wilford was overwhelmed and the local officials anticipated a huge flow of traffic bringing big spenders with deep pockets to the new downtown Santa Fe.

All this good news was happening while the trial of Hunt Dalton and Duce Dawson was underway. The big trial of Nimrod would follow, but these two criminals were first. The town was full of newspaper reporters because anything revolving around the Ohara's was big news now. The trial was big news in the media, but the Oharas were changing the face of Santa Fe, and that was big news too.

After the lawyers for Hunt Dalton and Duce Dawson discovered that the prosecution had three eyewitnesses to the killing of the Ohara brothers, and five witnesses for the attempted murder of Cielito, they urged their clients to plead guilty and throw themselves on the mercy of the court. Hunt and Duce did that and were sentenced to be put to death by hanging. Mexican Bob came out better than those two, as he was sentenced to life without parole for attempted murder. Nimrod had yet to have his "day in court," but based on what happened to Hunt and Duce and Mexican Bob, things didn't look good for Nimrod Bloom.

The newspaper reporter was able to get a rendering of the whole Monte Carlo project, which was published in the local newspaper and thru out the surrounding states. As the remodeling of the casino was going on, Nimrod had his lawyer to ask for a court order to halt construction because he claimed to be the owner. The Magistrate's Court Clerk was a friend of the Toilet brothers, and he called them to tell them what was happening. He said he would hold up completing the paperwork for the request until Bax could look at it.

Bax dropped everything and hurried over to the courthouse to talk to the clerk and ask which judge would handle the request for the TRO (Temporary Restraining Order). It would be Judge Chamberlin. Bax said, "Go ahead and send it to the Judge and I will get Howell to put it on the civil court docket as soon as possible." Bloom will have to show probable cause, but we are not going to halt construction because his claim is fraudulent. Bax called Claudette and made her aware of the situation and advised her not to worry. There would be no halt to construction. She thanked him and thought, "Not Nimrod again!" She looked at the pups who were now two months old, and said, "Well, brothers, looks like we have another small problem on our hands." They barked as if they understood what she said.

Judge Chamberlin called Bax and said I am emptying my calendar and setting the hearing for two days from now. Bax thanked him and informed Bix to be ready in two days. Two days later the hearing in Santa Fe Magistrate Court was called to order. Judge Chamberlin asked Nimrod's attorney if he had evidence to show probable cause for the TRO against Ohara Inc. The attorney answered, "Yes, your Honor." The Judge asked, "Where is your client?" The lawyer responded that he was locked up. Judge Chamberlin glared at the lawyer and asked, "How long have you been practicing law?" "Three years, your Honor." Chamberlin took a sip of water before asking, "Did your law school teach you that all parties have to be present at the hearing? I am denying your request and directing you to advise your client that he cannot file another TRO for six months, no, I'm making it nine months, and meanwhile he will remain in custody." The attorney was speechless as he took his seat.

Bax asked if he could see the Judge in his chambers and his request was granted. He said "Howell, I know this is unorthodox, but you know his probable cause is fraudulent. We proved that in his first trial. Chamberlin responded, "Bax, you have been practicing law long enough to know this is unethical and I am going to forget you were here." Fair enough!

Meanwhile, Jeru, although pregnant, was taking care of the house and picking furniture. Wilford was busy hiring for the casino and hotel. He talked with Sarah about the restaurant in the casino. It was going to be smaller, but she would be manager of the hotel restaurant and the smaller one in the casino. She would have to interview and hire all of her staff. The upstairs apartment would be hers, but she was welcome to live with Wilford and Jeru at their new house across from Blossom.

Meanwhile, Wilford was having a problem with people coming by wanting to go inside the casino and hotel to look at everything before it was finished. He called on Brinson for extra security.

Brinson was happy to do that and hired enough men to have a twenty-four-hour presence seven days a week at both facilities. Blossom was kept busy checking on the expectant mothers. Each day was a flurry of activities and at day's end, all were tired souls, but they still found time for each other and to end each day with *Bible* study and prayer.

Chapter 23
"Mercy, Mercy Me!"

No amount of time and space can separate you from the person you are meant to be with in your life.

    It was cool for the beginning of spring in Santa Fe. People were moving with purpose, and it was a new day, a new year, with the national health issuing a statement that the flu virus was subsiding. All of the Ohara Inc projects were finished, and the push was on to get all the property on the strip sold. There was potential for much expected profitable first year. The newly establish Chamber of Commerce was pleased with the new tourist attraction -- the Monte Carlo Luxury Hotel and Casino. No one was happier than Sarah Twotrees. She had her new and important job, and she also would soon be a grandmother twice. She was so proud of her daughter, Jeru, and her husband Wilford. She had taken the evening off to shop for baby clothes and linen for her apartment.
    Sarah was not prepared for what happen next. As she walked through the store in the home section, from the back she thought she recognized the tall man standing with a female who appeared to be too young for the man. As she neared him, her

heart began to beat faster. She was not sure but had to find out. She spoke up and said, "Sgt Mercy? "He turned and couldn't believe his eyes. "Sarah, is it you?" She broke into a smile that lit up the store and he grabbed her and squeezed her so tightly that he almost cut off her breath. He said, "We have to sit down because I'm trembling." They sat on a display sofa, where he reached for her hand. She pulled it back, asking, "Is that your wife?" He laughed and said, "Serafina, meet the person I named you after. Meet Ms. Sarah Twotrees, the woman I talked about all the time since you were a little girl." The young lady said, "It is a pleasure to finally meet you; he talked about you all the time and I came to believe you were some Queen or Goddess.

Sarah asked where her mother was, and Sarafina replied that she never knew her mother. Sarah looked at Mercy as if to say, "Help me to understand." He said, "She is my daughter. I found her as a little baby in the Philippines where I was stationed. You are the only woman I loved and would consider marrying, or have you forgotten?" She said, "No, but I never heard from you after our brief encounter. I mean we were together such a short time that I thought you didn't care." With tears in his eyes, he told her that he had written her letters.

Sarah blushed and turned red. She glanced down at her hands and then said, "I am ashamed to say that in those days I couldn't read or write. Tell me what you are doing in Santa Fe." He said he worked for Ohara Inc. "I am Vice President of the mining division. She laughed. "I am manager of the hotel restaurant. Wait ... I must tell you this. You have a daughter and a granddaughter and one on the way." He got excited and asked to see her right away and introduce her to Sarafian. Sarah asked if he had a car, and since he did, they went to see his daughter right away. On the way Sarah asked him where he had been all those years. He said, "Right after we met, I was reassigned to Montana for a short time and then Cuba and Puerto Rico. After that I was in the Philippines for two years and Colorado for twelve years. That's when I had a chance to get a degree in engineering and mine safety, and when I retired from the army, I worked for the Ohara brothers, near Silver City. Sarafian said, "Don't you remember you were in New York training soldiers?" He said, "You are right, honey."

Sarah asked where he was living, and he shared that they just arrived today and were planning to get me a room at the Stockman Hotel. Sarah's face lit up. "You all can stay with me until you decide where you want to live." He spoke quietly, "No, people will talk and with my position I was told no scandals or even a hint of a scandal." Sarah said, "I know a good place right across the street from Jeru, but we can talk about that later. The next street is Buckhorn Road where Jeru and her husband, Wiford, live in their new house, which is right now the only house on that side of the street. We have about another five miles

When they reached the house Sarafina said, "Father, that is beautiful." Sarah exited the car and invited them in. She rang the doorbell. Jeru answered and said, "Mama, I am so glad to see you. Who is this with you? Sarah said "Honey, sit down. This is Jerusalem Mercy, your father, and his daughter, Sarafina, your sister." Jeru was shocked and suddenly got dizzy. Sarafina, who was a medical student, quickly checked her pulse and asked Sarah if there was a medicine cabinet in the house. "I need smelling salt." Sarah didn't know, but she went to the phone and called Blossom and ask her to come over. "Jeru fainted. Bring some smelling salt." Blossom rushed over knowing Jeru was pregnant. When she arrived, Sarafina had applied a cold compress to Jeru's forehead.

Blossom asked Sarafina to move back. Blossom announced that she is a midwife and needs to make sure the baby is all right. Blossom waved the salt under Jeru's nose, and she responded. Blossom asked Jeru to lay back, she asked Sarah for a glass. She asked Mercy to step out of the room. She raised Jeru's dress and discovered she was not wet, so she was all right. Sarah came back with the glass and Blossom placed it on Jeru's stomach and placed her ear on the glass and said the baby had a good heartbeat. Sarafina was surprised. "You could hear the heartbeat from that glass?" Blossom said yes. Sarafina said, "I am a medical student. Do you mind if I listen?" Sarafina placed the glass on Jeru and listened and smiled and said, "Thank you, Ma'am."

Once the drama was over, Sarah told Blossom, "This is Jeru's father, Jerusalem Mercy, and his daughter, Sarafina, Jeru's sister. Blossom said, "Pleasure to meet you all." Sarah said, "This is Ms. Blossom Blake." Mercy said he knew a man when he was in the army whose name was "Brownie Blake," and he was in Montana and also in the Philippines. Blossom said, "That was my husband." Mercy said, "He was much older than I was, and I learned a lot from him. He was in Cuba when I was there. Ma'am, he was a fine soldier." Blossom was moved. Sarah announced, "Blossom, Mercy and his daughter just arrived in town. He works for Claudette, and I thought since everyone has moved out you might put him up for a while." Blossom smiled and said, "I would be happy to. I will check with my son, since he is the man of the house, but I am sure he won't mind."

Jeru, with a hint of sarcasm because she was having a hard time digesting this news, asked Mercy, "Where have you been all this time, and did you not know you had a daughter?" Sarah said, "Hold on, honey, he is your father, and you have to respect that." Mercy looked at Jeru with compassion and said, "No, it is okay, I don't mind. Jeru, honey, I didn't know because I was in the army, and two weeks after I met Sarah, I fell in love with her and planned to ask her to marry me, but my unit was reassigned to Montana. I wrote to her, but she never got the letters." Sarah repeated that's because she couldn't read or write then, they lost touch. "I never married because he was the only man I ever loved. He treated me like a human being, at a time when to everyone else I was a dirty Indian squaw. I didn't want that for you, so I was never interested in another man. I longed for Mercy and didn't understand why he didn't want me, but now I know the whole story. He never married because he was in love with me."

Sarafina and Mercy, and even Blossom were moved by Sarah's story. But Jeru still felt hurt. She asked Sarah how Mercy got his second daughter, but Sarafina said she would explain. "My father found me in the jungles of the Philippines. I was just a baby and he adopted me, and I have no idea who my mother or father was." Blossom said Jeru, dear, I know this is all confusing to you to see your father for the first time and learn that you also have a little sister. But with as much as I taught you about love and understanding, it seems as though you're a little harsh with your words."

Jeru began to cry and apologized to Blossom. She said, "Mercy, or I should call you daddy or father? I'm sorry for my attitude. Please, you and Sarafina, forgive me for acting as I did. I hope you do live with Mama Blossom for a while. That way we can see each other often, and we have plenty of room here. Sarafina said, "I will only be here tonight. I have to get back to medical school. I graduate after two more semesters, but I would like to visit as often as I can. I want to get to know and love you. Before we go, can I see my niece?" Then, Mercy said he wanted to meet his granddaughter. Jeru said, "Of course. I just put her down and she is sleeping but follow me. Jeru whispered as they walked toward Connie.

"Sarafina, you and Connie have something in common because her mother died in childbirth, and I adopted her." Sarafina looked at Connie and asked Jeru, " is Connie her name?" Jeru said with pride, "Consuela, but we call her Connie." Sarafina kissed a finger and touched Connie's forehead and said, "Bless you, my niece." Mercy did the same thing to his granddaughter and whispered that he would see them tomorrow. Wilford arrived home from work and walked into the kitchen asking whose car was outside. Jeru said, "Darling, come and meet my father and my sister." Wilford entered and kissed Jeru and rubbed her stomach and asked if Connie was asleep. He said, Darling, you never mentioned your father." She said she had just met him. "It's a long story. I will tell you all about it later, but Honey, this is my father, Jerusalem Mercy, and my sister, Sarafina, named after my mother, Sarah. Everyone, this is my husband, Wilford Dunford. They all shook hands and Wilford welcomed them to their home.

"I want you to meet our best friends and the couple that lives here also, and you must stay for dinner." Blossom said, "Speaking of dinner, I have to get back across the street and get the rest of my dinner started. Mr. Mercy, if you and Sarafina would like to come with me you can see the house and come back." Wilford insisted that Blossom and the whole family come over for dinner. Blossom begged off, saying, "You all just moved in and to feed that many people might be a little much for Jeru." He suggested she bring what she was cooking. "We have plenty of room and enough chairs and eating utensils. I will drive over and load the food into the car, along with Shy, JB and the babies. I will call Cielito and Brinson and invite them over too. Please, Mama Blossom, we have been away from you three days, and we miss you." Blossom said, "Mr. Mercy, you see what I am up against? Okay, son, whenever you are ready, come on over. I will walk with Mr. Mercy."

As Mercy and Blossom walked, he asked Blossom whatever happened to Sgt. Blake. Blossom answered in a voice loaded with sadness. "Mr. Mercy ..." He stopped her and said, "Please call me Jerusalem or Abraham or just plain old Abe." Blossom agreed if he would address her as Blossom or Mama, as all the children do. She went on to say, "I received a two-year-old letter some time ago stating that he was missing and presumed dead." Mercy said, "He was in the Philippines when I was there, although we were not in the same company. I never would have thought that would happen to him because he was too good of a soldier. Sometime later, I would like to discuss that with you." She thanked him and said, "We are home." He said, "Blossom, you said all your children. How many do you have?" She said, "I Have two that God sent me and the rest, we were brought together by tragedy. I will tell you about that sometime. My son, JB, is mute. He hears good and can draw like nothing you have ever seen. We communicate by sign language. And Shy, my daughter, is as smart as a whip. They have triplets. Come on in and you can meet Shy. JB is in the field. He has a cleaning company, and he farms fifteen hundred and thirty acres. That's where he is right now, but he will be home in about an hour.

They entered the house, and Mercy commented on how clean and big the house was. Blossom took him upstairs to see the extra bedrooms, all furnished, and said anytime Sarafina wants to come she is welcome. He thanked her, and after seeing the rooms, he said, "I will take one. How much is it?" Blossom said, "Son, you will find that I am a God-fearing woman, and I believe in prayer and the scriptures. It won't cost you one dime. This house was a gift, and I will not take money for a gift. If you have read the *Bible*, didn't Jesus say you were given free so you must give freely? Now that we have settled that, let's go downstairs." She took him to meet Shy, who was on the phone, and showed him the babies. Shy concluded her call and Blossom said, "Mercy, this is my daughter, Ms. Shyanne Blake." Shy stood up and shook his hand and said, "Pleasure to meet you, Sir."

Blossom told Shy that Mercy had consented to live with them for a while. He's employed by Ohara Inc. and is Jeru's father and has another daughter, Sarafina, who is a medical student in Albuquerque. "You will meet her tonight. We are having dinner across the street." She added that Mr. Mercy asked to be called Abe or Jerusalem. Shy asked Mercy what his job was with Ohara Inc. "I am Vice President of the Mines Division. She congratulated him and said, "I am Vice President of Ohara Inc Agriculture Division." Mercy stated "You appear to be quite young for such a big job, but

Blossom repeated that she was smart as whip and managed their fifteen hundred acres and her husband's cleaning company, plus another fifteen thousand acres and a large cattle ranch. He said, "My, my, I must commend you. For such a tiny lady, you have mighty broad shoulders to handle all of that." Shy thanked him and said to feel free to call on her for any help he might need. Mercy said, "I didn't mean any disrespect by saying you were young. I joined the army at age fifteen and was leading a platoon of men at seventeen."

A minute later, JB was home from the fields and went through his regular routine of kissing Blossom and Shy and the babies. He noticed the tall man in the office. Before JB could sign a question Blossom signed and said, "JB, this is Mercy, and he is going to live with us for a while if it is okay with you." To Blossom's surprise, Mercy signed to JB. "Mr. Blake, I am pleased to meet you. I knew your father, Sgt. Brownie Blake. Blossom was quick to state that Brownie was JB's stepfather. "I said that I had two children whom God provided to me -- JB and Shy. I was rendered incapable of bearing children at an early age." JB signed "Where did you learn sign language?" Mercy said, "in the army." Blossom excused herself to remove her ham and sweet potatoes from the oven. "JB, son, wash up. We are having dinner across the street."

Chapter 24
The Extended Family Meets Mercy

It's seven o'clock and all is well. Dinner is served and there are many stories and secrets to tell.
Prior to Wilford's return with the Blakes, Mercy and Blossom, the Beauchamp's had arrived from work, and Brinson and Cielito were there with their dinner. There was a whirlwind of conversation going on. Jeru had introduced Sarafina to everyone and announced that their father was on the way from across the street. Blossom was the first to enter with ham and sweet potatoes, followed by Shy and the triplets and JB, while Mercy was the last, carrying the highchairs and diaper bag. Shy was the first to speak after the pleasantries of the day. She said to Cielito and Jeru, "This is what you two have to look forward to soon."

After Mercy sat the highchairs down, Jeru went to him and placed her arm in his, and with Wilford standing on the other side of him, she announced, "Everyone, this is my father, Jerusalem Mercy." Cielito approached him, as everyone else had met him prior. She said, "This is my husband, Brinson DuBois." Brinson shook his hand and declared to Jeru, "Now I can see where you got your name and height from. It is a pleasure meeting you, Mr. Mercy."

Wilford announced, "If everyone will be seated dinner is ready, and if no one objects, then I will ask for the blessings." No one objected, so he thanked God for all of them to be together. He prayed for the unborn and the blessings that all of them were able to enjoy. Lastly, he thanked God for Jeru and their everlasting love. Everyone said "Amen," and Mercy added, "Bless this house and all who dwell in it." Blossom whispered to Wilford, "Son, I am so proud of you. I couldn't have said it better." He kissed her and said, "Mama, that was you speaking through me."

Wilford cleared his throat and said, "Claudette, I have good news. All of the strip is sold, and I am waiting for you to approve the contracts and sign off on them." He went on to explain how four companies came together and bought the whole strip minus the hotel and casino. Shy asked if their stores would be that big. Wilford responded, "I don't think so. I suspect they did it to keep their competitors from buying in because the way it is subdivided, they can sell to whomever they want."

After dinner Shy said, "By now you all know how much I love each one of you, and now we have further extended our family with Mercy and Sarafina. I am sorry we have to go, but JB has to get to sleep, and I got three to bathe and put to sleep. Remember, Sunday dinner at our house." Claudette suggested that they rotate, but Blossom said, "If I may say something, because of Cielito's and Jeru's condition and the fact that they are going to be busy for some time, let's not shoulder them with that responsibility. After a year we can plan to rotate." Claudette said, "As usual, Mama, you are right. That was my selfish person surfacing, but I am working on it. Jean Claude can attest to that, right, darling?" She went to Blossom and hugged and kissed her.

Mercy added, "I guess we will leave also." Jeru said, "No! I am not going to let you go this soon you have been away from me for thirty some odd years. Please, Daddy, spend the night here. We have plenty of room for you, Mama, and Sarafina." Jeru was holding onto him. He said, "I have to get Sarafina back to school tomorrow." She replied, "You can do that from here as well as across the street." He looked at Blossom as if to say, "What should I do?" Blossom said, "She is right, the door is always open to you. I feel you all have a lot to catch upon." Sarah said, "Wait a minute. How is that going to look?" Jeru said, "Mama, quit. It's not like you two haven't been together, and besides, we have four guest rooms." Sarah protested that she didn't bring anything to sleep in and has to work tomorrow, but Wilford told her she could take tomorrow off. He asked her, "Don't you want to spend some time with Mercy to catch up on the years he was missing, and to see Sarafina before she goes back to school?"

Jeru solved Sarah's wardrobe problem by offering one of her robes, and with that, there were no more excuses. Blossom told Jeru that she was going to leave what was left of the ham and sweet potatoes so that she wouldn't have to cook tomorrow. Blossom said, "Good night," and asked Shy and JB to go on ahead of her because she needed to think about some things and wanted to walk home alone. Shy was apprehensive, saying, "Mama, it is dark out there." Blossom made her aware that she was not afraid of the dark. "Child, your Mama has spent many nights walking in the dark." As Blossom walked away, she was thinking,

"Mercy had something he wanted to say to me, but I won't push it. He will tell me when he is ready."

Meanwhile, Mercy and Sarah were still at the table talking. Wilford showed Sarafina her room. Jeru removed the dishes, and she and Claudette were in the kitchen washing dishes and talking. Claudette expressed her undying love for Jeru and was so happy she had met her father. "Isn't that something? After more than thirty years they found each other. I think that is so romantic to think he still loves her." Jeru added, "I think Mama is afraid of being hurt so I don't know how that will turn out. I do like Sarafina and hope she will visit as much as she can. I wonder if she would be interested in going to school at the university here in Santa Fe. Wouldn't it be nice to have her in our circle of sisters?" Claudette said they should ask her when they finished the dishes.

They went to talk with Sarafina, who was sitting on the bed reading from *Gray's Anatomy.* Jeru declared, "I hope we are not disturbing you, Sister." Sarafina indicated she was just catching up on her reading assignment for the upcoming semester. Claudette said, "This won't take too long. I don't know if you know it, but we have a campus here in Santa Fe, and it would be great if you could finish here, and we can be close to each other." Sarafina said, "That would be nice, but as I have said, I only have two semesters before I graduate, and after this semester, it will begin "Match Day." Claudette asked what Match Day meant, and Sarafina said, "That is when we get matched up with the hospital where we will do our residency. I was hoping to get matched up with a hospital in Colorado, which is where my boyfriend is."

Claudette said, "You met my sister, Cielito, and she and her husband are building a state-of-the-art hospital here. I wish you could be matched up here, since you have family here. Just say the word and she can get you accepted." Sarafina got quiet as if to carefully choose her next words. "Please do not think I am ungrateful for what you two are trying to do, but Donald and I – that's his name -- he graduated last year, and we have been apart for a year." Claudette said, "Say no more. I understand. Not long after I got married, I was agonizing over my husband planning a business trip where he would be gone three weeks. And then I thought about the fact that when Jeru and I were in school, I was so distraught over the death of my parents that I left campus and insisted Jeru stay and graduate. We only had a few weeks before graduation, and those were the worst days of my life." Jeru added, "So, Sister, as much as we want you close by, we understand." The three of them hugged and said, "Love you and good night."

As the clock struck eleven, in the kitchen Mercy and Sarah were still talking. Jeru stuck her head in and uttered, "When you two love birds finish, there are towels on your beds, and Mama, I put one of my robes there for you. Good night." Mercy asked, "Can I get a kiss from my little girl?" Jeru responded, "Of course, Daddy, uh hearing you say that makes me feel good all over. I love you." Sarah asked, "How about your mother?" Jeru expressed love and kissed her. "I have an idea. Why don't you kiss, for old times' sake?" Sarah smiled and said, "This is your house, but get out of here." Jeru responded playfully, "I am going, but you know you want to." Sarah said, "I wish I had something to throw at you; have you no shame?" She said, "Not when it comes to love. Night, night."

Sarah looked at Mercy and said, "She's your daughter and I don't know where she gets such notions." Mercy said, "I think what she said is a good idea. You know, when I heard your voice and turned and saw it was you, the same girl I remembered, my heart almost leaped out of my chest." Sarah was thinking that hers did the same thing. Mercy stood and moved closer to her and said, "How about it" He reached out his arms, and Sarah just fell into them, and they shared one long, passionate kiss. But then, Sarah pushed away and said, "This is not right." He asked, "What was wrong with that? Does your heart belong to someone else?" She said, "No, but this could lead to something wrong. do you know how long I ached for you and wanted that feeling the night we made Jeru." He gently held both her hands and replied, "Don't you know that a man can ache for the woman he loves and that I, too, was aching for you?" Sarah said good night and left the kitchen.

Mercy sat for a while before going to the car to get his bag, only to find it was not there. He turned and went back in the house to the room assigned to him, only to find his bag was there. Obviously, Wilford had brought his and Sarafina's bags inside. He retrieved his robe and went to the bathroom and started the shower. The bathroom was situated between the bedrooms assigned to Sarah and Mercy.

As she lay in the bed listening to the water running, she rolled over and covered her ears; but try as she may, she could not get the image of Mercy in there with that hot water running all over him out of her head. She covered her mouth and cried, "No! no! I won't. I will fight it." The sound from the shower stopped and she heard the door to the bathroom close shut. Her heart was beating fast as if she had been running. She beat the pillow and attempted to fall asleep, but sleep would not come.

Finally, she tossed the cover away and quietly got out of bed and gently turned the doorknob and stepped out of the room and tiptoed to Mercy's door and gently tapped on his door. She did not hear any sound or movement, so, she turned the doorknob and pushed the door, which suddenly flew open. There they were face to face. She fell into his arms. Mercy closed the door and they moved to the bed. Sarah said, "I tried to fight it but I couldn't. I am yours, so promise me you won't go away." Mercy picked her up and placed her on the bed, laid next to her, and said, "Only when the good Lord comes to get me."

After they had made love Mercy rolled over on his stomach as she lay on her back. He said, "Of course, you know what this means. She said she didn't, as she ran her hands over his arm and chest and asked, "Is it really you or am I dreaming?" He said, "No, it is me in the flesh. Now answer my question. Do you know what this means?" She didn't. Mercy said, "We have to get married tomorrow." She protested. Mercy asked, "Are you telling me you don't want to get married?" She reached up and pulled his head to hers and said, "Mercy, I was trying to say this must be a dream. I've been waiting for that for thirty years." Mercy said, "And did I make you feel as loved as I did thirty years ago?" They lay there for a while and finally fell asleep.

About eight o'clock the next morning Jeru had fix breakfast. She went to Sarafina's room and tapped on the door, announcing, "Breakfast is ready, and I thought you might want to see your niece." Sarafina asked if she could hold her, which she did while Jeru woke up Mama and Daddy. She went to Sarah's room and didn't hear anything, so, she went to Mercy's room and tapped on the door.

Mercy answered. Jeru said, "Daddy, breakfast is ready if you two are hungry for food." Sarah and Mercy were together, and Sarah whispered, "She knows." Mercy said, "It's okay, we are two adults, and besides, didn't she suggest it?" Sarah still felt embarrassed. Mercy asked, "Darling, don't you think she knows all about sex and love making? Honey, she's pregnant."

Sarah rolled over and kissed him and said, "I love you and I want the whole world to know." Mercy suggested that they not mention to the family that they were getting married. "Let's just get married on our way back from Albuquerque." She replied, "If you say so, my love." When they went down for breakfast everyone was eating. Wilford and Jean Claude were reading the newspaper. JB would always stop on his way home and purchase three sets of newspapers and leave them at the door for Cielito and Brinson and for the Dunford's and Beauchamp's, plus one set for Shy.

Mercy and Sarah walked in and spoke to everyone. Jeru said, "Good morning, Mama and Daddy. Did you sleep well, among other things?" Everyone stopped what they were doing. Mercy said, "My darling, we certainly did sleep good and other things as well. Now come and let me hug you and hold my granddaughter." Sarah, with a sheepish look, was quiet and looking down. Jeru commented, "Mama, you don't have anything to say?" Sarah, without looking up, said, "No, and stop kidding me." Now everyone was curious.

Wilford changed the conversation by addressing Claudette. "Will you look at this? How did they get this? I sent those contracts over to you around three, just before I left for the day." Claudette looked at the article and said, "Don't worry, it didn't come from our end." A few minutes later, Claudette, Jean Claude, and Wilford rushed out of the house heading for town.

Mercy asked Jeru, "Are those wolves that follow her all the time? I noticed that when we had our meeting, they were sitting at her feet, and when she got up, they followed her." Jeru said, "Daddy, it's the darndest thing you will ever hear. A mama wolf left two pups at Blossom's door, and she was in the yard watching. When we picked them up, the mama wolf turned and walked away with the other pups."

Jeru asked Sarah if she would help her with the dishes. When they cleared the table and went into the kitchen and placed the dishes in the sink, Jeru turned to Sarah and said, "Mama, I am so happy for you. I have never seen you with a glow on your face" She hugged her and said, "I wasn't making fun of you; I am just so happy that I am about to burst." Sarah responded. "When we get back from dropping Sarafina off at school, I will tell you something that will make you happier, if there is any such thing." She asked Jeru if she really loved Mercy. "Yes, Mama, he is my father."

Sarah said, "Let me tell you the kind of man he really is, honey. "Don't think bad of your Mama, but I was a prostitute when I met him. I was thirteen and got fired for having sex with the Negro soldiers. I couldn't make any money from the White men who called me a filthy Indian squaw. It is a long story, but Mercy took me from that place and rented me a little shack. He would come by and bring me food and a little money. He confessed his love for me and said he didn't care what I was because he loved me. I liked what he was doing for me, but the only thing I could do for him was to make love with him. Because he was loving and romantic, he kissed me. No other man had done that. All they did was get on top of me and use me until they were through. But not Mercy."

Sarah continued. "He must have kissed me ten times and that was the last I saw of him. I would ask the other soldiers where he was, and they said he came down on orders. I didn't know what that meant, and I was devastated. I thought he didn't want me anymore. I was advised to change the way I looked and went to work at the *Santa Fe Social Club* as a prostitute, and it wasn't long before I found I was pregnant with you. When you were born you were so large and long when Blossom delivered you that she said, 'Child, this precious baby has torn your insides, but you will heal.' I could no longer work as a prostitute and had to do whatever I could to take care of you. At the time I couldn't read or write, but I would do anything for you to get that opportunity. I sent you to school, where you met Claudette, and by then you were old enough to know the rest."

Sarah asked Jeru if she could forgive her. Jeru said, "Mama, I don't need to forgive you, you did what you had to do." She had tears in her eyes and running down her cheeks. She said compassionately, "Mama, you have had a rough life. I am wealthy now, thanks to the Ohara's. I want to make the rest of your life better." Sarah said she could do that by loving Mercy with all her your heart and being. "He will make sure I live a good and happy life. I wish you and Connie could go with us, but he told me last night he has some things to talk over with Blossom concerning her husband, so he wants her to go with us. Jeru pleaded with Sarah. "Mama, please promise me we will see each other often."

Chapter 25
Blossom Hears Truth, and Sarafina Meets Her New Mother

"Ye shall know the truth and the truth will set you free." After Mercy loaded the bags and they all hugged and said their goodbyes, he drove across the street to talk to Blossom. He asked her to ride with them to Albuquerque, but she couldn't leave Shy there alone with the babies. Mercy said they would be gone approximately three hours and he needed to tell her the truth about her husband. Blossom went to Shy's office and told her she was going to ride with Mercy to take Sarafina back to school. "Will you be okay for three or four hours?" Shy assured her she would be okay. I have the female employees here, so don't worry, go on." "Ok, daughter, I love you." She kissed her and the babies and left.

  The trip to college was uneventful until Mercy mentioned that he and Sarah were going to get married when they returned to Santa Fe. Sarafina was studying in the back seat, but hearing this news, she was happy she now had a mother. She was not satisfied to remain in the back seat away from Sarah, so she asked Mercy to stop so mother and daughter could sit together.

After the hugs and kisses and goodbyes, Mercy asked Blossom to sit up front with him and Sarah. "On the way back, we want to make one stop at the Cathedral to see if the Priest will marry us." Blossom said, "My goodness gracious, praise God. Yes, by all means stop."

Mercy said, "Blossom, I must tell you the truth about your husband. I told you we were both in Cuba and the Philippines, which was the last time I saw him. That's true, but what I am about to tell you may come as a shock. I had said earlier that whatever he was, I knew him to be a good soldier. When we first went to the Philippines, most of us Negro soldiers knew nothing of the country and its people. We just knew we were told we were going there to liberate the people from Spain. When we got there, we saw the people were dark-skinned like us, and we were happy to do our part."

Blossom felt a little anxious at what she had yet to hear, but she was patient. Marcy continued. "After the Spanish surrendered, which was a folly, they made an agreement to not surrender to the Philippines, but to the Americans. They set up a mock battle where the Americans would fire over their heads, and they would surrender. Afterwards, we learned America had no intentions of granting the people their independence but were going to keep the Island for themselves.

There was a large Island called the "Republic of Negro" or "Negros Republic." They were not going to take it lying down, so war was declared, and we were sent to fight them. Well, a lot of the soldiers decided to not fight against those Black people, but to join them, and Sgt. Brownie Blake was among them. He went over to the other side and was fighting against us at the time I was promoted to a Lieutenant. I was a Company Commander.

Most of our duties were pacifying the villages, which was all that we did for the whole time I was there. On one of our patrols, I made a big mistake, and my squad was surrounded by the enemy and taken to their headquarters. We must have marched two days before we finally arrived at their jungle headquarters where I believed we would be executed."

"Well, to my surprise, the Commanders were none other than Sgt. Brownie Blake and Sgt David Fagan. I knew that some of the men from the 24th and 25th had refused to fight against the rebels. I didn't know he was one of them. He had tried to get me to join him, but I refused. I had taken an oath to defend the country against all enemies, both foreign and domestic. He said, 'Mercy you know what we do to any American soldier we capture.' I told him I had heard. He inquired as to when I was due to rotate (return stateside), and I told him in ninety days."

"Ms. Blake, he said he would let me and my men go if I would do him a favor. I said it depend upon the favor. He said he had this baby girl whose mother was one of my rebels. She was wounded in an ambush and later died, but not before the baby came. He wanted me to take her back to the states with me. I didn't know how I would do that, but I told him I would. I would have told him anything to save my men."

"Long story short, as an officer we had women who washed and ironed our uniforms and shined our boots. I promised her that I would bring her back to the states if she would care for the baby. She said she would if her husband could come also.

Now, Sarah, I hope you understand this. I had to lie to get her into the states. The rule was that in order for me to get her here I had to show that I had married her, and her husband was my son.

The lie held and I was able to get the three of them here. When I got to Colorado, which was my next duty station, I found housing for them. I filed for a birth certificate for Sarafina, showing her as my dependent, and I divorced from Mandanaga and gave the paperwork to the army. She and her husband didn't like the weather and wanted to go to California, so, I gave them the money and never heard from them again. God was watching over me because one of the men captured with me was assigned to my company here in the states. He was married and said he and his wife owed me. It was because of me and Sarafina that his life was spared, and they would be glad to take care of Sarafina for me, which they did for the next fifteen years."

"Now, Ms. Blake, when I left the Philippines in 1902, Sgt Blake was alive. It is my understanding that the army did not want it out that these members of the American military had deserted, so they listed all of them as missing and presumed dead. There was a bounty on his head for six hundred dollars. I don't know if Sarafina was his daughter or not, but the word was that she was. At any rate, she is my daughter now and I love her like she was my own birth child. And I say this again -- Sgt Blake was a good soldier as far as I am concerned."

Mercy said he knew he told a very long story, but he wanted Blossom and everyone to know the story of Sarafina. "Anyway, I thought I owed it to you to know the truth." Blossom thanked him and added, "Abraham, God knows I loved that man and, alive or dead, I still love him, but you know God has sent all of you to me, so my love is not wasted."

Sarah said, "Honey, I don't need to see the divorce papers. I love you and believe you. We are here. Let's go in this church and get married." Fifty-five minutes I after they left the church as husband and wife, they all arrived at Blossom's house. She said to Mercy, "I guess you won't be needing that room." He replied, "I still want the room for right now. I haven't talked it over with Sarah, but I would like to stay here for a while until we can get a piece of land on this street. I want to be near Jeru and my grandchildren."

Sarah said, "Mercy, you took the words right out of my mouth and that will complete the circle." Blossom said they should go in and tell Shy the good news. As soon as Blossom walked into Shy's office, the phone rang. It was Brinson. Shy said, "Yes, she just walked in. I will tell her." She hung up and said, "Mama, Cielito has gone into labor, and they need you." Blossom responded, "Tell him I am on the way. I just need to grab my bag."

Sarah said while you are doing that we can run into town and get my clothes and come back. Blossom rushed across the yard and entered the barn and panicked. She was so excited that she couldn't find her way upstairs. She yelled out to Brinson, "Where are the stairs to come up to you?" He told her to just stay where she was, and he would come down in the lift and get her. He kissed Cielito and said, "Be right back, honey." She said, "Brinson Francois Dubois, you better not leave me." He said, "Honey, I am just going down in the lift to get Blossom." He ran in the lift and moved it downstairs. Blossom was standing there confused and bewildered. He opened the gate and said, "Over here." She went to him, and he moved the lever and the lift started to move up. Blossom asked, "This thing won't fall, will it? He said they would be fine.

"I have towels, sheets blankets, and water heating." Blossom said, "Good, son, you did good. Let me get to her." She could hear Cielito yelling, and she called out, "I am here, baby. Lay back and let me look at you." She checked her and said, "It's not time. When did your water break?" Cielito said it happened about fifteen minutes ago. Blossom said, "It is going to be little while because the baby is just moving into the birth canal. Leave your legs up and open. I will be with you, so just hold my hand."

After fifteen minutes Blossom checked her and said, "OK, it's crowning. I need you to push really hard." Cielito said she was afraid. Blossom said, "No, I want you to place your feet against my shoulders and push." Cielito screamed, "Mama it hurts." Blossom said to give me one more hard push and the baby would be there. Cielito grunted and pushed, as Blossom backed away and grabbed her scissors and cut the cord and spanked the baby. She cried, and Cielito heard her and told Mama to give her the baby.

Blossom wiped her off and wrapped her first. As she handed her the baby, she said, "You have a most beautiful baby girl!"

Cielito called for Brinson. Blossom said, "Not yet. You have to pass the after birth and I will clean you up and then he can come in." Blossom moved as fast as possible, as she could hear Brinson pacing and praying. The after birth came and Blossom went through the procedure of getting rid of it. She returned and cleaned Cielito, changed the bed and put Cielito and baby in the bed and told Brinson he had a beautiful baby girl. He rushed in the room, kissed Cielito, and confessed his love for her. Cielito handed him the baby and said, "Here's your daughter, darling." He looked at her and began to shed tears. "Darling, these are tears of joy. I love her. I can't help but love her because she looks just like you."

Blossom interrupted. "It is time to give her a name." Brinson said, "Cielito" should be her name, but Cielito asked what his mother's name was. "Sophia." She wanted her to have his mother's name. They both looked at Blossom, who thought for a moment and asked, "How about Sophia Guadalupe Cielito, since your mother was Guadalupe." They said, "Mama, you are wonderful; that will be her name." Blossom said, "Hand her to me, and Cielito, hold my hand and Brinson you hold Cielito's hand and with your other hand touch the baby. I will say her name because I was the first person she saw, and I will hand her to you, Cielito, and you repeat her name and tell her that is her name. Afterwards, you hand her to Brinson, and he will do the same."

They all did as Blossom had instructed. She said, "Now, she will always know who she is." She asked Cielito to squeeze her breast to make sure she had milk. She began to nurse. Blossom said, "For the next several weeks, let her lay on you on the left side so she can get used to your heartbeat. If you are feeling okay, I will go and you two enjoy being Mama and Daddy. She told Brinson that for a few weeks she would bring Cielito meals and check on her and Sophia. "I will call Dr. Joe come out tomorrow and check Sophia. I always like to have Dr. Joe to check behind me."

Blossom returned to the house to tell Shy that Cielito had a baby girl whose name is Sophia Guadalupe Cielito." Shy had gone to the door where Mercy and Sarah had returned from town. Blossom entered the parlor and told all three the news, and they express their happiness. Mercy and Sarah said they would tell Jeru after they moved into their room. Blossom went to the phone to call Dr. Joe. He said he would come over, and he needed to talk to her and Brinson. Blossom asked if he could also check on Jeru because they had a scare the other day.

Mercy and Sarah moved their clothes in and advised Blossom that they were going across the street to tell all the good news. As they walked across the street, Jeru was adjusting the picture window curtains and noticed them walking hand-in-hand. She went out to meet them. She yelled, "Hey, you two, are you in love or what?" Mercy kissed Sarah and asked, "Does that answer your question?" Sarah said, "That's not all, darling daughter, we are married." Jeru said, "Are you kidding me?" Mercy said, "We stopped on the way back from Albuquerque and got married at the Cathedral. Jeru said, "Is that any way to treat your daughter whom you claim to love so much?" Mercy hugged and kissed her. "We did it that way so there would not be any delay. Last night we made love and decided that we needed to get married right away, which is something that should have happened thirty years ago.

When Mercy made the statement about making love last night, Sarah was blushing and trying to hide her face. Jeru said, "Aw, Mama, when I found you both in the same room, I didn't think you were just playing hide and seek. I think that is so romantic. I love you and I have to do something special for you both. I can't wait to tell Claudette." Mercy said, "By the way, Cielito had a baby girl, and they named her Sophia Guadalupe Cielito, and Dr. Joe is coming by to check on Cielito and you.

Jeru said she had to call Wilford to tell him the good news. She called the hotel and the receptionist said Mr. Dunford was not in. She identified herself and was told that he went to Corporate headquarters for a meeting with Ms. Beauchamp. Jeru thanked her and called Claudette, who was meeting with Wilford. Jeru asked the receptionist to have them to call home when they finished the meeting. Wilford called his wife and asked if everything was okay. She assured him she was okay, but said, "Mama and Daddy got married today and Cielito had a baby girl." He said that was good news.

Jeru asked what they could do to celebrate. Wilford replied, "Let's have everyone to come to the hotel and celebrate here. Why don't you get a hold of Blossom and have her to get JB to bring the family. Claudette and Jean Claude are here, and I will let them know. I guess that leaves Cielito and Brinson out, but we don't want to delay this celebration, after thirty years of waiting for this." He asked Jeru to bring him a change of clothes, and maybe Jean Claude and Claudette might need a change of clothes too. Jeru promised to talk with Brinson and Cielito, saying she was sure they would understand. Jeru called Brinson saying she didn't want to disturb Cielito, but wanted to offer congratulations. She also said that her Mama and Daddy got married and they all were going to celebrate at the hotel. Brinson said, "Please wish them all the happiness from us, and you all come by and see Sophia soon."

Jeru promised they would come by tomorrow. She called Blossom and told her about the plans for the whole family to be at the hotel, including the children. Blossom said she had to fix dinner for Cielito and Brinson first. Then she checked with

Shy, who was excited to get dressed up. Blossom called Brinson and advised that she would bring dinner early. She asked if Dr. Joe had been by, and Brinson said he came and said the baby was in good shape and he was leaving to check on Jeru. When JB got home, Shy was busy dressing the triplets. He signed, "What are you dressing the babies for?" She said and signed all the news of the day, ending with them being invited to a marriage celebration at the new hotel.

Blossom returned and rushed to her bedroom to get dressed. She went to Shy and asked how she looked. Shy said "Mama, you look great. We are going to have to watch to keep the men from flocking to you." Blossom said, "Hush up, child. You and the babies look so good." When JB entered the room, Blossom signed and said, "JB, you look so handsome. Tell your wife how pretty she looks and the babies, too." JB kissed his family and signed that they were ready. They went to their new car and were off to the hotel. When they arrived, the valet opened the door and asked for the keys to park their vehicle.

They walked up to the door and a man in a uniform opened the door and they stepped inside. Another man came up and asked if they had reservations. Shy said they were guests of the Dunfords, and he led them to a closed door and opened it. None of them had seen such a place before. He led them to a table that had their names on it, and he said the Dunford's, the Mercys and the Beauchamp's would be in shortly. He walked away and came back with a bottle of champagne. Shy asked, "What is that?" "Champagne." Shy said they would have of water. At that time, the rest of the party entered and apologized for being late.

Claudette complimented Shy on how good her family looked.

Wilford whispered to the waiter that they could bring in the food. Blossom was asked to pray for the food and for Mercy and Sarah, who were congratulated and toasted for a long and happy union. After dinner, Wilford took everyone on a short tour and was showered with praises for the work he had done. Everyone departed for home. Jeru wanted Mercy and Sarah to spend the night with them, but Claudette offered a comment to Jeru. "My love, who was with you and Wilford on your honeymoon? I believe they want to be away from family for theirs." Jeru blushed and had to agree.

Chapter 26
Claudette's Response to Nimrod

They say, "If at first you don't succeed, then try, try again." However, trying could land you in a place you don't want to be. Several weeks after the whole family, except for new parents, Cielito and Wilford, celebrated the marriage of Mercy and Sarah, Claudette was becoming a seasoned CEO. She reviewed contracts and reports, and she held daily meetings with division heads and contractor, Streeter Finley. There were conference calls with Bax Toilet's law firm, which had grown substantially. Even that could not keep her from being a loving and affectionate wife and not allowing her business to interfering with her personal responsibilities. That's something she learned from Shy.

It seemed there were always vacancies to fill, until one morning Streeter introduced her to Lesly Smythe Bellows, a young lady from New York who was a college classmate of his son. Lesly had earned a degree in Business Management with a specialty in Human Resources and Risk Management from the renowned *Cromwell School of Business at New York University.* She came highly recommended by her professors and the president of the school. Streeter suggested from what little he knew of her, that Claudette should offer her the position of VP of Personnel, which would relive Claudette from having to interview and handle other personnel matters. He also suggested that all employees undergo a Criminal History Background check by Brinson's security company. "You need that because you never know when Nimrod is going to plant a spy in the organization." Claudette said, "Pleased to meet you, Lesly, and welcome aboard. By tomorrow we will have you an office and you can start to hire your staff. One of your first assignments is to put out a memo to division heads to have all personnel records forwarded to your office by the end of business three days from now. If you would like to tour the facility, I will have someone escort you." She said she would like that. Claudette opened her intercom and asked the receptionist to have someone from security to come to her office to give a new person a tour.

Streeter commented to Claudette that she was adapting to her role as CEO admirably. "If I may suggest for the time being, maybe you should have her work from the old office building until we can have a building with a security fence. We should never allow people seeking employment to have access to the headquarters building without some form of security in place." She thanked him and asked where he would suggest they put the building. He showed her the rendering of the headquarters building. "I think this is a good place, and on the other side for future use will be a large parking lot. The building should be facing the lot." Claudette thanked him and asked if he could get Scott McKenzie started on it right away and she would sign off on it. He assured her he would get on it as soon as he got back from taking Ms. Bellows to the Stockman Hotel.

Claudette said, "We can't have a VP at that hotel, so please take her to our hotel on the strip and I will alert Wilford." Claudette asked Streeter if he gave her a copy of the Corporate folder and he had. He said she looked over it and was surprised that this large enterprise had no insurance. He said he was still talking with industrial insurers. "I told you she is on the ball. When I talked with her yesterday, she had done her research, so, before her interview she wanted to be ready for any questions. She said she would have a portfolio for you in the morning. Claudette added I guess she is on the ball. Streeter asked Claudette if she mind if he made a personal observation. Claudette said, "No, go right ahead." He said, "Those are two strange dogs." She said they were wolves and, yes, they were strange indeed.

Lesly returned from her tour and noticed that there were a lot of empty offices. Streeter said they had just moved into the headquarters building and were still in the process of organizing and hiring. "Most of the divisions are stand-alone entities; for example, our mines are South of here in the Silver City area, Ohara Oil is thirty miles away on the Ohara's High Spade Cattle Ranch, along with the Agriculture arm which consists of fifteen thousand acres. And then, of course, you saw the Monte Carlo strip with the luxury hotel. Ms. Beauchamp has asked me to put you up there until you can secure permanent housing.

Claudette apologized, but Mr. Bax Toilet and another gentleman were on their way to see her. As Finley and Lesly were leaving they passed by Bax and the gentleman entering Claudette's office. Lesly asked out loud, "Doug, is that you?" Doug was asked if they knew each other. "Yes, we were on campus at the same time. She was attending the

Cromwell School of Business, and I was at *Adams School of Law.*" She asked what he was doing there, and he replied that he was looking for a job. She said, "So was I. I just got hire; hope you land a position, good seeing you."

Bax and Doug entered Claudette's office. Bax said, "Good day, Ms. Beauchamp, this is the young man I was telling you about." Doug rushed over and introduced himself as "A. Douglas Baldwin," and wanted to be sure the two animals wouldn't bite. Claudette said, "So, you want to head our Legal Department? On Mr. Toilet's recommendation you have the job. Do you have a resume? He set it on her desk. She commented, "It is mighty thick. And by the way, I hope you do not have a problem having a woman as your boss." He said, "Ma'am, I am happy to have you at the helm." Claudette replied, "I was not speaking of me. The young lady you just greeted will be the VP of the Personnel Division and the Legal Department is under that umbrella." Doug was fine with that.

Bax advised Doug that he would be with him shortly, as there was another matter he needed to discuss with Ms. Beauchamp before he departed. He turned to Claudette and alerted her. "Nimrod is at it again. He has filed a suit against you as CEO of *Ohara Inc.* I got the news late last night and you should be served with papers sometime today. I want to be here when it happens. I have asked the Governor for a *Stay of Execution* for Hunt and Duce so I can get them to testify against Nimrod and we can try him for conspiracy to commit murder."

The wolves stood up, as if they understood his comment, but Claudette commanded them to sit. "Before you do anything, I learned something from Blossom that I will never forget. She said you can't render a rattle snake safe by pulling his fangs because they will grow back each time you do that. The only way you can render it harmless is to take everything it have -- cut out its genitals and bleed it dry. I am going to take everything he has -- all the farmland, mines, and money he stole from us and murdered other people to enrich himself."

Bax asked how she planned to do that. She said, "He claimed he owned the casino, so I am going to sucker him into a game of poker, winner take all, and after that, I'll counter sue him." Bax thought that was taking a serious risk, but Claudette said that no one had ever beaten her at poker except her mother who is dead. "Do you think you can sucker him into putting up all he owns?" She responded confidently, "I know his kind. He won't put up all of it, and that's where the counter suit comes into play. I will run ads in the paper that say anyone with five million dollars can get in the game, and I will humiliate him until his ego will force him to get in the game."

Bax said, "You know he will be out of jail soon from the contempt charges. You've got to do it within ninety days, which is probably all I can get the Judge to delay hearing the case." Claudette said she only needed thirty-four days.

After Bax and Doug left, Claudette asked the receptionist to get Greta D Gossiper of the *Santa Fe Gazette* on the line. She was away from her desk but called back within an hour. Claudette immediately suggested that they could help each other. "How would you like to name your salary, have your own office, and be the spokesperson for *Ohara Inc.*?" Greta was interested and asked for details. Claudette said, "Come to Ohara's corporate headquarters as soon as you can." Greta arrived within thirty minutes and was shown to Claudette's office. She said, "I heard about the dogs. Will they bite?" Claudette said they would not bite. "We have to become close friends because it is you who will tell the world about *Ohara Inc.*, the first large corporation to be run by women, and you'll tell our story.

I am sure you know who Nimrod Bloom is. He had my brothers murdered and thinks he has gotten away with it. The courts let him off, but I plan to break him and take everything he has. It is not revenge or anger, but I do plan to get even. There are men and women out there hoping we fail, but as long as I have women who are loyal and want to see this corporation rise and be profitable, we will show them." Greta's eyes widened, as this promised to be the "story of the Century." "Your first job is to advertise countrywide that one can own the *Santa Fe Monte Carlo Casino* by beating me at poker. It's five million dollars in cash to play the game. You must direct it at Nimrod, but anyone interested can contact Mr. Wilford Dunford at Monte Carlo strip luxury hotel. Every day I want an article needling Nimrod until he can't wait to get in the game and allow me to strip him of his manhood. Do everything you can to humiliate him, OK?"

Greta understood but wanted to talk salary. Claudette asked how much she wanted to be paid. She said, "I make fifty-five dollars every two weeks and I want double that." Claudette agreed and they shook hands. Greta said, "I will write you a byline when I get back to the office and show it to you for your approval before you leave for the day." As soon as she left, Claudette had her receptionist to get Bax Toilet on the phone and get ahold of Doug, too, because she had an assignment for him. She told Bax, "I am about to do something, and I want to know if it is legal." He said he and Doug would see Claudette shortly. She called Greta to make three copies of the article she was preparing, and Greta said she would do it within the hour.

Bax and Doug arrived, and Greta would be there soon. Claudette informed Bax that she had hired Greta as their Communication Spokesperson. Bax commented that she continued to surprise him. She challenged him by asking if he implied that a man would grasp the CEO role quicker than she, but Bax apologized and altered his words. She affirmed that, as CEO, she was determined to take this company to new heights of success and profitability, and anyone in her company without the same, serious attitude was in the wrong place. Greta had arrived and presented Claudette with a draft and three copies for Claudette's review and revision. Claudette handed a copy each to Bax and Doug. "You were out of the office when Bax and I discussed this, but it is my tool to get Nimrod to bite." Bax explained who Nimrod was and his fraudulent claim to owning the Casino. He elaborated upon Claudette's plan to break him financially and to sue him for whatever assets and cash he is trying to hide.

Doug said that, if it is known that his claim is fraudulent, why not go after him in court? Bax explained that he had been in court a few times, but he always came up with some trick to get away. Doug suggested some word changes in the article, or else Nimrod could sue them for slander. "Ms. Gozipper, why don't you dispense with using his name and instead use something like 'the person making the claim knows his claim is fraudulent.' That way, he can't sue for *Deformation of Character*, I would like to work with you on this, if you don't mind. I understand you are quite the poker expert, and I wonder how many players you expect to draw." She hadn't given much thought to that.

He said, "If you are going to do this, I would imagine that a lot of men out there with means would be thinking of signing up. I suggest you might as well make money off this by promoting it as a tournament, I can draw it up for you tonight and have it ready for you in the morning." Claudette asked Bax to look over what Doug drafted in the morning. Doug asked Greta if she would like to spend the rest of the afternoon working on the article, and she jumped at the chance to spend the afternoon with Doug, since he was quite a handsome man. Just before Jean Claude arrived, Greta and Doug returned to Claudette's office and handed her the rewritten article. She promised to look it over later that evening, as she was about to pack up and wait for Jean Claude.

As soon as she opened her office door, the wolves ran for the front entrance. The guard let them out and they began to mark their territory. Jean Claude opened his rear door and they jumped into his vehicle. He could see Claudette walking toward the front entrance, and when she reached the car, Jean Claude was standing and waiting for her. They hugged and kissed, and he asked her if she wanted to drive home. She said she had something to read while they drove home.

When they arrived, Jeru asked how their day went, and then she announced, "I promised Mama Blossom I would take Cielito and Brinson their dinner. Wilford is going with me so we can see the baby, and you two can go with us, or else dinner is ready whenever you all are. We shouldn't be gone longer than an hour." Claudette said she and Jean Claude would come tomorrow or maybe later. Claudette asked Jeru what Dr. Joe had said when he came by yesterday. Jeru said. "He said that the baby sounded good, and I was doing good. He thinks the baby should arrive in three to four months." Claudette said that was good news.

Cielito and Brinson were glad to see Wilford and Jeru and especially proud to show off Sophia. Wilford commented, "She looks just like you and got a head full of hair already. Connie's hair has grown, and we are feeding her mashed up food. Jeru told Dr. Joe that Connie felt a little warm, but he said that was not unusual, as she was teething." Cielito asked Jeru to come and sit by her on the bed. "Did you think it was going to be this wonderful?" Jeru answered, "Not in a thousand years! I never thought I would have someone like Wilford. He's so loving and attentive. Honey, did you know he was rubbing my stomach before I was showing?" She whispered, "And he asked me if we could we still make love because he was afraid it might hurt the baby." Cielito burst out laughing and covered her mouth. Sophia made a little noise.

Cielito looked at her and she began moving her lips. Cielito picked her up and placed her breast in Sophia's mouth and whispered to Jeru, "Brinson asked me the same thing when we found I was pregnant. Mama Blossom told him that we could make love right up to the eighth month. To tell you the truth, sometimes he was too gentle and caused me some frustration. I don't know about you, but I like passionate love making." Jeru did, too. You know, I can't wait for Claudette to get pregnant. It is such a feeling to know you have a live person growing inside of you. I love Connie with all my heart, but I felt so special when I learned I was pregnant." Cielito said, "Yes, it seemed Brinson loved me more."

Brinson entered the room with a tray and asked if Cielito was hungry. She lay Sophia down, winked at Jeru, and sat down to dinner. Brinson asked what she would like to drink, and she replied that anything was fine. Wilford took Jeru by the hand and said, "We need to get back across the street. Claudette and Jean Claude said they will come by tomorrow. Love you both and hope you enjoy your dinner.

As they walked away from the new barn, Jeru asked Wilford if he left the painting of her in his old studio. He remembered that he did. She said, "Honey, can you get it? I want it hanging in our home." He went in the barn and retrieved it and revealed to her that he planned to hang it in the hotel behind the check-in counter. Jeru said, "I love that painting; it was like you were saying how much you loved me, and I could see your love for me in it." He put one arm around her as they continued walking. "You know, I will paint a larger one to go in the hotel, and we can hang this one in the house." She stopped and kissed him, and he said, "God knows I love you, Claudette, and to me, my love, you make me feel special in a way I can't explain." They paused for a minute and embraced.

Shy had gone out to bring in laundry from the clothesline. She saw them and yelled, "Hey, stop that kissing in my back yard." They turned to see Shy. Jeru said, "Hey, yourself, little sister. We are coming over to say hello to Mama Blossom, but we have to hurry back because Claudette and Jean Claude are watching Connie. We just delivered dinner to Cielito and Brinson. Shy said, "I take it you saw the beautiful Miss Sophia." Wilford said, "She is a doll!"

They all went inside where Blossom was getting dinner ready. She said, "Come here, let me get a hug and a kiss. What is that you are carrying, Son?" He unwrapped the painting and Blossom said, "Ooh my goodness, did you do this?" He grinned and said he had. "I couldn't have done it if JB hadn't taught me to sketch. Mama, someday I want to do a painting of all of us. If JB will sketch it, then I will paint it. I love you, Mama. I expect we should get home." Jeru asked where her Mama and Daddy went, since she had seen his car when they were walking over to the Dubose's. Blossom answered, "I suspect they are honeymooning." Jeru said, "When they come up for air, tell them we asked about them and we would like to see them soon." Blossom jokingly said, "Get out of here, child."

When they got home, Claudette and Jean Claude had set the table and were waiting for them. Jeru said they didn't need to wait, but Claudette responded, "We didn't want to dine alone. We love you, and you are so much a part of our lives that we didn't mind waiting." Jean Claude asked what Wilford was carrying, and he said it was his painting of Jeru and Connie. You've seen it before, remember?" Claudette chimed in, "We still want you to paint us." Jeru said with great pride that he was going to paint a bigger painting of this one to hang in the lobby of the hotel. Wilford added, "Hey, that just gave me an idea. Suppose I paint a large one of you two and hang it in the Casino when Jeru is up to helping me with the Entertainment Division?" Claudette said she had a picture of her mother and father from which Wilford might paint them and hang the picture in the Casino.

Claudette had something she wanted Wilford to review tomorrow, but for now, it was time for them to eat. Jeru said, "You all get started. I need to check on Connie." While she was out of earshot, Claudette asked Wilford if he knew that Jeru's birthday was Thursday next week. He didn't know that but was open to ideas. Claudette replied, "She is getting bigger, so get her some sexy underwear to make her feel she is still desirable and that you want to make love to her as much as you ever did. Wilford thanked her. After dinner, Jean Claude winked at Claudette and leaned his head in the direction of the bedroom. Claudette signaled that she understood, and she asked Jeru if she needed help in the kitchen. Jeru said she could handle it, noting that she had seen the look between Claudette and Jean Claude. Claudette asked her if there was anything she didn't see!" She was tired but she would not allow that to get in the way of her love and duty to her husband.

After they left, Wilford helped Jeru with the dishes, after which he leaned forward and gave her a long, passionate kiss. Jeru asked, "Honey, what was that all about?" He whispered, "Let's make love right here and now, in the kitchen. I've been missing you all day." She said, "What about Connie, and what if Claudette or Jean Claude come to the kitchen?" He responded, "I don't think anyone is coming this way, and besides, this will be like 'stealing,' which will make it more exciting! Remember the second time we made love?" She said, "Oh, yes." She began to unbutton his shirt and before long, they were following Wilford's plan. Afterwards they hurried down the hallway to the bedroom. Jeru lay on the bed and rolled over and asked Wilford If she could have a "do over." Once again, they were locked in a passionate embrace. Now both were breathing heavily, as Wilford rolled over on his back and Jeru snuggled up to him, as they fell asleep until the next morning when Connie's crying woke them up.

She looked at the clock and called out to Wilford. "Wake up, darling, it is nine o'clock. I will hurry and fix breakfast. She washed up and threw on a robe and hurried to the kitchen, only to find a note from Claudette which read, "You two were sleeping so soundly that we decided to get breakfast in town. Ask Wilford to come to my office before he goes to the hotel."

Jeru sat down and began to nurse Connie. Before long, Wilford showed up and said he didn't need breakfast before leaving for work. She said, "Claudette left a note asking you to meet her in her office before you go to the hotel." He thanked her, kissed her and Connie, and left. She looked at sleeping Connie and said, "I guess it is just you and me." She lay Connie down and went to take a bath. As she was bathing, she thought about last night and smiled, musing to herself, "I wonder how many women have what I do." For some reason she remembered the toast Blossom made to her and Wilford: "May you have everything you want in life and want everything you have." It was time to thank God. Jeru kneeled at the bed and gave thanks for her loving husband, for Connie, and for the unborn child she was carrying, and also for Sarah and her father, Claudette, Jean Claude, Cielito, and Brinson. She gave special thanks for the whole Blake family and asked God to please help her to remain humble.

Jeru heard a knock at the door and answered. It was Sarah without Mercy. She said, "Mama, I am going to give you a key. Where is Daddy?" Sarah said he had to go to the office to hire a Mine Superintendent, and Wilford gave her time off for her honeymoon. "So, I decided to spend the day with you and my granddaughter. Is she asleep?" Jeru asked if she had breakfast and Sarah said she and Mercy had eaten with Blossom. "So, then, what do you want to do?" Jeru said she had something to show her mother, and she took her to

Wilford's studio which was a small room at the back of the house. She showed Sarah the painting of her and Connie.

Sarah was overcome with pride to see her daughter so beautiful. "Wilford did this? Honey, that man loves you and I can see that in the painting." Jeru replied, "Mama, that is not all. He is going to paint a larger one of this and hang it in the lobby of the hotel." Sarah said, "My goodness, darling, no wonder you pray!" She hugged Jeru and repeated over and over, "Thank you, Jesus, please continue to bless my child." Jeru said, "Mama, now that you are near, I am going to continue my driving lessons so we can do so much together." Sarah said, "I would love to do that, and before the baby comes, we can drive to see Sarafina." Jeru said, "Oh, Mama, I would love to do that. I need to get her address from Daddy so I can write to her. Let's go in the kitchen and have a cup of coffee."

Chapter 27
"Power Couples"

"There are more things in Heaven and Earth, Horatio, Than are dreamt of in your philosophy." Shakespeare

At the *Oharas Inc.* headquarters, it was a requirement for all division heads to meet in the conference room in Claudette's suite weekly for morning briefing at 9:00 a.m. Claudette opened the first meeting by introducing all the VPs, new and old, adding that two are missing -- newly promoted Chief Financial Officer Gregor Finley, on assignment with Corporate Attorney Aberham Toilet, and the Entertainment VP is running late because of a personal matter that had to be solved right away. "In the meantime, I want to introduce you to Greta D Gossiper, head of our Communications Department. Any questions from the outside should be referred to her. If any your employees or you have a problem with females heading divisions or departments, they can exit right now." Nobody moved to leave.

"I see Mr. Dunford has made it. Mr. Dunford, you will find a folder in front of your name card, and you can read over the material. I want you all to meet Mr. Streeter Finlay, a trusted advisor who will pass each of you a folder. Please turn to your section and he will go in order explaining the Organizational Chart." Streeter explained each division's budget for the year. "If you will notice, the Personnel Division has no budget because it is a nonrevenue-producing division." Everyone seemed to follow what he was saying, but at the end, he added, "If there are any questions, I will be here all day." Claudette thanked him and dismissed the meeting, asking Greta, Doug, and Wilford to come to her office.

Claudette asked Wilford what he thought about her proposed poker tournament. He said, "I think it could work, but it is going to take me some time to work out the logistics. I suppose you want this in the large ballroom. *Cinco de Mayo* might be cutting it close, but we can work to make it happen on that day. Claudette said it was just December. She told him to get together with Doug and study his plan. "By the way, Doug, I like your idea of having our dealers involved." Wilford said, "I want you all to know that Claudette is the only one who can pull this off. I have been with her for three years in Paris and Monte Carlo, and I never witnessed her losing a hand." He asked Greta how soon she could get the story out, and she replied she only needed for Bax to make sure everything was legal, and nothing could backfire on them. She said, "Team, let's make this happen!"

After Doug and Greta left, Wilford told Claudette, "Yesterday, Jeru and I decided we don't want a salary. We have enough money and don't owe anybody. "Her dividend checks continue to add to our wealth, and we are truly blessed. We just want to continue living and loving you and Jean Claude." Claudette was visibly moved, and she said, "Come here so I can hug you." She said, "I never intended to take a salary either. My satisfaction will come from seeing this company show a profit, and have the employees feel this is the best company to work for.

Wilford left to get back to the hotel and the receptionist advised Claudette that Ms. Blake was on line one. She picked up and said, "Little sister, how are you all doing?" Shy replied, "Everything is going great. The triplets are walking and trying to talk. JB is doing well. We got contracts with two more buildings -- *Channel* and Cartier. Did Wilford tell you that a company called *Bailey, Banks, and Biddle* has bought a lot from *Channel,* so I guess that we will get that building, which will require only one person to clean it. I have great news from Al. They have turned over the cover crops and planted all ten thousand acres with wheat and five thousand with soybeans, and we should have a bumper crop of spring wheat. We have a contract from *Mitchel Blane*, and the Department of Agriculture is going to buy most of our wheat. I will get that contract over to you. Also, I spoke with our ranch foreman who said come spring we are going to have a good calving season."

Claudette took a deep breath over the phone as if to say, "Phew!" She said, "I love you, little sister, and from now on when you get a contract, I will send a lawyer over to look at, and if all is legal, you both can sign off right then. I will try and stop by this evening when I go to see my niece, Sophia." Shy said, "She is so pretty, like a little angel. I'm looking forward to seeing you. Hey, since you are coming this way, I can give that contract to you." Claudette said to send it instead. "I learned something from you. I will not allow anything to interfere with my home life. Honey, yesterday I had a hard day, but last night Jean Claude wanted to be intimate. I was tired, but I did it anyway." Shy responded that she knew the feeling.

Claudette called the University and asked Jean Claude if he could come by early so they could see Cielito and Sophia. He said he would be there in an hour. She packed up her stuff and said to the wolves, "Come on, boys, let's go see your niece." As usual, Jean Claude was standing outside with the back passenger side door open for the wolves. He held the door for her and kissed her, and they were off for home. First, Claudette asked him to turn into Blossom's yard and drive around back to the new barn. They went in and looked for the stairs. Jean Claude yell out, "How do we get upstairs?" Brinson hollered back, "Stay there. I will send the lift down." When they got upstairs, Brinson said Cielito was sitting in the bedroom and he had to run back to his office.

Cielito was reading the paper while Sophia was sleeping. She pulled the blanket backet from her face, and Claudette confirmed that she was a little angel. Jean Claude said, "She looks just like you." She said that was what Francois said, too. Claudette asked her how she was feeling, and she said she should be up and around tomorrow. "Mama Blossom comes by and check on me and wash diapers and other laundry for me. Soon, I will be able to do all those things." Claudette commented on what a beautiful place Cielito had, adding that she looked forward to going together to shop for her niece. "Oh, that will be great, and I am looking forward to the day when you are with child." Claudette said, "On that note, we better get going."

At the house Jeru was giving Sarah a shampoo. Jean Claude said had just seen Cielito and the baby. Jeru asked, "Is Daddy coming home early?" Claudette responded that he would not be early, as he was getting ready for government safety inspection." Sarah said she and Mercy would be driving to Silver City tomorrow for three days." Jeru didn't know that. Sarah apologized and said, "Honey, Daddy was going to tell you this evening, and that's why I wanted you to do my hair." "Sorry if I sounded abrupt, Mama, but I don't want to lose him again."

Claudette said Wilford would be late because he was working to get a project out by tomorrow. The phone rang, and it was Wilford needing to speak to Claudette. "My love, I know how you feel about not talking business at home, but we need to have a picture of the casino with this article. Doug and Greta agree with me, but how do you feel about that?" She said that as long as everything was legal to go head. He anticipated getting the article in the papers the next day.

Wilford turned to Doug and Greta. "Greta, can you get photographer over to the casino and have him take several shots from different viewpoints and get them to us right away?" Greta assured him she would get on it right away as she was leaving. When she returned, Wilford was explaining to Doug that there needed to be a lot more information in the article. Greta was a little offended by his comments, and Wilford admitted he knew nothing about writing a newspaper article. "What I was saying is that if I were going to put out a million dollars, I would need to know more about the event, such as who and where could I contact someone for further information." Greta understood and agreed. Wilford suggested they add, "any interested party could contact the Monte Carlo Luxury Hotel at 1 Monte Carlo Strip, Santa Fe, New Mexico, phone number Santa Fe 7-7000."

Wilford told Greta and Doug that by tomorrow there would be an extra switchboard and women to operate it by 5 P.M. Greta promised to get the revised article out, and Doug had the breakdown of the tournament. "I suggest that those who are interested should obtain a bank draft from the bank here in Santa Fe, and we can send them a copy of the tournament rules." As they continued to work, the photographer arrived with the shots of the casino, and Greta rushed to the *Gazette* office to file her article for the morning edition.

When Wilford arrived home and went through his usual ritual, Jeru asked if her father was still there when he left. Wilford said he was right behind him and should be home soon. Sarah told Jeru not to worry about her Dad, but she said, "Mama, I worry because I love him so much. I guess I am going to have to get used to the fact that he has things to do. Is that being selfish on my part?" Sarah offered comforting words. "Honey, when he was gone, it was not because he wanted to be away, but because the army was his life. I get nervous too. I wish you all could have seen him the first time I met him. I was working at the Dixieland Plantation Saloon owned by a low-down man and wife from the South. They didn't care for Negro soldiers and wouldn't serve them in the saloon. The soldiers would hang around out back in a little wooded area, and that is where we would sneak off to be with them. I was thirteen at the time and green as gall."

Sarah paused for a moment as she changed to a sad, serious tone. "One of the White girls was missing, and the owner's wife found her out back with a soldier. She came back and told her husband, and he and some of the men in the saloon caught him and hanged him outside in the front of the saloon. When the soldiers discovered the body still hanging, I don't know what happened, but I was upstairs where the Madam was scolding us for being with 'Niggers.' I said something and she grabbed me by the hair and was dragging me down the stairs. She pushed me down and I landed at the bottom on the floor, and this tall, handsome soldier picked me up and turned his attention to the Madam and said, 'Touch her again and I will kick your ass so far up your back you will look like you are wearing shoulder pads!' He said, 'Girl, stand behind me." The other soldier was Sgt Fagin, who told my brave defender, Mercy, that he had some fighting to do."

Everyone was engrossed in the story when Mercy came in. Sarah kissed him and said, "I was telling them how we met how you were standing there so tall and handsome, and you told the Madam how far you would kick her behind. Tell them the rest of the story." He said, "Aww, they don't want to hear that." But Jeru said, "I want to hear more of how you protected Mama from the Madam. Everyone, come and sit, and I will bring the food in, and Daddy can finish the story as we eat." Mercy needed to wash up first. When he returned, everyone was sitting and waiting for him to tell the rest of the story. Jeru asked Jean Claude to say the blessing first. He said, "When I saw Sarah, she was such a fragile, pretty girl. I pushed her behind me and Fagin was holding the twelve or so White men at gunpoint. He yelled to me to lock the door and anyone who got past him was mine. He said, 'All you yellow cowards, line up, and Mercy, let that girl go to the outhouse and bring in the *Sears Catalog*. I am going to beat the crap out everyone in here, and when I finish, they will need it to wipe. Fagin took them one at a time and I held my gun on them. It was like nothing I had ever witnessed. I tell you there were broken jaws, black eyes, missing teeth, and broken noses. The place was a wreck. Fagin and I left to get back to the Fort, and I took Sarah with me. I talked this Mexican into allowing me to rent an old adobe shack, and I gave Sarah some money and told her to remain there until I came to her the next day."

He looked around the room to see he had everyone's attention. "However, the next day the sheriff came to the Fort with the saloon owner and his wife and some of the men. The General had the whole regiment to fall out in formation, and he walked with the men to identify us. Captain Pearson said under his breath, 'Don't say anything; let me do the talking.' The saloon owner said, 'That tall Nigger is one of them," and the Captain turned and punched him in the mouth. The General yelled at the Captain to stand at attention, and the wife identified Fagin. 'His hands are swollen. That's him!' The Captain asked if he could speak, and the General allowed him. He said, 'Sir, Mercy was in the barracks all night sewing his Sgt. stripes on his uniform. The men in his squad will swear to that. And Sgt. Fagan was getting ready for the boxing tournament next week, and Corporal Billups, his sparring partner, is at the post surgeon.' Well, then I asked the Captain for a pass because I had some urgent business that need my attention. I had to see Sarah. I had fallen in love with her at first site and confessed my love for her when I told her to wait for me a day. Two weeks later the whole regiment headed to Montana. I can't swear to it, but I will always believe the Captain volunteered us for that assignment to get us out of New Mexico."

Sarah admitted that she was puzzled and afraid when he didn't return. But she shared with the group, "He was the only man who saw me as a person instead of a dirty Squaw. That's what the White men called me, and he must have kissed me ten times as I said I was thirteen and he was seventeen. But I loved him and made love with him that one night where we had just a few hours together. Jeru, that is how you got here." Jeru got up from the table and sat in Mercy's lap and hugged him and said, "Daddy, I love you. That was so romantic." Everyone else said something about hearing this incredible story.

Mercy asked to hold his granddaughter before they left. "Sarah and I need to pack. We might be gone three days. Before we go, I want to thank all of you for loving my daughter, Jeru." When he and Sarah departed, there was not a dry eye at the table, including the two men. Jeru cleared the table and washed dishes, while Wilford gave Connie her bath. Claudette volunteered to help Jeru with the dishes, but she told Claudette to go and take care of Jean Claude. "I love you, and before you go, call Cielito and see how your other niece is doing." Good idea.

The next morning Claudette and Jean Claude were about to leave when the phone rang. Jeru answered and it was Bix for Claudette. She signaled to Jeru to tell him they just drove off. When Claudette walked into her office, the receptionist said that Mr. Toilet was on the line. The first thing he asked her was, "Are you crazy? Have you seen the morning paper?" She said, "No, I just walked in." He said, "You can't do this. It says you are giving away the casino for a poker game! She said, "Didn't Bax tell you that Nimrod is trying to take me to court again and I am going to put a stop to that? I am going to take him for everything he owns." Bix was confused, nervous and angry. "But, Claudette, you are taking a chance and there is no guarantee you will win." She replied, "No one can beat me at poker except my mother and she is dead. How do you think Jeru and I were able to pay for our lavish lifestyle in Paris and Monaco and not spend any of our dividends? The only way I will lose is if he is cheating, and the game will be set up so that no one can cheat." He admitted being nervous until this thing was over.

When Wilford arrived at the hotel, the phone people were there installing the switchboard. He immediately called Cielito and asked if the young ladies from her school would be there. All six of them were coming in the door with an Instructor. Wilford advised them that the job was temporary but could lead to a permanent position. He handed them folders containing answers to any question that they might have. They could call him also. "There are three positions and the other three of you will act as relief operators. While the phone company is hooking everything up, I will have someone to show you around. You have free access to the restaurant, and you will be paid every two weeks. You'll make a note of all callers' names and addresses and give your lists to me." The young ladies were agreeable and eager to begin.

There was a different article every day poking Nimrod without mentioning his name, but calling him a "gutless yellow coward," accusing him of wearing female underwear and sleeping with men and announcing that a certain company was taking bets with odds of one thousand to one that he wouldn't show up for the world to see him beaten at poker by a female. After three weeks Nimrod couldn't stand it anymore. He was sure everyone knew the articles were referencing him. He thought of suing the *Gazette*, but if he did, then everyone would know for sure it was him the articles were alluding to. He had his attorney to call in and register for him. The attorney said he could call in on Nimrod's behalf. According to the rules, in order to be considered, a person had to purchase a bank draft of five million dollars in his name before receiving the qualification rules. Nimrod used his own name.

Two days later, as Wilford was looking over the list of names that the ladies had provided to him, he noticed Nimrod's name. He called Claudette's office and ask the receptionist to ring her. She answered the phone and Wilford said, "Your plan worked! Nimrod's name showed up on today's list. And did you know the news of the poker tournament is reaching Europe? She asked how he knew that, and Wilford said, "I can tell by the names. While we were there, did you ever meet the *Grand Duke and Dutchess of Corsica*?" Claudette answered in a long "Yes.... I saw them in Paris and Monte Carlo several times but never played with them. It's strange that every time I saw them, they had a table near me and Jeru, but we never noticed them. Well, anyway, three more months and Nimrod gets his 'come upping's."

Claudette was leaving for the day, but Wilford planned to stick around. "I am meeting an artist in order to have some artwork in the lobby and hallways and suites." Claudette said he should get home to his wife and two babies. He told her, "Now that we got Nimrod on the hook, I plan to start leaving early and limit my time on the weekends." He decided to call Jeru and tell her he was going to be a little late, but just then two artists walked in. He greeted and seated them before calling Jeru. "Hello, darling, how are my two favorite girls? I was calling to tell you I am going to be a few minutes late, but I have some good news I will share when I get home. Love you."

While he was on the phone the last artist walked in. Wilford asked if they had brought some of their work, but all three men said they didn't realize they should bring work samples. He said, "Gentlemen, your work is your resume. Let's call this meeting over, and you can leave work samples tomorrow." Before they left, he asked what kind of work each one did. They did portraits, landscapes, and impressionistic art. They would provide samples for Wilford's consideration the next day.
Wilford closed and locked his office door and left for home.

Jeru was waiting to hear what news he had for her. He said, "Guess who signed up today to play in the poker tournament?" She said, "It has to be Nimrod because he's the big fish you all were trying to catch." He asked where Connie was and Jeru said she was asleep, but it was time to wake her for dinner. Wilford asked if it was ok for him to play with her before dinner. Jeru looked at him and they embraced and kissed. "Of course, but you might have to change her diaper." He didn't mind. Jeru said, "Honey, I want to ask you something and I don't want you to misunderstand. Are you going to love the baby more than Connie?" Wilford said, "No, honey, I am hurt by that because I thought you knew that I would love them the same." She apologized and said, "It's just that Mama Blossom was checking on me today and she thinks it is going to be a boy from the heartbeat." He asked how Mama Blossom could tell. Jeru said, "She put a glass on my stomach and listened." He replied, "Well I'll be!"

After dinner Jeru asked Claudette if she felt like talking while they did the dishes. Jeru told her what Blossom said. Claudette was excited and hugged her and kissed her and ask if she had told

Wilford. She said he was beside himself. "There is one more thing where I want to know what you think. I want to build Mama and Daddy a house near us or on our land. I checked today and found who owned the small plot of land next to us which is about twelve acres." Claudette said, "My love, it's a fine idea when it was just you and me, but we have to clear it with Jean Claude and Wilford. They will probably say it is ok, and you might need to ask Mercy and Sarah how they feel about it. I think it is wonderful!" Jeru said, "Thank you, honey, you seem to always come up with good answers. I love you. Now I need to go in and give Connie a bath and love on my husband. You know, when he came home, he asked if he could wake Connie before dinner so he could play with her. My heart just melted because he really does love her." Claudette said he always appeared to be a sweet person and she said good night.

When Jeru went into her bedroom, she heard Wilford in the bathroom singing a children's nursery rhyme and water splashing. Wilford had Connie sitting in the face bowl giving her a bath, and he was singing, "You are going to have a little brother and you are going to be a big sister." She walked up behind him and wrapped her arms around his waist and nuzzled her face against his back and said, "What we did that first time might have been wrong, but God knew what he was doing when he put us together. Loving Claudette was good, but as Mama Blossom said, it was not whole and complete. With you I feel whole and complete. You are the sweetest man God ever created, and every day you surprise me in the many ways you show your love. I love you a zillion times. Dry her and I will dress her for bed and then let's take a bath together." Wilford said that was a good idea. "I think I will run cold water; I got a feeling before we finish it will be steaming." Jeru laughed. "You better shut up or we won't make it to the tub."

As they sat in the tub talking, Jeru told him about her idea of building a house for Sarah and Mercy on their property or buying twelve acres next to their property. He agreed but said she should first ask them their thoughts. She promised to do that when they returned from Silver City. She asked him to make love like they did the second time, but he wanted to be sure it wouldn't hurt their son. By the time the two went to bed they were exhausted.

Just as Jeru was drifting off to sleep, Wilford sprang up and said, "Why didn't I think of it before?" Jeru asked in a sleepy voice, "Before what, darling?" He said, "Yes, that's it – JB! Darling, remember the painting I did of you? I plan to have a fifteen-foot recreation of that done to hang in the lobby of the hotel, with pictures of the extended family of Blossom in the hallways and the four meeting and ballrooms, and remember I said I couldn't have done it without JB? Well, he can sketch really good, whereas I can paint, so why not have him sketch and I will paint.?" Jeru asked if he thought they'd have the time. He lay back down and said he would ask JB tomorrow. They snuggled up and went back to sleep.

The next morning, Wilford left for his office earlier than usual. Jeru was preparing breakfast. He rushed into the kitchen, picked up Connie from the highchair and kissed her, and spun around with her and said, "You little lump of sugar, Daddy loves you!" She was grinning and making noise and kicking. "Your little brother will be here soon." He sat her back in the highchair. Jeru could do nothing but marvel at her husband and think, "God, I don't know why you had me wait this long. I thank you and praise you for sending me such a sweet and loving man. Watch over him because his little family loves him so much." Wilford interrupted her train of thought when he kissed her on the back of her neck. He could feel her slipping out of his grip as if she was going to fall to the floor. She said it felt so good when he kissed her on the neck. He had no time for breakfast, as he had to catch up with JB. She asked what he was going to do with the painting he was carrying, and he said she would see soon.

Wilford drove to Main street in the new downtown looking for JB's van at the *Wells Fargo* building. JB was standing outside engaged with someone, and he parked behind JB's van and walked over to him. Wilford asked JB if he had time to stop at the hotel for a few minutes. JB pulled out his tablet and wrote that he could in about thirty minutes. Wilford said that was fine. When he arrived at the hotel carrying the painting of Jeru and Connie, he noticed the switchboard operators were busy already. He unlocked his door and found some paintings from the artists he talked to yesterday. He left his office and went to the lobby carrying the painting of Jeru. He walked out near the doors, turned, and looked at the wall behind the registration counter.

JB arrived and Wilford said he had a large project and needed JB's help, if he had the time. JB wrote that he would make the time. Wilford asked if he could sketch this painting on the wall behind the counter, and Wilford would paint it. JB wrote that he should just hang the painting there, but Wilford thought it was too small. "I want people to see it as soon as they come through the doors." JB understood that he wanted it to be the length of the wall. JB wrote, "It will have to be done at night, and the area has to be covered. Or, if you can find a large enough canvas, I can do it at home in the new barn." Wilford thought that would work. JB wrote, "But how would we get it from the barn to here?" Wilford said he could get a contractor's truck that hauls lumber. JB wrote that it would work with that kind of truck, but he asked where they would find such a large canvas. Wilford suggested that they might sew several big pieces of canvas together, and when he painted it, he could hide the seams. JB would stop at the University bookstore to see if they sold the canvas, and Mama could sew them together.

Chapter 28
Claudette's Paranormal Encounters Revealed

At Ohara Inc. Headquarters, Claudette was speaking with Bax Toilet about the number of inquiries they were getting regarding the Poker Tournament. Most wanted to know if they were selling tickets to the event, and a few have also committed to play. Bax added, "We should know how serious they are when we hear from the bank how and who has purchased the five-million-dollar bank draft. I think you should hire your brother-in-law to have his firm run checks on those people, and regarding the selling of tickets, charge one thousand dollars, and if they stay two or more nights at the hotel, you'll cut the price of the ticket in half." She said she would speak to Wilford about that.

Bax asked how Doug was working out, and Claudette added that he appeared to be a "team player" and a good fit for their operation. Bax switched subjects. "I will have that civil suit filed on Nimrod the day after you have taken what little cash he has, and we will go after all of his fraudulent assets. And the grand jury advised me that they are ready to indict him on criminal charges soon." She thanked Bax and promised to keep him up to date on everything.

As Claudette was about to call Wilford, she noticed Mercy and Sarah going into his office. She opened her intercom to his office and asked him how things went in Silver City. He replied, "Madam CEO, let me file these government papers and I will come to your office and give you the profit reports." She said fine see you in a minute. Mercy asked Sarah to make herself comfortable and feel free to look around, promising his business with Claudette shouldn't take long. He went into Claudette's office and said, "Madam CEO, I had plan to do this when I had all of this on display boards for you and the rest to see at our meeting in the morning, but if you want to see it now, I will attempt to explain it. She just wanted a brief overview and would study it later.

He started with the government findings. "We received high marks for safety, and I commended all of the superintendents and said they should expect to receive a letter from you on that. I am pleased to say all the mines continue to show quarterly profits over last year, and I expect the fiscal year profits to exceed Finley's predictions." She said, "Mercy, you are doing a fantastic job, and it appears that I am going to have to depend on you above your present position. Turn that stuff over to your secretary and tell her to have everything you will need for tomorrow's briefing, and you get out of here and I will see you in the morning. And let's not forget the men who deserve a raise in pay. Sometime in the next two weeks let's meet with Finley and figure out how much of a raise for them and what your next year's budget should be. And stop referring to me as 'Madam CEO.' You know my name." He said, "That I do, but I also respect your position. At home it is 'Claudette,' but here it's 'Madam CEO.' All of us in the Executive Division must set the example." "Okay, Mr. Senior Vice President."

Claudette called Wilford to discuss his thoughts on selling tickets to the event. He responded, "If I were making the decision, I would make it two-tier. My plan was to have the main event in one of the large ballrooms with fewer people attending, but with a higher price of admission. The preliminaries can take place in the casino's main room, and we could charge less for tickets to that event." Claudette told him to do what he wanted, as he had her approval. He said, "Thank you. I will make it a memorable event that people will talk about for years to come." After talking to Claudette, he thought to himself how she had gone from a carefree girl to a savvy businesswoman. He walked out of his office and noticed JB in the lobby and asked if he was looking for him. JB wrote "Yes, I am. When you get a chance, come by the barn give me your opinion on something I've been working on."

Wilford asked if he was headed home, and he was. Wilford said he would follow JB and they could take a look. When they arrived, Wilford was amazed at how much JB had accomplished in a few days. "JB, I hope this is not taking you from your other duties." JB wrote, "No, this is called "laying by season." The spring wheat is in the ground, and with the new barn there is nothing to fix, so I was able to get this far on the sketching of just one subject." Wilford said he also wanted to paint JB, Shy, and the triplets, plus a big one of Blossom alone, and finally a painting of Blossom with the rest of us. He would hang them all somewhere in the hotel. JB smile and wrote, "I would enjoy doing that." Wilford hugged JB and said, "I love you, Brother," and he left to go back to work.

After a few weeks, the painting of Jeru and Connie was finished and taken to the hotel and placed in the lobby. JB had done the other sketches, and Wilford had begun to paint them. By the time he finished, it was two weeks from *Cinco de Mayo*. He had them moved to the hotel and mounted. Soon after, Wilford met with Brinson to discuss security at the casino and the hotel. He returned to the hotel to draw out the VIP section of the main ballroom, which was now renamed the "Blossom Benbow Blake Ballroom." He sketched for the maintenance crew a gradually elevated seating area for the family and the VIPs and their guests. Wilford was called to the front desk to meet the sign contractor, who advised that the neon sign he ordered was up and ready for approval. They walked from the hotel to the casino's main gambling room where there was a neon sign saying, "Jade and Bybel Ohara Main Gambling Room." Wilford stood and studied the sign and told the contractor he liked it.

    The next thing was to see if Claudette approved. He called the Ohara building and left a message for her to go by the casino to check the sign and the painting over the main gambling door. Wilford returned to his office at the hotel and pulled out his notebook to make sure everything was ready. After ascertaining everything was in place, he called the house to check on Jeru. Sarah answered the phone and said Jeru was resting. He asked if he needed to come home, but Sarah assured him that Jeru was just feeling a little tired. "By the way, I will be back to work next week." He responded, "According to Blossom and Dr. Joe, the baby should arrive any day now, and I know you will want to be there for her when the baby comes."

    The day finally arrived -- *Cinco de Mayo*! There were celebrations going on all over Santa Fe and all of New Mexico. All employees of Ohara Inc.

were given a holiday, except for security. Of course, most of the employees were interested in the outcome of the Poker Tournament, especially the ones who worked at the casino and might be under a new owner. The tournament was scheduled to begin at 4:30 P.M. with the play for the grand prize at 7:30 P.M.

At the three households on Buckhorn Road, everyone was preparing for the evening festivities. At the Blakes, the females were making last-minute decisions on what they would wear. Shy was deciding the outfits for the triplets, JB and Mercy were on the front porch playing with the triplets in the swing and talking. Brinson and Cielito had selected outfits for themselves and baby Sophia. Across the street at the Dunford's and Beauchamp's home, Jeru, being pregnant, didn't have much choice for her attire, and she was putting Wilford through some things that would drive the average husband batty. Wilford was so much in love with Jeru and Connie that he was willing to put up with almost anything to please them. Wilford needed to be at the casino at 2:00 P.M. Jeru asked to watch him dress, and then she held onto him as they walked to the kitchen. He said tenderly, "Honey, you have to let go. I have to get to the casino. He kissed her and asked Sarah to bring Connie so he could kiss her. He kissed Connie and left.

When Wilford arrived, the spectator area was almost full. The waiters were busy taking orders and bringing food and drinks to the patrons. The contestants were at the tables. Wilford called Rooster, the Floor Manager, and reminded him that at 2:30 P.M., all the contestants must go to the #1 private room to be searched by security before the games began. Rooster assured him that everything was in place, and after each set a new deck would be introduced.

At the hotel, it appeared that things there were just like the casino, with spectators gathering at the restaurant and a line of patrons waiting to be seated. The bar was looking the same. Wilford had the clerk at the counter to page the shift manager, who hurried to Wilford's office. "Bob, I just wanted to ask you if everything is set up and ready to go in the "3B Room (Blossom Benbow Blake Room)." Bob replied affirmatively. "What about the microphone and speakers? Have you made a sound check? He answered, "No, Sir, I will do that as soon as I leave here. Sir, should I introduce Ms. Beauchamp first?" Wilford said, "By protocol, the Duke and Duchess of Corsica are first, Claudette next, and the winner and the runner up last. I will have the names of the preliminary tournament winners for you, along with Nimrod Bloom, who will be the final entrant. Now let me hear your speech." After Bob did his speech, Wilford commented, "Ask yourself if anyone hearing that was ready to buy. I need you to put some salesmanship into this event.

Bob spoke, "Good evening, ladies, and gentlemen. I am Bob Mobley, Shift Manager here at this magnificent hotel and resort. While you are here with us, if you have any problems or concerns, you only need to call me for immediate assistance. Let me say that today, you are a part of history that you can tell your children and relatives about. Please stand while I recognize three unforgettable people: the Duke and Duchess of Corsica, and next the beautiful Ms. Claudette Beauchamp, escorted by her husband, Jean Claude Beauchamp. Now, hold onto your seats, as the suspense will soon be over. One lucky person could leave here tonight as the new owner of the *Santa Fe Monte Carlo Casino,* but first they have to beat Mrs. Beauchamp in the Poker Tournament. And rounding out the list of participants are ... so and so and so ... and Nimrod Bloom. The third unforgettable person for you to meet is the President of this magnificent and luxurious hotel and casino, Mr. Wilford Dunford, escorted by his beautiful wife and soon-to-be mother for a second time, Jeru Mercy Dunford.

I know I said there were three unforgettable people here, but there's one more. I want to introduce you to the person for whom this luxurious ballroom was named – Ms. Blossom Benbow Blake -- and if you turn to the rear, you will see a life size painting of her by Mr. Dunford. There was a round of applause. Just one more thing, folks. For your entertainment and pleasure, the casino and bar will be open all night." Wilford commented to Bob, "I was sold this time. Do it like that and you will have everyone excited." Wilford asked Bob to check out front and have the additional doormen hired for the night to escort the twelve VIPs to the private ballroom.

Wilford sent four limousines to pick up Blossom and her family; one for Cielito and Brinson; and one for Jeru, Claudette, Jean Claude, which, of course, included the two wolves who never left Claudette's side; and one for Mercy and Sarah. They all arrived at 6:40 P.M., with all the females except Jeru wearing gowns. Jeru was happy to show off her pregnancy in the dressy, but shorter outfit she had chosen. The five guys wore tuxedos. They all were stunning and turned heads as soon as they walked into the casino. Bix and his family were there, and so was brother Bax, who whispered to Claudette, "As soon as the last hand is over, I will present Nimrod with the summons." All the VIPs were escorted to their seats in the gallery, except for

Claudette and Jean Claude, who waited in the anti-room with the wolves until they would be formally introduced.

The Duke and Duchess were late. Nevertheless, Bob thought it appropriate to begin the ceremony. As soon as he began his welcome, the Duke and Duchess arrived with a heavy guard escort presence. Claudette and Jean Claude moved swiftly toward them to formally greet them. They had been a presence in Claudette's and Jeru's lives when they were all in Monte Carlo, but this time, the security around the Duke and Duchess stood in front of them, so Claudette and Jean Claude returned to their places in line.

Bob introduced the Duke and Duchess first, and was preparing to introduce Claudette next, when the wolves who had stood quietly by her side rose and ran to the Duke and Duchess and perched on either side of them. Instinctively, Claudette was not bothered by it. She was introduced next, and she and Jean Claude were seated. The two tourney winners were seated next, and Nimrod took his seat last without any fanfare. Then Wilford, Jeru and Connie were acknowledged and seated. When Blossom was introduced the audience attention was directed to the back of the room to see her life-size portrait, she was taken by surprise at that and her name over the door. She was proud when JB, Shy and the triplets were introduced, along with their business titles. Cielito, Brinson, and Sophia were next, and Bob asked for a round of applause for the Dubois family, who had the new state-of-the-art hospital built and was instrumental in the development of the new downtown Santa Fe. The Duke and Duchess' security detail remained positioned next to the Duke and Duchess the entire evening.

The guests were breathless with anticipation for the Poker Tournament to commence when Bob announced, "Let the games begin!" The dealer opened a new deck and shuffled the cards and asked one of the security men to cut the card, and he shuffled again and began to deal. Nimrod announced he would play the cards he had, as did the royals and Claudette. The two tourney winners each asked for two cards. The Duke said he "stands," and so did Claudette and Nimrod. The Duke opened with one million dollars, and another player matched it. Nimrod said, "I will see you and raise two million." The security guard who could see his hand thought, "This guy is crazy trying to bluff with a hand like that." Claudette raised with three million, and the Duke said he would pass. Nimrod laid his hand and said, "Aces and Eights." Claudette said, "You better look again."

He looked and saw that he actually had a handful of mixed cards. He yelled, "That ain't right! I had Aces and Eights!" The referee, Judge Chamberlin, told security to please advise Mr. Bloom that if he has one more outburst he will be disqualified and forfeit all his money and be dismissed. Nimrod asked to speak to the Judge, who agreed and had security to escort Nimrod to the Judge's private space. He repeated his claim to have "Aces and Eights," but the security monitor interjected, "Judge, these are the cards he was dealt. I was wondering why he made the bet with a hand like this." He showed the Judge the cards, and the Judge said, "You need glasses." They all went back to the table.

The dealer showed everyone the new sealed deck and handed it around so they could see it was sealed. After everyone had agreed, he broke the seal and shuffled the deck and asked another security man to cut. He proceeded to deal, and Nimrod asked for two cards. Claudette asked for two, and the tourney winners each asked for three. The Duke said he would stand, and when it was all said and done the Duke had a Royal Flush. Nimrod again had a hand full of mixed cards. Claudette had a Straight Flush. The tourney winners decided to cut their losses and fold. In the preliminary tournament they had won twelve million and lost two million at the Grand Prize table, so they were way ahead. So, now it was just The Duke, Claudette, and Nimrod. One of the Duke's guards slid a sealed envelope to Claudette that said, "Do not open until the end of the game."

    She laid it in her lap and the dealer passed the new, sealed deck around and broke the seal and asked a security man to cut the cards. He dealt the cards. Nimrod asked for three, and those three made his hand worse than before. Claudette said she would stand. The Duke opened with five million. Claudette thought he must have another Royal Flush or a Straight Flush. As much as she didn't want to, she had to fold holding Four of a Kind. Nimrod, angry as hell, yelled, "This game was rigged." Judge Chamberlin said, "According to the rules, Mr. Bloom, you must now forfeit everything." To Nimrod's surprise, Bax approached him and handed him two subpoenas to show up in Civil and Criminal Court. Brother Bix was stunned, thinking Claudette should not have taken that chance. He thought she had lost the casino to the Duke and Duchess. Judge Chamberlain attempted to give the Duke the deed, when one of the Duke's guards stopped him and instructed him to bring the deed to Claudette. The Duke and his entourage, all of his security, along with the wolves, disappeared into the night.

Claudette couldn't believe she had lost the casino, which would have been the first loss in her entire life, and the highest stakes she had ever put up in a Poker game. She felt weak, and Jean Claude rushed to her, as the letter in her lap dropped to the floor. He noticed that the Duke had left without the deed. Still feeling a little sick, Claudette opened the envelope and began to read it:

"Our dear loved one, we have to let you know you didn't lose the casino. It is still yours. Because of our condition, we cannot take material things where we are going. We are part of the Fifth Dimension, and we belong to the Cosmos. What you have been seeing over the past years was our spirit, which is, in fact, the spirit of your ancestors. When we met you in Monte Carlo, we were in the Fifth Dimension so that you could see and converse with us. After your brothers were brutally murdered, we were granted the ability to move into the Fifth Dimension to help you and your sister to grieve and to bring your brothers' spirits with us. Mama Blossom helped you understand why these two wolves who suddenly appeared outside your door were drawn to you and never left you until tonight.

We will be penalized for telling you what I am about to convey in this letter, but we want to explain that after you pass, your spirit leaves your body and you become part of the Cosmos. There are different stages. As a living being, you can only understand height, depth, and width, which is the Third Dimension. In the Fourth Dimension, one can only come to you in a dream, but in the Fifth, one is granted the ability to materialize as you have been seeing us, although we are not allowed to touch or be touched. We can't interfere with earthly matters *without risking loss of our gift and being returned to the Fourth. We did something tonight that will return us to the Fourth.*

You did not win or lose. We made that Nimrod person think he had a winning hand when he didn't. So, we violated our position and for that we may become lost and banned from the Heavenly Host. We love you, and your brothers send their love. They are no longer wolves, as their spirits are with us. At some point you may be alone just thinking, and a gust of wind will touch your face and encircle you. It may interrupt your thoughts and feel strange, but do not worry. It is a hug and a kiss from us." Your feeling of invincibility at playing Poker came to you from your grandparents through your mother, Jade, which is why she alone could beat you at Poker. Tonight, we made certain that Nimrod would be disqualified and lose everything he valued, while we elevated you and your family to your rightful place within your tribe. Be well and happy, and after you have read this, the page will become blank.

After she read the letter, she ran to the door to see if she could see the Duke and Duchess and the wolves, but they had already disappeared. She fainted, and Jean Claude called for Dr. Joe. He and the two female doctors who were with him as part of the VIP group came and checked on her. Dr. Smith had her bag with some smelling salts, and she waved it under Claudette's nose while checking her pulse. She also used her stethoscope to listen to her heart and lungs, then her eyes, and finally her stomach. She turned to Jean Claude and said, "She is fine, and in about seven months you will become a father." He was stunned and speechless at first. Then he said in an excited and happy voice, "No, it can't be, could it?" The doctor said, "I haven't been wrong yet." He yelled out, "Did you all here that? I am going to be a father!" Everyone who was still there laughed. He cradled Claudette in his arms. "Honey, did you hear the doctor say that we are going to have a baby?"

About the same time Jeru was moved to the private room in Wilford's office. Her water broke and Blossom said it was too late to try to get her to a hospital. Jeru said, "I want you to deliver my baby, Mama Blossom." Wilford said, "I want that too." She told him to go and see if Dr. Joe was still there. He found Dr. Joe and Dr. Smith with Claudette. When Jean Claude saw him, he said, "Hey, buddy, I am going to be a father in about seven months." Wilford said, "I beat you to it. I am about to become a father for the second time in a few minutes. That is why I need Dr. Joe. Claudette said she was all right and the doctors should go and see about Jeru. She asked Jean Claude to bring her to Jeru, and they followed Wilford to his private suite. Blossom asked Wilford for some towels and hot water. He quickly complied.

By that time Jean Claude had arrive with Claudette. Blossom asked Sarah to shoo all the men out. Jeru asked for Mama Blossom to let Wilford stay. Blossom said, "No, I need to work, and I don't need a nervous father in here." Claudette went to the bed and took Jeru's hand and kissed her on the forehead and reassured her that everything was going to be all right. Blossom asked Jeru to prop her legs up and open them. She could see the head crowning and told Jeru to give a good, strong push. Doctors Joe and Smith entered the room, and seeing that Blossom had everything under control. Dr. Smith went to the head of the bed where Sarah was holding one of Jeru's hands and asked Sarah to let her check Jeru's pulse. Sarah asked if she was OK, and Dr. Smith said she was doing well. At that moment, they heard the baby cry. Dr. Smith reached in her bag and offered to cut the cord and clean the baby boy up. She did that so she could circumcise him without alarming Jeru.

Sarah said, "Did you hear that, honey, you have a baby boy!" A few minutes later Dr. Smith returned with the baby swaddled up in towels and handed him to Jeru. She asked for Wilford to come in and see his son, but Blossom said she had to first pass the placenta and let Blossom clean her up. Blossom caught the placenta in a towel and was instructing Sarah what to do with it. Dr. Smith took it, as Dr. Joe went out with the baby to show Wilford his son. He asked Wilford if he could find him a large pan and some ice. Dr. Joe understood why Dr. Smith wanted the placenta. It would be a good teaching tool for the student doctors. He took the baby from Wilford and returned to the room and handed the baby to Jeru, assuring her that Wilford would be in in a minute. "You might want to feed that little one. I expect he is hungry, and I want to make sure your milk is flowing." Blossom was finished cleaning up Jeru and putting fresh linen on the bed. Doctors Joe and Smith commended Blossom on her fast thinking and professionalism, saying they could not have done a better job.

Wilford returned with a pan and Dr. Smith placed the placenta in it and said they should go. Blossom asked Jeru if she and Wilford had a name yet. "We need to tell him who he is." Jeru asked Wilford what his father's name was, and Wilford hesitated before saying, "Wilford, yes I am a Junior." Jeru said, "Mama, go and get Daddy, and Connie needs to be here, too. Sarah came back with Mercy and Connie, who was asleep. Jeru said, "Ok, everyone, meet Wilford Jerusalem Dunford, III." Having gone through the naming with Connie, Jeru stopped the baby from nursing and looked at him and said, "Hello, Wilford Jerusalem, III." She handed him to Wilford, Jr., who spoke the same words. She said, "Daddy, you are next." The whole room did the same.

After everyone had their turn, Jeru said, "I wish Sarafina was here to meet her nephew." Dr. Smith advised all that Sarafina was on duty in the emergency room and could not be there. Blossom suggested Jeru spend the next four days in Wilford's private suite. Claudette wanted to stay with her if Mercy would take over duties for the next few days. Sarah said she was going to stay also, and Wilford would find rooms for them. Blossom reminded everyone that Wilford and Jeru should be alone to enjoy this special time for them. Jeru added, "Mama Blossom is right. If I need something Wilford can take care of that. I love you all and my heart is light seeing how much you care for me."

After the last of the loved ones had departed, Jeru called for Wilford, who was about to take a bath. He jumped to her side to see what he could do for her. They were alone with their new baby boy. She said, "I am all right. I just wanted to kiss you and thank you for loving me. Come closer so I can kiss you." Then she told him to go ahead and take his bath. He went back to the bathroom and returned wearing a hotel robe. "It is one of the amenities we offer when you spend the night in the hotel. Here, I will get you one." He returned with a robe for Jeru. She told him that tomorrow he would have to go home and bring her some night gowns and underwear for a couple of days, plus diapers and little gowns for their little one. She got up and pulled off the slip and slipped on the robe. She asked him to come and lay beside her. "Let's give thanks to God for this handsome and healthy baby boy and a beautiful baby girl and for each other and reuniting Mama and Daddy."

Afterwards, she said, "Wilford, honey, I never dreamed life could be like this. You know, I am so blessed to be a mother and I love being a wife and mother. That's all I want to be. We have enough money, and my quarterly dividends continue to add to our wealth. I don't need to work. I understand how Shy feels when she says she will not let anything interfere with her duties as a wife and mother." Wilford said "Speaking of being a mother, while you were going into labor, Claudette fainted and Jean Claude called for Drs. Joe and Smith, who told him that in seven months he would be a father. Jeru sat up in happy disbelief. Wilford said Jean Claude was beside himself. Jeru said, "Honey, that is great news. I can't wait until morning. You know, I wish this had happened sooner." Wilford replied, "No, honey, it happened when God wanted it to happen."

On the way home, Shy said to JB and Blossom "When we get home, I will tell Cielito about Jeru, since they had to leave early and missed all the excitement." Blossom added, "I am happy for Jeru. She and Cielito are going to make fine mothers and wives, just like you, Shy." Shy said, "Ah, Mama." Blossom said, "You are younger in age but have been married and been a mother longer." Shy asked about Claudette, and Blossom said she would be all right, but definitely a changed person after tonight. Shy asked if it was because Claudette had lost the casino, but Blossom explained that first, she was pregnant, and second, earlier in the evening, she had had an out-of-body experience. "I can't tell you now but will explain later. We are home, so, let's get the babies inside, undressed, and in bed. They are growing so fast that at some point you and JB must have them sleeping in their own beds." Shy said, "You are so right, Mama, it's going to be hard, but it must be done."

Once inside and having taken care of the triplets, Shy called Cielito to tell her the news. Brinson answered the phone and said she and Sophia were asleep. He received the news with gladness and promised to tell Cielito in the morning. Meanwhile, in Hotel room #75, the vacant room Wilford had provided for Claudette and Jean Claude, Claudette was propped up in bed going over some preliminary figures Wilford had given her on the profits from different entities connected with the Poker Tournament. Jean Claude was excited that she was pregnant, but Claudette attempted to avoid talking about it. He reached and pulled the papers from her hands, asking, "Why are you avoiding talking about being pregnant when I am so happy and excited?"

She began to tear up and stated, "Darling, I am afraid," and she buried her face in his chest. He pulled away and raised her head up so he could look her in the eyes. "Darling, what are you afraid of?" He grabbed tissues from the nightstand and gave them to her to dry her eyes. She said, "I told you before that I have Negro blood in me, and what if the baby is dark- skinned. You might not like it." He attempted to speak, but she stopped him and insisted that she finish. "The other reason I am afraid is that I want be a good mother, and I don't know if I can be that." Jean Claude took a deep breath and said, I thought you knew me! Yes, you told me that before. Honey, you can't continue to go through life allowing that to make you feel guilty. I told you the first time I saw you walking up that gang plank that I fell in love with you. As for the complexion of our baby, that means nothing to me. It will be like all of us at that stage, where we just want to be loved and taken care of. This child is going to have both of our blood flowing through its veins. It will be ours and I am going to love it with every fiber of my being, just as I love you."

She reached up and pulled him to her and started kissing him all over his face. She said, "I love you. Let's make love." He asked if she was sure that it would be okay, and she said of course. "I heard Mama Blossom tell Cielito it was okay. I hope it's a girl and I will name her Claudia. What was your mother's name?" He replied, "Millicent." She said, "That's it; her name will be Claudia Millicent." "What if it is a boy?" She said it was going to be a girl. After their loving, she rolled over from her position and he rolled onto his stomach. She rested her head on his back and, at that moment, as far as Claudette was concerned, all was right with the world. She was in the process of taking Nimrod down, and she and Wilford's numbers from the Poker Tournament totaling close to forty-five million dollars, not counting food and liquor. She drifted off to sleep with a smile on her face.

Epilogue

The saga of the special and unusual families that were touched by Blossom Benbow Blake grew outwards. What was left of The Oharas became two different families: Dubois and Beauchamp. The Twotrees became the Dunford and Mercy families. Claudette Ohara, after going through the tragedy of having her brothers murdered, became the CEO of Ohara Inc. She married Jean Claude Beauchamp, and they had one child, Claudia Millicent Beauchamp, who, like her mother and grandmother, grew into a beautiful and shapely woman. Like Jade, her grandmother, she had certain European features; however, her physique was without a doubt Negroid. Claudia Millicent followed her mother, Claudette, by attending the *St. Augustine School* in New Orleans with her best friend, Consuela Dunford. Although younger, Claudia possessed a high IQ. At an early age she came to sit atop Ohara Inc. as the CEO. When Claudette stepped down, based on her middle name "Millicent," it was her destiny to step into Claudette's executive shoes. She was "strong in work," armed with a tenacious perseverance and skill at cultivation.

Jean Claude established an agriculture experimental station on the *High Spade Ranch*. He continued to write books on dishes made from soybeans. He surprised Claudette when he purchased two marble headstones for the Ohara brothers and took the lead in planning a fitting memorial. Claudette and Jean Claude lived to a ripe old age of ninety-five and eighty, respectively.

Cielito Ohara, renowned philanthropist and businesswoman, married Brinson Dubois, who was a respected detective on two Continents and owner of a security company that was much in demand. They had two children. Sophia Guadalupe Cielito Dubois, like her father, became a successful detective. A son, Francois Ohara Dubois, became Mayor of Santa Fe and later an activist for Mexican rights, and like his mother, he was a renowned Philanthropist.

Jeru Twotrees Mercy married Wilford Dunford, who established the *Santa Fe Monte Carlo Strip,* a project with a luxury hotel and gambling casino, plus high-end stores, and boutiques -- the first of its kind in the nation. It preceded Las Vagas in popularity by several years. The Dunford's had two children: a girl, Consuela Sarah Dunford, who, like her mother attended the *St. Augustine School* in New Orleans with her best friend, Claudia Millicent Beauchamp. Although being independently wealthy, she was well known as a recognized expert in interpreting peace treaties between the United States and all indigenous tribes throughout the country. The son, Wilford Jerusalem Dunford, after graduating from West Point Academy, went on to have a stellar military career as one of the youngest and most decorated two-star generals in the army.

Sarah Twotrees, mother of Jeru Twotrees, and Mercy, after thirty years, reunited by divine providence. She had found her long lost love and father of daughter, Jeru. Jerusalem Mercy, who had an adopted daughter, Sarafina Mercy, who became a well-respected physician and expert in Indigenous medicine. Sarah and Mercy married and lived "happily ever after," loving their two daughters and two grandchildren.

Blossom Benbow Blake, who was the anchor for the entire family clan, was independently wealthy, along with her two adopted children and three grandchildren. They continued to live their uncomplicated lifestyle and to set examples for the extended family. Blossom was proud of JB and Shy, and their three children added to that sense of pride.

Andrew Bexley helped his father, JB, to run the janitorial company and the farm. Paul Baxley became a real estate investor and helped his mother, Shyanne, with her endeavors. Also, at harvest and planting time, he helped his father and brother. Blossom Shyanne became Professor of Divinity at *New Mexico State University.*

Life at what was now called the community of "Blossom Place" went on as more families moved into the area and learned to live in peace and harmony, thanks to Doctor Blossom Shyanne Blake, who continued providing her grandmother's legacy of wisdom and compassion for the scripture to anyone with whom she encountered. She lived by Mathew 6:33, always performing her oaths to the Lord.

Nimrod Bloom, after all the years of robbery, fraud, forgery, arson, and conspiracy to commit murder, attempted murder, and assault, was finally taken down by Claudette Ohara and her lawyers. They won a seventy-million-dollar civil case in court where he was sued for defamation and character assassination. He had to this point been successful in avoiding all convictions, due to crooked judges and negligent law enforcement officials, but he was now indicted in criminal court on two counts of murder, one on attempted murder, fraud, and forgery. His lawyers argued that, since he had been tried for those things and found not guilty, that would be "Double Jeopardy." In addition, the Defense argued that the charges of fraud and forgery should be dropped.

The Prosecution pointed out that Nimrod Bloom was not being tried for the previous acts. This was against the Oharas, and all the charges should remain. They presented into evidence the document showing that the date on the forged bill of sale was two days after the Ohara brothers' bodies were discovered. The jury agreed and he was found guilty on all counts and was sentenced to fifty years in prison without parole. Needless to say, he was never worth more than twenty million dollars in cash and assets combined. All the land he had was seized and any other assets were attached and sold to be paid to the Ohara Corporation. So, it was fitting to say that Nimrod didn't have a "pot to PP" (peel potatoes) in.

Some months after the trial, the State Attorney General, based upon evidence found in J Arthur Begg's files, began proceedings against the crooked Judges and law enforcement officials.

THE END

How to Reach the Author

SK Bentley Davis, aka Jim Scott, is available for book signings, lectures, panel discussions, keynote speaking engagements about how his fiction narratives fit into the fabric of the historical accuracy of the "wild, wild West."

He can be reached at 404-569-8878 or jimscott1121@gmail.com.

Made in the USA
Columbia, SC
31 December 2024